Fairy Tales

26th July 2015
~~2015~~ 2005

Here is a collection of
stories from the part of
your future!

Should we stay or
should we go?

Tim   Kirsten

HANS CHRISTIAN ANDERSEN
Fairy Tales

Translated by TIINA NUNNALLY
Edited and Introduced by JACKIE WULLSCHLAGER

VIKING

VIKING

Published by the Penguin Group

Penguin Group (USA) Inc., 375 Hudson Street,
New York, New York 10014, U.S.A.
Penguin Group (Canada), 10 Alcorn Avenue,
Toronto, Ontario, Canada M4V 3B2
(a division of Pearson Penguin Canada Inc.)
Penguin Books Ltd, 80 Strand, London WC2R 0RL, England
Penguin Ireland, 25 St. Stephen's Green, Dublin 2, Ireland
(a division of Penguin Books Ltd)
Penguin Books Australia Ltd, 250 Camberwell Road, Camberwell, Victoria 3124, Australia
(a division of Pearson Australia Group Pty Ltd)
Penguin Books India Pvt Ltd, 11 Community Centre, Panchsheel Park,
New Delhi – 110 017, India
Penguin Group (NZ), Cnr Airborne and Rosedale Roads, Albany, Auckland 1310, New Zealand
(a division of Pearson New Zealand Ltd)
Penguin Books (South Africa) (Pty) Ltd, 24 Sturdee Avenue, Rosebank,
Johannesburg 2196, South Africa

Penguin Books Ltd, Registered Offices: 80 Strand, London WC2R 0RL, England

First American edition
Published in 2005 by Viking Penguin,
a member of Penguin Group (USA) Inc.

1 3 5 7 9 10 8 6 4 2

Translation copyright © Tiina Nunnally, 2004

Introduction, notes and selection copyright © Jackie Wullschlager, 2004
All rights reserved

Paper cutouts of Hans Christian Andersen reproduced by agreement with and thanks to Odense
City Museums (all illustrations except as listed below):
The Royal Library, Copenhagen (pages 3, 27, 45, 123, 161, 205)
and Silkeborg Kunstmuseum (pages 65, 409).

LIBRARY OF CONGRESS CATALOGING IN PUBLICATION DATA

Andersen, H. C. (Hans Christian), 1805–1875.
[Tales. English.]
Fairy tales / Hans Christian Andersen ; translated by Tiina Nunnally ;
edited and introduced by Jackie Wullschlager.
p. cm.

ISBN 0-670-03377-4

1. Fairy tales—Denmark. 2. Children's stories, Danish—Translations into English.
I. Nunnally, Tiina, 1952– II. Title.
PT8116.E5N86 2005
839.8'136—dc22   2004053622

This book is printed on acid-free paper. ∞

Printed in the United States of America
Set in 12/14 Monotype Bembo

Contents

Acknowledgments

These new translations of stories by Hans Christian Andersen are the result of the dedicated collaboration of several key people. I am especially grateful to Andersen's biographer, Jackie Wullschlager, for bringing her unique insight to the selection of the tales and for contributing the highly informative introduction and notes. I was also fortunate to work with two wonderful editors. In London at Penguin/Allen Lane, Laura Barber, who has a keen eye for details, offered enthusiastic support from the very beginning and took a special interest in choosing the illustrations for the book. In New York, Caroline White, my longtime editor at Viking Penguin, coordinated all aspects of the project with unflagging patience and tenacity, giving me much-needed encouragement along the way. I would also like to thank Marianne Stecher-Hansen, an Andersen scholar and professor at the University of Washington, for answering all my questions about the eccentricities of Andersen's Danish. And I could not have done these translations without the brilliant linguistic and literary assistance of Steven T. Murray. Finally, I would like to dedicate these translations to my parents, Eeva and Elam Nunnally, who blessed me with a love of literature that has made my own ventures out into "the wide world" both joyous and deeply rewarding.

—Tiina Nunnally

Special thanks to Odense City Museums; The Royal Library, Copenhagen; and Silkeborg Kunstmuseum for permission to reproduce Hans Christian Andersen's paper cutouts in this volume.

Chronology

1805 (April 2) Hans Christian Andersen is born in Odense. He is the son of Hans Andersen, a cobbler, and his wife, Anne Marie, a washerwoman. He is also brought up by his grandmother; who tells him folktales.

1812 His father leaves Odense to join Napoleon's army in Germany, returning in 1814.

1816 His father, weakened by illness contracted during his years in the army, dies.

1818 His mother remarries; her second husband is also a shoemaker.

The Royal Theater from Copenhagen visit Odense; Andersen is given a walk-on part. He becomes known in Odense as "the little Nightingale of Fyn" because of the fine singing voice with which he entertains middle-class families in the town.

1819 Andersen leaves Odense to seek his fortune in Copenhagen.

1819–22 Andersen lives in lodgings in Copenhagen, supported by benefactors including the composer C. E. F. Weyse and the poet Jens Baggesen. He has singing lessons, makes his debut on the stage of the Royal Theater in Copenhagen as a troll, and writes plays that are rejected by theater management.

1822 Andersen's grandmother dies without seeing him again. She is buried in a pauper's grave.

1822–27 Andersen attends grammar school in Slagelse, a provincial Danish town fifty miles from Copenhagen. He is sponsored under a proposal put together by the Copenhagen philanthropist Jonas Collin. On his first holiday in 1823, he returns home to Odense, by ship and on foot, to see his mother for the first time in four years. Beginning of friendship with B. S. Ingemann, a romantic poet living near Slagelse.

1827 Andersen returns to Copenhagen to study for his university matriculation, which he passes in 1829, but chooses not to go to university. Dines in weekly rotation with leading cultured families of Copenhagen, as was typical for students at the time; thus the beginning of friendships with Edvard Collin, son of Jonas Collin, with the physicist Hans Christian Ørsted, and with the naval family of Admiral Wulff and his daughter Henriette; all become lifelong supporters.

First publication of his work, a poem called "The Dying Child," in the newspaper *Copenhagen Post*.

1829 First book publication, *A Walking Tour from the Holmen Canal to the Eastern Point of Amager*, a comic fantasy in the style of E. T. A. Hoffmann. First play, *Love at St. Nicholas Tower*, performed at the Royal Theater in Copenhagen.

1830 In the summer, travels to Jutland and Fyn, where he falls in love with Riborg Voigt, who is engaged; in October she turns down his proposal of marriage.

1831 First journey abroad, to Germany, where he meets romantic writers Ludwig Tieck in Dresden and Adelbert von Chamisso in Berlin. Publishes an account of his trip, *Skyggebilleder (Shadow Pictures)*.

1832 Visits his mother, dying of alcoholism in Odense, for the last time. Unsuccessfully courts Louise Collin, sister of Edvard.

Writes his first autobiography, *Levendsbogen (The Book of My Life)*, written not for publication but to explain his life to a few close friends, especially the Collin family. The most honest and reliable of his three autobiographies, it is not published until 1926.

1833–34 First long journey of cultural formation in Europe, visiting Paris, Switzerland, and Italy.

In Rome on December 16, 1833, hears that his mother has died. A few days later he begins his first novel, *The Improvisatore*, set in Rome and Naples.

1835 (April 9) The publisher Reitzel issues *The Improvisatore*, dedicated to the Collin family. It is Andersen's breakthrough—

an immediate success, quickly reprinted, and translated into German.

(May 8) Reitzel publishes first installment of *Eventyr, fortalte for Børn (Fairy Tales, Told for Children)*, containing four tales: "The Tinderbox," "Little Claus and Big Claus," "The Princess on the Pea," and "Little Ida's Flowers." Andersen receives 30 *rigsdaler* (equivalent of £300/$450 today) for it.

December 16, second installment of *Eventyr*, containing "Thumbelina"; "The Naughty Boy," based on Anacreon's poem about Cupid; and "The Traveling Companion."

1836 Publication of second novel, *O.T.*, subtitled *Life in Denmark*; it is much less successful than *The Improvisatore*.

Spends summer on Fyn, avoiding Edvard Collin's wedding and writing "The Little Mermaid."

1837 Publication of third installment of *Eventyr*, containing "The Little Mermaid" and "The Emperor's New Clothes."

Publication of third novel, *Only a Fiddler*, about "the terrible struggle that went on in me between my poet nature and my hard surroundings," which is very successful. Søren Kierkegaard, then an unknown theology student, dedicates his entire first book, *From the Papers of a Person Still Alive, Published Against His Will*, to a critique of it.

1838 Awarded annual grant of 400 *rigsdaler* by the king of Denmark. This gives Andersen financial security and releases him from having to write novels. For the next ten years he concentrates on fairy tales. On December 1, he moves into a suite of rooms at the Hotel du Nord, Copenhagen's grandest hotel, his Danish home for the next decade.

1840 *The Mulatto*, his most successful play, opens at the Royal Theater in Copenhagen. Begins a long journey to Italy, Greece, and Constantinople; it includes his first train ride. An account of the trip is published as *A Poet's Bazaar* in 1842.

1843 Falls in love with opera singer Jenny Lind, the "Swedish nightingale"; she does not return his affection but inspires his fairy tale "The Nightingale." He also has a brief affair with a Danish aristocrat, Henrik Stampe; soon afterward Stampe marries Edvard Collin's niece Jonna and Andersen feels used and rejected.

Nye Eventyr (New Fairy Tales), containing "The Ugly Duckling," "The Nightingale," "The Sweethearts," and "The Angel," is Andersen's breakthrough in Denmark as a writer of fairy tales: it is a bestseller and a critical success.

1844   Visits Weimar, former home of Goethe and Schiller and unofficial capital of German culture. He is extremely drawn to the Hereditary Grand Duke of the principality, Carl Alexander: "I quite love the young duke, he is the first of all princes that I find really attractive." He considers Weimar his second home and visits often over the next five years.

Second installment of *Nye Eventyr*, containing "The Snow Queen" and "The Fir Tree."

1846   Travels to Germany and Italy, where he writes his second autobiography, *Das Märchen meines Leben ohne Dichtung (The True Story of My Life)* commissioned by the German publisher Lorck to introduce a German edition of his collected works. At the same time writes the fairy tale "The Shadow."

First publication of his tales in English, translated by Mary Howitt; reviews are in general enthusiastic.

1847   Visits England for the first time. He is the lion of the London season, sought after by all the leading society hostesses. For Andersen, the highlight is meeting Charles Dickens. He returns home via Weimar.

1848   Revolution in Europe leads to conflict between Denmark and Prussia over the duchies of Schleswig and Holstein and the 1848–51 Three Year War. Andersen is bitterly divided between Danish patriotism and his German friends.

His patriotic novel *The Two Baronesses* appears; he also writes the poem "In Denmark I Was Born," which becomes a rallying wartime song and is still popular today.

1851   Publishes *Pictures of Sweden*, an account of his travels there at a time when war prevented him visiting Germany.

1852   Publishes first collection of fairy tales in four years, now under the title *Historier (Stories)*. It includes "She Was No Good," a romantic but indignant portrait of his mother as a hardworking washerwoman destroyed by harsh social circumstances.

Visits Weimar for the first time in five years.

1855   Third autobiography, *Mit Livs Eventyr (The Fairy Tale of My Life)*, published.

1857   Stays for five weeks with Charles Dickens in England; he outstays his welcome and Dickens never writes to him again. Publication of philosophical novel *To Be or Not to Be*.

1858   *Eventyr og Historier (New Tales and Stories)* opens a new phase of experimental tales including "The Marsh King's Daughter." Four volumes appear in the series between 1858 and 1859.

1861–63   Andersen falls in love with Harald Scharff, a ballet dancer with the Royal Theater in Copenhagen. They have a brief affair, which Andersen cannot resist publicizing ("I told all about my erotic time").

1864   A second Prussian-Danish war leads Andersen to break definitively with Carl Alexander of Weimar, and causes him great unhappiness.

1865   Beginning of close friendship with the Melchiors and the Henriques, two wealthy Jewish families who help make his old age comfortable and productive. Stays extensively at Rolighed ("Tranquillity") and Petershøi, their estates north of Copenhagen.

1867   Awarded the Freedom of Odense; his home town is illuminated in his honor during a daylong festival.

1867–68   Makes three trips to Paris, where the World Exposition inspires his tale "The Wood Nymph" and, as an observer, he visits brothels for the first time.

1872   Last volume of stories, including "Old Johanna's Tale" and "Auntie Toothache," appears in November and sells out at once. Shortly afterward Andersen experiences the first symptoms of the liver cancer that is to kill him.

1874   King makes him a Privy Councillor (*Konferensraad*).

He illness is now widely known; Carl Alexander of Weimar, with whom he has had no contact since 1864, sends a telegram inquiring about his health, and communications between them reopen.

Spends much of the year ill at Rolighed.

1875   Celebrates his seventieth birthday with a banquet at the Melchiors for 244 people, with each dish and wine named after one of his fairy tales ("The Wild Swans," "The Ice Maiden," and "The Snowman").

Dies in his sleep at Rolighed on August 4. Among the hundreds present at his funeral, including the king and crown prince of Denmark, there is not one blood relation of Andersen's. His estate of 30,000 *rigsdaler*, plus rights to his works sold for 20,000 *rigsdaler*, are left to Edvard Collin.

Introduction

HANS CHRISTIAN ANDERSEN, 1805–2005

In one of Hans Christian Andersen's last tales, the search is on for "the most incredible thing." A young artist has wrought an extraordinary clock from which different tableaux of figures emerge as each hour strikes—three Wise Men, five Senses, seven Deadly Sins. He is about to win the princess and inherit half the kingdom when a huge thug of a man bursts in and smashes the clock to bits. The verdict switches, for " 'Destroying a work of art like that,' said the judges. 'Yes, that is the most incredible thing!' Everyone said the same, and so he was to have the princess and half the kingdom, because a law is a law, even if it's the most incredible thing."

You will have to read "The Most Incredible Thing" to see whether artist or thug ultimately gets the princess—in Andersen, who oscillated wildly between faith and pessimism, either is possible. But the moment is one to which no twenty-first-century audience can fail to respond: In his anxiety over the future of civilized values in a changing world, Andersen is one of us. To current readers, echoes of war and the terrorist attacks across Europe, the United States, Asia, and the Middle East with which the twenty-first century opened, sound through the tale. The battle between culture and aggression, though, is timeless. The story was inspired by the Franco-Prussian conflicts of the 1860s and 1870s, but between 1940 and 1945, during the Second World War, it was widely circulated, with anti-Nazi illustrations, among the Danish Resistance to German occupation. Yet it also vividly calls to mind Kenneth Clark's comment on Delacroix's "The Crusaders Entering Constantinople": "they have conquered the civilised world and will destroy it out of sheer embarrassment."

We do not think of Andersen as a political artist, or even, usually, as a writer for grown-ups. We tend, in fact, not to consider him an author at all, but rather the curator of his stories, the most famous of which are as deeply imbedded in our culture as myth and legend. But while over centuries collectors like Charles Perrault in France and the Grimm brothers in Germany recounted tales from oral lore, drawing on the shared inventory of motifs and conventions that are part of our common remembrance, Andersen was different. He was the first writer who was not only skilled at adapting existing stories in an original and lasting manner, he was also capable of creating new tales that entered the collective consciousness with the same mythic power as the ancient, anonymous ones. This individual achievement has never been matched. Almost two centuries after he wrote them, "The Emperor's New Clothes" and "The Ugly Duckling" are still bywords for elements of the human condition, while his Snow Queen, Little Mermaid, and Steadfast Tin Soldier belong with characters of folk memory.

Yet these stories were either invented or given definitive form by Hans Christian Andersen, a very modern literary artist. It is no accident that self-portraits open and close the fairy-tale oeuvre of this most self-conscious writer. When Andersen, young, obscure, and penniless, composed his first story, "The Tinderbox," he dreamt that, like his soldier hero, he would overcome the world's demons—witches and tyrannical kings—to win fame and riches for himself. By the time of his tale "Auntie Toothache" in 1872, the position was reversed. From his standpoint as the most famous author in Europe, he looked back, through the lens of a still-aspiring poet, on the work that had brought him wealth and success and dismissed it all as personal agony and meaningless rubbish—because, as he wrote in the first edition of the tale, "everything" ends "in the bin."

In the nearly forty years in between he became master of the genre that he could reshape like soft clay, into tales classical or modernist, heroic or ridiculous, tragic or comic. Above all, there was from the start the double audience. At first he aimed at children "while always remembering that Father and Mother often listen, and you must also give them something for their minds"[1]—thus the gentle, nudging satire of "The Emperor's New Clothes" or "The Ugly Duckling." But as Andersen grew older, a darker outlook asserted itself; he left behind the traditional genre to create a pioneering new style, a high-voltage short story for adults. The terror of psychological disintegration in "The Shadow," the disturbing sexual symbolism of "The Ice Maiden," the grotesque muse pointing to death not art in "Auntie Toothache"—the themes of such stories, rarely included in Andersen anthologies, combine the fatalism of ancient folktales with an almost contemporary sense of the chaotic chance and absurdity of human existence. These tales were largely forgotten when nineteenth-century Britain and America relegated Andersen to the nursery. In the Anglo-Saxon world, he has mostly been encouraged to stay there—partly because our simplified image of him became fixed, partly because poor translations did no justice to the complexity of his vision or the dazzle of his style. Yet they complete the circle with which Andersen evolved a fundamentally peasant genre into a sophisticated proto-modernist one, and they confirm his reputation as a very individual storyteller. While the glacier mass of the world's fairy tales is anonymous, Andersen holds a unique place in it.

"THE HISTORY OF MY LIFE WILL BE THE BEST COMMENTARY ON MY WORK."[2]

So said Andersen, and much in his inspired fantasy had its direct reflection in his own experiences. Born in 1805 in Odense, a provincial Danish town, Andersen was the only son of a cobbler and an illiterate washerwoman. A lonely, ugly, gawky, dreamy boy, he was regarded as a freak by the other town children, and spent his time apart from them, sewing doll's clothes and playing with puppets: a classic ugly duckling. His father, depressive, frustrated, and self-educated, died when he was eleven. His illiterate mother came from a dirt-poor, harsh, promiscuous background—her own mother had four children by four different men, her sister ran a brothel, and she herself had an illegitimate daughter, six years older than Andersen, who never lived in the family home. But she was a mild-mannered, superstitious, hardworking, and loving woman who brought her son up as best she could and gave him two inestimable gifts: an unshakable conviction in his own genius, and a connection with the folk mind-set still surviving in parts of Europe. She believed in trolls and ghosts, she consulted fortune-tellers in times of crisis, she stuck pieces of St. John's wort into the clefts between the beams in her ceiling, judging from their growth whether her friends and acquaintances would live long or die soon.

Andersen was growing up, in the first decade of the 1800s, at a time when folktales were no longer current in cities like Copenhagen but survived in country areas, though they were on the wane there, too. This was the decade when the Grimm brothers were collecting tales from German peasants, aware that an oral tradition was dying out—their first collection appeared in 1812. So it was in Odense, a small rural town on the island of Fyn, separated from both Copenhagen and the Danish mainland by stretches of the Baltic Sea. The tales that made a lasting impression on the young Andersen were told by his paternal grandmother, who worked with other poor old women in the spinning room of the local lunatic asylum. These stories included such Nordic characters as ice maidens, trolls, and the water-spirits living in the "bell-deep" in the Odense river, as well as a cast of witches and soldiers and princesses, which would make up his first published collection thirty years later. "The stories told by these old ladies, and the insane figures which I saw around me in the asylum, operated so powerfully upon me, that when it grew dark I scarcely dared to go out of the house," Andersen recalled. "I was therefore permitted, generally at sunset, to lie down in my parents' bed . . . here I lay in a waking dream as if the actual world did not concern me."[3] A mad paternal grandfather, a woodcarver, with whom Andersen felt some dreaded connection, completed the cast of characters influential on the writer as a child. This grandfather used to parade through the town singing at the top of his voice, covered in garlands of flowers. "One day . . . I heard the boys in the street shouting after him," remembered Andersen. "I hid myself behind a flight of steps in terror for I knew that I was of his flesh and blood."[4]

Neither a rudimentary schooling nor a couple of brief stints as an apprentice roused the young Andersen from his reverie of stories and songs, or from the sense that a special destiny relating to them

awaited him. He had a fine soprano voice and at the start of one of
his apprenticeships he was relieved of his duties and asked rather
to entertain the workmen with his songs. So beautiful was his
high-pitched voice that they soon decided that he must be a girl,
and forcibly undressed him to find out—whereupon he fled home
to his mother, who promised he need never return. Instead, by the
age of thirteen, when the other town boys of his age and class were
already working, he was inveigling himself into the homes of
the Odense bourgeoisie as a precocious singer and actor, soon
nicknamed "the little Nightingale from Fyn." He conceived the
impossible ambition of becoming a performer, in any capacity
whatsoever, at the Royal Theater in Copenhagen—a touring
troupe had visited Odense in 1818. Saving the "pocket money"
rewards from his local performances, he pleaded with his mother
to let him leave Odense forever. He had never traveled more than
a few miles before and she told her neighbors that "when he sees
the rough sea, he will be frightened and turn back."[5] But in 1819,
the fourteen-year-old Andersen set off alone to Copenhagen, then
two days' journey away, to make his fortune. He had 10 *rigsdaler*
(equivalent of about £100/$150 today) in his pocket and knew no
one in the capital.

Little in his bizarre personality and harrowed youth gave grounds
for hope that anything would become of him, save his obstinate
self-belief and a certain ability to inspire others to look after him.
Like the Ugly Duckling, the teenage Andersen in Copenhagen
nearly starved, nearly froze, and thrust himself into all sorts of
middle-class environments where he was not wanted. He lived in
slum lodgings, supported initially by cultivated benefactors including the composer C. E. F. Weyse and the poet Jens Baggesen, to
whom he had presented himself on his arrival. They arranged for
him to have singing lessons; he made his debut as a troll on the
stage of the Royal Theater, where he also took dancing lessons,
and he wrote plays that were rejected as abysmally ignorant of even
basic grammar and spelling by the theater management.

After three years of living on the margins of society, he was
rescued by kindly patrons who put together a fund to educate
him. He was sent off to grammar school at Slagelse, a provincial
backwater fifty miles from Copenhagen—it was chosen partly

to remove Andersen from the distractions of the theater, which remained his goal in life. He was seventeen, a gawky overgrown ignoramus in a class of nicely schooled eleven-year-olds. Asked on his first day to point out Copenhagen on a map, he had to admit he had not a clue how to find it. Andersen called his five traumatic school years in Slagelse and, later, in another grammar school at Helsingør—under the same bullying, tyrannical headmaster—the most miserable of his life. He could not learn, he could not concentrate: "My nasty vanity sneaks in," he wrote at the age of twenty-one, "there is a kind of unpleasant dreaminess in me, something restless and impulsive in my soul."[6]

But he completed the curriculum, and moved back to Copenhagen, an educated veneer now coating the peasant fatalism and the inherited tendency to depression that would never leave him. Among the capital's intelligentsia, however, he was still a figure of fun, mocked as "the little clamator" because he could not refrain from declaiming his writings to all and sundry. He still felt isolated and misunderstood: Around this time, in 1832, he wrote his first autobiography, the most honest and reliable of the three accounts of his life, to explain his difficulties and hardships to a few close friends. But it would be another decade of floundering with poetry, drama, and the novel, in all of which Andersen believed lay his vocation, before he found, as if by accident, his authentic voice. In 1833, he left Denmark for a yearlong trip to Italy, which was a vital formative influence, maturing his vision and adding a classical rigor to his writing. He returned to pubish a novel about Italian life, *The Improvisatore*, an immediate critical and popular success, soon translated into German. While it was at the printer in 1835 Andersen wrote to a friend "I have also written some fairy tales for children. Ørsted [the Danish physicist Hans Christian Ørsted] says . . . that these tales will make me immortal, for they are the most perfect things I have ever written; but I myself do not think so."[7] Weeks after the successful appearance of *The Improvisatore*, the publisher, Reitzel, paid Andersen 30 *rigsdaler* (£300/$450 today) to bring out a slim, unbound pamphlet, sixty-one pages long, called *Eventyr, fortalte for Børn (Fairy Tales, Told for Children)*.

FIRST FAIRY TALES AND THE NINETEENTH-CENTURY INVENTION OF CHILDHOOD

It is hard now to imagine the astonishment of a child in 1835 who opened a small unknown book called *Eventyr* and read these opening words:

A soldier came marching along the road: left, right! left, right! He had his knapsack on his back and a sword at his side, because he had been off to war, and now he was on his way home. Then he met an old witch on the road. She was so hideous, her lower lip hung all the way down to her breast.

Now, we assume imaginative, anarchic stories as the bedrock of good children's books, from *Alice's Adventures in Wonderland* to the Harry Potter series. But when Andersen wrote his first tales, children's books were not about enjoyment; they were humorless moralizing prose meant to educate rather than amuse young readers. Fairy tales, moreover, had been disapproved of as frighteningly or irrelevantly imaginative by generations of educators since the Enlightenment. The Grimms' collections (1812–15) had given them a recent respectability, and there were now also the German *Kunstmärchen* (art fairy tales) of Romantic writers such as E. T. A. Hoffmann and Ludwig Tieck. These were elaborate, convoluted long stories for adults that Andersen admired, although they were very different from his own work. But no one had yet taken the form as a model for creative writing for children. The volume called *Eventyr* transformed the folktale into a new genre that blew like a gust of fresh air through the European literary establishment. Here was a genuine storytelling voice, truthful, convincing, straightforward but not banal, which everyone understood. The influence on children's books was to be inestimable.

It was inspired luck to open with "The Tinderbox." A confident, typical young man's tale, lively and fast-moving, it rejoices in the triumph of youth over age with the force and optimism of traditional folktales such as "Jack and the Beanstalk" or "Puss in

Boots," whose penniless heroes overcome hardship and end successful and happy. Yet what distinguishes it immediately from the folktale on which it is based—a Danish variant of the Aladdin story—is the humor and detail. When the soldier finds gold, for example, he could "buy all of Copenhagen and every single sugarpig sold by the cake-wives, and all the tin soldiers, whips, and rocking horses in the whole world!" The double adult/child readership Andersen intended is also marked in the social satire: When the soldier loses his money and lives in a garret, "none of his friends came to see him because there were too many stairs to climb."

With this first tale, Andersen challenged the Danish literary establishment and especially Adam Oehlenschläger's five-act drama *Aladdin* (1805), the most esteemed play of the day, written in the ornate style Andersen rejected. It is no accident that the first three fairy tales Andersen chose to adapt—"The Tinderbox," "Little Claus and Big Claus," and "The Princess on the Pea"—are all fantasies of social climbing and class revenge. Two have plots in which random violence upturns the established order (" 'Tell me right now what you want it for or I'll pull out my sword and chop off your head!' 'No,' said the witch. So the soldier chopped off her head. There she lay!"). In Andersen's second volume of *Eventyr*, published later in 1835, he reworked in a more consciously individual manner two further folk stories, "Thumbelina" and "The Traveling Companion," which also revel in the unlikely triumph of the poor and obscure. Then, over the next nine years came the tales that dramatize in an ever more autobiographical way the suffering of the outsider: "The Little Mermaid," "The Steadfast Tin Soldier," "The Wild Swans," "The Ugly Duckling," "The Nightingale," "The Fir Tree." Had he written nothing else, his reputation would have been assured by the stories of this decade.

Behind them lay half a lifetime of struggle, rejection, and alienation; ahead lay the future of the genre that was to be children's literature. The two cannot be separated, for, as Andersen delved into his childhood memories of folklore, there surfaced all the resentments and injustices of his life in the underclass. Through a revolutionary shift in perspective, Andersen talked to the child in the adult. With his child heroes and heroines, his speaking toys and farmyard animals, he gave a voice—compelling, colloquial, funny—to groups that had been traditionally silent and oppressed: children, the poor, those outside the standard social or sexual stereotypes. Like Lewis Carroll, who used similar anarchic elements ("Off with her head") in *Alice's Adventures in Wonderland* as his rebellion against middle-class Victorian Oxford thirty years later, Andersen identified with children because he felt excluded from the conventional adult world. Both he and Carroll used fantasy as a form in which to express forbidden emotions of rage and inadequacy without, as it were, being caught.

If children's books were a characteristic invention of the democratizing nineteenth century, among whose crowning social achievements was enlarged sympathy with children, then the life and work of Andersen embodies that process. He is the penniless but ambitious young heroes of "The Tinderbox" and "Little Claus and Big Claus," and the fatalistic, thoughtful orphaned Johannes in "The Traveling Companion." He is the morbidly sensitive heroine of "The Princess on the Pea," able to perceive a pea through twenty mattresses and so prove a sensibility equal to that of the upper classes, and the thumb-size Thumbelina, made to feel small and out of control of her fate. Throughout his tales he drew himself as other creatures beyond the mainstream, notably birds. Swans—like Andersen, clumsy on dry land but gloriously elegant in the artistry of their own milieu—make a frequent appearance in his tales, from "The Traveling Companion" through "The Wild Swans" to "The Marsh King's Daughter." He depicted himself clearly as the Ugly Duckling; he is too the fragile but heroic swallow in "Thumbelina," whose migratory habits he followed in his travels every year, and the Nightingale, cast out in favor of cheap artifice but finally acknowledged as the real artist. Many people compared his appearance to that of a stork or crane, and he laughed at himself in his portrayal of the gauche, chattering storks that narrate "The Marsh King's Daughter." Through all of them, Andersen mythologized his own humiliations to make of the folktale his own art.

It was his historical luck to be born on the cusp of two worlds; without this chance he would have been a very different artist. He grew up during the last period in history when, in backward Odense at least, primitive folk culture was still alive, and he absorbed it naturally in a way that was impossible for middle-class, conscious collectors of tales such as the Grimms. Yet his education and ambition propelled him into a wider society that offered, at the beginning of the nineteenth century, the possibility of social mobility for the first time. Had Andersen been born just a little earlier, into the feudal eighteenth century, this chance would have been denied him. Had he been born later, the folk culture that formed his art would already have disappeared.

The particular trauma of Andersen's rapid move up the social scale—even today it is difficult for the child of an illiterate mother to overcome the social and emotional obstacles to education—and the hardship and rejection he encountered along the way, color much of his writing. Many of his stories are powerful because he held on to the primitive folk aspects and vernacular of his childhood, merging them with the social climber's idealization of the bourgeoisie, with whom as an adult he at once belonged and did not belong. As he moved away from the folk motif and made up his own tales, he favored the domestic setting of toys and inanimate objects coming to life, shooting it through incongruously with the folktale's inexorable sense of fate and death. So masterly are his comic touches that it is a shock to calculate that of his more than 150 tales, over three-quarters include references to death, including many whose plots turn on or end with it. This perhaps is what gives the coziness of his bourgeois drawing rooms the hard edge that has made them last.

Certainly tales like "The Steadfast Tin Soldier," the first with no folk source, written in 1838; "The Sweethearts"; "The Fir Tree"; and "The Shepherdess and the Chimney Sweep" made him loved across nineteenth-century Europe as the recorder of the romanticized, cultivated world of middle-class childhood. Introducing comedy and fantasy as the essential components in children's literature, he shaped and continues to shape the agenda of children's culture, from *Winnie the Pooh* to *Toy Story*. Discarding the didactic impulse that had previously governed writing for children, he overturned readers expectations of a moral message to show, in the words of his latest great descendant Philip Pullman, that " 'Thou shalt not' is soon forgotten, but once upon a time lasts forever."[8]

THE GREAT MIDDLE YEARS—ANDERSEN AND THE EUROPEAN ROMANTIC TRADITION

"My name is gradually beginning to shine, and that is the only thing I live for . . . I covet honour in the same way as a miser covets gold,"[9] Andersen admitted in 1837. Gradually, he achieved the critical and social success he craved—first with his novels, then, by the early 1840s, with the fairy tales; both were translated into most European languages and he became known across the continent. As he did so, the vengefulness of his heroes dwindled, to be replaced by drives that were much sadder, and which dogged Andersen all his life: loneliness, a sense of inexorable apartness, and sexual neurosis.

For even when he was famous, Andersen felt isolated, confused in his sexuality, constantly rejected by those he attempted to love, and aware that he was endlessly mocked for idiosyncrasies that made him appear an outsider everywhere. "He was certainly something of an 'oddity'. In person tall, gaunt, rather ungainly . . . most decidedly disconcerting in his general manner . . . 'gauche': so much so that I am afraid the small boys of the family rather laughed at him behind his back,"[10] recalled Henry Dickens, the novelist's son, after Andersen had stayed for five weeks—"which seemed to the family AGES," said Charles Dickens in a cruel note pinned to his guest's room after his departure. A Danish writer described Andersen in 1872 as "strange and bizarre in his movements and carriage. His arms and legs were long and thin and out of all proportion, his hands were broad and flat, and his feet of such gigantic dimensions that no one would ever have thought of stealing his boots."[11] He was, moreover, a mass of highly strung nerves: hypochondriac, pathologically vain, hypersensitive to criticism (Dickens once found him prostrate on the lawn, sobbing his heart out over a bad review), so terrified of being buried alive that he slept with a note—"I only seem dead"—by his side, fearful of dogs, of eating pork, of fire (a rope went everywhere with him in his luggage). It was not surprising that he felt unloved and unlovable, and that this is a central concern of his work.

Many readers comment on an overwhelming difference between

Andersen's stories and the traditional folktale: Andersen's frequently unhappy endings. In *The Uses of Enchantment*, the child psychoanalyst Bruno Bettelheim showed how folktales allow a child to face unconscious problems through fantasy—sibling rivalry in "Cinderella," mother-daughter jealousy in "Snow White," fear of desertion in "Hansel and Gretel." "Through the centuries (if not millennia) during which, in their retelling, fairy tales became ever more refined," writes Bettelheim, "they came to convey at the same time overt and covert meanings—came to speak simultaneously to all levels of the human personality, communicating in a manner which reaches the uneducated mind of the child as well as that of the sophisticated adult."[12] A satisfying ending is essential to the psychological workings of these tales, almost a reason for their survival from generation to generation. Andersen by contrast rarely provides that satisfaction and consolation. Indeed he cannot, because, although he managed to create tales that match the resonance and double articulation of the traditional forms, his stories are not pared down over generations, but are the individual imaginings of a particular consciousness governed by a culturally specific zeitgeist—one tended to the romantic and the tragic.

Among his friends were the writers Balzac, Hugo, and Heine, and the musicians Mendelssohn, Liszt, and Schumann. With them, Andersen was a representative figure of the European Romantic spirit, and an essential part of that spirit was the transmutation of inner suffering into art—Romanticism's autobiographical imperative. Andersen's compulsion was to understand his own life, to transform the pain and emptiness he felt into artistic order. This Romantic chord shaped the superb archetypal works of his middle years, and although he wrote in a minor key, his achievement was no less rooted in his own psychological distress than, say, that of Dickens, Carlyle, or Ruskin—early Victorian contemporaries who, like him, published their first works in the 1830s and 1840s, combining, as he did, comedy and tragedy to convey both a bitter personal vision and a radical political message.

Andersen was a typical Romantic in the enjoyment with which he broadcast his unhappy love affairs with women. He was immature and prudish—a reaction perhaps against his mother's family, with its association of promiscuity and poverty—and he fell in love for the first time at twenty-five with Riborg Voigt, a Fyn merchant's daughter safely engaged to someone else. "She is so beautiful, so gentle, and good, you would love her, so would all the world," he wrote to the poet B. S. Ingemann. "Oh it is killing me to think of it! Dear, dear Ingemann, I wish I were dead!—dead!—even if death were annihilation; but it cannot be."[13] He made just as much noise thirteen years later when he fell in love with the singer Jenny Lind, also safely unattainable: "Now do you understand that all my thoughts are about such a pearl? And yet, she won't be mine—can't be mine, but she shall seem to me like a good and kind spirit."[14] In between there were a few minor infatuations. But by 1837, when one girl, sixteen-year-old Sophie Ørsted, got engaged, he confided with relief to his diary "Now I shall never be married, no young woman grows up for me any more, day by day I'm getting to be more and more a bachelor!"[15]

The truth was less simple, for each time Andersen fell seriously in love with a woman he quietly and simultaneously courted a young man—liaisons that he did not broadcast. He especially favored a triangular relationship in which he turned his attentions to both a sister and a brother. In 1830, he was as engrossed with Christian Voigt as with his sister Riborg, and the most lasting obsession of his life, with the Danish civil servant and bibliophile Edvard Collin, was partly expressed through a courtship of his sister Louise in 1832. In 1843, when he was announcing his love for Jenny Lind, he was secretly conducting an affair with Danish aristocrat Henrik Stampe: "My darling Henrik—you whom I believe I could many times feel inclined to sacrifice my life for."[16] Two years later, he and Jenny were addressing one another as "sister" and "brother" and staying at the court in Weimar, and there was another triangle involving Weimar's Hereditary Grand Duke Carl Alexander, with whom Andersen was also in love. The two men held hands and sobbed over their adoration of Jenny, "[He] told me he loved me and pressed his cheek to mine . . . received me in his shirt with only a gown around himself," he panted to his diary. "He pressed me to his breast, we kissed . . . 'Think of this hour,' he said, 'as being yesterday. We are friends for life.' We both wept."[17]

In his novel *The Improvisatore*, Andersen describes the hero Antonio, a self-portrait, as "one of those intellectually amphibious creatures . . . only a poetical being, not a man, like the rest of you." His second novel, *O.T.* (1836), contains a daring scene of cross-dressing in which two men are in love with one another's sisters but dress up at a party in such a way that, encouraged by sibling likenesses, they caress each other: "When Wilhelm seated himself on his knee, and pressed his cheek to his, Otto felt his heart beat as in a fever; it sent a stream of fire through his blood . . ." And Andersen's third novel, *Only a Fiddler* (1837), has a heroine whose sexual identity is constantly blurred, who spends much of the story dressed and behaving as a man, a "little moustache on her beautiful upper lip" as "in her male attire" she publicly kisses and flirts with her male lover.

None of these come fully alive as fiction. Not until he discovered the fairy tale did Andersen find a literary genre whose obvious gap from reality freed him to write as he was and felt. Already in "The Traveling Companion" (1835) the sexual malaise of a frigid princess turning into different-hued swans, at the mercy of a sorcerer and an innocent youth, carries some of Andersen's unease, but from "The Little Mermaid" (1837) onward, his tales, comically or tragically, are the story of himself as failed lover and struggling artist, a man tormented by liabilities of temperament against which he fought a lifelong battle.

He began writing "The Little Mermaid" in 1836 when his unrequited love for Edvard was at its height: "I long for you, yes, this moment I long for you as if you were a lovely girl . . . I never had a brother, but if I did, I could not have loved him as I love you . . . No one have I wanted to thrash as much as you, no one has brought more tears to my eyes, but neither has anyone been loved so much by me as you."[18] He composed other, more intimate letters that he dared not send, and then he cast himself as the little mermaid, sexless, voiceless companion to her prince, who, like him, cannot express what she feels and is denied the reality of love as the prince marries someone else. Andersen wrote the tale on the island of Fyn where he had gone to escape Edvard's wedding. "If you looked down to the bottom of my soul, you would understand fully the source of my longing and—pity me. Even the open transparent lake has its unknown depths which no divers know,"[19] he told Edvard.

Alone, silent, unlovable, yet with an unswerving sense of his own unalterable self—that is Andersen's quintessential hero. Examples span his oeuvre: the one-legged toy in "The Steadfast Tin Soldier" (1838); the glittering top in the comedy "The Sweethearts," a self-portrait composed in 1843 when, now famous, he met middle-aged frumpy Riborg (the ball) thirteen years after she had turned him down; the pining Snowman, melting from love for a stove, whom he created in 1861 after falling in love with Harald Scharff, a young dancer. Doomed love is a recurring Andersen theme; like many children's writers, he was perhaps too childlike to understand or to even genuinely want an adult sexual relationship. Observing his little vanities, his sulks if not served first at dinner, his fuss over the slightest discomfort, Annie Wood, an English visitor to the grand Danish country estates, where Andersen spent much time visiting his aristocratic friends, concluded that he was "a child according to the ideal of childhood; keenly sensitive, entirely egoistical, innocently vain, the centre of life, interest, concern and meaning to himself . . . taking it for granted that everywhere he was to be first and all . . . He had no notion of time, and as pertinaciously required everyone to be at his beck and call as any curled darling in the nursery who is at once the plague and the joy of his household."[20]

Andersen's vision was childlike to the core, as is shown not only by his sympathy with the child's struggle to survive, believe, be listened to (Gerda in "The Snow Queen," Elsa in "The Wild Swans," the Ugly Duckling) but by his empathy with plants, toys, domestic objects, as living things—a shirt collar, a spinning top, a darning needle with pretensions to being an embroidery needle, a butterfly unable to make up its mind. Any random object, it appeared, would do as an alter ego—and of course the natural egoism of the child, seeing its own concerns in all things, was the mirror image of that empathetic ability. "It often seems to me as if every hoarding, every little flower is saying to me, 'Look at me, just for a moment, and then my story will go right through you,' and then, if I feel like it, I have the story," he said. "[Ideas] lay in my thoughts like a seed corn, requiring only a flowing stream, a ray of sunshine, a drop from the cup of bitterness, for them to spring forth and burst into bloom."[21]

Yet like the child in "The Emperor's New Clothes"—that perfect comedy of Romanticism's innocent penetration to the heart of things—he saw clearly and deeply not only how people think and feel, but into the wider world around him, and portrayed it with a comic genius accessible to all. Everywhere shafts of satire or bathos light up his narratives: the ridiculous opening to "The Nightingale": "In China, as you probably know, the Emperor is Chinese, and everyone around him is Chinese too"; the crows asking for a pension in "The Snow Queen"; the matches in "The Flying Trunk" boasting of their noble "family tree," the great pine in the forest of which they were the little sticks, for "then came the woodcutters. It was the great revolution, and our family was split apart." Andersen complained when people failed to see "that naivety was only a part of my tales, that humor was really what gave them their flavor."[22] But beneath the comedy and fantasy, the intent is deadly serious.

"In a utilitarian age, of all other times, it is a matter of grave importance that Fairy Tales should be respected," Dickens wrote in 1853, just after Andersen had visited England but before English children's literature had taken root. "Everyone who has considered the subject knows full well that a nation without fancy, without some romance, never did, never can, never will, hold a great place under the sun."[23] Both Dickens and Andersen wrote against the brutal, rational mercantile values of fast-industrializing Europe, prioritizing the emotional, the sentimental, the individual. Two of Andersen's greatest masterpieces come out of that battle: the perfect miniature of "The Little Match Girl," in which the creative imagination battles with a cold hard society where outsiders are left to die, and "The Snow Queen," an epic drama of a spiritual quest celebrating the triumph of love over reason.

"I heard Dickens read the death-bed scene of Little Nell," wrote a contemporary observer, "and I was moved to tears, but I knew that the author himself was reading the story; but when I heard Andersen read the story of the Little Girl with the Matches, I did not think of the author at all, but wept like a child, unconscious of everything around me."[24] The conviction of the storytelling in

"The Snow Queen," too, the galloping word pictures and passion-
ate evocation of the changing seasons—Andersen wrote that the
tale "permeated my mind in such a way that it came out dancing
over the paper"—surely emerged from his deep alignment with
and longing for Gerda's innocent view of love, which propels the
narrative and saves Kai from the grown-up, threatening sexuality
of the Snow Queen:

They had forgotten all about the cold, empty splendor of the Snow
Queen's castle as if it had been a bad dream. Grandmother was sitting in
God's bright sunshine and reading aloud from the Bible: "Unless you
become as little children, you shall not enter the kingdom of Heaven."
And Kai and Gerda looked into each other's eyes, and all of a sudden
they understood the old hymn: "In the valley where roses grow wild /
There we will speak to the Christ Child!" There they sat, two grown-ups,
and yet they were children—children at heart—and it was summer.
Warm, blissful summer.

It was not just northern Denmark that prompted Andersen's
many wintry settings. He also feared that the splinter of ice in his
own heart made him unlovable, emotionally frozen, even as the
chant "love nourishes life" choruses through his work. He had the
artist's essential detachment as well as involvement—that misery,
says Ellen Handler Spitz, "was the deep ground of his genius . . .
the source of the profoundest grief in the story of the little match
girl . . . The story is only four pages long, but it epitomizes all that
Andersen understood about the gap between desire and truth. In
it, he honoured the rough matter of his own earliest childhood,
brought it through fire, and cut a gem."[25]
  In postfeminist times, Andersen is sometimes criticized for
enjoying the suffering of his major female characters. To a public
raised on Disney, it is almost too painful to read of the sacrificial
love of the Little Mermaid, walking on knives for her prince, or
the freezing, starving Match Girl, or the agony of Karen in "The
Red Shoes" dancing to death in punishment for vanity. Many
parents today choose not to read these particular Andersen tales to
their children, and it is a debatable point whether they are suitable
for them. They certainly lack the consolation of a happy ending,

the redemption of suffering, with which the traditional folktale appealed to younger readers, and which the twentieth century, more cosseting of children than the nineteenth, made virtually universal in children's literature. Just because unhappy endings in children's fiction are now so rare, however, some parents have found that stories such as "The Little Mermaid" are extraordinarily effective in capturing a child's interest and opening a window for them to ask deeper, life-and-death questions.

Suitable for today's children or not, such stories express an important part of Andersen's vision. They are not sadistic outpourings of a patriarchal culture but masochistic self-portraits—a link emphasized by the use of feet to symbolize suffering in "The Little Mermaid" and "The Red Shoes," casting back to Andersen's memories of his cobbler father. In them Andersen, the self-confessed "amphibious creature," part male, part female, punishes himself for the weaknesses that caused him the most suffering in life. He castigates himself for inappropriate love in "The Little Mermaid," for the frozen emotions shutting out human relationships in "The Little Match Girl," while "The Red Shoes," written in 1845, the year of his first triumphal journey across Germany, is symbolic of the restless vanity that sent him dancing across the courts of Europe. And if they emphasize Andersen's perception of himself as a passive sufferer, they have their counterpoints in another Romantic tradition to which Andersen contributed some of the great nineteenth-century archetypes—the femmes fatales the Snow Queen, the Ice Maiden, and Auntie Toothache, whose victims are all boys or young men and whose peculiar psychological power embodies the strange shifting tones of his late works.

LATE ANDERSEN—THE SELF AND THE SHADOW

By 1847, when he visited London for the first time, Andersen was the most famous writer in Europe. English aristocratic salons, German princely courts and the Danish royal family all competed for his attentions. "Twenty-five years ago," he gasped in 1844, "I arrived with my small parcel in Copenhagen, a poor stranger of a boy, and today I have drunk my chocolate with the [Danish] Queen, sitting opposite her and the King at the table."[26] And a few years later, "Tears came into my eyes, I thought that I, the poor shoemaker and washerwoman's son, was being kissed by the Czar of Russia's grandson. How the extremes were meeting."[27] The Ugly Duckling had become the Swan of his tale: a poetic but tame bird applauded by children and fed titbits from the tables of the rich. All his life Andersen swooned before royalty. "He is a lean man with a hollow lantern-jawed face, and in his outward appearance he betrays a servile lack of self-confidence which is appreciated by dukes and princes. He fulfills exactly a prince's idea of a poet," recalled Heinrich Heine. "When he visited me he had decked himself out with a big tie-pin; I asked him what it was that he had put there. He replied very unctuously, 'It is a present which the Electress of Hessen has been gracious enough to bestow on me.' Otherwise Andersen is a man of some spirit."[28]

His rise had indeed been meteoric, and it is a measure of his ruthlessness and integrity as an artist, and his continuing eagerness to engage freshly with the world around him, that in his fairy tales he was never overcome by his fame. That he did not sink into sentimentality or a pastiche of his rags-to-riches story—except in his fraudulent autobiography *The Fairy Tale of My Life*—is a mark, too, of how deeply alienated from his society this complex, restless man was. "Enthusiastic listeners frequently asked him to read 'The Ugly Duckling,'" recalled the critic Edvard Brandes, "to listen to it . . . was a partial insight into that which this rare and *abused* soul of a human being had felt and suffered in order to be able to create this immortal little work of art . . . He had led his war against everyone and he seemed to be a significant and exceptional spirit, sitting there in his chair and bending his splendid head over the book whose words he knew by heart."[29]

Although now financially comfortable, Andersen never acquired a home, but traveled ceaselessly, allowing himself to be pampered at the estates of the rich but unable to commit himself to any fixed place or person. "Oh, to travel, to travel! If one could only spend one's life fluttering from one place to another!"[30] That typical Romantic cry, uttered first when he was in his twenties, lasted a lifetime as Andersen acquired the economic means to flutter endlessly from place to place. (Travel in the nineteenth century was very expensive, and restricted to the privileged few.) But the restlessness fed into his work, too, and as he aged it was no longer aimed even in part at a child audience; it was steadily becoming more divided and fragmentary within itself, more disturbing, more pessimistic, though saved from unremitting bleakness by humor. "I looked where no one else can look, and I saw what no one else can see, what no one ought to see!" says his character the Shadow. "What an ignoble world it really is! I wouldn't even want to be a man except that being human is considered worthwhile."

"The Shadow" (1847) expresses Andersen's deep self-divisions. On a superficial reading, the story was inspired by his humiliation fifteen years earlier at the hands of Edvard Collin, who had kept his distance by declining Andersen's suggestion in 1831 that they use the familiar *du* form (equivalent of French *tu*). The rejection rankled Andersen for the rest of his life, and he spoke daily of his isolation. The shadow uses almost verbatim the language in which Edvard couched his refusal, and Andersen wrote to Edvard in 1847, "Well, I expect you have understood that the malice is aimed against you."[31] But this is only the first level at which the story works. Andersen felt so close to Edvard that he used him here as his alter ego. Andersen himself is at once the learned man, serious and civilized, and the Shadow, a shifty dark figure behind the scenes, the artist as a man without his own identity but honed to all experiences. "I am like water, everything moves me, everything is reflected in me, I suppose this is part of my nature as a poet . . . but often it also torments me,"[32] Andersen confided in a letter in 1855. He feared the void in himself while recognizing that it contributed to his creativity: the agony of the Romantic doppel-gänger is that its two sides are one divided soul, and throughout Andersen's life and work this dualism is apparent.

"The contrasts in this complex person are legion," wrote Andersen scholar Elias Bredsdorff. "He was a Christian rejecting the main dogmas of Christianity; he was a generous miser; he was a social snob who invariably stood up for the underdog; he was more intense both in his hatred and in his love of his native land than any other writer of his time; he was scared stiff of all the dangers connected with travelling, and yet no other contemporary European writer travelled more than he did."[33] The contradictions in his outlook are everywhere apparent in his tales. The divisions within "The Shadow" are answered by the harmony of "The Bell," where rich and poor, artist and scientist, find the truth their own way. The victory of true art and nature in "The Nightingale" is offset by the princess's preference for the artificial musical rattle over the real bird in "The Swineherd." The triumph of love over death in "The Snow Queen" is undone by "The Ice Maiden," where the elderly Andersen reasserts his fatalism and death outmaneuvers love. The hope that art is greater than tyranny, that it confers immortality—"Dead people can't walk again . . . but a work of art can"—expressed in "The Most Incredible Thing" is rejected two years later in "Auntie Toothache," where art is dismissed as rubbish.

Georg Brandes read "The Shadow" as Andersen's sense of the triumph of the second-rate, which gives the story a contemporary ring in our age of mass culture and dumbing down. Its mix of comedy and nihilism is certainly modern. Here we see the decent well-meaning hero out of control; the stylistic tour de force by which Andersen has the learned man killed offstage and in a subordinate clause, too frail and blank to be worth a sentence of his own; the reversal of fairy-tale expectations, the villain marrying the princess and ruling the kingdom. All this has more in common with the black-humored modernism of Kafka or Evelyn Waugh than with the work of Andersen's contemporaries.

"The Shadow" opened a new phase of stylistic experimentation in which Andersen reinvented the fairy tale as a modern self-referential genre, publishing his tales from the 1850s on under the new, more general title *Historier* (*Stories*). In tales such as "The Marsh King's Daughter," "Anne Lisbeth," "A Story of the Dunes," and "Psyche," he now anticipated aspects of modernism—the expression of meaning chiefly through style, form, and image; fluid, changing characters and a portrayal of the irrational, unconscious mind; a decreasing importance of plot. "One of these stories, 'The Wind Tells of Valdemar Daae and His Daughters,' is, perhaps, regarding the construction, of special significance," he wrote to Duke Carl Alexander. "I have tried, and I hope I have succeeded, in giving the whole narrative a tone as if one heard the wind itself."[34] He reworked the story many times to capture the sound of the rushing wind, and form is content here—the transience of life conveyed by the language of the howling wind-narrator. Similarly, the long, complicated "The Marsh King's Daughter" reaches a sophisticated modulation of comedy and tragedy by using the parochial storks as an ironic, dramatic chorus to comment on and contribute to the action; in the conclusion, Andersen mocks those readers who dismiss him as just a children's author:

"That was a new ending to the story!" said Stork Father. "That's not what I expected at all. But I like it very much."

"What do you think the children will say about it?" asked Stork Mother.

"Well, of course that's what counts the most," said Stork Father.

"Our time is the time of fairy tales," Andersen wrote in "The Wood Nymph." Like many self-made men, he saw the future as a source of opportunity, excitement, and pleasure rather than cause for nostalgia. In this respect he belonged with the optimists of the nineteenth century, who saw the world getting better, more equal, less harsh. He embraced the new inventions that occurred in his lifetime, such as the railway—he called it "the steam serpent"—and the telegraph as extensions of his magical universe; thus he effortlessly incorporated the Paris World Exposition of 1867 into his fairy tale "The Wood Nymph."

In art as in life Andersen was innovative, forward-looking, preternaturally attuned to what was new and of the moment in the zeitgeist. In the 1830s and 1840s, tales such as "The Little Mermaid," "The Ugly Duckling," and "The Snow Queen" had chimed with the early Victorian novel, with its child-heroes and fixed characters and the strong linear narrative deriving from its biographical drive. By the 1860s and 1870s, he had left behind these grand classical archetypes and was writing like the mid-nineteenth-century European novelists—of psychological disintegration, of the battle between individual instinct and social control. In strokes of vivid local color, he paints his Wood Nymph, touring the demimonde of Paris, of chartreuse-drinkers and cancan dancers, as a worldly fallen woman who might have tripped off the pages of contemporary French novels—Flaubert's *Madame Bovary*, or Zola's *Thérèse Raquin*. The hallucinatory quality that he gives to his two great late femmes fatales, the Ice Maiden and Auntie Toothache, suggests that both are less living women than nightmare visions brought forth by the victims whom they torment to death. Both young men, therefore, are destroyed by the power of their own imaginations, by their inner divisions and doubts.

Religious doubt concerned Andersen especially in this period of his life. His mother had brought him up in the Lutheran faith that was standard in nineteenth-century Denmark, though her own version of Christianity was so close to pagan superstition that it is not hard to see the origins of her son's colorful melding of the two traditions in tales such as "The Little Mermaid" and "The Snow Queen," each peopled with creatures of legend yet peppered with references to good works, God's Heaven, or the words of a hymn. In his carefully constructed autobiography, Andersen overlaid her unquestioning faith with the skepticism of his father, with whom he identified and whose quoted words we can take as Andersen's own viewpoint, safely camouflaged as the dead man's thoughts to avoid giving offense to religiously orthodox friends. "Christ was a man like us, but an extraordinary man!" and "There is no other devil than that which we have in our own hearts," Andersen has his father say; whereupon his mother promptly discovered three nail marks on her husband's arm, a sign "that the devil had been to visit him in the night, in order to prove to him that he really existed."[35]

But if, intellectually, Andersen aligned himself with modern, man, rather than God-centered Christianity, instinctively he held to some of his mother's primitivism: In the spiritual as in all other aspects of his temperament he was inescapably the child of both his parents. As a lonely young man, he chats to God in his diary as to his only friend—"O Lord I could kiss you!"—at the end of a particularly successful day,[36] while, when things go badly, the twenty-year-old schoolboy resorts to the fantastical bargaining of a small child—"God, I swear by my eternal salvation never again within my heart to mistrust Your fatherly hand, if only I might this time be promoted to the fourth form."[37] He was promoted—and embarked on a lifetime of doubt, ceaselessly, romantically, aware that education and modernity played its part in prizing him from the peasant convictions of his mother. "He's now dust and ashes, dead, extinguished, burned out like a light which is no more!" he wrote when a friend died in 1872. "My Lord God, can You let us vanish completely? I'm afraid of that, and I've gotten too clever—and unhappy."[38] Yet all his life he clung to the central Christian tenets of providence, grace, and immortality, which he saw as compensation for the pain and injustices of mortal life in general and his own loneliness in particular. His love letters to Edvard are full of hopes for a happier unity: "I look up to you and then I love you as I could love the one whom I shall tell you about when with God . . . oh is there an eternal life . . . there we shall learn to understand and appreciate each other. There I shall no longer be the destitute one, needing friends and appreciation, there we shall be equal."[39]

Like many nineteenth-century intellectuals hovering on the edge of agnosticism, he rarely went to church but took comfort from some Christian ritual, scrupulously observing the Sabbath and noting approvingly that "the good old fashion of saying grace before meals is still observed in Dickens's home." On his visits to England, he flung himself into ostentatious Victorian Christianity; a young fan staying with his publisher Richard Bentley recalled that after a happy breakfast party Andersen suddenly rose and announced he would say grace, "then raising his hands and bowing his gaunt figure low over the table, he said in a reverential, hushed but audible tone, 'I thank Thee, O Lord, that Thou has permitted me to enjoy another breakfast such as I had at Mr. Bentley's! Amen!' For a moment I thought the dear old man [he was then forty-two!] had lost his senses or was making fun, but a glance at his earnest face rebuked the idea, and I felt ashamed of my mistake."[40]

The scene conjures exactly the nineteenth-century milieu, caught between old pieties and a new secularism, in which Andersen moved. The nit-picking religious squabbles of some of his narrow-minded Danish friends incensed him: "A big unpleasant argument this evening," he noted at the aristocratic estate of Basnæs in 1870, "about Christ and religion. I said Christian dogma was from God and it was a blessing, but that although the circumstances of the birth and family were of interest, they were not necessary for me.

Then the fur began to fly—if one didn't take His birth and death into account, then His teachings would be meaningless! . . . Since I didn't believe in the Father, the Son, and the Holy Ghost, I wasn't a Christian. I answered that I believed in them as concepts but not as people, corporeal beings. They almost gave up on me . . ."[41] Sometimes he almost gave up himself, and during the Danish-Prussian wars of the mid-1860s particularly, when he wrote that "I lost for a moment my hold on God, and felt myself as wretched as a man can be. Days followed in which I cared for nobody, and I believed nobody cared for me,"[42] loss of faith in religion flowed into doubts about the future of culture, which are palpable in his last works.

Living on the cusp of our modern world, he was able to see all around him the first signs of the battle between high and popular culture that was inevitable in an increasingly democratic age. "The Most Incredible Thing," which acts out this debate in the form of a masque enclosed within a modern legend, was written in 1870, just a year after Matthew Arnold's *Culture and Anarchy*. Andersen is unlikely to have known Arnold's work, but he echoes his fear of the incursion of the philistine. And few nineteenth-century works deal as bravely with the artist's preoccupations as "Auntie Toothache," where Andersen explores the link between suffering and creativity, the terror of a mind beyond control, the fear that art is as meaningless and short-lived as wrapping paper—and that so is life itself. The valedictory story recalls elements from every period of his fairy-tale writing: the oversensitive poet recalls "The Princess on the Pea," the fatalistic conclusion echoes the bittersweet "The Fir Tree" ("over, over, and that's what happens to every story!"), the mix of psychology and fantasy, and the anxiety over the future of culture, suggests "The Shadow." Through it all threads the fear of insanity that had haunted Andersen intermittently—his grandfather had died mad—but became constant in old age. "God has given me imagination for my vocation as a poet but not to make me a candidate for the madhouse!"[43] he told his diary in 1871, and later variations of "once again I feel I am on my way to the madhouse" are common.

The tone of Andersen's late tales was not far from the symbolic elements in Ibsen, whose work alarmed him, and the fin de siècle symbolists Mallarmé, Huysmann, Wilde. The sexual fears that fueled much of his work creep nearer the surface here. The identification of sex with death, suggested in "The Little Mermaid" and "The Snow Queen," is consciously played out in several tales of the 1860s—"The Ice Maiden," where Rudy is kissed to death, "Psyche," and "The Wood Nymph." Andersen visited several brothels while researching this last tale, merely chatting to the girls who "said I was indeed very innocent for a man . . . Many might call me a fool—have I been one here?"

That kernel of innocence was at once his unique strength and his limitation as an artist, one of the aspects of his genius that allowed him to come so close to the pared-down archetypes of the folktale, to see, as it were, despite his own emotional ups and downs, beyond the clutter of human desire. Toward the end of his life when he was too ill to write, he occupied himself with the paper cutouts that he had made since childhood, and whose mix of refinement and simplicity seem to embody his style; their stark outlines and silhouette forms appear modern today, and a revelatory match to a twenty-first-century translation of his tales. "He always cut with an enormous pair of paper scissors—and it was a mystery to me how he could cut such dainty delicate things with his big hands and those enormous scissors,"[44] remembered Baroness Bodild Donner, whose estate Andersen often visited at Christmas. "The Christmas tree was lit . . . I had cut out and pasted the figures that hung on the branches. The snow fell, the sleigh bells jingled, the wild swans sang on the seashore; it was charming without, it was snug within,"[45] he wrote—and this coziness is as much part of Andersen's outlook as the inner rage and terror that reacted against it. In his final years he achieved a measure of contentment from being made much of in such settings, and he died after a short illness at the estate of Rolighed north of Copenhagen in 1875, four months after his seventieth birthday. At his request, he was buried in a triple plot where the bodies of Edvard Collin and his wife joined him in 1886 and 1894, but a few years later they were moved to a family vault, and Andersen was left in the original grave alone.

Since it had been obvious that his seventieth birthday would be his last, the occasion was marked by national and international tributes that already had the tone of obituaries—fitting for a writer of such insatiable vanity, for it gave him the pleasure of reading them. None delighted him more than the acclaim in the London *Daily News* of April 5, 1875, in a review whose reading of Andersen still holds true today:

It has been given to *Hans Andersen* to fashion beings, it may almost be said, of a new kind, to breathe life into the toys of childhood, and the forms of antique superstition. The tin soldier, the ugly duckling, the mermaid, the little match girl, are no less real and living in their way than *Othello*, or *Mr Pickwick*, or *Helen of Troy*. It seems a very humble field in which to work, this of nursery legend and childish fancy. Yet the Danish poet alone, of all who have laboured in it, has succeeded in recovering, and reproducing, the kind of imagination which constructed the old fairy tales. . . . It is only a writer who can write for men that is fit to write for children.

THE SOUGHING OF THE CONCH SHELL—
ANDERSEN'S LANGUAGE, 1835–2005

Grown-up, modern, far-ranging, evolving, unfamiliar as well as greatly loved—this is the Andersen whom the new Penguin selection attempts to capture on the two hundredth anniversary of his birth. This volume reflects the broad three phases of his work as a storyteller—the early tales, derived from folklore; the great classical stories of his middle years, the high point of his art; and the revolutionary late experiments with the form, where his preoccupations with symbolism, the unconscious, and the absurd chime with the concerns we have today. All appear in new translations that bring many revelations, for language and style are Andersen's essential hallmarks, and it was his raw and unpolished Danish, his individual colloquial manner, which most startled audiences in his day, and which Tiina Nunnally has caught here.

It is one of the elusive achievements of great literature that translations date while fine writing remains timeless. Goethe, Dostoevsky, Proust—we need new translations every few generations in order to keep in touch with the brilliance of the original language, which may acquire the patina of its times but is never labored, old-fashioned, or difficult. The earliest Andersen versions in English are a particularly acute example of how translations are made through the prism of their times, for the very revolutionary language that so shocked yet enticed Danish readers was simply filtered out by the sentimental Victorians. The colloquialisms and chatty manner, the abruptness and humorous asides, the mix of warmth and satire, all were ignored and even replaced by the florid diction that Andersen had deliberately rejected. For almost a century from the 1840s on, Andersen translations ranged from the inadequate to the abysmal, with translators working mostly from German versions repeating errors and adding their own as they went. Mary Howitt, his first translator, was the most competent but made basic errors such as translating *Svalen* as "the breeze" instead of "the swallow"; her rival Charles Boner embellished Andersen's style with ludicrously fanciful language—"see" became "behold," "sweetheart" became "the affianced one." Other Victorian translators destroyed the meaning of certain works spectacularly; in one version "The Ugly Duckling"—*den grimme Ælling* in Danish—became "The Green Duck," following a German mistranslation of *grimme* into *grün* (green); in another, the translator was so upset by the court's preference, in "The Nightingale," for the artificial bird—a point on which the story depends—that he added his own explanation: "But the reader must recollect that they were only Chinese." Only the powerful structure of Andersen's tales, and their emotively unmissable messages, allowed them to survive in translation at all.

Things improved greatly from the 1930s in the works of a few translators of rigorous standards working directly from the Danish, but still an elegance crept in which stopped English-speaking readers from hearing just how odd Andersen actually sounds. This oddness, which is part of his originality, was probably what Dickens had heard about from Victorian translators when he wrote dismissively to a friend in 1857 that "Hans Christian Andersen may perhaps be with us, but you won't mind *him*—especially as he speaks no language but his own Danish, and is suspected of not even knowing that."[46]

"The whimsical traditions of speech, the small words that are so alive, the unmisunderstandable breaches in logic—all these were ingredients in what was in addition poetic prose of great breadth of expression," writes Erik Dal, co-editor of the complete Danish critical edition (1963–90) of the tales. "We find ourselves listening to the most intimate shades of meaning our language has to offer, shades so fine that even the best translators often have given up trying to grasp, or at all events reproduce, the full combination of overtones in the unmistakable soughing of the conch-shell."[47]

Tiina Nunnally's translation comes in my view closest to that magical turn. Her feel for Andersen's slightly eccentric yet beautifully fluent and easy use of language makes this translation at once accurate, loyal to the original, and a joy to read—proof that the adage "translations (like wives) are seldom faithful if they are in the least attractive" does not have to be true. Natural and colloquial without ever being jarringly modern, Nunnally's version is a pleasure to speak aloud, and it makes one imagine the fun of those early sessions when Andersen read his tales to their first audiences, refining the language and tone according to the eager responses of his listeners. Nunnally also captures how effectively Andersen works through the smallest details, many of which come most fully alive when spoken. Her progression from "Ooh" to "Eeek" to "Oh how hideous," for instance, makes us shudder *with* the soldier in "The Tinderbox" as he encounters the increasingly monstrous dogs. Similarly, she has noticed, in "The Ugly Duckling," that Andersen deliberately withholds the word *ugly* until the end, substituting similes like "hideous" to give the final point greater punch. And she is the first significant translator to render correctly into English the title "The Princess on the Pea"—that small preposition an example of the still-surprising earthiness and literalness in Andersen that often unnerves translators and diverts them from his true tone. In all the major twentieth-century editions in English the story is decorously called "The Princess and the Pea," losing both the immediacy and the sense of the ridiculous that Andersen worked so hard to achieve.

"He enjoyed giving his humour free rein," recalled Edvard Collin, "his speaking was without stop, richly adorned with the figures of speech well known to children, and with gestures to match the situation. Even the driest sentences came to life. He did not say, 'The children got into the carriage and then drove away', but 'They got in to the carriage—'Goodbye, Dad! Goodbye,

Mum!'—the whip cracked smack! Smack! And away they went, come on! Gee up!' People who later heard him reading his tales will be able to form only a dim idea of the exceptional liveliness with which he told them to children.''[48] Nunnally's translation too draws teller and listener together in the light touch of its humor, in the fresh, vivid rendering of the jokes against the pompous and powerful, yet sacrifices none of the graceful, classical simplicity that links Andersen to the tradition of folktale and legend.

A note on translations in this introduction: As this book is for English-speaking readers, where possible I have used a published English source and credited it below. Extracts from the stories in this volume are by Tiina Nunnally. All other translations from Danish sources are my own unless otherwise specified.

NOTES

1. Andersen to B. S. Ingemann, November 20, 1843, *Breve fra Hans Christian Andersen*, ed. C. S. A. Bille and N. Bøgh (Copenhagen, 1878) II:94.

2. Hans Christian Andersen, *The Fairy Tale of My Life*, trans. Horace Scudder (New York, 1870; reprinted in Denmark, 1955, and in London: British Book Centre, 1975), 274.

3. Ibid., 8.

4. Ibid.

5. Ibid., 23.

6. Andersen to Jonas Collin, July 2, 1826, *H. C. Andersens Brevveksling med Jonas Collin den Ældre og andre Medlemmer af det Collinske Hus*, ed. H. Topsøe-Jensen (Copenhagen 1945–48), I:55.

7. Andersen to Henriette Wulff, March 16, 1834, *Hans Christian Andersen's Correspondence with the late Grand-Duke of Saxe-Weimar, Charles Dickens etc. etc.*, ed. Frederick Crawford (London: Deen & Son, 1891), 141.

8. Philip Pullman, Acceptance Speech for the Carnegie Medal 1996, reproduced on www.randomhouse.com.

9. Andersen to Henriette Hanck, September 20, 1837, "H. C. Andersens Brevveksling med Henriette Hanck 1830–46," in *Anderseniana* IX–XIII, ed. Svend Larsen (1941–46), X:199.

10. *The Recollections of Sir Henry Dickens KC* (London: Heinemann, 1934), 35.

11. William Bloch, *Paa Rejse med H. C. Andersen* (Copenhagen, 1942), trans. Reginald Spink in Danish Ministry of Foreign Affairs, *Danish Journal* (Copenhagen, 1975), 13.

12. Bruno Bettelheim, *The Uses of Enchantment* (London: Peguin, 1978), 5–6.

13. Andersen to B. S. Ingemann, January 18, 1831, *Andersen's Correspondence with the late Grand-Duke of Saxe-Weimar* (London: Deen & Son, 1891), 66–67.

14. Andersen to Henriette Wulff, December 10, 1843, *H. C. Andersen og Henriette Wulff. En Brevveksling*, ed. H. Topsøe-Jensen (Copenhagen 1959–60), 1:347.

15. *The Diaries of Hans Christian Andersen*, selected and translated by Patricia L. Conroy and Sven H. Rossel (Seattle: University of Washington Press, and London 1990), December 11, 1837, 95.

16. Andersen to Henrik Stampe, December 27, 1843, Collin collection of Andersen's letters at the Royal Library, Copenhagen, XVII H, 32, no. 588.

17. *The Diaries of Hans Christian Andersen*, February 7, 1846, 57.

18. Andersen to Edvard Collin, August 28, 1835, *H.C. Andersens Brevveksling med Edvard og Henriette Collin*, ed. H. Topsøe-Jensen (Copenhagen 1933–37), 1:238.

19. Ibid., July 5, 1835, 226.

20. Annie Wood writing anonymously in the *Spectator*, August 17, 1875, quoted in *H. C. Andersen og England*, ed. Elias Bredsdorff (Copenhagen, 1954), 292.

21. Andersen to B. S. Ingemann, November 20, 1843, *Breve fra Hans Christian Andersen*, II:95, quoted and translated in Svend Larsen, Introduction to *Hans Christian Andersen Fairy Tales* (Odense: Forlag, 1951), 20–21.

22. *The Diaries of Hans Christian Andersen*, June 4, 1875, 422.

23. Charles Dickens, "Frauds on the Fairies," *Household Words*, October 1, 1853.

24. G. W. Griffin, *My Danish Days* (Philadelphia: Claxton, 1875), 209.

25. Ellen Handler Spitz, "The Real Nightingale," *New Republic*, June 25, 2001.

26. Andersen to Edvard Collin, September 5, 1844, *H. C. Andersens Brevveksling med Edvard og Henriette Collin*, II:13.

27. *H. C. Andersens Dagbøger 1825–1875*, ed. H. Topsøe-Jensen and Kåre Olsen (Copenhagen, 1971–76), June 25, 1856, vol. 4, 213.

28. *Adam International Review*, 1955, 248–49:3.

29. Edvard Brandes, "H. C. Andersen Personlighed og Værk," *Litterære Tendenser*, ed. C Bergstrøem-Nielsen (Copenhagen, 1968), 249.

30. *The Diaries of Hans Christian Andersen*, May 31, 1831, 28.

31. Andersen to Edvard Collin, June 27, 1847, *H. C. Andersens Brevveksling med Edvard og Henriette Collin*, II:141.

32. Ibid., September 8, 1855, 261.

33. Elias Bredsdorff, *Hans Christian Andersen: A Biography* (Oxford: Phaidon Press, 1975), 305.

34. Andersen to Carl Alexander, March 21, 1859, *Andersen's Correspondence with the late Grand-Duke of Saxe-Weimar*, 395.

35. Andersen, *The Fairy Tale of My Life*, 11.

36. *The Diaries of Hans Christian Andersen*, December 19, 1825, 15.

37. Ibid., September 20, 1825, 8.

38. Ibid., March 5, 1872, 379.

39. Andersen to Edvard Collin, quoted in Wilhelm von Rosen, "Venskabets Mysterier," *Anderseniana* 3.3.1980, 170, and Andersen to Edvard Collin, August 28, 1835, *H. C. Andersens Brevveksling med Edvard og Henriette*, 1:238.

40. Annie Wood in *Temple Bar* magazine, December 1877.

41. *The Diaries of Hans Christian Andersen*, June 13–14, 1870, 359.

42. Andersen, *The Fairy Tale of My Life*, 501.

43. *H. C. Andersens Dagbøger 1825–1875*, March 2, 1871, IX:29.

44. Bodild Donner in a memoir, 1926, quoted in *Hans Christian Andersen as an Artist*, ed. Kjeld Heltoft (Copenhagen, 1977), 106.

45. Andersen, *The Fairy Tale of My Life*, 451.

46. Charles Dickens to Angela Burdett-Coutts, June 3, 1857, quoted in Bredsdorff, *H. C. Andersen og England*, 120.

47. Erik Dal, introduction to *The Little Mermaid* (Copenhagen: Høst and Son, 1994), 8–9.

48. Edvard Collin, *H. C. Andersen og det Collinske Hus* (Copenhagen, 1929, second edition), 299.

Further Reading

Andersen, Hans Christian. *The Fairy Tale of My Life*. Translated by Horace Scudder. London, British Book Centre, 1975.

The Diaries of Hans Christian Andersen. Selected and translated by Patricia L. Conroy and Sven H. Rossel. Seattle and London: University of Washington Press, 1990.

Hans Christian Andersen's Correspondence with the late Grand-Duke of Saxe-Weimar, Charles Dickens, etc. etc. Edited by Frederick Crawford. London: Deen & Son, 1891. The only selection of Andersen's letters in English, but very unrepresentative.

Bettelheim, Bruno. *The Uses of Enchantment*. London: Penguin, 1978.

Bredsdorff, Elias. *Hans Christian Andersen: A Biography*. Oxford: Phaidon Press, 1975.

Heltoft, Kjeld. *Hans Christian Andersen as an Artist*. Copenhagen: Royal Danish Ministry of Foreign Affairs, 1977. Only available in libraries; for those interested in Andersen's paper cutouts.

Rossel, Sven H., ed. *Hans Christian Andersen: Danish Writer and Citizen of the World*. Amsterdam: Rodopi Bv Editions, 1996. Academic essays of some interest to the general reader.

Wullschlager, Jackie. *Hans Christian Andersen: The Life of a Storyteller*. London: Penguin, 2000 and New York, Alfred Knopft, 2001.

Translator's Note

I was introduced to the stories of Hans Christian Andersen long before I learned Danish and discovered how poorly the previous English translations have represented his work. When I was three or four I had a little yellow record with a song about Thumbelina that I played over and over on our portable record player. As I grew older I read "The Ugly Duckling," "The Princess on the Pea," "The Little Match Girl," "The Nightingale," "The Emperor's New Clothes," and "The Wild Swans," and these were the other Andersen stories that made the biggest impression on me. It was the characters of his stories that appealed to me: the duckling who was bullied and teased because he didn't fit in, the sensitive princess who couldn't sleep, the lonely little girl dreaming of luxuries that would never be part of her own life. In Andersen's world animals and tea kettles could talk, emperors could be fooled, and even kings might open the door if you knocked. He made the fabulous and extraordinary seem plausible and familiar. And he had no qualms about presenting the reader with frightening images, such as the figure of Death perched on the chest of the Emperor or the angry crowd taunting the mute princess on her way to the gallows as she knits one last shirt to break the spell cast over her brothers.

For almost two hundred years, Andersen's stories have colored the imagination of children and adults alike. So why do we need another English translation of his stories? Aren't there enough of them already? This brings me to the history of the English translations of Andersen's work. In Jackie Wullschlager's biography of Hans Christian Andersen she discusses many of the problems exhibited by the first English translations. She also describes the fierce competition that arose in the mid-nineteenth century among those who were vying to be Andersen's English translators. In an earlier Andersen biography, the Danish scholar Elias Bredsdorff devotes an entire chapter to the topic of the early translations, and in 1949, he also wrote an article on the subject, entitled "How a Genius Is Murdered."

Bredsdorff reports that most of the nineteenth-century English translations were "very unsatisfactory," to put it mildly. The fact is that Andersen's style of writing is extremely difficult to translate. He uses colloquialisms, slang, and special idioms. He peppers his narrative with little "filler" words and phrases such as, "you know," "after all," "I suppose," "of course"—phrases that often don't fall naturally into an English text. He also loves to make up words, especially when inanimate objects are talking, and he's very fond of puns and wordplay. He uses a familiar, conversational tone that was quite radical for the literature of his day. And the stories often have an undercurrent of irony, ridicule, or scorn. He's also very funny, and humor is one of the hardest things to translate from one language to another. The translator often can't rely on a direct translation, but instead must come up with something that is equivalent.

Many of Andersen's early translators didn't even know Danish. They based their work on German versions, which were frequently quite terrible. Others who claimed that they *did* know Danish had such a limited understanding of the language that they made outrageous mistakes. For example, Mary Howitt, who produced the first published English translation, knew German and some Swedish, which she assumed would give her a basic reading knowledge of Danish. But some of her mistakes, as reported by Bredsdorff, were both ludicrous and unforgivable. For example, she translated "the soft ground" (*den bløde jord*) as "the bloody earth," while "butterflies" (*sommerfugle*) became "summer birds." She was also known to censor passages that she thought might be offensive to English readers. For example, she changed the opening lines of "Thumbelina" so there would be no possible discussion of where babies come from.

Other English translators took it upon themselves to "improve" Andersen's writing, substituting more flowery words for Andersen's plain prose, or even adding adjectives or adverbs that weren't in the Danish at all, which could radically change the tone of a story. These early translations did great damage to the way in which English readers have perceived Andersen's stories and his style of writing. And the enormous number of English-language "adaptations," "versions," and "retellings" hasn't helped matters.

Translations done in the twentieth century were usually more faithful to the words of the text, aiming for greater accuracy, but most of the translators still largely ignored Andersen's unique voice. Since so many generations have grown up reading the flawed, embellished, and censored English translations of Andersen's work, I've long wondered whether readers would be willing to accept his *real* voice. And I also wondered whether it was even possible to convey that voice in English.

When I was first asked to translate this volume of thirty tales by Hans Christian Andersen, I hesitated for a long time before saying yes. I knew from past experience that Andersen can be extremely difficult to translate, but I decided that I wanted to try to get closer to his style and tone—I wanted to do greater justice to his voice.

While I was working on the translation I began to notice certain keys to Andersen's style. He has a great love of repetition—he is especially fond of the word *lovely*—and I tried to keep this repetition in the English. He also has a preference for a plain, straightforward prose, especially in the early tales, which were specifically intended for children. In the later stories, such as "The Wood Nymph," his vocabulary is much more sophisticated and complex. The real test was to figure out when he was being sarcastic or humorous, and to try to match his wordplay and rhymes in English. It can be challenging to make a poem or phrase rhyme without changing the meaning.

I also wanted to make the stories sound lively and natural without sounding too "modern." Most translators will agree that the farther away you get in time from the origin of the work, the harder it is to find the proper tone. In the twenty-first century, we really don't know how these stories sounded to a nineteenth-century reader, or which parts would have been considered especially funny or odd.

There were other things that I noticed as well. For example, in

"The Nightingale," Andersen indicates with only one word that the bird is female. The question of gender is a crucial issue because in Danish it's possible to use a neutral pronoun to identify a person or other living creature, but in English this is rarely done. For example, in Danish a child is often referred to as "it," as is the case in the opening paragraph of "The Story of a Mother." Since referring to the child in this way would sound odd, or even heartless, in English, I chose to use male pronouns right from the beginning, since the second paragraph of the story reveals that the child is a boy. In "The Shadow," the pronoun used for the title character deliberately shifts from "it" to "he" when the Shadow assumes the role of a human being.

The dilemma was even greater with inanimate objects, and in most cases I chose to identify the gender of objects, based on the context of the story. The one exception was the little fir tree, where the use of "it" seemed perfectly natural.

While I was working on these translations, I was fortunate to have the help of extensive notes to the stories compiled by two Danish Andersen scholars, Erling Nielsen and Flemming Hovmann. This collection of notes is part of the seven-volume definitive edition of Andersen stories, published in Denmark by C. A. Reitzel between 1963 and 1990. These excellent notes often gave me a clue as to what Andersen probably intended with certain words or phrases, which I otherwise might not have understood. The notes also pointed out stylistic idiosyncrasies. For example, Andersen purposely uses French words when he wants his characters to sound especially snobbish. So, in "The Emperor's New Clothes," when the court officials are asked about the invisible cloth, they don't call it "magnificent," they say, "Yes, isn't it *magnifique?*"

There are countless other examples of the odd sentence structure and quirky word choices in Andersen's stories. The translator's goal should always be to get as close as possible to the tone and intent of the author, but it's a process that involves endless decisions and choices. It's an art, not a science, and no two translations of the same text will ever be alike.

For example, here are seven different translations of one of the most famous lines from "The Ugly Duckling":

It does not matter in the least having been born in a duckyard, if only you come out of a swan's egg! [Anonymous]

Being born in a duck yard does not matter, if only you are hatched from a swan's egg. [Jean Hersholt]

It doesn't matter about being born in a duckyard, as long as you are hatched from a swan's egg. [R. P. Keigwin]

Being born in a duck yard doesn't matter if one has lain in a swan's egg! [Pat Shaw Iversen]

It does not matter that one has been born in the henyard as long as one has lain in a swan's egg. [Erik Christian Haugaard]

It doesn't matter if one is born in a duckyard, when one has lain in a swan's egg! [Patricia L. Conroy & Sven H. Rossel]

It doesn't matter if you're born in a duck yard when you've been lying inside a swan's egg. [Tiina Nunnally]

You might think of a translator as a musician, interpreting the work of a composer, or as an actor, inhabiting the voice of the author and giving up her own personality to play the part. It's important for a translator not to insert too much of her own voice into a translation, though, of course, every translator brings her own cultural background, experience, and linguistic skill to the work. A translator is also like an alchemist who uses a mysterious distilling process to transform one substance into another, always hoping that it will be the longed-for gold, that the translation, in its new form, will reflect the richness and beauty of the original.

Before I started on this project I asked myself: What would the world be like *without* the stories of Hans Christian Andersen? Some people might shrug their shoulders and say: Well, they're just children's stories, aren't they? And I would reply: Yes, they *are* stories for children, but they're also for adults. In spite of the flawed English translations, Andersen's tales have managed to resonate in our hearts for so many years because he recognized that life is both ruthless and full of joy. His stories tell us something about the human condition while at the same time they entertain and sometimes scare us. They show us that going out into the "wide world" can be both dangerous and wonderful. There will be many obstacles and trials, but it will also be adventurous and fun, and unexpected help will appear along the way.

Now I can say that this project is one of the most challenging I've ever undertaken. But I can also say that it was both a privilege and a pleasure. I loved discovering Andersen's wit and humor, and I was also amazed by the startling cruelty of some of the stories that I hadn't read before, such as "The Ice Maiden." It is my hope that these new translations will bring readers of English closer to the world of Hans Christian Andersen as he portrayed it in his unique and unforgettable voice.

Tiina Nunnally
Albuquerque, New Mexico
March 2004

A Note on the Illustrations

Like many creative people, Hans Christian Andersen was gifted in several artistic spheres, and in his youth and adolescence it was not clear whether singing, drawing, or writing would in the end predominate in his life. Once he had become a writer, he channelled his abilities as a visual artist into a peculiarly original form, that of paper cutouts, with which he entertained friends and consoled himself for some fifty years. In an early work he includes a self-portrait as a student with a gift for making cutouts, "now a man hanging from a gibbet and holding in his hand a heart, because he was a stealer of hearts; now an old witch riding a broomstick and carrying her husband on her nose." The cast list in the cutouts is similar to those in his fairy tales; both are rooted in the legends and folktales of his childhood. And as in the fairy tales, themes of love, death, and fate are resonant in the cutouts, which often suggest both comedy and grief.

These wonderful works are little known even to Andersen fans, and it is a pleasure to reproduce them here. How contemporary and fresh they look today, how ahead of their time they were in the nineteenth century, when narrative realism was the dominant artistic style; even as late as the 1950s the art world took a little time to accommodate to Henri Matisse's paper cutouts, which now we accept as a vital chapter of late modernism. Simplicity of form, a pared-down style that gets to the heart of things with strong lines and a powerful central image; an elegant overarching structure: In all these aspects the cutouts bear the hallmark of the author of the fairy tales and express his modernity.

"He had one beautiful accomplishment," admitted Henry Dickens of the visitor who plagued the Dickens household for five weeks, "which was the cutting out in paper, of lovely little figures of sprites and elves, gnomes, fairies, and animals of all kinds, which might have stepped out of the pages of his books. These figures turned out to be quite delightful in their refinement and delicate in design and touch."[1] An English visitor to Denmark in the 1860s also remembered the paper figures "so absurd in their expression and attitudes that roars of laughter always follow their appearance on the table."[2] As Andersen traveled feverishly across Europe in his quest to be a figure of international stature, finding himself frequently in milieux where he did not feel at home or could not speak the language, the paper cutouts were, then as now, an engaging way of instant communication.

NOTES

1. *The Recollections of Sir Henry Dickens KC* (London, 1934), 35.
2. Annie Woods, *Temple Bar* magazine (London, February 1875).

Fairy Tales

The Tinderbox

A soldier came marching along the road: left, right! left, right! He had his knapsack on his back and a sword at his side, because he had been off to war, and now he was on his way home. Then he met an old witch on the road. She was so hideous, her lower lip hung all the way down to her breast. She said, "Good evening, soldier. What a nice sword and big knapsack you have—you must be a real soldier! Now you shall have all the money you could ask for!"

"Well, thanks a lot, you old witch," said the soldier.

"Do you see that big tree?" said the witch, pointing at a tree right next to them. "It's completely hollow inside. Climb up to the top and you'll find a hole that you can slip into and slide all the way down inside the tree. I'll tie a rope around your waist so I can hoist you back up when you call me."

"Why would I go inside that tree?" asked the soldier.

"To get the money!" said the witch. "You see, when you reach the bottom of the tree, you'll be in a huge passageway that's very bright because it's lit by more than a hundred lamps. Then you'll see three doors, and you'll be able to open them because the keys are in the locks. If you go inside the first chamber you'll see a big chest in the middle of the room, and on top of it sits a dog. He has eyes as big as a pair of teacups, but never mind that. I'll give you my blue-checked apron that you can spread on the floor. Go right over and pick up the dog and set him on my apron. Then open the chest and take as many *skillings* as you like. They're all made of copper, but if you'd rather have silver, then go into the next room. In there is a dog with eyes as big as a pair of mill wheels, but never mind that. Set him on my apron and take the money. But if it's gold you want, you can have that too, and as much as you can carry, if you go into the third chamber. But the dog sitting on the money chest has two eyes that are each as big as the Round Tower. Now that's a real dog, believe me! But never you mind. Just set him on my apron and he won't harm you. Then take from the chest as much gold as you like."

"Not bad," said the soldier. "But what do I have to give you in return, you old witch? Because I imagine there must be something you want."

"No," said the witch, "I don't want a single *skilling*. All you have to bring me is an old tinderbox that my grandmother left behind when she was down there last."

"Fine. Then let's have that rope around my waist," said the soldier.

"Here it is," said the witch. "And here is my blue-checked apron."

So the soldier climbed up the tree, tumbled down the hole, and then, just as the witch had said, he stood inside the huge passageway where hundreds of lamps were burning.

He opened the first door. Ooh! There sat the dog with eyes as big as teacups, staring at him.

"You're a handsome fellow!" said the soldier and set him on the witch's apron. Then he took as many copper *skillings* as his pockets would hold, closed the chest, put the dog back, and went into the second room. Eeek! There sat the dog with eyes as big as mill wheels.

"You shouldn't look at me so hard," said the soldier. "You might hurt your eyes!" And then he set the dog on the witch's apron, but when he saw all the silver coins inside the chest he threw away the copper coins he was carrying and filled his pockets and his knapsack with nothing but silver. Next he went into the third chamber. Oh, how hideous! The dog in there really did have eyes as big as round towers, and they were spinning around in his head like wheels.

"Good evening," said the soldier and doffed his cap, for he had never seen a dog like that before. But after he'd looked at him for a while, he thought to himself, "All right, that's enough." And he lifted him onto the floor and opened the chest. Good Lord, there was a lot of gold! Enough to buy all of Copenhagen and every single sugar-pig sold by the cake-wives, and all the tin soldiers, whips, and rocking horses in the whole world! Yes, there was certainly plenty of money! So the soldier threw away all the silver coins that filled his pockets and knapsack and took the gold instead. Yes, all his pockets, his knapsack, his cap, and his boots were so full that he could hardly walk. Now he had money! He put the dog back on the chest, slammed the door shut, and called up through the tree:

"Hoist me up now, you old witch!"

"Do you have the tinderbox?" asked the witch.

"Oh, that's right," said the soldier. "I forgot all about it." And he went over and picked it up. The witch hoisted him up and he once again stood on the road, with his pockets, boots, knapsack, and cap full of money.

"What do you want the tinderbox for?" asked the soldier.

"That's none of your business," said the witch. "You've got the money. Now just give me the tinderbox."

"Pish posh!" said the soldier. "Tell me right now what you want it for or I'll pull out my sword and chop off your head!"

"No," said the witch.

So the soldier chopped off her head. There she lay! But he wrapped up all his money in her apron, slung it in a bundle over his shoulder, stuffed the tinderbox in his pocket, and headed straight for the city.

It was a lovely city, and he went inside the loveliest of inns and demanded the very best rooms and his favorite food, because now he had so much money that he was rich.

The servant who was supposed to polish his boots thought they were rather strange old boots for such a rich gentleman to be wearing, but he hadn't yet bought himself new ones. By the next day he had a good pair of boots and fine clothes to wear. The soldier was now a distinguished gentleman, and the people told him about all the splendid things to be found in their city, and about their king and what a charming princess his daughter was.

"Where might I catch a glimpse of her?" asked the soldier.

"It's impossible to catch a glimpse of her," they all said. "She lives in an enormous copper palace surrounded by dozens of walls and towers. No one but the king dares visit her, because it was foretold that she would marry a simple soldier, and that certainly did not please the king."

"She's someone I'd like to see," thought the soldier, but that wasn't possible.

He was now leading a merry life, going to the theater, taking drives in the king's gardens, and giving away a great deal of money to the poor, which was a very nice gesture. No doubt he remembered from the old days how miserable it was not to have even a *skilling*. He was now rich and wore fine clothes, and had so many friends who all said that he was a pleasant fellow, a real gentleman, and that certainly pleased the soldier. But since he was spending money each day and not taking any in, he finally had no more than two *skillings* left and had to move out of the beautiful rooms where he had been living and into a tiny little garret room right under the roof. He had to brush his own boots and mend them with a darning needle, and none of his friends came to see him because there were too many stairs to climb.

It was a very dark evening, and he couldn't even afford to buy a candle, but then he remembered there was a little stump of one in the tinderbox he had taken from the hollow tree when the witch had helped him inside. He took out the tinderbox and the candle stump, but the minute he struck fire and sparks leaped from the flint, the door flew open and the dog that he had seen inside the tree, the one with eyes as big as two teacups, stood before him and said, "What is my master's command?"

"What's this?" said the soldier. "What an amusing tinderbox, if I can wish for whatever I want! Bring me some money," he said to the dog, and zip, he was gone; zip, he was back, holding a big sack of *skillings* in his mouth.

Now the soldier realized what a wonderful tinderbox it was. If he struck it once, the dog who sat on the chest of copper coins came; if he struck it twice, the one with the silver coins came; and if he struck it three times, the one with the gold came. Now the soldier moved back downstairs to the beautiful rooms, dressed in fine clothing, and all his friends recognized him again, because they were so fond of him.

One day he thought, "How odd that no one is allowed to see that princess. Everyone says she's supposed to be so lovely. But what good is it if she's always kept inside that enormous copper palace with all the towers? Couldn't I possibly have a look at her? Where's my tinderbox?" And then he struck fire and zip, the dog with eyes as big as teacups appeared.

"I know it's the middle of the night," said the soldier, "but I have such a great desire to see the princess, if only for a moment."

The dog was out the door at once, and before the soldier knew it, he was back with the princess. She was sitting on the dog's back, asleep, and she was so lovely that anyone could see she was a real princess. The soldier couldn't resist, he had to kiss her, because he was a real soldier.

Then the dog ran back with the princess, but when morning came and the king and queen were pouring their tea, the princess said that she'd had a strange dream in the night about a dog and a soldier. She was riding on the dog's back, and the soldier had kissed her.

"That's certainly a fine story!" said the queen.

One of the old ladies-in-waiting was then ordered to keep watch at the bedside of the princess on the following night, to see if it was really a dream, or what else it might be.

The soldier was longing terribly to see the lovely princess once more, so the dog appeared in the night, picked her up, and ran as fast as he could, but the old lady-in-waiting put on her wading boots and ran just as swiftly right behind. When she saw them disappear inside a large building, she thought to herself: Now I know where it is. And with a piece of chalk she drew a big cross on the door. Then she returned home and went to bed, and the dog came back too, bringing the princess. But when he saw that a cross had been drawn on the door where the soldier lived, he took another piece of chalk and put a cross on all the doors in the whole city. That was a clever thing to do, because now the lady-in-waiting wouldn't be able to find the right door, since there were crosses on all of them.

Early the next morning the king and queen, the old lady-in-waiting, and all the officers went out to see where the princess had been.

"There it is!" said the king when he saw the first door with a cross on it.

"No, it's over there, my dear husband," said the queen, who saw another door with a cross on it.

"But there's one there, and one there!" they all said. Wherever they looked, there was a cross on every door. Then they realized it was no use to go on searching.

But the queen was a very clever woman who was capable of more than just riding around in a coach. She took her big golden scissors, cut a large piece of silk into pieces, and then stitched together a charming little pouch, which she filled with fine grains of buckwheat. She tied it to the back of the princess, and when that was done, she cut a tiny hole in the pouch so the grains would sprinkle out wherever the princess went.

That night the dog appeared once again, put the princess on his back, and ran off with her to the soldier, who loved her so much and wanted dearly to be a prince so that he could make her his wife.

The dog didn't notice the grain sprinkling out all the way from the palace to the soldier's window, as he ran along the wall, carrying the princess. In the morning the king and queen could see quite well where their daughter had been, and they seized the soldier and threw him into jail.

And there he sat. Oh, how dark and dreary it was, and then they told him, "Tomorrow you will hang." That was not a pleasant thing to hear, and he had left his tinderbox behind at the inn. In the morning he could see through the iron bars on the little window that people were hurrying to the outskirts of the city to watch him hang. He heard the drums and saw the marching soldiers. Everyone was in a great rush, including a shoemaker's apprentice wearing a leather apron and slippers. He was moving along at such a gallop that one of his slippers flew off and struck the wall right where the soldier was sitting, peering out through the iron bars.

"Hey, shoemaker's apprentice! You don't have to be in such a rush," said the soldier. "Nothing's going to happen until I get there. But if you run over to the place where I was staying and bring me my tinderbox, I'll give you four *skillings*. But you have to be quick about it!" The shoemaker's apprentice wanted those four *skillings*, so he raced off to get the tinderbox, brought it to the soldier, and . . . well, let's hear what happened.

Outside the city a huge gallows had been built, and around it stood the soldiers and many hundreds of thousands of people. The king and queen sat on a lovely throne right across from the judge and the entire council.

The soldier was already standing on the ladder, but as they were about to put the rope around his neck, he said that before a sinner faced his punishment he was always allowed one harmless request. He dearly wanted to smoke a pipe of tobacco; it would be the last pipe he had in this world.

Now, that was not something the king could refuse, and so the soldier took out his tinderbox and struck fire, one, two, three! And there stood all three dogs: the one with eyes as big as teacups, the one with eyes like mill wheels, and the one with eyes as big as the Round Tower.

"Help me now, so I won't be hanged!" said the soldier, and then the dogs rushed at the judge and the entire council, seizing one by the leg and one by the nose, and flinging them high into the air so they fell back down and were crushed to bits.

"Not me!" said the king, but the biggest dog seized both him and the queen and tossed them after all the others. Then the soldiers were afraid, and all the people shouted, "Little soldier, you shall be our king and wed the lovely princess!"

They put the soldier in the king's coach, and all three dogs danced before it, shouting, "Hurrah!" The boys whistled through their fingers, and the soldiers presented arms. The princess came out of the copper palace and became queen, and that certainly pleased her! The wedding celebration lasted for a week, and the dogs sat at the table too, making big eyes.

Little Claus and Big Claus

There was a town where two men had the very same name. Both of them were named Claus, but one owned four horses while the other had only one. In order to tell them apart, people called the man with four horses Big Claus, and the man with only one horse Little Claus. Now we're going to hear what happened between those two, because this is a real story!

All week long Little Claus had to do the plowing for Big Claus, lending him his only horse. Then Big Claus would help him in return with all four of his horses, but only once a week, and that was on Sunday. Hee-ya! How Little Claus would crack his whip at all five horses. They might as well have belonged to him on that one day. The sun shone so wondrously, and all the bells in the tower rang, summoning people to church. Everyone was dressed in their best, walking with their hymnals under their arms, on their way to hear the pastor preach. And they looked at Little Claus, who was plowing with five horses, and he was so pleased that he cracked his whip again and shouted, "Giddy-up, all my horses!"

"You shouldn't say that," said Big Claus. "Only one of those horses is yours."

But when someone else passed by on his way to church, Little Claus forgot that he wasn't supposed to say that and he shouted, "Giddy-up, all my horses!"

"All right, now I really must ask you to stop that," said Big Claus. "Because if you say it one more time, I'm going to strike your horse on the forehead, and he'll drop dead on the spot, and that will be the end of him."

"Well, I certainly won't say it again," said Little Claus, but when people came past and nodded hello, he was so pleased and thought it looked so splendid that he had five horses plowing his field that he cracked his whip and shouted, "Giddy-up, all my horses!"

"I'll giddy-up your horses!" said Big Claus, and he seized the tethering mallet and struck Little Claus's only horse on the forehead so that it fell to the ground, stone dead.

"Oh no, now I have no horse at all!" said Little Claus and began to cry. Later he flayed the horse and let the hide dry in the wind. Then he stuffed it in a sack that he hoisted onto his back and set off for town to sell his horsehide.

He had such a long way to go. He had to pass through a big, dark forest, and a terrible storm came up. He completely lost his way, and before he found the right road, dusk had fallen, and it was much too far to reach town or to go back home before night came.

Close to the road stood a large farm. The shutters on all the windows were closed, and yet there was a glimpse of light above. Surely they'll let me spend the night here, thought Little Claus, and he went over and knocked.

The farmer's wife opened the door, but when she heard what he wanted, she told him to keep on going. Her husband wasn't home, and she didn't take in strangers.

"Well, then I guess I'll have to sleep outside," said Little Claus, and the farmer's wife shut the door in his face.

Nearby stood a big haystack, and between the haystack and house a little shed had been built with a flat, thatched roof.

"I can sleep up there," said Little Claus when he saw the roof. "That would make a lovely bed, and I'm sure the stork isn't going to fly down and bite me on the leg." A real live stork was standing on the roof, where it had made a nest.

So Little Claus climbed up onto the shed, lay down, and turned onto his side to settle in properly. The wooden shutters on the windows of the house didn't quite meet at the top, which meant that he could peek into the room.

A great feast had been laid out with wine and a roast and such a lovely fish. The farmer's wife and the deacon were sitting at the table, all alone. She was pouring wine for him, and he began with the fish, because he was awfully fond of fish.

"If only I could have a bite too," said Little Claus, craning his neck toward the window. Lord, what a lovely cake he could see in there. Oh yes, it was quite a feast.

Then he heard someone come riding along the road toward the house. It was the woman's husband, on his way home.

Now, it's true that he was a good man, but he had a strange affliction: He couldn't stand to see deacons. If he caught sight of a deacon, he would grow quite furious. That was also why the deacon had come to visit the woman when he knew that her husband wasn't home, and that's why the good woman had set out for him the best food she could offer. When they heard her husband coming, they were both terrified. The woman told the deacon to climb into a big empty chest that stood in the corner, which he did, because he knew full well that the poor man couldn't stand the sight of a deacon. The woman quickly hid all the wonderful food and wine inside her baking oven, because if her husband saw it, he was sure to ask what was going on.

"Oh no!" sighed Little Claus up on the shed when he saw all the food disappear.

"Is somebody up there?" asked the farmer, peering up at Little Claus. "Why are you lying up there? Come on into the house!"

Then Little Claus told him how he had lost his way and asked if he might stay the night.

"Yes, of course," said the farmer. "But first we'll have a bite to eat."

The woman welcomed them both, set dishes on a long table, and brought them a big bowl of porridge. The farmer was hungry and ate with gusto, but Little Claus couldn't help thinking about the wonderful roast, fish, and cake that he knew were hidden in the oven.

Under the table at his feet he had put the sack with the horsehide in it, because we know, after all, that this was what he had brought from home to sell in town. The porridge was not at all to his liking, and so he stepped on his sack, and the dry horsehide inside creaked quite loudly.

"Hush!" said Little Claus to his sack, but at the same instant he stepped on it again, and it creaked even louder than before.

"Tell me, what do you have in your bag?" asked the farmer.

"Oh, it's a troll," said Little Claus. "He says we shouldn't eat the porridge because he has conjured a whole oven full of roast and fish and cake.''

"Is that right?" said the farmer and quickly opened the oven. There he saw all the wonderful food that his wife had hidden, but he now thought the troll in the bag had conjured it up. His wife didn't dare say a word but set the food on the table at once, and so they ate the fish and the roast and the cake. Then Little Claus stepped on his sack again, making the hide creak.

"What's he saying now?" asked the farmer.

"He says," said Little Claus, "that he has also conjured up three bottles of wine for us, and they're standing over in the corner by the oven." Then the woman had to bring out the wine she had hidden, and the farmer drank and grew quite merry. A troll like the one that Little Claus had in his bag was something that he would certainly like to own.

"Can he also conjure up the Devil?" asked the farmer. "That's someone I'd really like to see, now that I'm feeling so merry."

"Yes," said Little Claus, "my troll can do anything I ask. Isn't that right?" he said as he stepped on the bag, making it creak. "Did you hear him say yes? But the Devil looks so horrid that you wouldn't want to look at him."

"Oh, I'm not the least bit afraid. How bad do you think he could look?"

"Well, he's going to look exactly like a deacon."

"Whoa!" said the farmer. "That's ghastly, all right. I must tell you that I can't stand the sight of deacons. But that doesn't matter, because I'll know it's the Devil, so it won't bother me as much. I'm feeling brave now. But don't let him come too close."

"Let me ask my troll," said Little Claus, and he stepped on the bag, cupping his ear.

"What does he say?"

"He says that you can go over and open the chest that's standing in the corner, and you'll see the Devil moping inside, but you have to hold on to the lid so he doesn't get out."

"Come and help me hold on to it," said the farmer, and he went over to the chest where his wife had hidden the real deacon, who sat there completely terrified.

The farmer lifted the lid slightly and peeked inside. "Whoa!" he yelled, jumping back. "I saw him all right, and he looks just like our deacon! Oh, that was terrible!"

After that they had to have a drink, and then they kept on drinking until late into the night.

"You've got to sell me that troll," said the farmer. "Ask whatever price you like. Why, I'd even give you a whole bushelful of money!"

"No, I can't do that," said Claus. "Just think how much I'll gain from owning this troll."

"Oh, but I'd certainly like to have it," said the farmer, and he kept on begging.

"All right," said Little Claus at last. "Since you've been kind enough to give me shelter for the night, I can't refuse. You can have the troll for a bushel of money, but I want the bushel to be full to the brim."

"And that's what you'll get," said the farmer, "but you have to take that chest over there with you. I refuse to have it in the house for even an hour longer. There's no telling whether he's still inside."

Little Claus gave the farmer the sack with the dried horsehide and got in return a whole bushel of money, full to the brim. The farmer even presented him with a big wheelbarrow for carrying the money and the chest.

"Farewell!" said Little Claus, and then he set off with his money and the big chest in which the deacon was still sitting.

On the other side of the woods was a big, deep river. The water was running so fast that it was almost impossible to swim against the current. A big new bridge had been built across it. Little Claus stopped in the middle of the bridge and said very loudly so that the deacon inside the chest would hear him:

"Well, what do I need this stupid chest for? It's so heavy it feels like it's full of rocks. I'm getting awfully tired of carting it around, so I think I'll throw it in the river. If it floats home to me, that's fine, but if it doesn't, it won't matter at all."

Then he grabbed one handle of the chest and lifted it slightly, as if he were going to shove it into the water.

"No, stop!" yelled the deacon inside the chest. "Let me out!"

"Ooh!" said Little Claus, pretending to be scared. "He's still inside! I've got to toss it in the river as quick as I can so he'll drown."

"Oh no, oh no!" shouted the deacon. "I'll give you a whole bushelful of money if you don't."

"Well, that's a different story," said Little Claus, and opened the chest. The deacon crawled out at once, shoved the empty chest into the water, and went off to his house, where he gave Little Claus a whole bushelful of money. Little Claus already had one bushel from the farmer; now his whole wheelbarrow was full of money.

"Look at that, I certainly did get a good price for that horse," he said to himself when he came back to his own house and dumped all the money in a big heap in the middle of the floor. "Big Claus will be annoyed when he finds out how rich I've become from my only horse, but I'm not going to come right out and tell him about it."

Then he sent a boy over to Big Claus to borrow a bushel measure.

"I wonder what he wants it for," thought Big Claus, and smeared tar inside the bottom so that a little of whatever was being weighed would stick to it. And it did, because when he got the bushel measure back, there were three new silver eight-*skilling* coins stuck to it.

"What's this?" said Big Claus and ran right over to see Little Claus. "Where did you get all this money?"

"Oh, I got it for my horsehide. I sold it last night."

"That was certainly a good price!" said Big Claus, and he raced back home, picked up an ax, and struck every one of his four horses on the forehead. Then he skinned them and drove into town with the hides.

"Hides! Hides! Who wants to buy hides?" he shouted through the streets.

All the shoemakers and tanners came running and asked him how much he wanted for the hides.

"A bushel of money for each of them," said Big Claus.

"Are you crazy?" they all said. "Do you think we have bushels of money?"

"Hides, hides! Who wants to buy hides?" he shouted again, but to everyone who asked how much the hides cost, he replied, "A bushel of money."

"He's trying to make fools of us," they all said. Then the shoemakers picked up their straps and the tanners their leather aprons, and they all started beating Big Claus.

"Hides, hides!" they jeered at him. "Oh yes, we'll give you a hide that bleeds like a pig! Now get out of town!" they shouted, and Big Claus had to rush off as fast as he could. He had never been beaten so badly in his life.

"Well!" he said when he got home. "Little Claus is going to pay for this. I'm going to murder him for this!"

But back at Little Claus's house his grandmother had just died. Now, it's true that she had been terribly ill-tempered and mean toward him, but even so he was quite sad. He took the dead woman and put her in his warm bed to see whether she might come back to life. There she would lie all night long while he slept in the corner, sitting on a chair; that was something he had done before.

As he was sitting there that night, the door opened and Big Claus came in with an ax. He knew where Little Claus's bed stood, and he went right over and struck the dead grandmother on the forehead, thinking that it was Little Claus.

"Take that!" he said. "Now you won't make a fool of me anymore." And then he went back home.

"What a mean and evil man," said Little Claus. "He wanted to murder me, but it's a good thing the old lady was already dead, or he would have taken her life."

Then he dressed his old grandmother in her Sunday best, borrowed a horse from his neighbor, harnessed it to his wagon, and put his old grandmother on the back seat so that she wouldn't fall out when he started driving. Then they headed off through the woods. When the sun came up, they were outside a big inn, where Little Claus stopped and went inside to get a bite to eat.

The innkeeper was very, very rich, and he was also a good man, but hot-tempered, as if there were pepper and tobacco inside of him.

"Good morning," he said to Little Claus. "You've put on your fine clothes awfully early today."

"Yes," said Little Claus, "I'm going to town with my old grandmother. She's sitting outside in the wagon, and I can't get her to come indoors. Would you mind taking her a glass of mead? But you'll have to speak up because she doesn't hear very well."

"Why, certainly," said the innkeeper. He poured a big glass of mead and took it outside to the dead grandmother, who was propped up in the wagon.

"Here's a glass of mead from your grandson," said the innkeeper, but the dead woman didn't say a word, just sat there without moving.

"Didn't you hear me?" shouted the innkeeper as loud as he could. "Here's a glass of mead from your grandson!"

Once again he shouted the same thing, and then one more time, but when she didn't budge in the slightest, he got angry and tossed the glass of mead right in her face so it ran down her nose. And she toppled over backward into the wagon, because she had merely been propped up but wasn't tied down.

"What's this?" shouted Little Claus as he came running out the door and grabbed the innkeeper by the shirtfront. "You've gone and killed my grandmother! Just look at that big hole in her forehead!"

"Oh, what bad luck!" cried the innkeeper, wringing his hands. "It's all the fault of my bad temper. Dear Little Claus, I'll give you a whole bushelful of money and pay for your grandmother's burial as if she were my own, but don't say a word or they'll chop off my head, and that would be awful!"

So Little Claus got a whole bushelful of money, and the innkeeper buried the old grandmother as if she were his own.

As soon as Little Claus got back home with all the money, he at once sent his boy over to see Big Claus, to ask if he could borrow a bushel measure.

"What's this?" said Big Claus. "I thought I killed him! I'm going to have to see this for myself." And so he took the bushel measure over to Little Claus in person.

"Where on earth did you get all that money?" he asked, opening his eyes wide when he saw how much more Little Claus had accumulated.

"It was my grandmother, not me that you killed," said Little Claus. "But now I've sold her for a bushelful of money."

"That was certainly a good price," said Big Claus, and he rushed home, picked up an ax, and promptly killed his old grandmother.

He put her in his wagon, drove into town to the apothecary's shop, and asked him whether he wanted to buy a dead body.

"Who is it, and where did you get it?" asked the apothecary.

"It's my grandmother," said Big Claus. "I've killed her for a bushelful of money."

"Good Lord!" said the apothecary. "You don't know what you're saying! Don't say things like that or you could lose your head." And then he told him exactly what a dreadful, evil thing he had done, and what a bad person he was, and that he ought to be punished. Big Claus was so scared that he leaped straight from the apothecary's shop into his wagon, cracked his whip at the horses, and raced off home. The apothecary and everyone else thought he was mad, and so they let him go where he liked.

"You're going to pay for this!" said Big Claus when he was out on the road. "Oh yes, you're going to pay for this, Little Claus!" As soon as he got home he took the biggest sack he could find and went over to Little Claus and said, "You've made a fool of me again. First I killed my horses, and then my old grandmother. It's all your fault, but you're never going to trick me again." And he grabbed Little Claus around the waist and stuffed him into the sack. Then he slung him over his back and shouted, "Now I'm going to take you out and drown you!"

It was a long walk to reach the river, and Little Claus wasn't easy to carry. The road passed very close to the church, where the organ was playing and people were singing so beautifully inside. Then Big Claus put down the sack holding Little Claus right next to the church door, thinking that it might do him good to go inside and listen to a hymn first, before continuing on his way. Little Claus couldn't get out, and everyone else was in church, so Big Claus went inside.

"Oh me, oh my!" sighed Little Claus from inside the sack. He twisted and turned, but it was impossible for him to loosen the cord. At that moment an old, old cattle-driver with chalk-white hair and a big walking stick in his hand came by. He was driving a big herd of cows and bulls in front of him. They trampled over the sack that Claus was in, tumbling it onto its side.

"Oh my," sighed Little Claus. "I'm so young, but I'm already headed for Heaven."

"And what a poor man am I," said the cattle-driver. "Here I am so old but it's not yet my time to go."

"Open the sack!" shouted Little Claus. "Climb in and take my place, and you'll end up in Heaven at once."

"Oh, I'd like that very much," said the cattle-driver, untying the sack. And Little Claus jumped right out.

"Could you take care of the cattle?" said the old man, and he climbed into the bag, which Little Claus tied up and then went on his way, taking along the cows and bulls.

A little while later Big Claus came out of the church and hoisted the sack onto his back, thinking that it certainly was a lot lighter, because the old cattle-driver was no more than half the weight of Little Claus. "How easy it is to carry him now! Well, that's probably because I've been listening to a hymn." Then he went over to the river, which was deep and wide, threw the sack with the old cattle-driver into the water, and shouted after him, thinking he was Little Claus, "Take that! Now you won't be making a fool of me anymore!"

Then he headed home, but when he came to the crossroads, he met Little Claus walking along with all his cattle.

"What's this?" said Big Claus. "Didn't I drown you?"

"Yes, you did," said Little Claus. "You threw me in the river less than half an hour ago."

"But where did you get all these wonderful cattle?" asked Big Claus.

"They're sea cattle," said Little Claus. "Let me tell you the whole story. And by the way, thanks for drowning me, because now I'm back on my feet and let me tell you, I'm as rich as can be! I was so scared when I was inside that sack, and the wind whistled in my ears when you threw me off the bridge and into the cold water. I sank straight to the bottom, but I didn't hurt myself because the loveliest soft grass grows down there. That's where I landed, and the bag was opened at once. The loveliest maiden, wearing chalk-white clothing and with a green wreath on her wet hair, took my hand and said, "Is that you, Little Claus? Well, first let me give you these cattle. Five miles up the road there's another whole herd that I want you to have." Then I saw that the river was a great highway for the sea folk. Down on the bottom they were walking and driving all the way from the sea toward land, to the place where the river ends. It was so lovely with flowers and the freshest of grass, and fish swimming in the water; they flitted around my ears like the birds in the air. How handsome the people were and how many cattle there were, ambling along the ditches and fences."

"But why did you come back to us so soon?" asked Big Claus. "That's not what I would have done if it was so charming down there."

"Well, you see," said Little Claus, "it was really very cunning of me. You heard me say that the mermaid told me that five miles up the road—and by road she meant the river, of course, since she can't travel any other way—there was a whole herd of cattle waiting for me. I happen to know where the river starts to bend, first one way and then the other, making a whole detour. It's much shorter, if you can do it, to come up here on land and head straight across to the river. That way I saved almost two and a half miles and reached my sea cattle much quicker."

"Oh, you certainly are a lucky man!" said Big Claus. "Do you think I could get some sea cattle too, if I went down to the bottom of the river?"

"Oh yes, I imagine so," said Little Claus. "But I can't carry you in a sack to the river; you're much too heavy for me. But if you walk there yourself and then climb into the bag, I'd be more than happy to throw you in."

"Thanks so much," said Big Claus. "But if I don't get any sea cattle when I get there, I'm going to give you a beating, believe you me!"

"Oh no! Don't be so mean!" And then they went down to the river. The cattle were so thirsty that when they saw the water, they ran as fast as they could down the slope to drink.

"Look how fast they're moving," said Little Claus. "They're longing to go back down to the bottom."

"Yes, but help me first," said Big Claus. "Otherwise I'll give you a beating!" And then he climbed into the big sack that was lying across the back of one of the bulls. "Put a rock inside, because otherwise I'm afraid I won't sink," said Big Claus.

"Oh, I'm sure you will," said Little Claus, but just the same, he put a big rock in the sack, tied the cord tight, and then gave it a shove. Plop! Big Claus landed in the river and promptly sank to the bottom.

"I'm afraid he's not going to find any cattle," said Little Claus, and then he headed home with all he had.

The Princess on the Pea

Once upon a time there was a prince. He wanted a princess, but she had to be a real princess. So he traveled all over the world to find one, but wherever he went there was something wrong. There were plenty of princesses, but he wasn't quite sure if they were real princesses. There was always something that wasn't quite right. Then he went back home and was so sad because he dearly wanted to have a real princess.

One evening there was a terrible storm. Lightning flashed and thunder roared, the rain poured down, it was simply dreadful! Then there was a knock at the town gate, and the old king went to open it.

There was a princess standing outside. But good Lord how she looked because of the rain and terrible weather! Water was streaming from her hair and her clothes, running in the toes of her shoes and out of the heels. Then she said that she was a real princess.

"Well, we'll see about that," thought the old queen, but she didn't say a word. She went into the bedroom, took off all the bedclothes, and placed a pea at the bottom of the bed. Then she took twenty mattresses and put them on top of the pea, and another twenty eiderdown quilts on top of the mattresses.

That's where the princess was to sleep that night.

The next morning they asked her how she had slept.

"Oh, dreadfully!" said the princess. "I hardly closed my eyes all night. Lord knows what there was in my bed. I was lying on something hard, and I'm black and blue all over! It's simply dreadful!"

Then they could see that she was a real princess, since she had felt the pea through those twenty mattresses and those twenty eiderdown quilts. No one else could have such tender skin except for a real princess.

And so the prince took her as his wife, because now he knew that he had a real princess. And the pea was placed in the Royal Curiosity Cabinet, where it can still be seen today, as long as no one has taken it.

Now you see, that was a real story!

Thumbelina

Once upon a time there was a woman who dearly wanted to have a tiny little child, but she had no idea where to get one. So she went to an old witch and said to her, "I want so much to have a little child. Won't you tell me where I might get one?"

"Oh yes, I think we can manage that!" said the witch. "Here's a grain of barley, but it's not the kind that grows in the farmer's field or the kind that chickens are given to eat. Put it in a flowerpot, and then you'll have something to see!"

"Thank you so much!" said the woman and gave the witch twelve *skillings*. She went home, planted the grain of barley, and a lovely big flower sprang up at once. It looked exactly like a tulip, but its petals were closed tight, as if it were still a bud.

"What a charming flower!" said the woman and kissed the beautiful red and yellow petals, but just as she kissed them, the flower gave a loud bang and opened. It was a real tulip, she could see that now, but in the middle of the flower, on the green stool, sat a tiny little girl, so delicate and charming. She was no taller than a thumb, and that's why she was named Thumbelina.

She was given a charming lacquered walnut shell for a cradle, blue violet petals for her mattresses, and a rose petal for her comforter. That's where she slept at night, but in the daytime she played on the table where the woman had set a dish. Around it she had placed an entire wreath of flowers with their stems sticking into the water where a big tulip petal floated. This was where Thumbelina sat, sailing from one side of the dish to the other. She had two white horsehairs to use as oars. It looked perfectly lovely.

She could also sing. Her voice was elegant and charming, like nothing anyone had ever heard.

One night, as she lay in her beautiful bed, a hideous toad hopped through the window—one of the panes was broken. The toad was vile, big and wet, and she jumped right down onto the table where Thumbelina lay sleeping under the red rose petal.

"What a lovely wife for my son!" said the toad, and she seized hold of the walnut shell where Thumbelina was sleeping and hopped out the window with her, down to the garden.

There a big, wide stream ran, but near the bank it was marshy and muddy, and that was where the toad lived with her son. Ugh! He was so vile and horrid, he looked exactly like his mother. "Ko-ax, ko-ax, brekke-ke-kex!" was all he could say when he saw the charming little girl in the walnut shell.

"Don't talk so loud or you'll wake her up!" said the old toad. "She might still run away from us because she's as light as swan down. We'll put her in the stream on one of the big water-lily pads. Since she's so little and light, it will seem just like an island to her. She won't be able to escape while we fix up the good parlor down in the mud where the two of you will live together."

So many water lilies grew in the stream, with big green pads that looked as if they were floating on the water. The pad that was farthest away was also the biggest. The old toad swam out to it, and there she left the walnut shell with Thumbelina in it.

The poor tiny little girl woke up quite early the next morning, and when she saw where she was, she began to cry bitterly, because there was water on all sides of the big green lily pad, and it was impossible for her to reach land.

The old toad was sitting in the mud, decorating her parlor with reeds and yellow water lilies; everything was going to be so fine for her new daughter-in-law. Then she swam with her vile son out to the lily pad where Thumbelina stood. They wanted to get her pretty bed and set it up in the bridal chamber before she arrived. The old toad made a deep curtsy before her in the water and said, "Here you see my son. He's going to be your husband, and the two of you will live so splendidly down in the mud."

"Ko-ax, ko-ax! Brekke-ke-kex!" was all the son could say.

Then they took the charming little bed and swam off with it.

Thumbelina sat all alone on the green lily pad, weeping, because she didn't want to live with the horrid toad or have the hideous son for her husband. The little fish swimming in the water must have seen the toad and heard what she said because they poked their heads up and wanted to see the little girl. As soon as they caught sight of her, they found her quite charming, and they felt terrible that she would have to go live with the vile toad. No, that was never going to happen. Down in the water they gathered around the green stem that held the lily pad she was standing on. With their teeth they chewed through the stem, and then the lily pad floated downstream, carrying off Thumbelina, far away where the toad could never go.

Thumbelina sailed past scores of towns, and the little birds sitting in the bushes saw her and sang, "What a charming little maiden!" The lily pad carrying her drifted farther and farther away; that was how Thumbelina ended up traveling abroad.

A charming little white butterfly kept on flying around her and finally landed on the lily pad, because he was quite fond of Thumbelina. She was so happy because now the toad couldn't reach her, and everywhere she sailed was so lovely. The sun shone on the water; it was like the loveliest gold. She took off her sash and tied one end to the butterfly. The other end of the ribbon she fastened to the lily pad. Then it moved much faster and she did too, because she was standing on the pad, after all.

At that moment a big cockchafer beetle came flying past. He caught sight of her and in a flash fastened his claw around her slender waist and flew up into a tree with her. But the green lily pad kept floating downstream, and the butterfly flew along with it, because he was tied to the lily pad and could not pull free.

Lord, how frightened Thumbelina was when the beetle flew up into the tree with her! But she was even sadder about the beautiful white butterfly that she had tied to the lily pad. If he couldn't get free he would starve to death. But the beetle didn't care about that. He set her on the biggest green leaf of the tree, gave her blossom nectar to eat, and said that she was very charming, even though she didn't look at all like a cockchafter beetle.

Then all the other beetles that lived in the tree came to visit. They looked at Thumbelina, and the lady beetles tugged at their antennae and one of them said, "But she has only two legs. How pitiful she looks!"

"She has no antennae," said another.

"She's so thin around the waist. Ugh! She looks like a human being! How horrid she is!" said all the female beetles, and yet Thumbelina was so charming. That's what the beetle who had brought her thought, but all the others said she was hideous. In the end he thought so too, and didn't want to keep her anymore; she could go wherever she liked. They flew down from the tree with her and set her on a daisy. There she sat and wept because she was so ugly that the cockchafer beetles didn't want to keep her, and yet she was the loveliest creature imaginable, as delicate and radiant as the most beautiful rose petal.

All summer long poor Thumbelina lived all alone in the big forest. She wove a bed for herself out of blades of grass and hung it under a big dock leaf to keep off the rain. She plucked nectar from flowers to eat and drank from the dew that settled on the leaves each morning. In this way the summer and autumn passed, but then came winter, the long, cold winter. All the birds who had sung so beautifully for her flew off, and the trees and flowers withered. The big dock leaf she had been living under curled up, becoming nothing more than a withered yellow stalk. She was dreadfully cold, because her clothes were tattered and she was so tiny and delicate. Poor Thumbelina, she was about to freeze to death. Snow began to fall, and every snowflake that fell on her was like having an entire shovelful thrown at us, because they were big and she was only as tall as a thumb. Then she wrapped herself in a withered leaf, but it gave no warmth, and she shivered with cold.

At the edge of the forest where she had ended up stood a big field of grain, but the grain had long since disappeared and only the bare dry stubble was left standing in the frozen ground. For her it seemed like an entire forest to walk through, and oh, how she shivered from the cold. Then she came to the field mouse's door. It was a little hole under the grain stubble. That's where the field mouse lived, warm and snug, with a whole room full of grain, a lovely kitchen, and a pantry. Poor Thumbelina stood outside the door like any other poor beggar girl and asked for a little bit of barley; she hadn't had a scrap to eat in two days.

"You poor little thing!" said the field mouse, because she was actually a kind old field mouse. "Come inside my warm house and eat with me."

Since she had taken a liking to Thumbelina she said, "You're welcome to stay with me this winter, but you have to keep my house nice and clean and tell me stories, because I'm quite fond of stories." And Thumbelina did as the kind old field mouse asked and settled in quite comfortably.

"We'll be having a visitor soon," said the field mouse. "My neighbor usually comes to visit me once a week. He's even more well-off than I am. He has big rooms and wears such a lovely black velvet coat. If only you could win him as your husband, you would be well provided for. But he can't see. You have to tell him the most charming stories you know."

But Thumbelina didn't much like that idea, and she had no desire to have the neighbor as her husband, because he was a mole. He came to visit in his black velvet coat. He was very rich and cultivated, said the field mouse. His lodgings were also more than twenty times bigger than hers, and he had book-learning. But he didn't like the sun or the beautiful flowers; he had nothing good to say about them because he had never seen them. Thumbelina had to sing, and she sang both "Beetle, Fly, Fly Away" and "The Monk Walks Through the Meadow." And the mole fell in love with her because of her beautiful voice, though he said nothing, because he was a sober-minded man.

He had recently dug a long passageway through the earth from his house to theirs, and the field mouse and Thumbelina were invited to promenade along it whenever they liked. He told them not to be frightened by the dead bird lying in the passageway. It was a whole bird with feathers and beak, and it must have died not long ago when winter came. Now it lay buried in the very spot where he had made his passage.

The mole took a stick of touchwood in his mouth because it shines like fire in the dark. He went first, lighting the way for them in the long, dark passage. When they reached the place where the dead bird lay, the mole shoved his wide nose against the ceiling and pushed up the earth, making a big hole so the light could shine through. In the middle of the floor lay a dead swallow with his beautiful wings pressed tightly to his sides, his legs and head tucked under his feathers. The poor bird had undoubtedly died from the cold. Thumbelina felt very sorry for him. She was so fond of all the little birds. All summer long they had sung and chirped so beautifully for her. But the mole kicked at the bird with his stubby legs and said, "He's not going to do any more peeping! What a pitiful thing to be born a little bird. Thank the Lord that won't happen to any of my own children. A bird like this has nothing but his chirping and then ends up starving to death in the wintertime."

"Yes, you're right about that, sensible man that you are," said the field mouse. "What does the bird have for all his chirping when winter comes? He ends up starving and freezing. But that's supposed to be so noble."

Thumbelina didn't say a word, yet when the other two had turned their backs on the bird, she bent down, pushed the feathers aside that lay over his head, and kissed his closed eyes. "Maybe this was the one who sang so beautifully to me this summer," she thought. "What great joy you brought me, you dear, beautiful bird."

Then the mole closed up the hole through which the daylight was shining and escorted the ladies home. That night Thumbelina couldn't sleep a wink, so she got out of bed and wove a big beautiful blanket out of hay and then carried it down and tucked it around the dead bird. She placed some soft cotton she had found in the field mouse's house alongside the bird so that he would be warm in the cold earth.

"Farewell, you beautiful little bird," she said. "Farewell and thank you for your lovely song this summer, when all the trees were green and the sun shone so warm on all of us." Then she laid her head on the bird's breast, but at that instant she grew quite frightened for it sounded as if something were beating inside. It was the bird's heart. The bird wasn't dead. He was in a deep slumber, and now that he was warm, he had revived.

In the autumn the swallows all fly off to the warm countries, but if one of them lingers, he freezes and then falls to the ground quite dead. He lies where he falls, and the cold snow covers him up.

Thumbelina was so frightened that she was shaking all over, because the bird was very, very big compared to her; she was only as tall as a thumb. But she gathered her courage, pulled the cotton closer around the poor swallow, and went to get a mint leaf that she had been using as a coverlet. She placed it over the bird's head.

The following night she went back down to see the bird. By then he was very much alive, but so weak that he could open his eyes only for a brief moment to look at Thumbelina, who stood with a piece of touchwood in her hand, because she had no other lantern.

"Thank you, my charming little child," said the sick swallow. "I feel so wondrously warm. Soon I'll have my strength back and can fly again, out into the warm sunshine."

"Oh," she said, "it's so cold outside, it's snowing and frosty. Stay here in your warm bed, and I'll take care of you."

She brought the swallow some water in a flower petal, and the bird drank and told her how he had torn a wing on a hawthorn bush. That's why he couldn't fly as well as the other swallows when they flew far, far away to the warm countries. Finally he had fallen to the ground, but he couldn't remember anything more and had no idea how he had ended up here.

All winter long he stayed down there, and Thumbelina was kind to him and grew quite fond of him. Neither the mole nor the field mouse had even an inkling about this, because, after all, they cared nothing for the poor pitiful swallow.

As soon as spring arrived and the sun warmed up the earth, the swallow said farewell to Thumbelina, who opened up the hole that the mole had made overhead. The sun flooded in so wondrously, and the swallow asked if she wanted to come with him. She could sit on his back, and they would fly far away into the green forest. But Thumbelina knew it would make the field mouse sad if she left her like that.

"No, I can't," said Thumbelina.

"Farewell, farewell! You kind, charming girl," said the swallow and flew out into the sunlight. Thumbelina gazed after him, and tears rose in her eyes, because she was very fond of the poor swallow.

"Vit-vit! Vit-vit!" sang the bird and flew into the green forest.

Thumbelina was very sad. She wasn't allowed to go out into the warm sunshine. The grain that had been sown on the ground above the field mouse's house grew so high into the air that it too seemed like a great dense forest to the poor little girl who was only as tall as a thumb.

"This summer you need to start sewing your trousseau," the field mouse told her, because her neighbor, the dreary mole in the black velvet coat, had now proposed to Thumbelina. "You'll need both woolens and linens. You'll need cushions and bedding when you become the mole's wife."

Thumbelina had to use the spindle, and the field mouse hired four spiders to spin and weave, day and night. Every evening the mole would come to visit, and he always talked about when the summer would end and the sun was no longer so hot. Right now it was scorching the earth as hard as stone. Yes, when the summer was over he would celebrate his wedding with Thumbelina. But she was not pleased at all, because she wasn't the least bit fond of the dreary mole. Every morning when the sun came up and every evening when it went down, she would slip out to the doorway. And when the wind parted the tops of the grain so she could see the blue sky, then she thought about how bright and beautiful it was outside and wished that she might once again see the dear swallow. But he never came back. No doubt he was flying far away in the beautiful green forest.

By the time autumn came, Thumbelina's trousseau was finished.

"In four weeks you'll celebrate your wedding," the field mouse told her. But Thumbelina wept and said that she didn't want to marry the dreary mole.

"Pish posh!" said the field mouse. "Don't be obstinate or I'll have to bite you with my white tooth. You're getting a lovely husband. Even the queen doesn't have the likes of his black velvet coat. Both his kitchen and cellar are full. You should thank the Lord for him."

Then it was time for the wedding. The mole had already come to get Thumbelina. She was going to live with him, deep underground, and never come out into the warm sunlight, because he didn't like the sun. The poor child was so sad because she now had to bid farewell to the sun. At least she had been allowed to look at it from the field mouse's doorway.

"Farewell, bright sun!" she said, stretching her arms high into the air as she took a few steps outside the field mouse's house. By now the grain had been harvested, and all that remained was the dry stubble. "Farewell, farewell!" she said and threw her tiny arms around a little red flower standing there. "Say hello to the little swallow for me if you ever see him."

"Vit-vit, vit-vit!" she suddenly heard overhead. She looked up, and there was the little swallow just flying past. As soon as he saw Thumbelina he was overjoyed. She told him how unwilling she was to have the hideous mole for her husband, and that she was going to live deep underground where the sun never shone. And then she couldn't help crying.

"The cold winter is coming," said the little swallow, "and I'm going to fly far away to the warm countries. Do you want to come with me? You can sit on my back. Tie yourself on with your sash, and we'll fly away from the hideous mole and his dark house, far away over the mountains to the warm countries where the sun shines more beautifully than here, where it's always summer with lovely flowers. Fly with me, sweet little Thumbelina. You saved my life when I lay frozen in the dark earth cellar."

"Yes, I'll go with you," said Thumbelina, and she climbed onto the bird's back, put her feet on his outspread wings, and tied her belt onto one of the strongest feathers. Then the swallow flew up into the sky, over forests and over lakes, high up over the great mountains that are always covered with snow. And Thumbelina shivered in the cold air, but then she crept under the bird's warm feathers and stuck out her little head to see all the delights below.

At last they came to the warm countries. There the sun shone much brighter than here. The sky was twice as high, and along ditches and fences grew the loveliest green and blue grapes. Lemons and oranges hung in the forests that were fragrant with myrtle and mint. The most charming children ran along the road and played with big, colorful butterflies. But the swallow flew even farther, and everything was more and more beautiful. Under the loveliest of green trees near the blue lake stood a dazzling white marble palace from ancient times. Grapevines twined around the tall pillars, and on the very top perched scores of swallow nests. In one of them lived the swallow who was carrying Thumbelina.

"There's my house," said the swallow. "But if you want to choose one of the magnificent flowers down below, then I'll take you there and you'll be as comfortable as you can imagine!"

"How wonderful!" she said, clapping her tiny hands.

There was a huge white marble column that had fallen to the ground and broken into three pieces, but among them grew the most beautiful big white flowers. The swallow flew down there with Thumbelina and set her on one of the wide petals. How surprised she was! There sat a little man in the middle of the flower, as white and transparent as if he were made of glass. He had the most charming golden crown on his head and the loveliest bright wings on his shoulders. He was no bigger than Thumbelina. He was the flower's angel. In every flower lived a little man or woman just like him, but he was king of them all.

"Good Lord, how handsome he is," whispered Thumbelina to the swallow. The little prince was terribly frightened by the swallow because the bird was gigantic compared to him. He was quite tiny and delicate. But when he saw Thumbelina, he was so happy. She was the most beautiful girl he had ever seen. That's why he took the golden crown from his head and put it on hers, asking her what her name was and whether she would be his wife. Then she would be queen of all the flowers! Yes, he was certainly quite a man, not like the toad's son or the mole with the black velvet coat. That's why she said yes to the lovely prince, and from every flower came a lady or gentleman—all so charming that they were a joy to see. Each of them brought a gift for Thumbelina, but the best of all was a pair of beautiful wings from a big white fly. They were fastened to Thumbelina's back, and then she too could fly from flower to flower. Everyone rejoiced, and the little swallow sat up in his nest and sang for them as best he could. But in his heart he was sad because he was so fond of Thumbelina and had never wanted to be parted from her.

"Your name will no longer be Thumbelina," the flower's angel told her. "That's a horrid name, and you're so beautiful. We'll call you Maja!"

"Farewell! Farewell!" said the little swallow and flew off again, far from the warm countries, far away back to Denmark. There he had a little nest above a window where the man lives who tells fairy tales. He's the one for whom the swallow sang "Vit–vit, vit–vit!" And that's where we heard the whole story.

The Traveling Companion

Poor Johannes was so sad because his father was very ill and about to die. There was no one else but the two of them in the little room. The lamp on the table was about to go out, and it was quite late in the evening.

"You've been a good son, Johannes," said the sick father. "Our Lord will surely help you make your way in the world." And he fixed his somber, gentle eyes on him, took a big, deep breath, and died. It was as if he fell asleep. But Johannes wept. Now he had no one in the whole world, no father or mother, sister or brother. Poor Johannes! He knelt down beside the bed and kissed the hand of his dead father, shedding many salty tears. Finally he closed his eyes and fell asleep with his head against the hard bed frame.

Then he dreamed a strange dream. He saw the sun and the moon bowing to him; he saw his father healthy and vigorous once more and heard him laugh the way he always laughed when he was truly pleased. A lovely girl with a golden crown on her beautiful long hair held out her hand to Johannes, and his father said, "Do you see what a bride you've won? She's the loveliest in the whole world." Then he woke up and all the beauty was gone. His father lay dead and cold in his bed; there was no one else with them. Poor Johannes!

The following week the dead man was buried. Johannes walked right behind the coffin. He would no longer be able to see his good father, who had loved him so much. He heard them toss dirt onto the coffin, and looked down at the last visible corner; but with the next shovelful of earth, it too was gone. Then his heart felt as if it would break, he was so sad. Around him they were singing a hymn. It sounded quite beautiful, and tears came to Johannes's eyes. He wept, and in his grief this did him good. The sun shone splendidly on the green trees, as if it wanted to say, "You mustn't be sad, Johannes. See what a beautiful blue the sky is. Your father is up there now, asking the good Lord to see that things always go well for you."

"I will always be good," said Johannes. "Then I'll go up to Heaven to my father. What a joy it will be to see each other again! I will have so much to tell him, and he in turn will show me so many things, and teach me about all the splendors in Heaven, just as he taught me here on earth. Oh, what a joy that will be!"

Johannes imagined it all so clearly that it made him smile, though the tears still ran down his cheeks. The little birds sat high in the chestnut trees and said, "Vit-vit, vit-vit!" They were quite cheerful even though they were at a funeral. No doubt they knew that the dead man was now up in Heaven, with wings much bigger and more beautiful than their own. And he was happy because he had been good here on earth, and that pleased them. Johannes saw them fly from the green trees far away into the world, and he suddenly had such a desire to fly with them. But first he carved a big wooden cross to put on his father's grave. When he brought it there in the evening, the grave was decorated with sand and flowers. Strangers had done this, because they were all terribly fond of the dear father who was now dead.

Early the next morning Johannes packed up his small bundle, hiding in his belt his entire inheritance, which consisted of 50 *rigsdaler* and a couple of silver *skillings*. Now he was ready to set out into the world. But first he went over to the churchyard to his father's grave, recited the Lord's Prayer, and said, "Farewell, dear Father! I will always be a good person, so don't hesitate to ask the good Lord to see that things go well for me."

Out in the field where Johannes was walking, all the flowers stood fresh and lovely in the warm sunlight. They nodded in the wind as if to say, "Nature welcomes you! Isn't it charming?" But Johannes turned around one more time to look at the old church where as a little child he was baptized, where he had sat every Sunday with his old father and sung hymns. Then he noticed that high up in one of the openings in the tower stood the church-elf wearing his little pointed red cap. He was shading his face in the crook of his arm because otherwise the sun would have hurt his eyes. Johannes nodded farewell to him. The little elf waved his red cap, put his hand to his heart, and kissed his fingers over and over, to show what good wishes he was sending him for a happy journey.

Johannes thought about all the beautiful things he was now going to see in the great, magnificent world. He walked farther and farther away, farther than he had ever been before. He didn't know the towns he passed through or the people he met. Now he was far away among strangers.

The first night he had to sleep in a haystack out in a field; he had no other bed. But it was quite charming, he thought. Surely the king couldn't be any more comfortable. The whole field, with the stream, the haystack, and the blue sky above made such a beautiful bedchamber. The green grass with the tiny red and white flowers was the carpet, the elderberry bushes and the wild rose hedges were flower bouquets. For his washbasin he had the whole stream with its clear, fresh water, where the reeds bowed, saying both good evening and good morning. The moon was an enormous night-light, high above beneath the blue vault, and it wouldn't set the curtains on fire. Johannes could sleep quite peacefully, and that's what he did, waking only when the sun came up and all the little birds around him sang, "Good morning! Good morning! Aren't you up yet?"

The bells rang, summoning everyone to church. It was Sunday. People went inside to hear the pastor, and Johannes followed along, singing a hymn and listening to God's Word. It seemed to him that he was back in his own church where he was baptized and used to sing hymns with his father.

Out in the churchyard there were many graves, and on some of them grew tall grass. Then Johannes thought about his own father's grave that would also end up looking like this since he wouldn't be there to weed and tend it. So he sat down and pulled out the grass, put back the wooden crosses that had fallen over, and replaced the wreaths that the wind had torn from the graves, all the while thinking, "Maybe someone will do the same for my father's grave, now that I can't do it myself."

Outside the churchyard gate stood an old beggar, leaning on his

crutch. Johannes gave him all the silver *skillings* that he had and
then continued on, happy and content, out into the wide world.

Toward evening a terrible storm came up. Johannes hurried to
find shelter, but soon it was night and pitch dark. Finally he came
to a little church that stood all alone on a hill. Fortunately the door
stood open, and he slipped inside; here he would stay until the bad
weather had passed.

"I'll sit down here in the corner," he said. "I'm quite tired and
could use a little rest." Then he sat down, folded his hands, and
said his evening prayer. Before he knew it he fell asleep and was
dreaming as lightning flashed and thunder roared outside.

When he awoke it was the middle of the night, but the storm
had passed and the moon was shining through the windows. In the
middle of the church stood an open coffin with a dead man inside,
because he had not yet been buried. Johannes was not the least bit
frightened because he had a pure conscience, and he knew that the
dead hurt no one. It's people who are alive and evil who cause
harm. Two such alive and evil men stood close to the dead man
who had been brought inside the church before being placed in his
grave. They wanted to do him harm. They didn't want to let him
lie in his coffin; they meant to throw him out the church door, that
poor dead man.

"Why do you want to do that?" asked Johannes. "That's an evil
and mean thing to do. In Christ's name, let him sleep!"

"Oh, pish posh!" said the two vile men. "He cheated us. He
owes us money but he couldn't repay it. Now, on top of everything
else, he's dead and we won't get a single *skilling*. That's why we
want to take our revenge. He's going to lie like a dog outside the
church door!"

"I have only fifty *rigsdaler*," said Johannes. "That's my whole
inheritance, but I'll gladly give it to you if you will honestly promise
me to leave the poor dead man in peace. I'm sure I can get by
without the money. I have strong, healthy limbs, and our Lord will
always help me."

"All right," said the nasty men. "If you want to pay his debts
this way, then we won't do him any harm, you can be certain of
that!" And then they took the money Johannes gave them, laughed
uproariously at his kindness, and went on their way. But Johannes

put the body back into the coffin, folded the man's hands, and said farewell. Then, feeling content, he set off once more through the vast forest.

All around, wherever the moon managed to shine through the trees, he could see charming little fairies playing merrily. They weren't disturbed by him, because they undoubtedly knew he was a good and innocent person. Only evil people are not allowed to see fairies. Some of them were no bigger than a finger, with their long yellow hair pinned up with golden combs. Two by two they teetered on the big drops of dew that lay on the leaves and the tall grass. Now and then a drop would begin to roll, and they would fall off among the tall blades of grass. Then a chorus of laughter would rise up from the tiny fairies. It was tremendous fun! They were singing, and Johannes recognized quite clearly all the beautiful songs he had learned as a little boy. From one hedge to the other, big colorful spiders with silver crowns on their heads were spinning long hanging bridges and palaces. When the fine dew fell, they looked like shimmering glass in the bright moonlight. Things continued this way, right until the sun came up. Then the little fairies crept into the flower buds, and the wind seized hold of their bridges and castles, which flew off into the air like big spiderwebs.

Johannes had just come out of the forest when a man's powerful voice boomed behind him, "Hello there, friend! Where are you headed?"

"Out into the wide world," said Johannes. "I have neither father nor mother. I'm a poor lad, but surely Our Lord will help me."

"I'm also headed out into the wide world," said the stranger. "Should we keep each other company?"

"Why, of course!" said Johannes, and the two of them set off together. They soon grew quite fond of each other, since they were both good people. But Johannes noticed that the stranger was much wiser than he was. He'd been nearly everywhere in the world and could talk about practically everything in existence.

The sun was already high overhead when they sat down under a big tree to eat their lunch. At that moment an old woman appeared. Oh, she was very old, and she walked all hunched over, leaning on a crutch. On her back she carried a load of firewood that she had gathered in the forest. Her apron was tucked up, and

Johannes saw three big bundles of ferns and willow branches sticking out of it. When she was quite close, her foot slipped and she
fell, uttering a loud shriek, because she had broken her leg. That
poor old woman!

Johannes wanted them to carry her back to where she lived at
once, but the stranger opened his knapsack, took out a jar, and said
that he had a salve that would instantly make her leg healthy and
whole. Then she could walk home on her own, as if she had never
broken her leg at all. But in return he wanted her to give him the
three bundles that she had in her apron.

"That's certainly a high price!" said the old woman, nodding
her head in an odd way. She wasn't eager to part with her bundles,
but then again it wasn't very pleasant to be lying there with a
broken leg. So she gave him the bundles, and as soon as the stranger
had rubbed the salve on her leg, the old woman stood up and
walked much better than she had before. That's what the salve
could do. But it was not something that could be bought in an
apothecary's shop.

"What do you want those bundles for?" Johannes asked his new
traveling companion.

"The three of them make such pretty bouquets," he said. "I just
happen to like them, because I'm a peculiar fellow."

Then they continued on for a good distance.

"Oh, there's a real storm brewing," said Johannes, pointing
straight ahead. "Look at those dreadful, thick clouds!"

"No," said his traveling companion, "those aren't clouds, they're
mountains. Lovely huge mountains where you can climb high
above the clouds into the fresh air. It's glorious, let me tell you! By
tomorrow we're bound to make it that far in the world."

But the mountains weren't as close as they looked. They walked
for an entire day before they reached the mountains where the
black forests grew right up to the heavens and where the boulders
were as big as a whole town. It would certainly be a difficult passage
to make their way over them. That's why Johannes and his traveling
companion stopped at an inn to have a good rest and gather their
strength for the hike the next morning.

Scores of people were crowded into the big tavern of the inn
because a man there was staging a marionette show. He had just set

up his little theater, and a crowd was gathering round to watch the play. In the very front row a fat old butcher had sat down in the best seat of all. His big bulldog—oh, how fierce he looked!—was sitting next to him and making eyes, along with everyone else.

Then the play started, and it was a nice play with a king and a queen. They sat on the loveliest of thrones, with golden crowns on their heads and long trains on their garments, because they could afford it. The most charming wooden marionettes with glass eyes and big handlebar mustaches stood at all the doors, opening and closing them to let fresh air into the room. It was quite a charming play, and it wasn't the least bit sad. But just as the queen stood up and walked across the stage, then . . . Well, God only knows what that big bulldog was thinking. But since the fat butcher wasn't holding on to him, the dog leaped at the stage and grabbed the queen around her slender waist, making it say "crick, crack!" It was simply dreadful!

The poor man who was staging the play was so horrified and sad about his queen, because she was the most charming of all the marionettes he owned, and now the hideous bulldog had bitten her head off. But later, after everyone had left, the stranger, the one who had arrived with Johannes, said that he would repair her. And then he took out his jar and smeared the marionette with the salve that he had used to help the poor old woman when she broke her leg. As soon as the salve was rubbed on the marionette, she was suddenly whole again. Why, she could even move all her limbs on her own; it was no longer necessary to pull the strings. The marionette was like a live human being, except that she couldn't speak. The man who owned the little theater was overjoyed because he didn't have to hold on to the marionette; she could dance all by herself. None of the others could do that.

Later, when night fell and everyone at the inn had gone to bed, someone began sighing so heavily, and kept at it for so long, that they all got up to see who it could be. The man who had staged the play went over to his little theater, because it was inside there that someone was sighing. All the wooden marionettes lay jumbled together, the king and all his guardsmen. They were the ones who were sighing so pitifully, staring with their big glass eyes, because they dearly wanted to be rubbed with a little of the salve, like the queen, so they too could move all by themselves. The queen knelt down and held out her lovely golden crown as she pleaded, "Take this, but rub my consort and his courtiers with the salve!" Then the poor man who owned the theater and all the marionettes couldn't help crying, because he felt terribly sorry for them. He promised the traveling companion at once that he would give him all the money that he took in for his play on the following evening if only he would rub salve on four or five of his best marionettes. But the traveling companion said that he wanted nothing in return except for the big sword the man wore at his side. As soon as this was given to him, he rubbed salve on six marionettes, who promptly started dancing. It looked so charming that all the girls, the live human girls who were watching, began to dance too. The coachman and the cook danced, the waiter and the maid, all the guests, and the hearth shovel and tongs as well—though these two toppled over the minute they took their first steps. Oh, what a merry night that was!

The next morning Johannes and his traveling companion took leave of the others and set off up the steep mountains and through the big pine forests. They climbed so high that in the end the church towers far below looked like little red berries in the midst of all the green. They could see far, far off, for miles and miles, to places where they had never been. Johannes had never before seen so much beauty all at once in the lovely world, and the sun shone so warm in the clear blue sky. He could also hear the hunters blowing their horns in the mountains, sounding so beautiful and heavenly that his eyes filled with tears of joy, and he couldn't help saying, "My dear Lord! I could kiss You because You are so good to all of us and have given us all this splendor in the world!"

His traveling companion also stood with folded hands and gazed out over the forest and towns in the warm sunlight. At that moment there was a wondrously lovely sound overhead, and they looked up into the sky. A great white swan was hovering in the air. It was very beautiful and was singing like no bird they had ever heard sing before. But it grew fainter and fainter. The swan bowed its head and sank quite slowly to lie at their feet. It was dead, that beautiful bird.

"What lovely wings," said the traveling companion. "Wings as big and white as the ones on this bird are worth money. I'll take them along! Now you can see what a good thing it was that I got this sword." And then with a single blow he chopped both wings off the dead swan. He was going to keep them.

They now journeyed for miles and miles over the mountains until at last they saw before them an enormous city with more than a hundred towers, gleaming like silver in the sunlight. In the middle of the city stood a magnificent marble palace with a roof of red gold, and there lived the king.

Johannes and his traveling companion didn't want to enter the city at once, but stayed at an inn on the outskirts so they could put on their very best clothes. They wanted to look nice when they walked through the streets. The innkeeper told them that the king was such a good man who never did anyone any harm. His daughter, on the other hand . . . well, the Lord save us! She was a mean princess. She was not lacking in beauty—no one could be as beautiful or charming as she was. But what good did it do when she was a mean and evil witch who was to blame for so many handsome princes losing their lives? She had given permission for anyone to seek her hand. Anyone could come forward, whether he was a prince or a vagabond, it made no difference. All he had to do was guess three things that she asked of him. If he did, she would marry him, and he would be king of the whole land when her father died. But if he couldn't guess the three things, she would order him hanged or beheaded; that's how mean and evil the lovely princess was. Her father, the old king, was terribly sad about this, but he couldn't stop her from being so evil. He had once told her that he would never have the slightest thing to do with her sweethearts, so she could do as she pleased. Each time a prince appeared and tried to guess correctly to win the princess, he could never find the right answer, and then he was hanged or beheaded. They had warned him in advance, and he could have decided not to seek her hand. The old king was so sad about all this sorrow and misery that once a year for an entire day he would kneel along with all his soldiers and beg the princess to be good. But she refused to listen. The old women who drank aquavit would color the liquor completely black before they drank it to show their grief, but there was nothing else they could do.

"That hideous princess!" said Johannes. "She certainly deserves a whipping. It would do her good. If only I were the old king, she would bleed like a pig!"

At that moment they heard people outside shouting "Hurrah!" The princess was coming past. She was truly so lovely that everyone forgot how evil she was, and that's why they shouted "Hurrah." Twelve lovely maidens, dressed in white silk gowns and carrying golden tulips in their hands, rode coal-black horses at her side. The princess herself had a chalk-white horse adorned with diamonds and rubies. Her riding costume was of pure gold, and the whip in her hand looked like a ray of the sun. The gold crown on her head looked like little stars from the sky, and her cloak was made from the lovely wings of over a thousand butterflies. Yet she was even more beautiful than all her finery.

When Johannes caught sight of her, his face turned as red as dripping blood, and he could scarcely utter a word. The princess looked exactly like the lovely girl with the golden crown that he had dreamed about on the night his father died. He found her quite beautiful and couldn't help falling in love with her. It just couldn't be true, he said, that she was an evil witch who ordered people hanged or beheaded when they couldn't guess what she demanded of them. "Anyone has the right to seek her hand, even the poorest vagabond. I'm going up to the palace. I can't help myself!"

Everyone told him not to do it; the same thing was bound to happen to him that had happened to all the others. His traveling companion advised him against it, but Johannes thought things would go just fine. He brushed his shoes and his dress coat, washed his face and hands, combed his beautiful yellow hair, and then walked all alone into town and up to the palace.

"Come in!" said the old king when Johannes knocked on the door. Johannes opened the door and the old king, wearing a dressing gown and embroidered slippers, came to greet him. He had a golden crown on his head, a scepter in one hand, and a golden orb in the other. "Just a moment," he said and stuck the orb under his arm in order to shake hands with Johannes. But as soon as he heard that he was a suitor, he began to cry so hard that both the scepter and orb fell to the floor, and he had to wipe his eyes on his dressing gown. The poor old king!

"Don't do it!" he said. "Things won't turn out any better for you than for all the others. Just come and look at this!" And he led Johannes out to the flower garden that belonged to the princess, and what a horrible sight it was! High in every tree hung three or four princes who had sought the hand of the princess but couldn't guess the things that she had asked of them. With every gust of wind the bones rattled, frightening all the little birds so badly that they never dared enter the garden. All the flowers were tied up with human bones, and in the flowerpots sat grinning skulls. It was certainly quite a garden for a princess.

"There you see!" said the old king. "The same thing will happen to you as happened to all the others you see here, so don't do it. You're making me terribly unhappy, because I take it so much to heart."

Johannes kissed the hand of the kind old king and said that things would turn out just fine, because he was very fond of the lovely princess.

At that moment the princess herself, with all her ladies, came riding into the palace courtyard, and they went over to say hello. She was quite charming and gave Johannes her hand, which made him even more fond of her than before. Surely she couldn't be the mean, evil witch everyone said she was. They went up to the great hall, and the little pages served them jam and gingerbread cookies. The old king was so sad he couldn't eat a thing, and besides, the gingerbread cookies were too hard for him.

It was now decided that Johannes would come back to the palace the following morning. Then the judges and the entire council would be assembled to see whether he could manage to guess the answer. If he did well, he would have to return two more times. But so far no one had ever guessed more than once, and they had all lost their lives.

Johannes wasn't the least bit worried about how things would go for him. He was actually quite pleased and could think of nothing but the lovely princess. He no doubt believed that the good Lord would help him in some way that was unknown to him, and he refused to brood about it. He danced along the road as he made his way back to the inn where his traveling companion was waiting.

Johannes couldn't stop talking about how charming the princess had been toward him and how lovely she was. He was already longing for the next day when he would go back to the palace and try his luck at guessing.

But his traveling companion shook his head and was quite sad. "I'm so terribly fond of you," he said. "We could have continued on together for a long time, but now I'm going to lose you. Poor, dear Johannes, I feel like crying. But I don't want to disturb your joy on what might be the last evening we spend together. Let's be merry, truly merry! Tomorrow, when you're gone, I'll let myself cry."

Everyone in town had learned at once that a new suitor for the princess had appeared, and that's why there was great sadness. The theater was closed, all the cake-wives tied black crepe on their sugar-pigs, the king and the pastors were on their knees in church. There was such sorrow because Johannes couldn't possibly fare any better than all the other suitors.

Later that evening the traveling companion made a big bowl of punch and told Johannes that now they were going to be truly merry and drink a toast to the princess. But after Johannes had drunk two glasses, he grew so sleepy that it was impossible for him to keep his eyes open. He couldn't help falling asleep. The traveling companion gently lifted him from his chair and put him to bed. When dark night fell, he took the two big wings that he had chopped off the swan, and tied them to his shoulders. In his pocket he put the biggest bundle of branches that he had been given by the old woman who fell and broke her leg. Then he opened the window and flew over the city, right to the palace, where he perched in a corner under the window that opened onto the bedchamber of the princess.

The whole city was very quiet. Then the clock struck a quarter to twelve, the window opened, and the princess, wearing a big white cloak and long black wings, flew out over the city toward a huge mountain. The traveling companion made himself invisible so the princess wouldn't notice him and flew behind her, beating her with his branches so that blood flowed wherever he struck. Oh, how fast they flew through the air! The wind tore at her cloak, which spread out on all sides like a big sail, and the moon shone right through it.

"How it's hailing! How it's hailing!" said the princess with every lash of the branches, and she deserved it. Finally she reached the mountain and knocked. It sounded like thunder rumbling when the mountain opened and the princess went inside. The traveling companion followed, since no one could see him. He was invisible. They walked through a huge long passageway where the walls glistened quite strangely. Over a thousand glowing spiders were running up and down the walls, shining like fire. Then they came to an enormous hall made of silver and gold. Flowers as big as sunflowers, red and blue, gleamed from the walls. But no one could pick these flowers, because their stems were horrid poisonous snakes, and the blossoms were flames spewing from their mouths. The entire ceiling was covered with shimmering glowworms and sky-blue bats who were flapping their transparent wings. How peculiar it all looked! In the middle of the hall stood a throne resting on four horse skeletons with harnesses of red fire-spiders. The throne itself was made of milk-white glass, and the cushions on the seat were little black mice who were biting each other's tails. Above was a canopy of rose-colored spiderwebs, studded with the most exquisite little green flies that sparkled like gemstones. In the center of the throne sat an old troll with a crown on his ugly head and a scepter in his hand. He kissed the princess on the forehead, motioned for her to sit beside him on the precious throne, and then the music began. Big black grasshoppers played mouth harps, and the owl beat his belly because he didn't have any drums. It was a strange concert. Tiny black elves with will-o'-the-wisps on their caps danced around the hall. No one could see the traveling companion. He had taken up a position right behind the throne, watching and listening to everything. The members of the court, who now entered, looked quite elegant and handsome, but anyone who could truly see realized what they actually were. They were nothing but broomsticks topped by heads of cabbage that the troll had conjured to life, giving them embroidered garments. But it didn't much matter, since they were only there for decoration.

After the dancing had gone on for a while, the princess told the troll that she had a new suitor. She wanted to know what to ask him when he came to the palace the next morning.

"Now listen!" said the troll. "I'm going to tell you something.

Think of something very easy, because then it will never occur to him. Think about one of your shoes. He'll never guess that. Then have him beheaded. When you come back out here to see me tomorrow night, don't forget to bring me his eyes, because I want to eat them!"

The princess made a deep curtsy and said that she wouldn't forget the eyes. The troll opened the mountain, and she flew back home. The traveling companion followed behind, whipping her so hard with the branches that she sighed heavily at the terrible hailstorm and hurried as fast as she could back to her window and into her bedchamber. The traveling companion flew back to the inn where Johannes was still asleep. He took off his wings and lay down in bed as well, because of course he was tired.

It was quite early in the morning when Johannes awoke. The traveling companion got out of bed too and told him that in the night he had dreamed a very strange dream about the princess and her shoe. So he begged him to ask the princess if she might be thinking of her shoe. That, after all, is what he had heard the troll say inside the mountain, but he didn't want to tell Johannes anything about it. He merely told him to ask if she was thinking of her shoe.

"It doesn't much matter whether I ask about that or something else," said Johannes. "Maybe what you dreamed will be the correct answer, because I've always believed that Our Lord will help me. But even so, I'll say farewell to you now, because if I guess wrong, I'll never see you again."

Then they kissed each other, and Johannes went into the city and up to the palace. The entire hall was crowded with people. The judges were sitting in their armchairs with eiderdown cushions behind their heads because they had so much to think about. The old king stood up and wiped his eyes on a white handkerchief. Then the princess entered. She was even lovelier than the day before, and she greeted everyone with affection. She gave Johannes her hand and said, "Good morning, my dear!"

Now it was time for Johannes to guess what she was thinking about. Lord, how kindly she looked at him, but as soon as she heard the word *shoe*, her face turned chalk-white and she began shaking all over. But it did her no good, because he had guessed correctly!

Good Heavens, how happy the old king was! He turned a

magnificent somersault, and everyone applauded him and Johannes, who had guessed right the very first time.

The traveling companion was also pleased when he learned how well things had turned out. But Johannes folded his hands and thanked the good Lord, who no doubt would also help him the next two times. On the following day he would have to guess again.

The evening proceeded as it had the day before. When Johannes was asleep, the traveling companion flew behind the princess to the mountain, beating her even harder than the first time, because now he had brought along two bundles of branches. No one saw him, and he heard everything. The princess was going to think about her glove, and that's what he told Johannes, as if it were a dream. Johannes was able to guess correctly, and there was great joy at the palace. The entire court turned somersaults, just as they had seen the king do the first time. But the princess lay on the sofa and refused to say a single word. Now everything depended on whether Johannes could guess correctly the third time. If all went well, he would win the lovely princess and inherit the entire kingdom when the old king died. If he guessed wrong, he would lose his life, and the troll would eat his beautiful blue eyes.

That night, Johannes went to bed early, said his evening prayers, and slept quite peacefully. But the traveling companion attached the wings to his back, fastened the sword to his side, and took all three bundles of branches along as he flew over to the palace.

The night was pitch-black and so stormy that tiles were flying off the rooftops. In the garden where the skeletons hung, the trees were swaying like reeds in the wind. Lightning flashed every second, and thunder rolled as if it were one continuous thunderclap all night long. Then the window opened, and the princess flew out. She was as pale as death, but she laughed at the foul weather and seemed to think it wasn't nasty enough. Her white cloak whirled around in the air like a great sail, but the traveling companion beat her so hard with the three bundles of branches that blood dripped down to the ground, and in the end she could hardly keep flying. Finally she reached the mountain.

"It's hailing and blowing," she said. "I've never been out in such a storm before."

"Sometimes you can have too much of a good thing," said the troll. Then she told him that Johannes had guessed correctly the second time. If he did the same the next morning, he would win. She would never be able to come back to the mountain, would never be able to perform acts of magic as she had before. That was why she was terribly sad.

"He won't be able to guess," said the troll. "I'll think of something that would never occur to him. Or else he must be a greater sorcerer than I am. But right now let's be merry!" And he took the princess by both hands, and they danced in a circle with all the little elves and will-o'-the-wisps in the hall. The red spiders raced up and down the walls so merrily. The fire-blossoms seemed to be flashing sparks. The owl beat his drum, the crickets chirped, and the black grasshoppers played their mouth harps. What a merry ball it was!

After they had been dancing long enough, it was time for the princess to go home because otherwise she would be missed at the palace. The troll said that he would accompany her so they would have a little more time together.

They flew off into the storm, and the traveling companion wore out his three bundles of branches on their backs. The troll had never been out in such a hailstorm before. Outside the palace he said farewell to the princess as he whispered to her, "Think about my head." But the traveling companion heard what he said. The moment the princess slipped through the window into her bedchamber and the troll turned to leave, he grabbed his long black beard, and with the sword he chopped off the hideous troll's head right at the shoulders so that even the troll didn't see what happened. He tossed the body to the fish in the sea, but the head he merely dipped in the water. Then he wrapped it up in his silk handkerchief and took it back to the inn, where he lay down to sleep.

The next morning he gave the handkerchief to Johannes but told him not to open it until the princess asked him what she was thinking about.

There were so many people in the great hall of the palace that they were packed together like radishes tied in a bunch. The council sat in their chairs with the soft cushions behind their heads. The old king was wearing new clothes. His crown and scepter had been polished and looked quite exquisite. But the princess was very pale, and she wore a coal-black gown, as if attending a funeral.

"What am I thinking about?" she asked Johannes, who at once opened the handkerchief and was quite horrified when he saw the troll's vile head. Everyone shivered, because it was dreadful to look at, but the princess sat as if carved from stone and couldn't utter a single word. At last she rose and gave Johannes her hand, because he had guessed correctly, after all. She didn't look at anyone but gave a deep sigh. "You are my lord. Tonight we shall celebrate our wedding."

"Now that's to my liking," said the old king, "and that's how it will be!" Everyone shouted "Hurrah!" The guards played music in the streets, the bells rang, and the cake-wives took the black crepe off their sugar-pigs because now everyone was joyful. Three whole roasted oxen, stuffed with ducks and hens, were set in the middle of the marketplace, and anyone could cut himself a slice. The fountains spouted the loveliest wine, and if someone bought a *skilling* roll at the bakery, he would get six big buns as well, the kind filled with raisins.

That evening the entire city was lit up. The soldiers fired cannons, and the boys set off firecrackers. Everyone feasted and drank, clinking glasses and making merry up at the palace. All the distinguished gentlemen and the lovely maidens danced with each other. From far away their song could be heard:

> Here is many a pretty girl
> Who wants to take a little twirl.
> She sets off marching to the drum,
> Pretty girl, you dance and hum.
> Swaying, stamping, off she goes
> Till her shoes fall off her toes!

But the princess was still a witch and not the least bit fond of Johannes. The traveling companion realized this, and that's why he gave Johannes three feathers from the swan's wings, along with a little bottle containing several drops. He told him to order a big tub filled with water to be brought to the bridal bed. When the princess was about to climb into bed, he should give her a little push to make her fall into the tub. Then he should shove her under the water three times after first throwing the feathers and drops into the tub. That would release her from the spell, and she would end up feeling very fond of him.

Johannes did everything the traveling companion had advised. The princess screamed quite loudly as he shoved her under the water, flailing under his hands like a big, coal-black swan with flashing eyes. When she came to the surface the second time, the swan was white except for a single black ring around her neck. Johannes prayed piously to Our Lord and for the third time let the water play over the bird. At that instant she was transformed into the loveliest princess. She was even more beautiful than before, and she thanked him with tears in her lovely eyes because he had released her from the spell.

The next morning the old king came in with the entire royal household, and the congratulations continued half the day. Finally the traveling companion came in. He had his walking stick in his hand and his knapsack on his back. Johannes kissed him again and again, telling him not to leave. He had to stay because it was to him that Johannes owed all his happiness. But the traveling companion shook his head and said gently and kindly, "It's time for me to go now. I have repaid my debt. Do you remember the dead man that the evil men wanted to harm? You gave them everything you owned so that he would have peace in the grave. That dead man is me!"

At that instant he was gone.

The wedding celebration lasted an entire month. Johannes and the princess loved each other so much. The old king lived on for many pleasant years and let their tiny little children ride horsey on his knee and play with his scepter. But Johannes was king of the whole realm.

The Little Mermaid

Far out at sea the water is as blue as the petals of the loveliest cornflower and as clear as the purest glass, but it's very deep, deeper than any anchor line can reach. Scores of church towers would have to be set on top of each other to reach from the bottom up to the surface of the water. Down there live the sea folk.

Now, you mustn't think that there's nothing but a bare white, sandy bottom. No, the most wondrous trees and plants grow there, with such supple stems and leaves that at the slightest ripple in the water they move as if they were alive. All the fish, big and small, flit through the branches like the birds up here in the sky. At the very deepest spot stands the sea king's castle. The walls are made of coral, and the tall, arched windows are of the clearest amber. But the roof is made of seashells that open and close with the flow of the water. How lovely it looks, because in each of them lie dazzling pearls, any one of which would be a great jewel in the crown of a queen.

For many years the sea king had been a widower, though his old mother kept house for him. She was a wise woman, but proud of her noble birth, and that's why she had twelve oysters on her tail. The other nobles were only allowed to wear six. Otherwise she deserved high praise, especially because she was so fond of the little sea princesses, her granddaughters. All six were lovely children, but the youngest was the most beautiful of all. Her skin was as clear and soft as a rose petal, her eyes as blue as the deepest sea. Yet like the others she had no feet. Her body ended in a fish tail.

All day long they would play in the castle, in the great halls where living flowers grew out of the walls. When the big amber windows were opened, the fish swam in, just like the swallows fly in to us when we open our windows. The fish swam right up to the little princesses, ate out of their hands, and let themselves be petted.

Outside the castle there was a great garden with fiery red and dark blue trees. The fruit gleamed like gold, and the blossoms like a blazing fire as they constantly fluttered their stalks and leaves. The ground itself was of the finest sand, but blue like flaming sulfur. A wondrous blue glow hovered over everything down there. You might almost think you were high up in the air and could see nothing but sky both above and below, rather than being at the bottom of the ocean. In calm seas you could catch sight of the sun. It looked like a crimson flower from whose chalice all light streamed.

Each of the little princesses had her own small plot in the garden where she could dig and plant as she liked. One of them gave her flower bed the shape of a whale, another thought it better if hers looked like a little mermaid. But the youngest made hers perfectly round, like the sun, and planted only flowers that shone just as red. She was an odd child, quiet and pensive. While the other sisters adorned their gardens with the most wondrous things they had gathered from sunken ships, the only thing she wanted, other than the scarlet flowers that looked like the sun above, was a beautiful marble statue. It was a lovely boy carved from clear, white stone, which had come to the sea floor with a shipwreck. Next to the statue she planted a crimson weeping willow that grew so gloriously, draping its fresh boughs over the statue and down to the blue sandy bottom, casting a violet shadow that was in constant movement, like the boughs. It looked as if the treetop and the roots were pretending to kiss.

She had no greater joy than to hear about the human world up above. Her old grandmother had to tell her everything she knew about ships and cities, humans and animals. She thought it especially strange and lovely that up on earth the flowers had a fragrance, while those on the sea floor did not. And the forests were green, and the fish that could be seen among the branches could sing so loudly and beautifully that it was sheer delight. It was the little birds that their grandmother called fish, because otherwise they wouldn't understand her, since they had never seen a bird.

"When each of you turns fifteen," said their grandmother, "you'll be allowed to go up to the surface of the sea, sit in the moonlight on the rocks, and look at the great ships sailing past. You'll see forests and cities!" In the coming year one of the sisters would turn fifteen, but the others . . . Well, each was a year younger than the other, and the youngest of them still had a full five years before she could venture up from the bottom of the sea to find out what it looked like in our world. But each promised to tell the next what she had seen and what she found to be most lovely on her first day. Their grandmother hadn't told them enough, and there was so much they wanted to know.

None of them was as full of yearning as the youngest sister, the one who had the longest to wait and was so quiet and pensive. Many a night she would stand at the open window and gaze up through the dark blue water where the fish were flapping their fins and tails. She could see the moon and stars. Even though their glow was quite pale, through the water they looked much bigger than they do to our eyes. If a black cloud seemed to pass beneath them, she knew that it was either a whale swimming above her or a ship full of people. It probably never occurred to them that a lovely little mermaid was standing below, stretching her white hands up toward the keel.

Then the oldest princess turned fifteen and could venture up to the surface of the sea.

When she returned, she had hundreds of things to tell them. She said that loveliest of all was lying in the moonlight on a sandbar in the calm sea and looking at the great city close to shore where the lights sparkled like hundreds of stars, listening to the music and the noise and commotion of the coaches and people, seeing all the church towers and spires, and hearing the bells ring. The very fact that she couldn't go there made her yearn for it all the more.

Oh, how the youngest sister listened! And later that evening as she stood at the open window and gazed up through the dark blue water, she thought about the great city with all its noise and commotion, and then she imagined she could hear the sound of the church bells reaching down to her.

The following year the second sister was allowed to rise up through the water and swim wherever she liked. She reached the surface just as the sun went down, and that was the sight she found the loveliest of all. The whole sky looked like gold, she said, and the clouds, well, their loveliness she couldn't possibly describe! Red and violet, they had sailed above her. But even faster, like a long white veil, flew a flock of wild swans over the water in front of the sun. She swam toward it, but it sank, and the rosy glow was extinguished by the surface of the sea and the clouds.

The next year the third sister went up above. She was the most daring of them all, and that's why she swam along a wide river that flowed into the sea. She saw lovely green hills with grapevines, castles, and manor houses that peeked out from the magnificent forests. She heard all the birds singing, and the sunshine was so hot that she often had to dive underwater to cool her burning face. In a little bay she came upon a whole flock of tiny human children; quite naked, they ran around and splashed in the water. She wanted to play with them, but they ran off in fright, and a little black animal appeared. It was a dog, but she had never seen a dog before. It barked at her so fiercely that she was frightened and retreated to the open sea. But she would never forget the magnificent forests, the green hills, and the enchanting children who could swim in the water even though they had no fish tails.

The fourth sister was not as daring. She stayed out in the wild sea and claimed that it was the loveliest place of all. You could see for miles around, and the sky overhead was just like a great glass bell. She saw ships, but far away; they looked like black-backed seagulls. The amusing dolphins had turned somersaults, and the enormous whales had sprayed water out of their nostrils so it looked like hundreds of fountains all around.

Then it was the fifth sister's turn. Her birthday was in the winter, and that's why she saw what the others had not seen on their first time. The sea had turned quite green, and all around floated great icebergs. She said each of them looked like a pearl and yet was much bigger than the church towers that humans built. They appeared in the most wondrous of shapes and glittered like dia- monds. She sat down on one of the largest, and all the sailing ships tacked in terror around the place where she sat, as she let the wind blow through her long hair. But toward evening the sky was covered with clouds. Lightning flashed and thunder roared while the black sea lifted the icebergs high in the air, making them gleam with red lightning. On all the ships they took in the sails, while fear and horror reigned. But she sat calmly on her drifting iceberg and watched the blue lightning bolts zigzag down to strike the gleaming sea.

The first time one of the sisters went up to the surface she was always delighted by everything new and beautiful that she saw. But now that they were grown and allowed to go there whenever they liked, it no longer interested them. They longed for home, and after a month's time they would say that down below was the most beautiful place of all, and that's where they felt most comfortable.

Many an evening the five sisters would link arms and in a row rise up to the surface of the water. They had lovely voices, more beautiful than any human's. Whenever a storm was raging and they thought ships might be wrecked, they would swim before the ships and sing wondrously about how beautiful it was at the bottom of the sea, telling the sailors not to be afraid to go there. But the men couldn't understand their words. They thought it was the storm, and they never had a chance to see all the loveliness below because when the ship sank they would drown and come only as dead men to the sea king's castle.

In the evening, when the sisters would rise up, arm in arm, through the sea, their little sister would be left behind, all alone, to gaze after them. She felt as if she could cry, but a mermaid has no tears, and so she suffers even more.

"Oh, if only I were fifteen!" she said. "I'm sure that I will come to love the world up above and the human beings who live there!"

Finally she turned fifteen.

"Well, now we'll have you off our hands," said her grandmother, the old dowager queen. "Come here and let me dress you up like your sisters!" She put a wreath of white lilies on her hair, but every flower petal was half a pearl, and the old woman made eight big oysters clamp onto the tail of the princess to show her high birth.

"Ow, how that hurts!" said the little mermaid.

"Yes, but we do have to suffer a little for our finery," said the old woman.

Oh, how gladly she would have shaken off all that splendor and removed the heavy wreath. The red flowers in her garden suited her much better, but she didn't dare change things now. "Farewell!" she said and rose as easily and brightly as a bubble up through the water.

The sun had just gone down as she raised her head out of the sea, but all the clouds were still glittering like roses and gold, and in the midst of the pale pink sky gleamed the evening star, so lovely and clear. The air was mild and fresh, and the sea perfectly still. She saw a big ship with three masts. Only a single sail was raised, because not a gust of wind was blowing, and the sailors sat in all the rigging and on the yards. There was music and song, and as the evening grew darker, hundreds of colored lanterns were lit; they looked like the flags of every nation fluttering in the air. The little mermaid swam right up to the cabin window, and each time the waves lifted her in the air she could see through the mirrorlike panes at all the elegantly dressed people. Yet the most handsome of all was the young prince with the big dark eyes. He was probably no more than sixteen. It was his birthday, and that was the reason for all the splendor. The sailors danced on deck, and when the young prince stepped outside, more than a hundred rockets shot up into the sky. They lit up like bright daylight so the little mermaid grew quite frightened and dove down underwater, but she soon poked her head up again, and then all the stars in the sky seemed to be falling toward her. Never had she seen such fiery magic. Huge suns spun around, magnificent fire-fish swung in the blue sky, and everything was reflected in the clear, calm sea. On board the ship itself everything was so bright that you could see even the smallest line, not to mention all the people. Oh, how handsome the young prince was! He shook hands with all the men, laughing and smiling, as the music resounded through the lovely night.

It grew late, but the little mermaid couldn't tear her eyes away from the ship or the lovely prince. The colorful lanterns were put out, and rockets no longer rose up into the sky, nor were there any more cannon volleys, but deep down in the sea there was a droning and rumbling. And all the while she sat in the water, bobbing up and down so that she could look into the cabin. But the ship began picking up speed, one sail after the other catching the wind. Now the swells grew stronger, huge clouds gathered, lightning flashed in the distance. Oh, a terrible storm was coming! That's why the sailors were reefing the sails. The big ship pitched at a racing speed on the wild sea. The water rose up like great black mountains that threatened to pour over the mast, but the ship dove like a swan, down between the high waves, letting itself be lifted up again on the towering swells. The little mermaid thought the pace amusing, but the sailors did not. The ship creaked and crashed, the thick planks burst at the powerful thrusts the sea made at the ship. The mast snapped in half as if it were a reed, and the ship lurched onto its side as water rushed into the hold. Now the little mermaid saw that they were in danger. Even she had to watch out for debris and beams from the ship that were drifting around in the water. For an instant it was so pitch-black that she couldn't see a thing, but when lightning flashed it was once again so bright that she could make out everyone on board. Each person was managing as best he could. She looked in particular for the young prince, and when the ship broke apart she saw him sink down into the deep sea. She was at once filled with great joy, because now he would be coming down to her, but then she remembered that humans couldn't live in the water and that he couldn't come down to her father's castle, except as a dead man. No, he mustn't die. So she swam in among the timbers and planks floating in the sea, completely forgetting that they could have crushed her. She dove deeper underwater and then rose up high among the waves and at last reached the young prince, who couldn't swim much longer in the raging sea. His arms and legs had begun to tire, his beautiful eyes had closed; he would have died if the little mermaid hadn't come. She held his head above water and let the waves carry her with him, wherever they liked.

By morning the storm had passed. There was not a scrap of the ship in sight. The sun, red and glowing, rose up out of the water and seemed to bring life to the cheeks of the prince, but his eyes remained closed. The mermaid kissed his beautiful, high forehead and stroked back his wet hair. She thought he looked like the marble statue down in her little garden. She kissed him again and wished that he might live.

Now she saw before her dry land, with tall blue mountains. On the crest glinted white snow as if swans were resting there. Down near the shore stood lovely green forests, and in front of them a church or a cloister, she wasn't quite sure, but it was some kind of building. Lemon and orange trees grew in the garden, and before the gate stood tall palm trees. Here the sea formed a little bay that was perfectly still but very deep all the way up to the dunes where fine white sand had washed ashore. That's where she swam with the handsome prince and placed him on the sand, taking great care that his head lay high up in the warm sunshine.

Then the bells began ringing in the big white building, and scores of young girls came walking through the garden. The little mermaid swam farther out behind several high rocks that were sticking up out of the water. She put sea foam on her hair and breast so that no one could see her little face, and then she waited to see who would come for the poor prince.

It wasn't long before a young girl approached. She seemed to be quite frightened, though only for a moment. Then she summoned more people, and the mermaid saw that the prince began to revive and that he smiled at everyone standing around him. But he didn't smile at the mermaid, nor did he know that she had saved his life. She felt so sad, and when he was led inside the big building, she sorrowfully dove down into the water and made her way home to her father's castle.

She had always been quiet and pensive, but now she was even more so. Her sisters asked her what she had seen on her first time up above, but she told them nothing.

Many an evening and morning she would rise up to the spot where she had left the prince. She saw how the fruit in the garden grew ripe and was picked; she saw how the snow melted on the high mountains. But she did not see the prince, and so she always returned home sadder than before. There her only solace was to sit in her little garden and throw her arms around the beautiful marble statue that looked like the prince, but she neglected her flowers. As if in a wilderness they grew out over the pathways, weaving their long stalks and leaves into the branches of the trees so that it was quite dark.

Finally she could bear it no longer and told one of her sisters, and then all of the others instantly found out about it, but no one else, apart from a couple of other mermaids who didn't tell anyone except their closest girlfriends. One of them knew who the prince was. She had also seen the splendor aboard the ship and knew where he came from and where his kingdom lay.

"Come, little sister!" said the other princesses. With their arms around each other's shoulders they rose up out of the sea in a long row, right in front of the place where they knew the prince's castle stood.

The castle was built of gleaming, pale yellow stone, with great marble staircases, one of which reached all the way down to the sea. Magnificent gilded domes rose above the rooftop, and between the columns that surrounded the whole building stood marble images that looked alive. Through the clear panes of the tall windows they could look into the most splendid halls hung with costly silk curtains and tapestries, and all the walls were adorned with enormous paintings that were a pleasure to see. In the middle of the largest hall splashed a great fountain. The spray reached high up toward the glass dome in the roof through which the sun shone on the water and on the lovely plants growing in the huge basin.

Now she knew where he lived, and that's where she went, swimming through the water on many an evening and night. She swam much closer to land than any of the others had dared. She even went all the way up the narrow canal, beneath the magnificent marble balcony that cast a long shadow over the water. Here she would sit and gaze at the young prince, who thought he was quite alone in the clear moonlight.

Many an evening she watched him sail with music aboard his splendid ship, where the flags fluttered. She would peek out from the green reeds, and if the wind caught her long silvery white veil and anyone saw it, they thought it was a swan lifting its wings.

Many a night, when the fishermen lay anchored at sea by torchlight, she heard them say so many good things about the prince. It made her happy that she had saved his life when he was drifting on the waves half dead. And she remembered how firmly his head had rested on her breast and how fervently she had kissed him. He knew nothing of this, could not even dream about her.

She grew more and more fond of human beings; she wished more and more that she might rise up among them. Their world seemed to her much larger than her own. They could fly across the sea in ships, climb the highest mountains far above the clouds, and the lands they owned, with forests and fields, stretched much farther than she could see. There was so much she wanted to know, but her sisters couldn't answer all her questions. That's why she asked her old grandmother, who was very familiar with the world above, which she quite rightly called the lands above the sea.

"If humans don't drown," said the little mermaid, "can they live forever? Don't they die like we do down here in the sea?"

"Of course they do!" said the old woman. "They have to die too, and their lifetime is much shorter than ours. We can live three hundred years, but when we cease to exist, we become nothing more than foam on the water without even a grave down here among our loved ones. We have no immortal soul, there is no more life for us. We're like the green reed: Once it is cut, it will never be green again! Humans, on the other hand, have a soul that lives forever, lives on after the body has turned to dust. It rises up through the clear air, up to all the shining stars! Just as we rise up from the sea to look at the land of the humans, they rise up to the lovely unknown places that we will never see."

"Why weren't we given immortal souls?" asked the little mermaid sadly. "I would give all three hundred years of my life to be a human for just one day and then have a share in the heavenly world."

"You mustn't go around thinking about that," said the old woman. "We're much happier and better off than the humans up there."

"So I'm going to die and drift like foam on the sea, no longer hear the music of the waves, or see the lovely flowers and the crimson sun? Is there nothing I can do to win an eternal soul?"

"No," said the old woman. "Only if a human were to love you so much that you were dearer to him than his father or mother. If he clung to you with all his thoughts and love and had the priest put his right hand in yours, promising faithfulness now and for all eternity, then his soul would flow into your body, and you too would share in the happiness of humans. He would give you a soul and yet keep his own. But that will never happen! That which is so lovely here in the sea—your fish tail—they consider hideous up on earth. They don't know any better. Up there you have to have two clumsy pillars that they call legs in order to be beautiful."

Then the little mermaid sighed and looked sadly at her own fish tail.

"Let's be happy," said the old woman. "We should leap and bound for the three hundred years that are ours to live. Surely that's long enough, and later you can rest in your grave, all the more content. Tonight we're going to have a royal ball!"

And there was such splendor as has never been seen on earth. The walls and ceiling of the great ballroom were made of thick but clear glass. Hundreds of enormous seashells, rose-red and grass-green, were lined up on either side. A fire burning blue lit up the entire hall and shone through the walls so that the sea outside was illuminated. Countless fish were visible, big and small, swimming toward the glass wall. On some of them gleamed purplish red scales, on others they looked like silver and gold. Down the middle of the hall flowed a wide, rippling stream on which the mermen and mermaids were dancing to their own lovely songs. No humans on earth have such beautiful voices. The little mermaid sang more beautifully than anyone else, and they clapped their hands for her. For a moment she felt joy in her heart, because she knew that she had the most beautiful voice of anyone on earth or in the sea! But soon she started thinking once more about the world up above. She couldn't forget the handsome prince or her sorrow at not possessing, as he did, an immortal soul. That's why she slipped out of her father's castle, and while everything inside was song and merriment, she sat sadly in her little garden. Then she heard the sound of hunting horns echoing down through the water, and she thought, "Now he's probably sailing up there, the one I love more than my father or mother, the one my thoughts cling to and in whose hand I wish to place my life's happiness. I would risk everything to win him and an immortal soul! While my sisters are dancing inside my father's castle, I'll go to the sea witch, the one who has always terrified me; maybe she can offer help and advice."

Then the little mermaid left her garden and set off for the roaring maelstroms; beyond them lived the witch. She had never gone that way before, where no flowers grew, nor sea grass. Nothing but the bare, gray, sandy bottom stretched toward the maelstroms where the currents, like roaring mill wheels, swirled around and pulled everything they seized down into the depths. She would have to pass between these crushing whirlpools in order to reach the territory of the sea witch. For a long section there was no other path than over

hot bubbling mire; the witch called it her peat bog. Beyond it stood
her house in the midst of a peculiar forest. All the trees and
shrubs were polyps, half animal and half plant. They looked like
hundred-headed snakes growing out of the ground. All their
branches were long slimy arms, with fingers like slithery worms;
they rippled, joint by joint, from their roots to their very tips. They
wrapped tightly around anything in the sea that they could grab
and they never let go. The little mermaid was quite terrified as she
stood there at the edge. Her heart was pounding with fear. She
almost turned around, but then she thought about the prince and
a human soul, and that gave her courage. She tied up her long
fluttering hair so the polyps wouldn't be able to catch her by
grabbing hold of it. She pressed both hands to her breast and flew
off, the way a fish can fly through the water, in among the hideous
polyps that reached out their supple arms and fingers toward her.
She saw how each of them was holding something that it had
caught. Hundreds of tiny arms were wrapped around it, like strong
iron bands. Humans who had perished at sea and sunk into the
deep peered out, as white bones, from the arms of the polyps.
Rudders and sea chests were held in their grip, the skeletons of land
animals, and a little mermaid they had caught and strangled—for
her that was the most terrifying of all.

Then she came to a great slimy clearing in the forest where huge
fat water snakes romped, showing off their disgusting yellowish-
white bellies. In the middle of the clearing a house had been built
from the white bones of shipwrecked humans. There sat the sea
witch, letting a toad eat from her mouth, the way humans let little
canaries eat sugar. She called the hideous fat water snakes her little
chickens and let them swarm over her big spongy breasts.

"I know what you want!" said the sea witch. "How stupid of
you! But I'm going to grant you your wish, because it will bring
you misfortune, my lovely princess. You want to get rid of your
fish tail and instead have two stumps to walk on like a human being,
because then the young prince will fall in love with you, and you
can win him along with an immortal soul!" With that the witch
began laughing so loudly and horribly that the toad and the water
snakes fell to the ground, tumbling all around. "You've come just
in time," said the witch. "By tomorrow, when the sun comes up,

I wouldn't be able to help you until another year had passed. I'm going to make you a potion to take with you. Before the sun comes up, swim to land, sit down on the shore, and drink it. Then your tail will split in two and shrink to what the humans call charming legs, but it will be painful. It will feel like a sharp sword is passing through you. Everyone who sees you will say that you're the loveliest human child they've ever seen! You'll keep your graceful movements; no dancer will ever glide as you do, but every step you take will feel like you're treading on a sharp knife and make your blood flow. If you're willing to endure all that, then I'll help you."

"Yes," said the little mermaid in a quavering voice, thinking about the prince and about winning an immortal soul.

"But remember," said the witch, "once you've taken human form, you can never be a mermaid again. You can never come back into the water to your sisters or to your father's castle. And if you don't win the love of the prince so that he forgets his father and mother and clings to you with all his thoughts and lets the priest place your hand in his so that you become husband and wife, then you won't get an immortal soul! On the first morning after he marries another, your heart will burst, and you will become foam on the water."

"That's what I want," said the little mermaid, and she was as pale as death.

"But you also have to pay me!" said the witch. "And it's not a small thing that I demand. You have the loveliest voice of anyone here at the bottom of the sea. You're probably thinking of using it to charm him, but your voice you must give to me. I want the best thing you possess in return for my precious potion! My own blood I have to give you to make the drink as sharp as a double-edged sword."

"But if you take my voice," said the little mermaid, "what will I have left?"

"Your lovely figure," said the witch, "your graceful movements, and your expressive eyes; surely you can use them to captivate a human heart. Well, have you lost your courage? Stick out your little tongue. I'll cut it off as payment, and then I'll give you the powerful potion."

"Agreed," said the little mermaid, and the witch put on her kettle to brew the magic potion. "Cleanliness is a good thing," she said and scoured the kettle with the water snakes, which she tied into a knot. Then she made a cut on her breast and let her black blood ooze out. The steam formed the strangest shapes, fearsome and dreadful. The witch kept putting new things into the kettle, and when it was boiling properly, it sounded like a crocodile crying. Finally the potion was ready, and it looked like the clearest water.

"There you have it!" said the witch and cut off the little mermaid's tongue so she was now mute and could neither sing nor speak.

"If the polyps happen to grab you on your way back through my forest," said the witch, "toss a single drop of the potion at them, and their arms and fingers will burst into a thousand pieces!" But the little mermaid didn't have to do that. The polyps shrank from her in terror when they saw the shining potion that glowed in her hand, just as if it were a sparkling star. In this manner she quickly passed through the forest, the bog, and the roaring maelstroms.

She could see her father's castle. The torches had been extinguished in the grand ballroom, and no doubt everyone was asleep inside, but she didn't dare go to them, now that she was mute and about to leave them forever. Her heart felt as if it would break with sorrow. She slipped into the garden, took a flower from each of her sisters' flower beds, blew thousands of kisses toward the castle, and rose up through the dark blue sea.

The sun had not yet come up when she saw the prince's castle and mounted the magnificent marble staircase. The moon was shining wondrously bright. The little mermaid drank the fiery bitter potion, and it felt as if a double-edged sword passed through her delicate body. She fainted and lay there as if she were dead. When the sun was shining over the sea, she awoke and felt a searing pain, but right in front of her stood the handsome young prince. He fixed his coal-black eyes on her, making her lower her own, and she saw that her fish tail was gone. She had the most charming little white legs that any young girl could have, but she was quite naked—that's why she wrapped herself in her long, thick hair. The prince asked who she was and how she happened to come there, and she gave him a look that was so tender and yet so sad, with her dark blue eyes; not a word could she say. Then he took her by the hand and led her into the castle. Each step she took, as the witch had warned her, felt as if she were treading on pointed awls and sharp knives, but she gladly endured it. Hand in hand with the prince, she moved as lightly as a bubble, and he and everyone else marveled at her graceful, gliding walk.

She was given precious garments of silk and linen. In the castle she was the most beautiful of all, but she was mute; she could neither sing nor speak. Lovely slave girls, dressed in silk and gold, appeared to sing for the prince and his royal parents. One sang more beautifully than all the others, and the prince clapped his hands and smiled at her. Then the little mermaid grew sad; she knew that she used to sing much more beautifully. She thought, "Oh, if only he knew that in order to be with him I had to give up my voice for all eternity!"

Now the slaves were dancing a graceful swaying dance to the most glorious music. Then the little mermaid raised her beautiful white arms, stood up on her toes, and floated across the floor, dancing as no one had ever danced before. With every movement her loveliness became ever more apparent, and her eyes spoke deeper to the heart than all the songs of the slave girls.

Everyone was delighted, especially the prince, who called her his little foundling. She kept on dancing and dancing, even though every time her feet touched the ground it felt as if she were treading on sharp knives. The prince said that she would stay with him forever, and she was allowed to sleep outside his door on a velvet cushion.

He had men's clothing sewn for her so that she could go out riding with him. They rode through the fragrant forests where the green branches slapped at her shoulder and the little birds sang from behind the fresh leaves. With the prince she climbed up the steep mountains, and even though her delicate feet bled so that the others noticed, she merely laughed and followed him until they saw the clouds sailing below as if they were a flock of birds heading for foreign lands.

Back home at the prince's castle, when the others were asleep at night, she would go out to the wide marble stairs to cool her burning feet by standing in the cold seawater. Then she would think about everyone below in the deep.

One night her sisters came, arm in arm. They sang so sorrowfully as they swam through the water. She waved to them, and they recognized her and told her how sad she had made them all. Every night after that they visited her. One night she saw, far in the distance, her old grandmother who had not been to the surface for many years, and the sea king wearing his crown on his head. They stretched out their hands toward her but didn't dare come as close to land as her sisters.

Day by day the prince's affection for her grew. He loved her the way you might love a good, dear child, but it never occurred to him to make her his queen, and she had to become his wife or she would never have an immortal soul. On the morning after he was wed, she would become foam on the sea.

"Aren't you more fond of me than of all the others?" the little mermaid's eyes seemed to say whenever he took her in his arms and kissed her beautiful forehead.

"Yes, you are dearest of all to me," said the prince, "because you have the best heart of any of them, you are more devoted to me, and you look like a young girl I once saw but will probably never find again. I was on a ship that went down. The waves carried me to land near a holy temple where many young girls were in service. The youngest of them found me on the shore and saved my life. I saw her only twice. She was the only one I could love in this world. But you look like her; you have almost replaced her image in my soul. She belongs to the holy temple, and that's why my good fortune has sent you to me. We will never part!"

"Oh, he doesn't know that I saved his life!" thought the little mermaid. "I carried him across the sea to the forest where the temple stands. I sat behind the foam and watched to see if any humans would come. I saw the beautiful girl that he loves more than me!" And the mermaid sighed deeply; she could not cry. "The girl belongs to the holy temple, he said, and she'll never come out into the world. They will never meet again. But I'm here and see him every day. I will care for him, love him, offer him my life!"

Everyone said that now the prince was supposed to marry and take as his wife the lovely daughter of the neighboring king. That's why he was outfitting such a magnificent ship. People said the prince was going to visit the lands of the neighboring king, but it was actually to visit the neighboring king's daughter. He would take a large entourage with him. The little mermaid shook her head and laughed; she knew the prince's thoughts much better than anyone else. "I have to go!" he had told her. "I have to see the beautiful princess. My parents demand it, but they would never force me to bring her home as my bride. I cannot love her! She doesn't look like the beautiful girl in the temple, the one you resemble. If ever I should choose a bride, it would more likely be you, my mute foundling with the expressive eyes!" And he kissed her red lips, played with her long hair, and placed his head on her heart, making it dream of human happiness and an immortal soul.

"You're not afraid of the sea, my mute child, are you?" he said when they stood on board the magnificent ship that would carry him to the neighboring king's lands. And he told her about storms and becalmed seas, about strange fish in the deep and what his diver had seen there. She smiled at his tales because she knew better than anyone else about the bottom of the sea.

In the moonlit night, when everyone else was asleep except the helmsman who stood at the wheel, she sat near the railing of the ship and stared down into the clear water. She thought she could see her father's castle. At the very top stood her old grandmother with a silver crown on her head, staring up through the turbulent currents toward the ship's keel. Then her sisters rose up to the surface. They stared at her in sorrow and wrung their white hands. She waved to them, smiling and wanting to tell them that she was well and happy, but the cabin boy was approaching, and her sisters dove down, so he continued to think that the white he had seen was foam on the sea.

Next morning the ship sailed into the harbor of the neighboring king's magnificent city. All the church bells were ringing, and trumpets blew from the tall towers while soldiers stood with fluttering banners and flashing bayonets. Each day there was a celebration. Balls and banquets followed one after the other, but the princess was still not in attendance. They said she was being brought up far away in a holy temple where she was learning all the royal virtues. At last she arrived.

The little mermaid was eager to see her beauty, and she had to admit that she had never seen a more enchanting figure. Her skin was delicate and glowing, and behind her long dark lashes smiled a pair of deep blue loyal eyes.

"It's you!" said the prince. "You're the one who saved me when I lay like a corpse on the shore!" And he pulled his blushing bride into his arms. "Oh, I'm much too happy!" he said to the little mermaid. "The best thing of all, what I never dared hope for, has been granted to me. You'll rejoice at my happiness, since you are more fond of me that all the others." And the little mermaid kissed his hand, feeling as if her heart were already breaking. The morning after his wedding would bring her death and turn her into foam on the sea.

All the church bells rang, and the heralds rode through the streets proclaiming the betrothal. On all the altars burned fragrant oils in precious silver lamps. The priests swung vessels of incense, and the bride and groom joined hands and received the bishop's blessing. The little mermaid stood there in silk and gold, holding the bridal train, but her ears did not hear the festive music, her eyes did not see the holy ceremony. She was thinking about her death night, about all that she had lost in this world.

That very same night the bride and groom went on board the ship. Cannons roared, all the flags waved, and in the middle of the ship a costly tent of gold and purple had been raised, with the loveliest cushions. That's where the bridal couple would sleep in the cool, quiet night.

The sails billowed in the wind, and the ship glided easily and smoothly over the clear sea.

When it grew dark, colorful lamps were lit and the sailors danced merry dances on deck. The little mermaid couldn't help thinking about the first time she came to the surface and saw the same splendor and joy. She too began whirling along in the dance, darting like a swallow does when it's being pursued, and everyone cheered in admiration. Never had she danced so gloriously. It felt as if sharp knives were cutting into her delicate feet, but she didn't notice; the pain in her heart was much sharper. She knew that this was the last evening she would see the one for whom she had abandoned her family and her home, given up her lovely voice, and suffered endless daily torments, although he never knew. This was the last night that she would breathe the same air as he did, see the deep oceans and the starry blue sky. An eternal night without thought or dream awaited her, since she had no soul and could not win one. Everything was joy and merriment on the ship until long after midnight. She laughed and danced with the thought of death in her heart. The prince kissed his lovely bride, and she played with his black hair, and arm in arm they retired to the magnificent tent.

It grew quiet and still on the ship; only the helmsman stood at the wheel. The little mermaid rested her white arms on the railing and looked to the east for the red of dawn. She knew that the first ray of sunlight would kill her. Then she saw her sisters rise up from the sea. They were as pale as she was, and their beautiful long hair no longer fluttered in the breeze; it had been cut off.

"We gave it to the witch so she would help us and you wouldn't have to die tonight. She gave us a knife. Here it is! See how sharp it is? Before the sun comes up, you must stab the prince in the heart. When his warm blood drips on your feet, they'll grow together into a fish tail and you'll be a mermaid again and can come back into the water with us and live out your three hundred years until you turn into dead, salty sea foam. Hurry! Either he or you must die before the sun comes up! Our old grandmother is grieving so that her white hair has fallen out, just as ours fell to the witch's scissors. Kill the prince and come back! Hurry! Do you see that red stripe in the sky? In a few minutes the sun will come up and you must die!" And they uttered a strange, deep sigh and sank into the waves.

The little mermaid pulled aside the purple drapes of the tent and looked at the lovely bride sleeping with her head on the prince's breast. She bent down and kissed him on his beautiful forehead, looked up at the sky where the red of dawn was shining stronger and stronger, looked at the sharp knife, and then fixed her eyes once more on the prince, who in his dreams called his bride by name. She was the only one in his thoughts. The knife trembled in the mermaid's hand—but then she flung it far out into the waves. They shone red where it fell, and it looked as if drops of blood were trickling up from the water. One more time, with her eyes half glazed, she looked at the prince. Then she threw herself from the ship into the sea, and she felt her body dissolve into foam.

Now the sun rose out of the sea. Its rays fell so gentle and warm on the deadly cold sea foam, but the little mermaid did not feel death. She looked at the bright sun, and above her hovered hundreds of lovely, transparent creatures. Through them she could see the white sails of the ship and the red clouds of the sky. Their voices were melodious, but so ethereal that no human ear could hear them, just as no earthly eye could see them. Without wings they floated through the air, carried by their own lightness. The little mermaid saw that she had a body like theirs; it was rising higher and higher out of the foam.

"Who am I joining?" she said, and her voice rang like those of the other creatures, so ethereal that no earthly music could reproduce it.

"The daughters of the air!" the others replied. "A mermaid has no immortal soul and can never have one unless she wins the love of a human being! Her eternal life depends on an outside power. The daughters of the air have no eternal souls either, but through good deeds they can create one for themselves. We fly to the warm countries where the sultry, pestilent air is killing human beings; there we fan a cool breeze. We spread the scent of flowers through the air and bring relief and healing. After three hundred years of striving to do what good we can, we will be granted immortal souls and share in the eternal joy of humans. Poor little mermaid, you've tried with all your heart to do the same as we have. You've suffered and endured, raising yourself up to the world of the sylphs. Now, through good deeds, you too can create an immortal soul for yourself in three hundred years."

And the little mermaid raised her clear arms up toward God's sun, and for the first time she felt tears.

On the ship there was life and commotion once more. She saw the prince with his beautiful bride looking for her. Mournfully they stared out at the frothing foam, as if they knew that she had thrown herself into the waves. Invisible, she kissed the bride's forehead, smiled to the prince, and then rose up with the other children of the air into the crimson cloud that was sailing in the sky.

"In three hundred years we will float like this into God's kingdom."

"We might come there even sooner," one whispered. "Invisible, we float into human houses where there are children. For each day that we find a good child who makes his parents happy and deserves their love, God shortens our time of trial. The child doesn't know when we might fly through the room, and if we then can smile with joy at the child, one year is subtracted from the three hundred. But if we see a naughty and bad child, then we have to weep tears of sorrow, and every tear adds another day to our time of trial."

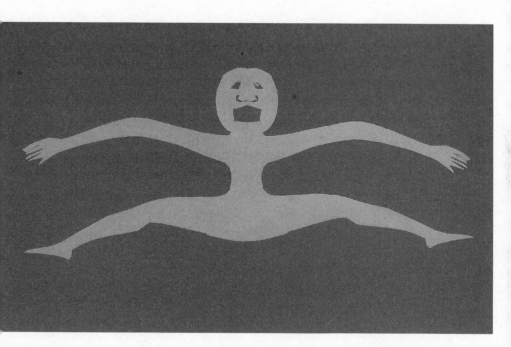

The Emperor's New Clothes

M any years ago there lived an Emperor who was so terribly fond of beautiful new clothes that he spent all his money on dressing elegantly. He didn't care about his soldiers, didn't care about the theater or driving in the woods; all he cared about was showing off his new clothes. He had a dress coat for every hour of the day, and just as people say of a king that he's in the council chambers, here they always said, "The Emperor is in the dressing room!"

In the big city where he lived everything was exceedingly pleasant, and every day scores of strangers appeared. One day two swindlers arrived. They claimed to be weavers and said they knew how to weave the loveliest cloth imaginable. Not only were the colors and patterns extraordinarily beautiful, but the garments they sewed from the cloth had the peculiar property of being invisible to any person who was unfit for his position or inexcusably stupid.

"What lovely clothes they must be," thought the Emperor. "By wearing them I could find out which men in my kingdom are unfit for the positions they hold; I could distinguish the clever from the stupid. Yes, I must have these clothes woven for me at once!"

And he gave the two swindlers a great deal of money so they would begin their work.

And they did set up two looms and pretend to work, but there was nothing at all on their looms. They promptly demanded the finest silk and the most magnificent gold, which they stuffed into their own bag. Then they sat at the empty looms and worked far into the night.

"I'd certainly like to know what progress they've made with the cloth," thought the Emperor, but he actually felt a bit uneasy about the idea that someone who was stupid or not suited to his position wouldn't be able to see it. Now, he certainly didn't think he needed to be afraid for his own sake, but he still wanted to send someone else first to see how things were going. Everyone in town knew what a wondrous power the cloth possessed, and everyone was eager to see how inferior or stupid his neighbor was.

"I'll send my honest old minister over to the weavers," thought the Emperor. "He's the best one to see how the cloth looks, because he is wise, and no one is more attentive to his position."

Then the venerable old minister went to the hall where the two swindlers sat working at the empty looms. "God save us!" thought the old minister and opened his eyes wide. "I can't see a thing!" But he didn't say that.

The two swindlers invited him to come closer and asked him if it wasn't a beautiful pattern and lovely colors. Then they pointed to the empty loom, and the poor old minister opened his eyes even wider, but he couldn't see a thing, because there was nothing to see.

"Good Lord!" he thought. "Could I be stupid? I've never thought so, and no one must find out. Am I unfit for my position? No, it won't do at all for me to say that I can't see the cloth."

"Well, you're not saying anything about it," said the one who was weaving.

"Oh, it's exquisite! Quite the most charming of all!" said the old minister, peering through his glasses. "That pattern and those colors! Yes, I shall tell the Emperor that it pleases me no end."

"That's very gratifying," said both weavers, and then they mentioned the colors by name and the unusual pattern. The old minister listened carefully so he would be able to repeat everything when he returned home to the Emperor, and he did.

Then the swindlers demanded more money, more silk and gold; they needed it for the weaving. They stuffed everything into their own pockets. Not a thread was put on the loom, though they continued, as before, to weave at the empty loom.

The Emperor then sent over another venerable official to see how the weaving was going and whether the cloth would soon be finished. The same thing happened to him; he looked and looked, but since there was nothing but the empty looms, he couldn't see a thing.

"Well, isn't it a beautiful piece of cloth?" said the two swindlers as they displayed and described the lovely pattern that wasn't there at all.

"I know I'm not stupid!" thought the man. "Am I supposed to be unfit for my position? That would certainly be ridiculous. But I can't let on."

Then he praised the cloth that he couldn't see and assured them of his joy at the beautiful colors and the lovely pattern. "Yes, it's quite the most charming of all!" he told the Emperor.

Everyone in town was talking about the magnificent cloth.

Then the Emperor wanted to see it for himself, while it was still on the loom. With an entire host of handpicked men, including both of the venerable officials who had been there before, he went over to visit the two cunning swindlers, who were now weaving with all their might, but without thread or yarn.

"Yes, isn't it *magnifique?*" said both of the venerable officials. "Just look, Your Majesty, what a pattern, what colors!" And then they pointed at the empty loom, because they thought that surely the others could see the cloth.

"What's this?" thought the Emperor. "I can't see a thing! This is terrible! Am I stupid? Am I unfit to be the Emperor? This is the most horrible thing that could happen to me!"

"Oh, it's very beautiful," the Emperor said. "I give it my highest approval." And he nodded contentedly and looked at the empty loom. He didn't want to say that he couldn't see a thing. The whole entourage he had brought with him looked and looked, but they could make no more of it than all the others. Yet, like the Emperor, they said, "Oh, it's very beautiful!" And they advised him to wear these splendid new clothes for the first time during the great procession. "It's *magnifique!*" "Exquisite!" "Excellent!" passed from mouth to mouth. Everyone was so genuinely pleased. The Emperor awarded each of the swindlers a Knight's Cross to put in his buttonhole and the title of Weaving Squire.

The swindlers stayed up all night long, with more than sixteen candles burning, before the morning of the procession. Everyone could see that they were busy finishing the Emperor's new clothes.

They pretended to take the cloth off the loom, they cut at the air with big shears, they sewed with needles but no thread, and at last they said, "See, now the clothes are done!"

The Emperor himself came, along with his most distinguished courtiers, and both the swindlers raised one arm in the air as if they were holding something up and said, "See, here are the trousers! Here is the dress coat! Here is the train!" and they kept on in this manner. "They're as light as spiderwebs. It's almost like having nothing on, but that's exactly their virtue."

"Yes," said all the courtiers, but they couldn't see a thing, because there was nothing to see.

"Would it please His Imperial Majesty most graciously to take off his clothes?" asked the swindlers. "Then we'll help him into the new ones in front of the big mirror."

The Emperor took off all his clothes, and the swindlers acted as if they were handing him each piece of new clothing that they had supposedly sewn, and the Emperor twisted and turned in front of the mirror.

"Lord, how well they suit you! How delightfully they fit!" they all said. "What a pattern! What colors! What priceless attire!"

"Outside they're waiting with the canopy that will be raised above His Majesty for the procession," said the Chief Master of Ceremonies.

"All right, I'm ready," said the Emperor. "They fit well, don't they?" And then he turned around one more time in front of the mirror, trying to look as if he were examining his finery.

The chamberlains who were going to carry the train fumbled their hands over the floor as if they were picking up the train. They started walking, holding on to air. They didn't dare let on that they couldn't see a thing.

Then the Emperor walked in the procession beneath the lovely canopy, and all the people on the street and in the windows said, "Good Lord, our Emperor's new clothes are beyond compare! What a lovely train he has on his coat! How heavenly it fits!" No one wanted to admit that he couldn't see a thing, because then he would have been unfit for his position or very stupid. None of the Emperor's clothes had ever aroused such admiration.

"But he doesn't have anything on!" said a little child.

"Good Lord, listen to the voice of the innocent," said the father. And one person whispered to the next what the child had said.

"But he doesn't have anything on!" the entire crowd cried at last. The Emperor cringed, because he thought they were right, but then he reasoned, "I have to make it through the procession." He held himself even prouder than before, and the chamberlains walked along carrying the train that was not there at all.

The Steadfast Tin Soldier

O nce upon a time there were twenty-five tin soldiers. They were brothers, because they were all born from an old tin spoon. Rifles they held at their shoulders, and their faces looked straight ahead. Red and blue, and oh so lovely were their uniforms. When the lid was removed from the box in which they lay, the very first words they heard in the world were, "Tin soldiers!" That's what a little boy cried, clapping his hands. They had been given to him because it was his birthday, and now he lined them up on the table. Each soldier looked exactly like the next, except for one who was slightly different. He had only one leg because he was the last to be cast, and there wasn't enough tin left. Yet he stood just as firmly on one leg as the others did on two, and he's the one who turned out to be remarkable.

On the table where they stood were many other toys, but the one that was most striking was a charming castle made of paper. Through the tiny windows you could see right into the halls. Outside stood small trees around a little mirror that was meant to look like a lake. Swans made of wax were swimming around on it, reflected in the mirror. The whole thing was so charming, and yet the most charming of all was a little maiden who stood in the open doorway to the castle. She had also been cut out of paper, but she was wearing a skirt of the sheerest tulle and a tiny narrow blue ribbon over her shoulder like a sash. In the middle sat a gleaming spangle as big as her face. The little maiden was stretching out both arms, because she was a dancer, and she was also lifting one leg so high in the air that the tin soldier couldn't see it at all, and he thought that she had only one leg, just like him.

"Now there's a wife for me!" he thought. "But she looks rather refined, and she lives in a castle. I have only a box, and it has to hold twenty-five of us. That's no place for her! Still, I have to see about making her acquaintance." And then he stretched out full-length behind a snuff box that stood on the table. From there he could get a good look at the elegant little lady, who continued to stand on one leg without losing her balance.

Later that evening all the other tin soldiers were put back in their box, and the people of the house went to bed. Then the toys began to play. They gave tea parties, fought battles, and danced. The tin soldiers rattled in their box because they wanted to play too, but they couldn't open the lid. The nutcracker turned somersaults, and the slate pencil scribbled all over the slate. There was such a commotion that the canary woke up and started chattering too, and in verse, of all things. The only two who didn't budge were the tin soldier and the little dancer. She held herself erect on her toes, with her arms held out. He was just as steadfast on one leg, and his eyes didn't leave her for a second.

Then the clock struck twelve, and *Bam!* the lid of the snuff box flew open, but there was no tobacco inside—no, there was a little black troll. What a wily trick that was.

"Tin soldier!" said the troll. "Keep your eyes to yourself!"

But the tin soldier pretended not to hear him.

"Well, just wait till morning," said the troll.

When morning came and the children got up, the tin soldier was moved over to the windowsill, and whether it was the troll or a gust of wind, all of a sudden the window flew open and the soldier plummeted headfirst from the fourth floor. What a terrifying speed, with his leg turned upward! He landed on his cap, with his bayonet stuck between the cobblestones.

The servant girl and the little boy went downstairs at once to look for him, but even though they nearly stepped on him, they couldn't see him. If the tin soldier had shouted "Here I am!" they probably would have found him, but he didn't think it was proper to yell when he was in uniform.

Then it started to rain. One drop came down faster than the other; it turned into a regular downpour. When it was over, two street urchins came along.

"Hey, look!" said one of them. "There's a tin soldier lying here. Let's send him out for a sail."

And so they made a boat out of newspaper, set the tin soldier in the middle of it, and he sailed off down the gutter. The two boys ran alongside, clapping their hands. God save us, what waves there were in that gutter, and what a current! Well, it's true that there had just been a downpour. The paper boat pitched up and down, and at times it would spin so fast that the tin soldier swayed. But he remained steadfast, his expression unflinching, standing erect with his rifle at his shoulder.

All of a sudden the boat washed in under a plank that lay over the gutter. It grew just as dark as inside his box.

"I wonder where I'll end up now," he thought. "Yes, well, this is all the troll's fault. Oh, if only the little maiden were sitting here in the boat, then I wouldn't care if it was twice as dark!"

At that moment a big water rat appeared. It lived under the gutter plank.

"Have you got a travel pass?" asked the rat. "Let's see your travel pass!"

But the tin soldier didn't say a word, holding his rifle even tighter. The boat raced along, with the rat right behind. Oh, how it gnashed its teeth, shouting to sticks and pieces of straw:

"Stop him! Stop him! He didn't pay the toll! He didn't show his travel pass!"

But the current grew stronger and stronger. The tin soldier could already glimpse daylight up ahead where the plank ended, but he also heard a roaring sound that would scare even a brave man. Just imagine: Where the plank ended, the gutter plunged right into a huge canal. For him it would be just as dangerous as for us to sail over an enormous waterfall.

He was already so close that he couldn't stop. The boat rushed forward; the poor tin soldier held himself as upright as he could. No one was going to say that he so much as blinked an eye. The boat spun around three or four times and filled with water up to the rim. It was going to sink. The tin soldier was standing in water up to his neck, and the boat sank deeper and deeper, the paper began dissolving faster and faster. Then the water was over the soldier's head. That's when he thought about the charming little dancer, whom he would never see again. And in his ears the soldier heard:

> "Flee, warrior, flee!
> Death is after you!"

Then the paper fell apart, and the tin soldier plunged right through. But at that very instant he was swallowed by a big fish.

Oh, how dark it was inside! It was even worse than under the gutter plank, and it was much more cramped. But the tin soldier was steadfast and stretched out full-length with his rifle at his shoulder.

The fish thrashed about, making the most terrifying movements. Finally it grew quite still, and what looked like a bolt of lightning flashed through it. The light shone so bright, and someone cried loudly, "Tin soldier!" The fish had been caught, brought to market, sold, and then ended up in a kitchen where the servant girl slit it open with a big knife. Putting two fingers around his waist, she plucked out the soldier and carried him into the parlor where everyone wanted to see the remarkable man who had traveled inside the belly of a fish. But the tin soldier was not the least bit proud of himself. They set him on the table and there . . . Oh, what strange things can happen in the world! The tin soldier was in the very same parlor where he had been before. He saw the very same children and the toys on the table and the lovely castle with the charming little dancer. She was still standing on one leg with the other lifted high in the air. She too was steadfast. The tin soldier was touched, he was just about to weep tears of tin, but that wouldn't be proper. He looked at her and she looked at him, but neither said a word.

At that moment one of the little boys picked up the soldier and tossed him right into the stove, giving no explanation at all. The troll in the box was most certainly to blame.

The tin soldier stood there, brightly lit, and felt a terrible heat, but whether it was from the actual fire or from love, he didn't know. The paint had worn right off him, but whether this had happened on his journey or from sorrow, no one could say. He looked at the little maiden, she looked at him, and he felt himself melting. But he still stood there, steadfast, with his rifle at his shoulder. Then a door opened, the wind seized hold of the dancer, and she flew like a sylph right into the stove to the tin soldier, burst into flame, and was gone. Then the tin soldier melted into a lump, and the next day, when the servant girl took out the ashes, she found him in the shape of a little tin heart. But all that was left of the dancer was the spangle, and that had been burned black as coal.

The Wild Swans

F ar away from here, where the swallows fly when we have winter, there lived a king who had eleven sons and one daughter, Elisa. The eleven brothers, who were princes, went to school wearing stars on their chest and swords at their side. They wrote on golden slates with diamond pencils and could recite just as well from memory as from a book. You could hear at once that they were princes. Their sister, Elisa, sat on a little stool made of mirrors, holding a picture book that had cost half the kingdom.

Oh, those children lived so well, but things wouldn't always be that way!

Their father, who was king of all the land, married an evil queen who was not the least bit kind to the poor children. Even on the very first day, they noticed it. Throughout the whole palace there were great festivities, and the children were playing tea party. But instead of giving them all the cakes and baked apples that could be found, the queen gave them only sand in a teacup and told them to make believe it was something good.

The following week the queen sent little Elisa out to the country to some farm folks, and it wasn't long before she had duped the king into thinking so badly of the poor princes that he no longer cared for them at all.

"Fly off into the world and fend for yourselves!" said the evil queen. "Fly like great birds, without a voice!" Yet she couldn't make it quite as bad as she intended; they turned into eleven lovely wild swans. Uttering a strange shriek they flew out the castle windows, over the park and forest.

It was still quite early in the morning when they came upon their sister, Elisa, who was sleeping in the farmer's house. Here they hovered above the roof, twisting their long necks and beating their wings, but no one saw or heard them. They had to take off again, climbing high up toward the clouds, far away into the wide world. There they flew into a big, dark forest that stretched all the way down to the shore.

Poor little Elisa stood in the farmer's house, playing with a green leaf; she had no other playthings. She stuck a hole in the leaf, peeking through it at the sun. Then she seemed to see the clear eyes of her brothers, and each time the warm rays of the sun shone on her cheek, she would think about all their kisses.

Each day passed like the one before. When the wind blew through the big rose hedges outside the house, it would whisper, "Who could be more beautiful than you?" But the roses shook their heads and said, "Elisa is." And if the old woman sat in the doorway on Sunday, reading her hymnal, the wind would turn the pages and say to the book, "Who could be more pious than you?" "Elisa is," said the hymnal: And that was the honest truth, what the roses and the hymnal had said.

When she was fifteen, Elisa returned home. And when the queen saw how beautiful Elisa was, she grew angry and hateful. She would gladly have turned her into a wild swan, like her brothers, but she didn't dare do so at once, since the king wanted to see his daughter.

Early in the morning the queen went into the bathhouse, which was built of marble and adorned with soft cushions and the loveliest tapestries. She brought three toads, kissed them, and said to the first one, "Sit on Elisa's head when she gets into the bath so that she grows as sluggish as you are!" To the second she said, "Sit on her forehead so she'll be as ugly as you are and her father won't recognize her!" To the third she whispered, "Rest on her heart, give her an evil soul that will make her suffer!" Then she put the toads into the clear water, which promptly turned a greenish color. She called for Elisa, undressed her, and made her step into the water. As she ducked under, one of the toads sat in her hair, the second on her forehead, and the third on her breast, but Elisa didn't seem to notice at all. As soon as she stood up, three red poppies appeared, floating in the water. If the animals hadn't been poisonous and kissed by the witch, they would have been transformed into red roses, but flowers they became all the same, by resting on her head and her heart. She was too innocent and pious for the sorcery to have any power over her.

When the evil queen saw this, she rubbed Elisa with walnut juice so she turned dark brown, smearing her beautiful face with a stinking salve and leaving her lovely hair all tangled. It was impossible to recognize the beautiful Elisa.

That's why, when her father saw her, he was quite horrified and said that she was not his daughter. No one else would have recognized her either, except for the watchdog and swallows, but they were humble creatures and had nothing to say in the matter.

Then poor Elisa wept and thought about her eleven brothers who had all vanished. Sadly she crept out of the castle and walked all day over field and marsh, and into the great forest. She had no idea where she was going, but she felt so sad and longed for her brothers. No doubt they too had been chased out into the world. She would go looking for them and find them.

Not long after she entered the forest, night fell. She had wandered far from any road or path. Then she lay down on the soft moss, said her evening prayer, and leaned her head against a stump. It was quiet, the air was mild, and all around in the grass and on the moss, like a green fire, shimmered more than a hundred glowworms. When she gently touched one of the branches with her hand, the glittering insects fell toward her like shooting stars.

All night long she dreamed about her brothers. They were playing again, as children, writing on the golden slates with diamond pencils and looking at the lovely picture book that had cost half the kingdom. But on the slate they didn't draw just circles and lines, as they had before, but rather the most daring deeds they had carried out, everything they had seen and experienced. And in the picture book everything was alive. The birds sang, and people stepped out of the book and spoke to Elisa and her brothers, but when she turned the page, they leaped back in so the pictures wouldn't get out of order.

When she awoke, the sun was already high overhead. She couldn't actually see it, because the tall trees had spread out their branches, thick and dense, but its rays played above her like a rippling golden veil. There was a fragrance of fresh nature, and the birds seemed about to land on her shoulders. She heard water splashing; there were many large springs, all feeding into a pond with the loveliest sandy bottom. It's true that thick shrubbery grew all around, but in one spot the deer had dug a big opening, and this was where Elisa went down to the water. It was so clear that if the wind hadn't rustled the branches and shrubs, making them move, she would have thought they were painted on the bottom, so sharply was each leaf reflected, both those that the sun shone through and those entirely in shadow.

As soon as she saw her own face, she grew quite frightened. It was so brown and horrid, but when she made her little hand wet and rubbed her eyes and forehead, her white skin shone through. Then she took off all her clothes and stepped into the fresh water. A more lovely royal child could not be found in this world.

When she had put her clothes back on and braided her long hair, she went over to the bubbling spring, drank from the hollow of her hand, and then wandered deeper into the forest without knowing where she was headed. She thought about her brothers, thought about the good Lord who surely would not abandon her. He had made the wild crabapples grow, to feed the hungry. He showed her such a tree where the branches were weighed down by fruit. Here she ate her midday meal, and then propped up its branches. Then she entered the darkest part of the forest. It was so quiet that she could hear every little withered leaf that crumpled underfoot. Not a bird was in sight, not a ray of sun could penetrate the huge, dense tree branches. The tall trunks stood so close together that when she looked straight ahead it was like a grating of timber surrounding her. Oh, here was a loneliness that she had never known before.

The night was so dark; not a single little glowworm gleamed from the moss. Sadly, she lay down to sleep. Then it seemed to her that the tree branches overhead moved aside and Our Lord looked down on her with gentle eyes, and little angels peeked out above His head and under His arms.

When she awoke in the morning, she didn't know whether she had dreamed it or whether it had actually happened.

She went on a few paces and came upon an old woman carrying a basket of berries. The old woman gave her some of them. Elisa asked whether she had seen eleven princes riding through the forest.

"No," said the old woman, "but yesterday I saw eleven swans with gold crowns on their heads swimming along the stream nearby."

And she led Elisa some distance away to a slope; down below wound a stream. The trees on its banks stretched out their long leafy branches toward each other, and wherever they couldn't reach because of their natural growth, there they had pulled their roots loose from the earth and leaned out over the water to intertwine their branches.

Elisa said farewell to the old woman and walked along the stream to the place where it flowed out onto the vast open seashore.

The whole lovely ocean lay before the young girl, but not a sailing ship was in sight, not a boat could be seen. How was she going to journey any farther? She looked at the countless pebbles along the shore; the water had worn all of them smooth. Glass, iron, stone, everything that had washed up had been shaped by the water, and yet it was even softer than her delicate hand. "It keeps on rolling, tirelessly, and then it smoothes out whatever is hard. I will be just as tireless! Thank you for your wisdom, you clear, rolling waves. My heart tells me that someday you will carry me to my dear brothers!"

Amid the washed-up seaweed lay eleven white swan feathers. She gathered them into a bouquet. Drops of water lay on them, but whether they were mist or tears it was impossible to tell. It was lonely at the seashore, but she didn't notice, because the sea offered endless variations; yes, more in a few hours than the inland lakes could display in a whole year. If a big black cloud passed by, it was as if the sea wanted to say, "I too can look dark." Then the wind would blow and the waves would turn their white side out. But when the clouds glowed crimson and the winds were asleep, the sea was like a rose petal. First it would turn green, then white, but no matter how calmly it rested, there was still a gentle movement at the shore. The water rose faintly, like the breast of a sleeping child.

When the sun was about to set, Elisa saw eleven wild swans with gold crowns on their heads come flying toward land. They glided one after the other like a long white ribbon. Then Elisa climbed up the slope and hid behind a shrub. The swans landed near her, flapping their great white wings.

As soon as the sun sank below the water, the swans shed their skins and there stood eleven handsome princes, Elisa's brothers. She uttered a loud cry, because even though they had changed greatly, she knew it was them, felt sure it had to be them. And she flung herself into their arms, calling them by name. They were so happy when they saw and recognized their little sister, who was now so grown-up and lovely. They laughed and they cried, and soon they understood how evil their stepmother had been to all of them.

"We brothers," said the eldest, "fly like wild swans as long as the sun is in the sky. When it goes down, we assume our human form. That's why at sundown we must always have a place to rest our feet, because if we're flying up there in the clouds, we would plunge, as humans, into the deep. This is not where we live. There's a land just as beautiful as this on the other side of the sea, but it's a long journey. We have to cross the vast ocean, and there is no island along the way where we might spend the night, only a lonely little rock jutting up midway across. There's barely room for us to stand on it, side by side. If the sea is rough, the water surges over us, and yet we thank Our Lord for it. That's where we can spend the night in our human form. Otherwise we would never be able to visit our dear homeland, because we must spend two of the longest days in the year in our flight. Only once a year are we allowed to visit the land of our ancestors. We dare stay here only eleven days, flying over the great forest. We can glimpse the castle where we were born and where our father lives, and see the tall tower of the church where Mother is buried. Here we feel the trees and shrubs are our kin, here the wild horses run across the plains the way we remember from our childhood, here the charcoal burner sings the old songs that we danced to as children. This is our homeland, to which we are drawn and where we found you, dear little sister! We dare stay here only two more days, then we must fly over the sea to a land that is lovely, though it is not our homeland. How can we take you with us? We have neither ship nor boat."

"How can I set you free?" said their sister.

And they talked almost all night long, dozing for only a few hours.

Elisa awoke to the sound of swans' wings rushing overhead. Her brothers were once again transformed, and they flew in great circles and were finally far away. But one of them, the youngest, stayed behind. The swan lay his head in her lap, and she stroked his white wings. All day long they stayed together. Toward evening the others returned, and when the sun went down, they stood there in their natural form.

"Tomorrow we must fly away from here, not daring to come back for another whole year, but we can't leave you like this! Do you have the courage to come along? My arm is strong enough to carry you through the forest—shouldn't all of us then have strong enough wings to carry you across the sea?"

"Yes, take me with you!" said Elisa.

They spent all night plaiting a net from the most supple willow bark and tough reeds, and it was big and strong. Elisa lay down on the net. When the sun came up and her brothers were changed into wild swans, they grabbed the net in their beaks and flew high up toward the clouds with their dear sister who was still asleep. Rays of sunlight fell across her face, and that's why one of the swans flew above her head so that his broad wings would give her shade.

They were far away from land when Elisa awoke. She thought she was still dreaming because it seemed so wondrous to be carried over the sea, high up in the air. At her side lay a branch with lovely ripe berries and a bunch of flavorful roots. Her youngest brother had gathered them and put them there for her. She smiled at him gratefully because she could tell that he was the one flying right above her head, shading her with his wings.

They were so high up that the first ship they saw below looked like a white gull floating in the water. A great cloud loomed behind them. It was a whole mountain, and on it Elisa saw the shadow of herself and the eleven swans, looking so huge as they flew. It was a painting more magnificent than any she had ever seen, but as the sun rose higher and the cloud fell farther behind them, the hovering shadow picture vanished.

All day they flew, like a racing arrow through the sky, yet they moved more slowly than usual now that they had their sister to carry. A bad storm was brewing, evening was approaching. Anxiously Elisa watched the sun sinking, and still there was no sign of the lonely rock in the sea. It seemed to her that the swans were flapping their wings harder. Oh, it was her fault that they couldn't make fast enough progress. When the sun went down, they would turn into humans, plunge to the sea, and drown. Then she prayed with all her heart to Our Lord, but still she could see no rock. The black cloud was coming closer; the strong gusts of wind heralded a storm. The clouds formed one vast menacing wave that was shooting forward, solid as lead. One lightning bolt flashed after another.

Now the sun had reached the rim of the sea. Elisa's heart was trembling. Suddenly the swans shot downward so swiftly that she thought they were falling, but then they were hovering again. The sun was halfway into the water when she first caught sight of the little rock below. It looked no bigger than a seal poking its head above water. The sun was sinking quickly; now it was no more than a star. Then her foot touched solid ground, and the sun was extinguished just like the last spark on a burning piece of paper. She saw her brothers, arm in arm, grouped around her, but there was no room on the rock for anything else. The sea pounded against the rock and washed over them like a downpour. The sky glowed in an ever-blazing fire, and thunder crashed, one peal after another. But the sister and her brothers held each other's hands and sang a hymn that gave them solace and courage.

At daybreak the air was clear and calm. As soon as the sun rose, the swans flew off with Elisa, away from the island. The sea was still rough. When they were high in the air it looked as if the white crests of foam on the greenish-black swells were millions of swans floating on the water.

When the sun rose higher, Elisa saw before them, half hovering in the air, a mountainous land with glittering masses of ice on the peaks, and in the midst stood a castle that was surely miles long, with one bold colonnade on top of another. Below swayed palm forests and magnificent flowers, as big as mill wheels. She asked whether this was the country she was going to, but the swans shook their heads. What she saw was Fata Morgana's lovely, ever-changing cloud castle; they didn't dare bring a human inside. Elisa stared at it. Then the mountains, forests, and castle collapsed, and there stood twenty proud churches, all exactly alike, with tall towers and arched windows. She thought she could hear the sound of an organ, but it was the sea she heard. She was quite close to the churches when they turned into an entire fleet sailing beneath her. She looked down, but it was only sea fog racing across the water. Yes, things changed constantly before her eyes, and then she saw the real country she was heading for. Lovely blue mountains rose up with cedar forests, cities, and castles. Long before the sun went down, she was sitting on a mountain in front of an enormous cave covered with fine, green vines that looked like embroidered tapestries.

"Now we'll see what you dream here tonight," said the youngest brother, showing her to her bedchamber.

"If only I would dream how I might set you free," she said, and this thought filled her whole mind. She prayed fervently to God for His help; yes, even in her sleep she continued to pray. Then it seemed to her that she was flying high up in the air, to Fata Morgana's cloud castle, and coming to greet her was the fairy, so beautiful and glittering. Yet she looked very much like the old woman who had given her berries in the forest and told her about the swans with the gold crowns.

"Your brothers can be freed," she said. "But do you have the courage and endurance? The sea may well be softer than your delicate hands, and yet it reshapes the hard stones, but it doesn't feel the pain that your fingers will feel. It has no heart, nor does it suffer the fear and agony that you must endure. Do you see these nettles that I'm holding in my hand? Many like this grow around the cave where you're sleeping. Only those and the ones that grow on graves in the churchyard can be used. Mark this well! These are the ones that you must pick even though they will burn blisters into your skin. Crush the nettles with your feet, and you will have flax. That's what you will use to spin and knit eleven shirts of mail with long sleeves. Throw these shirts over the eleven wild swans and the spell will be broken. But keep in mind that from the moment you begin this work and up until it is finished, even if it takes years, you must not speak. The first word you say will stab like a deadly dagger into the hearts of your brothers. Their lives depend on your tongue. Mark this well!"

And at that instant she touched Elisa's hand to the nettles. It felt like a blazing fire and woke her up. It was broad daylight, and close to where she was sleeping lay some nettles like the ones she had seen in her dream. Then she fell to her knees, thanked Our Lord, and went out of the cave to start her work.

With her delicate hands she reached down into the hideous nettles. They were like fire; they burned big blisters into her skin and arms, but this she would gladly endure if she could free her dear brothers. She crushed each nettle with her bare feet and spun the green flax.

When the sun went down, her brothers returned, and they were horrified to find Elisa so silent. They thought it was some new sorcery by their evil stepmother, but when they saw her hands they realized what she was doing for their sake, and the youngest brother wept. Wherever his tears fell, there she felt no pain, there the burning blisters vanished.

All night she spent at her task, for she would have no peace until she had freed her dear brothers. All the next day, while the swans were gone, she sat in solitude, but never had the time flown by so quickly. One shirt of mail was already finished; now she started on the next.

Then a hunting horn rang through the mountains. She grew quite frightened. The sound was coming closer, she heard the dogs barking. Terrified she ran inside the cave, bound the nettles she had gathered and spun into a bundle, and sat down on top of it.

At that moment a huge hound came leaping from the thickets, and right behind came another, and yet another. They were barking loudly, running back and forth. It was only a few minutes before all the hunters were standing in front of the cave, and the most handsome among them was the king of the land. He stepped over to Elisa. Never had he seen a more beautiful girl.

"How did you come here, you lovely child?" he said. Elisa shook her head, she didn't dare speak. It was a matter of her brothers' lives and salvation, and she hid her hands under her apron so the king wouldn't see what she had to endure.

"Come with me," he said. "You can't stay here. If you're as good as you are beautiful, then I will dress you in silk and velvet, set a golden crown on your head, and you shall live in my richest palace!" And then he lifted her onto his horse. She wept, wringing her hands, but the king said, "I wish only for your happiness. Someday you will thank me for this." And then he raced off through the mountains, holding her in front of him on his horse, and the hunters galloped behind.

When the sun went down, the magnificent royal city with its churches and domes lay before them. The king led her into his palace, where great fountains splashed in the vast marble halls, where the walls and ceiling were resplendent with paintings, but she had no eyes for any of that. She wept and grieved. Unresisting, she let the women dress her in royal garments, weave pearls into her hair, and pull fine gloves over her burned fingers.

When she stood there in all her splendor, she was so dazzlingly beautiful that the court bowed even lower to her. And the king chose her to be his bride, even though the archbishop shook his head and whispered that the beautiful forest girl was surely a witch. She had dazzled their eyes and deceived the king's heart.

But the king would not listen. He ordered music to be played, the costliest dishes to be served, the loveliest girls to dance around her, and she was led through the fragrant gardens into the magnificent halls. But not a smile crossed her lips or entered her eyes. Sorrow filled them as her eternal inheritance and possession. Then the king opened a little chamber close to the room where she was to sleep. It was adorned with the costliest green tapestries and looked exactly like the cave where she had been living. On the floor lay the bundle of flax that she had spun from the nettles, and from the ceiling hung the shirt of mail that she had finished knitting. All this one of the hunters had brought along, as a kind of curiosity.

"Here you can dream yourself back to your former home," said the king. "Here is what you were working on. Now, in the midst of all your splendor, it may amuse you to think back on those days."

When Elisa saw everything that was so close to her heart, a smile played across her lips, and the blood returned to her cheeks. She thought about her brothers' salvation and kissed the king's hand. He pressed her to his heart and ordered all the church bells to proclaim the wedding celebration. The lovely mute girl from the forest was to be queen of the land.

Then the archbishop whispered evil words in the king's ear, but they didn't reach his heart. The wedding took place, and the archbishop himself had to place the crown on her head. With evil intent he pressed the tight circlet so firmly on her forehead that it hurt. But an even heavier band gripped her heart: her sorrow for her brothers. She didn't notice the bodily pain. Her lips were mute; a single word would take her brothers' lives, but in her eyes dwelled a deep love for the kind, handsome king who had done everything to make her happy. With each day she came to love him more, with all her heart. Oh, if only she dared confide in him, tell him of her torment! But mute she had to remain, in silence she had to complete her task. That's why at night she would slip from his side and go into the little alcove that was adorned like the cave. She finished knitting one shirt of mail after the other, but when she started on the seventh, she had no more flax.

She knew that the nettles she needed grew in the churchyard, but she had to pick them herself. How was she going to get there?

"Oh, what is the pain in my fingers compared to the agony that my heart is suffering!" she thought. "I must attempt it! Our Lord will not abandon me!"

With fear in her heart, as if she were about to commit an evil deed, she crept out into the moonlit night, down to the garden. She walked down the long lanes out to the deserted streets and over to the churchyard. There she saw, sitting on one of the widest headstones, a group of Lamias, hideous witches. They were taking off their rags, as if they were going to bathe, and then they buried their long, gaunt fingers in the fresh graves, pulled out the bodies, and ate their flesh. Elisa had to pass close by, and they fixed their evil eyes on her, but she recited a prayer, gathered up the burning nettles, and carried them home to the palace.

Only one person had seen her: the archbishop. He was awake while the others slept. Now what he thought had been proven true: Things were not as they should be with the queen. She was a witch. That's why she had deceived the king and all the people.

In the confessional he told the king what he had seen and what he feared. As the harsh words fell from his tongue, the carved images of the saints shook their heads, as if to say, "That's not true. Elisa is innocent!" But the archbishop explained it differently, saying that they were bearing witness against her, that they were shaking their heads at her sin. Then two big tears rolled down the king's cheeks. He went home with doubt in his heart, and he pretended to sleep at night, but no peaceful sleep came to his eyes. He noticed that Elisa got up, and every night she did the same. Each time he quietly followed her and saw her disappear into the alcove.

Day by day his countenance grew darker. Elisa noticed but didn't know what it meant; yet it worried her. And what torments she suffered in her heart for her brothers! Over her royal purple and velvet robes ran her salty tears; they looked like glittering diamonds. Everyone who saw the rich splendor wished to be queen. Yet soon she would be finished with her work. Only one shirt of mail remained, but she had no more flax and not a single nettle. So once again, one last time, she would have to go to the churchyard and pick several handfuls. She thought with fear about the lonely walk and the terrifying Lamias, but her will was strong, as was her faith in Our Lord.

Elisa went out, but the king and the archbishop followed. They saw her disappear through the wrought-iron gate to the churchyard. When they approached, the Lamias were sitting on a headstone, just as Elisa had seen them. The king turned away, for among them he imagined the one whose head had rested on his breast that very evening.

"The people must judge her!" he said, and the people decided that she should be burned in the red flames.

From the splendid royal halls she was led to a dark, dank dungeon where the wind whistled through the grated window. Instead of velvet and silk they gave her the bundle of nettles that she had gathered; that's what she could lay her head on. The hard, burning shirts of mail that she had knit would be her comforter and coverlet, but they could have given her nothing more precious. Once again she set about her work and prayed to God. Outside, the street urchins sang spiteful songs about her. Not a soul comforted her with a loving word.

Then, toward evening, there was a rushing sound close to the grating: a swan's wing. It was the youngest of her brothers. He had found his sister. And she sobbed aloud with joy, even though she knew that the coming night might be her last. But now her work was almost finished and her brothers had come.

The archbishop arrived to spend the last hour with her. He had promised the king to do so, but she shook her head, begging him with her eyes and demeanor to leave. On this night she had to finish her work, otherwise it would all be for naught—everything, the pain, the tears, and the sleepless nights. The archbishop went away, speaking evil words against her, but poor Elisa knew that she was innocent and went on with her work.

Tiny mice ran across the floor, dragging the nettles over to her feet, trying to help a little. A thrush sat next to the window grating and sang all night long, as merrily as it could, so that she wouldn't lose her courage.

It was just barely daybreak, not until an hour later would the sun come up, when the eleven brothers stood at the palace gate, demanding to be taken before the king. But they were told this was impossible. It was still night, after all. The king was asleep, and no one dared wake him. They begged, they threatened; the guards came, yes, even the king stepped outside and asked what was the meaning of this. Then suddenly the sun came up, and there were no brothers to be seen, but over the palace flew eleven wild swans.

Out of the city gates streamed the entire populace; they wanted to see the witch burn. A wretched horse pulled the cart in which she sat. They had given her a smock to wear, made of rough sackcloth. Her lovely long hair hung loose around her beautiful face, her cheeks were deathly pale, her lips were moving faintly, but her fingers were twisting the green flax. Even on the way to her death she never stopped the work she had begun. The ten shirts of mail lay at her feet, the eleventh she was knitting. The mob jeered her.

"Look at the witch, see how she's muttering! She doesn't have a hymnal in her hand, no, she's sitting there with her odious sorcery. Take it away from her and tear it into a thousand pieces!"

And they all surged toward her, wanting to tear it to bits. Then eleven swans came flying; they alighted around her in the cart, beating their wings. The crowd drew back in horror.

"It's a sign from Heaven! She must be innocent!" many whispered, but they didn't dare say it aloud.

Then the executioner grabbed her by the hand. In haste she threw the eleven shirts over the swans. There stood eleven handsome princes, but the youngest had a swan's wing in place of one arm, because his shirt of mail was missing a sleeve; she hadn't managed to finish it.

"Now I dare to speak!" she said. "I am innocent!"

And when the people saw what had happened, they bowed to her as to a saint, but she sank lifeless into her brothers' arms, so deeply had the anguish, fear, and pain affected her.

"Yes, she is innocent!" said the eldest brother, and then he explained everything that had happened. As he spoke, the scent of millions of roses began to spread, for every piece of wood in the fire had grown roots and shot out branches. There stood a fragrant hedge, so tall and huge, with enormous red roses. At the very top sat one blossom, white and gleaming, that shone like a star. The king broke it off and placed it on Elisa's breast. Then she awoke with peace and happiness in her heart.

All the church bells began to ring of their own accord, birds appeared in great flocks, and back toward the palace headed a wedding procession like no king had ever seen before.

The Flying Trunk

Once upon a time there was a merchant who was so rich that he could pave the entire street as well as a small lane with silver coins, but that's not what he did. He knew of other ways to use his money, and if he spent a *skilling*, he would take in a *daler*. That's the kind of merchant he was. And then he died.

His son inherited all the money, and he led a merry life, going to masquerade balls every night, making paper kites out of *rigsdaler* bills, and skipping gold coins on the lake instead of stones. That way the money could quickly disappear, and it did. Finally he owned no more than four *skillings* and had no clothes but a pair of slippers and an old dressing gown. Then his friends no longer cared for him because they couldn't go out on the street together. But one of them who was kind sent him an old trunk and said, "Pack up and leave!" Well, that was all fine and good, but he didn't have anything to pack, so he put himself into the trunk.

It was a peculiar trunk. As soon as you pressed on the lock, the trunk could fly, and that's what it did. Zip, it flew, carrying him up through the chimney, high above the clouds, farther and farther away. The bottom creaked, and he was terrified that it would fall apart because then he would have taken quite an impressive tumble! God save us! Then he came to the land of the Turks. He hid the trunk in the forest under some withered leaves and walked back to town. He could easily do that because among the Turks everyone went around like he did in a dressing gown and slippers. Then he met a nursemaid with a little child. "Listen here, you Turkish nursemaid," he said. "What is that big castle right near the city with the windows way up high?"

"That's where the king's daughter lives," she said. "It was

prophesied that she would become terribly unhappy because of a sweetheart, and that's why no one is allowed to visit her unless accompanied by the king and queen."

"Thanks!" said the merchant's son, and then he went back to the forest, got into his trunk, flew up onto the rooftop, and crept in through the window to the princess.

She was lying on the sofa, asleep. She was so lovely that the merchant's son just had to kiss her. She woke up and was terribly frightened, but he told her that he was a Turkish god who had come to her through the air, and that pleased her.

Then they sat side by side, and he told stories about her eyes: They were the loveliest dark lakes, and her thoughts swam around in them like mermaids. And he told her about her forehead: It was a snowy mountain with the most magnificent halls and paintings. And he told her about the stork who brings the sweet little children.

Oh yes, they were lovely stories! Then he proposed to the princess, and she said yes at once.

"But you must come back on Saturday," she said. "Then the king and queen will be joining me for tea. They'll be so proud that I've won the Turkish god. See to it that you know a truly lovely tale, because my parents are especially fond of tales. My mother wants them to be moral and refined, and my father wants them merry, to make him laugh."

"Well, a tale is the only bridal gift I'll bring," he said, and then they parted. But the princess gave him a sword encrusted with gold coins, and that was something he could certainly use.

Then he flew off, bought himself a new dressing gown, and sat down in the forest to compose a tale. It had to be finished by Saturday, and that was not such an easy thing to do.

Finally he was done, and then it was Saturday.

The king, the queen, and all the members of the court were waiting with tea in the chambers of the princess. He was so charmingly received.

"Won't you tell us a story?" said the queen. "One that is profound and instructive."

"But one that will also make us laugh," said the king.

"Why, of course!" he said, and began to speak. Now you'll have to pay close attention:

Once upon a time there was a bundle of matches. They were exceptionally proud of the fact that they were of noble ancestry. Their family tree, meaning the great pine tree of which they were little sticks, had once been a huge old tree in the forest. The matches now lay on the shelf between a tinderbox and an old iron pot, and it was to them that they told the story of their youth. "Yes, when we sat on the green branch," they said, "then we were certainly sitting pretty! Every morning and evening we had diamond tea, which was the dew, and all day long we had sunshine when the sun shone, and all the little birds would tell us stories. We could certainly tell that we were rich because the leafy trees were only dressed in the summer, but our family could afford green clothes both summer and winter. But then came the woodcutters. It was the great revolution, and our family was split apart. The trunk won the post of mainmast on a magnificent ship that could sail around the world if it liked. The other branches found other positions, and now it's our job to light the candles for the lowly masses. That's how refined folks like us ended up here in the kitchen."

"Well, things have been quite different for me," said the iron pot standing next to the matches. "From the moment I came into the world I've been scoured and boiled over and over. I take care of practical matters and am actually considered the most important one in the house. My only joy, after the meal, is to stand nice and clean on the shelf and carry on sensible conversations with my friends. Except for the water bucket, which occasionally goes down to the courtyard, all of us always stay indoors. Our only news messenger is the market basket, but it talks so anxiously about the government and the people. Why, recently there was an old pot that was so terrified it fell down and was smashed to bits! And that basket is liberal-minded, let me tell you!"

"You talk too much," said the tinderbox, and steel struck flint so it sparked. "Aren't we going to have a merry evening?"

"Yes, let's talk about who's the most refined," said the matches.

"No, I don't like to talk about myself," said the stoneware pot. "Let's have an evening of entertainment. I'll start. I'm going to tell you about something that everyone has experienced. You don't have to think too hard about it, and that's quite pleasant: 'At the Baltic Sea by the Danish beech trees . . .' "

"What a lovely beginning!" said all the plates. "This is bound to be a story we'll like!"

"Yes, that's where I spent my youth with a quiet family. The furniture was polished, the floor washed, and clean curtains were put up every two weeks."

"What an interesting story you're telling," said the whisk broom. "You can hear at once that it's a woman talking. There's such an air of cleanliness through the whole story."

"Yes, you can sense that," said the water bucket, and then he gave a little leap of joy that made a slap against the floor.

And the pot continued her story, and the end was just as good as the beginning.

All the plates rattled with joy, and the whisk broom took some green parsley out of the sandbox and made a wreath for the pot because she knew this would annoy the others, and she thought: "If I crown her with a wreath today, then she'll crown me with a wreath tomorrow."

"Now I want to dance!" said the hearth tongs, and started dancing. Yes, God save us, how she could fling one leg in the air! The old upholstery on the chair in the corner split at the very sight. "Could I have a wreath too?" said the hearth tongs, and they gave her one.

"They're nothing but riffraff!" thought the matches.

Then the tea urn was supposed to sing, but she said she had a cold; she couldn't sing unless she was boiling. Yet that was sheer snobbishness. She didn't want to sing unless she was standing on the table in the parlor and the master and mistress of the house were there.

Over on the windowsill sat an old quill pen that the maid liked to use. There was nothing remarkable about him except that he had been dipped much too far into the inkwell, and that had turned his head. "If the tea urn doesn't want to sing," he said, "she doesn't have to. Outside there's a nightingale in a cage, and she can sing. Of course, she hasn't been trained, but tonight we won't even mention that!"

"I find that highly improper," said the teakettle, who was the kitchen singer and half sister to the tea urn. "Why should we listen to such a foreign bird? Is that patriotic? I'll let the market basket be the judge."

"I'm simply annoyed," said the market basket. "I'm more deeply annoyed than anyone could imagine. Is this any way to spend the evening? Wouldn't it be better to set the house in order? Then everyone could take his proper place, and I would govern the whole lot. That would certainly be a change!"

"Oh yes, let's raise a ruckus!" they all said. At that instant the door opened. It was the maid, so they all stood quite still. No one uttered a peep, but there wasn't a pot that didn't know what it was capable of and how refined it was. "Yes, if I had wanted to," they each thought, "this would certainly have been a merry evening!"

The maid picked up the matches and lit them. God save us, how they crackled and burst into flame!

"Now anyone can see," thought the matches, "that we are the most important! What a radiance we have! What light!"

And then they burned out.

"That was a lovely tale!" said the queen. "I felt as if I were right there in the kitchen with the matches. Yes, you shall marry our daughter."

"Yes, of course!" said the king. "You shall marry our daughter on Monday!" And they used the informal means of address because he was going to be part of the family.

The wedding day was now decided, and on the evening before, the whole city was lit up. Pastries and rolls were tossed to the crowds. The street urchins stood on their toes, shouting "Hurrah!" and whistling through their fingers. It was all so magnificent.

"Well, I suppose I ought to see about doing something too!" thought the merchant's son, and so he bought rockets, firecrackers, and all the fireworks imaginable, put them in his trunk, and then flew with them high into the air.

Whoosh, how they flared! How they crackled!

All the Turks jumped so high that their slippers flew up around their ears. They had never seen such a vision in the sky. Now they understood that it was the Turkish god himself who was to marry the princess.

As soon as the merchant's son came back down to the forest with his trunk, he thought, "I want to go to town to hear what kind of impression I made." And that was quite a reasonable wish.

And how the people did talk! Every single person he asked had his own version, but everyone agreed it had been lovely.

"I saw the Turkish god himself," said one person. "He had eyes as shiny as stars and a beard like foaming water!"

"He flew in a cloak of fire," said another. "The loveliest cherubs were peeking out of its folds!"

Yes, he heard lovely things, and the next day would be his wedding.

Then he went back to the forest to get into his trunk. But where was it? The trunk had burned up. A spark was left from the fireworks, the trunk had caught fire, and now it lay in ashes. He could no longer fly, no longer reach his bride.

She stood all day long on the rooftop and waited. She is still waiting, while he roams the world telling stories, though they're no longer as merry as the one he told about the matches.

The Nightingale

I n China, as you probably know, the Emperor is Chinese, and everyone around him is Chinese too. This story happened many years ago, but that's precisely why it's worth hearing, before it's forgotten. The Emperor's palace was the most magnificent in the world, made entirely of fine porcelain, so costly but so fragile, so delicate to the touch that you had to be extremely careful. In the garden you could see the most wondrous flowers. Tied to the most splendid of them were silver bells that jingled, and you couldn't walk past without noticing the flowers. Yes, everything was quite artful in the Emperor's garden, which stretched so far that even the gardener didn't know where it ended. If you kept on walking you would come to the loveliest forest with tall trees and deep lakes. The forest went right down to the sea, which was deep and blue. Great ships could sail right under the branches. And among the branches lived a nightingale who sang so blissfully that even the poor fisherman, who had many other things to tend to, would lie still and listen whenever he heard the nightingale as he pulled in his fishing nets at night. "Dear Lord, how beautiful she sounds!" he said.

But then he had to go back to his work and forget about the bird. Yet the next night when she sang again and the fisherman appeared, he would say the same thing, "Dear Lord, how beautiful she sounds!"

Travelers came from countries all over the world to admire the Emperor's city and the palace and the garden. But if they happened to hear the nightingale, they all said, "That's the best thing of all!"

The travelers would talk about everything when they went back home, and the learned men wrote many books about the city, the palace, and the garden, but they didn't forget the nightingale; she was esteemed above all else. Those who could write poetry wrote the loveliest poems, every single one about the nightingale in the forest by the deep sea.

These books circulated around the world, and one day some of them even reached the Emperor. He sat on his golden chair, reading and reading, as he kept nodding his head, because it pleased him to hear the magnificent descriptions of the city, the palace, and the garden. "Yet the nightingale is the best of all!" he read in the book.

"What's this?" said the Emperor. "The nightingale? I know nothing about it! Is there such a bird in my empire, let alone in my own garden? I've never heard of her. To think I had to learn about her from a book!"

And then he called for his Lord Chamberlain, who was so refined that if anyone lower in rank dared speak to him or ask him about something, his only reply was "P!" And that means nothing at all.

"Supposedly there is a truly extraordinary bird here called the nightingale," said the Emperor. "They say that she's the best thing in all my vast domain. Why hasn't anyone told me about her?"

"I've never heard her mentioned before," said the Lord Chamberlain. "She has never been presented at court."

"I want her to come here tonight and sing for me," said the Emperor. "The whole world knows what I have, but I do not."

"I've never heard her mentioned before," said the Lord Chamberlain. "I've search for her, I'll find her!"

But where was she to be found? The Lord Chamberlain ran up and down all the stairs, through the halls and corridors. Not a single person he met had ever heard mention of the nightingale. So the Lord Chamberlain ran back to the Emperor and said that she must be a fable concocted by those who write books. "Your Imperial Majesty should not believe what people write. It's all fabrication and what's called black magic."

"But the book I was reading was sent to me by the mighty Emperor of Japan," said the Emperor, "so it must be true. I want to hear the nightingale. She must be here tonight! I bestow on her my highest favor! And if she doesn't come, then all the members of the court will be punched in the stomach after they've eaten their supper."

"*Xing-pei!*" said the Lord Chamberlain, and once again he ran up and down all the stairs, through all the halls and corridors. And half the court ran along with him, because they didn't want to be punched in the stomach. Everyone was asking about the remarkable nightingale that was known to the whole world but to no one at court.

Finally they came upon a poor little girl in the kitchen, and she said, "Oh Lord, the nightingale! I know her well. Yes, how she can sing! Every evening I'm allowed to take home a few scraps from the table for my poor sick mother. She lives down near the shore, and when I walk back feeling tired, I take a rest in the forest, and then I hear the nightingale singing. It makes my eyes fill with tears. It's as if my mother were kissing me."

"Little kitchen maid," said the Lord Chamberlain, "I shall arrange a permanent post for you in the kitchen and permission to watch the Emperor eat if you can lead us to the nightingale. She has been summoned here tonight."

And so they all set off for the forest, to the place where the nightingale usually sang. Half the court went along. As they were walking, a cow began to moo.

"Oh!" said the royal squires. "Now we've found her. What remarkable power for such a small creature! We're quite certain we've heard her before."

"No, those are the cows mooing," said the little kitchen maid. "We're still quite far from the place."

Now the frogs began croaking in the bog.

"Lovely!" said the Chinese Court Chaplain. "Now I can hear her. It sounds just like little church bells."

"No, those are the frogs," said the little kitchen maid. "But I think we'll hear her soon."

Then the nightingale began to sing.

"There she is," said the little girl. "Listen! Listen! And there she sits!" And then she pointed at a little gray bird up in the branches.

"Is it possible?" said the Lord Chamberlain. "That's not at all how I imagined her. How plain she looks! She must have lost her color from seeing so many refined people all around."

"Little nightingale!" cried the little kitchen maid in a loud voice.

"Our Most Gracious Emperor would like so much for you to sing for him."

"With the greatest pleasure," said the nightingale and sang so it was sheer delight.

"It sounds just like glass bells," said the Lord Chamberlain. "And look at her little throat—she's singing with all her might. It's strange that we've never heard this bird before. She will be a huge success at court."

"Shall I sing some more for the Emperor?" asked the nightingale, who thought the Emperor was among them.

"My splendid little nightingale," said the Lord Chamberlain, "I have the great pleasure of summoning you to a royal celebration this evening, where you will enchant His Exalted Imperial Grace with your charming song."

"My song sounds best out in nature," said the nightingale, but she willingly went along with them when she heard that this was the Emperor's wish.

At the palace everything had been properly cleaned and polished. The walls and floors, which were made of porcelain, gleamed with thousands of golden lamps. The loveliest flowers, the ones with bells attached, had been placed in the corridors; there was a draft and a great commotion, making all the bells ring. You couldn't hear yourself think.

In the middle of the great hall, where the Emperor was seated, a golden perch had been placed, and that was where the nightingale was to sit. The entire court was present, and the little kitchen maid had been given permission to stand behind the door, since she now held the title of Real Kitchen Maid. Everyone was dressed in his very finest, and everyone was looking at the little gray bird, to whom the Emperor nodded.

And the nightingale sang so wondrously that tears filled the Emperor's eyes. Tears rolled down his cheeks, and then the nightingale sang even more beautifully; the song went straight to the heart. The Emperor was so happy that he said the nightingale must wear his golden slipper around her neck. But the nightingale thanked him and said that she had already received reward enough.

"I've seen tears in the Emperor's eyes. For me that is the richest treasure. An emperor's tears have a wondrous power. God knows, that is reward enough." And then she sang again in her sweet, blessed voice.

"This is the most lovable coquetry we've ever known," said the women all around, and then they put water in their mouths in order to cluck whenever anyone spoke to them. They thought they too could be nightingales. Even the lackeys and chambermaids announced that they were satisfied, and that is saying a great deal because they're the most difficult of all to please. Yes, the nightingale certainly was a success!

Now she would stay at court, and have her own cage, as well as the freedom to promenade twice a day and once at night. Twelve servants were sent along, each of them holding tight to a silk ribbon attached to her leg. There wasn't the least bit of pleasure in those excursions.

The whole city was talking about the extraordinary bird. If two people met, one of them would say to the other "Night!" and the other would say "Gale!" and then they would sigh, fully understanding each other. Why, eleven grocers' children were named after her, but not one of them could even carry a tune.

One day a big package arrived for the Emperor. On the outside it said: "Nightingale."

"Here we have a new book about our famous bird," said the Emperor. But it wasn't a book. A little work of art lay inside the box, a mechanical nightingale that was supposed to look like the live one, although it was completely encrusted with diamonds, rubies, and sapphires. As soon as they wound up the mechanical bird it sang one of the tunes that the real bird sang, and its tail moved up and down, glittering with silver and gold. Around its neck hung a little ribbon, and on it were the words: "The Emperor of Japan's nightingale is paltry compared to the Emperor of China's."

"It's lovely!" they all said, and the person who had brought the mechanical bird was at once given the title of Supreme Imperial Nightingale Bringer.

"Let's have them sing together. What a duet that will be!"

And then they had to sing together, but it was not a success, because the real nightingale sang in her own way, while the mechanical bird ran on cylinders. "There's nothing wrong with that," said the Music Master. "It keeps perfect time and is obviously a follower of my own methods." Then the mechanical bird had to sing alone. It brought just as much joy as the real bird, and on top of that it was much more charming in appearance. It glittered like bracelets and brooches.

Thirty-three times it sang the very same tune, and yet it never grew tired. Everyone could have listened to it all over again, but the Emperor felt that the live nightingale should also sing a little. But where was she? No one had noticed that she had flown out the open window, off to her green forests.

"Well, what sort of behavior is that?" said the Emperor. And all the members of court began scolding, saying that the nightingale was a most ungrateful creature. "Yet we have the best bird of all," they said, and then the mechanical bird had to sing some more, and that was the thirty-fourth time they heard the same tune. But they didn't yet know it by heart, because it was so complicated, and the Music Master lavished great praise on the bird. Yes, he assured them that it was better than the real nightingale, not only in terms of its attire and the scores of lovely diamonds, but also internally.

"For you see, ladies and gentlemen, and above all Your Imperial Highness! You can never count on what will come out of the real nightingale, but with the mechanical bird everything is certain. This is how it will sound, and no other way. You can explain it, you can open it up and demonstrate the human reasoning, how the cylinders are arranged, how they operate, and how one turns the other."

"Those are my thoughts exactly," they all said. And the Music Master was granted permission, on the following Sunday, to display the bird to the people. They too should hear it sing, said the Emperor. And they heard it and were as pleased as if they had drunk themselves giddy on tea; that was so typically Chinese. And everyone said "Oh!" and held up in the air the finger that we call "pot-licker" and then they nodded. But the poor fishermen who had heard the real nightingale said, "It sounds nice enough, and it does look quite like it, but something is missing, we don't know what."

The real nightingale was banished from the realm.

The mechanical bird had its place on a silk pillow close to the

Emperor's bed. All the gifts it had been given, gold and precious stones, were spread around it, and in title it had risen to Supreme Imperial Nightstand Singer. In rank it was number one on the left, because the Emperor considered the side of the heart to be the most noble, and even in an Emperor the heart is on the left. The Music Master wrote twenty-five volumes about the mechanical bird, books that were so learned and so lengthy, and written in the most difficult of Chinese words, that everyone said they had read and understood them, because otherwise they would have seemed stupid and then they would have been punched in the stomach.

A whole year passed in this fashion. The Emperor, the court, and all the other Chinese people knew by heart every little cluck of the mechanical bird's song, but that was precisely why they liked it above all else. They could sing it themselves, and they did. The street urchins sang "Xi-xi-xi! Cluck-cluck-cluck!" And the Emperor sang it too. Oh yes, it was certainly lovely!

But one evening when the mechanical bird was singing its best and the Emperor was lying in bed and listening, it went "Clunk!" inside. Something burst. "Buzzzzzz!" all the gears spun around, and then the music stopped.

The Emperor sprang out of bed at once and called for his royal physician, but what good could he do? Then they summoned the watchmaker. After much discussion and a great deal of study, he managed to get the bird working fairly well, but he said that it would have to be played sparingly because the cylinder pegs were worn out. It would be impossible to replace them with new ones so that the music would play properly. That was a terrible shame! Only once a year did they dare let the mechanical bird sing, and even that was almost too often. But then the Music Master gave a little speech using big words and said that it was just as good as new, and so it was just as good as new.

Five years passed, and the whole land suffered a great sadness, because everyone was truly very fond of their Emperor. Now they said he was ill and about to die. A new emperor had already been chosen, and the people stood outside on the street and asked the Lord Chamberlain how things were going with their Emperor.

"P!" he said and shook his head.

Cold and pale, the Emperor lay in his big, magnificent bed. The entire court thought he was dead, and all of them had run off to greet the new Emperor. The valets had run outside to talk about it, and the palace maids were holding a big coffee party. All around in the halls and corridors cloth had been laid down so that no one's footsteps could be heard. That's why it was so quiet, so quiet. But the Emperor was not yet dead. Rigid and pale, he lay in the magnificent bed with the long velvet curtains and the heavy gold tassels. High above, a window stood open, and the moon was shining on the Emperor and the mechanical bird.

The poor Emperor could hardly breathe; it felt as if something were sitting on his chest. He opened his eyes and saw that it was Death sitting on his chest. He had put on the gold crown and was holding in one hand the Emperor's gold sword, and in the other his magnificent banner. All around in the folds of the great velvet bed curtains peculiar heads were sticking out, some of them quite horrid, others so blessedly gentle. They were all of the Emperor's good and bad deeds, looking at him, now that Death was sitting on his heart.

"Do you remember this?" one after the other whispered. "Do you remember this?" And then they told him so many things that the sweat poured from his brow.

"I never knew that!" said the Emperor. "Music, music, the great Chinese drum!" he shouted. "So I won't have to listen to everything they're saying."

But they kept on, and Death nodded, as the Chinese do, at everything that was said.

"Music, music!" screamed the Emperor. "You blessed little golden bird! Sing now, sing! I've given you gold and precious things. I myself have hung my golden slipper around your neck. So sing now, sing!"

But the bird stood silent. There was no one to wind it up, and otherwise it couldn't sing. But Death kept on looking at the Emperor with his big, empty eye sockets, and it was so quiet, so horribly quiet.

At that moment, close to the window, the loveliest song was heard. It was the live little nightingale, who was sitting on a branch outside. She had heard about the Emperor's distress, and that's why she had come, to offer solace and hope. And as she sang, the figures grew more and more pale, the blood began to flow faster and faster through the Emperor's weak limbs, and Death himself listened and said, "Keep singing, little nightingale! Keep singing!"

"Yes, if you give me the magnificent gold sword! Yes, if you give me the opulent banner! If you give me the Emperor's crown!"

And Death returned each treasure for a song, and the nightingale still kept singing. She sang of the silent churchyard where the white roses grow, where the fragrant elder tree stands, and where the fresh grass is watered by the tears of the bereaved. Then Death had such a longing for his own garden that he floated out like a cold white fog, out the window.

"Thank you, thank you!" said the Emperor. "You heavenly little bird, of course I recognize you! You're the one I chased from my realm. And yet you have sung the evil visions away from my bed and driven Death from my heart. How shall I reward you?"

"You have already rewarded me," said the nightingale. "I won tears from your eyes the first time I sang. I will never forget that about you. They are the jewels that make a singer's heart glad. But sleep now and grow strong and healthy. I will sing for you."

And she sang. The Emperor fell into a sweet slumber, so gentle and refreshing was his sleep.

The sun was shining through the windows when he awoke, strong and healthy. None of his servants had yet returned, because they all thought he was dead. But the nightingale was still sitting there, singing.

"You must stay with me forever," said the Emperor. "You shall only sing when you want to, and I will smash the mechanical bird into a thousand pieces."

"Don't do that," said the nightingale. "It has done the best it could. Keep it as you always have. I can't live in the palace, but let me come whenever I wish. Then in the evening I will sit on the branch by your window and sing for you, to make you both joyous and pensive. I will sing about those who are happy and those who suffer. I will sing about the evil and the good that is kept hidden from you. The little songbird flies far and wide, to the poor fisherman, to the farmer's rooftop, to everyone who is far from you and your court. I love your heart more than your crown, and yet the crown has a scent of something sacred about it. I will come, I will sing for you. But one thing you must promise me."

"Anything!" said the Emperor, standing there in his imperial robes, which he had donned himself, and holding the sword that was heavy with gold pressed to his heart.

"One thing I ask of you. Tell no one that you have a little bird who tells you everything, and things will go even better."

And then the nightingale flew off.

The servants came in to tend to their dead Emperor. Oh yes, there they stood. And the Emperor said, "Good morning!"

The Sweethearts

A top and a ball lay in a drawer among the other toys, and then the top said to the ball, "Why don't we be sweethearts, since we're lying here in the drawer together?" But the ball, which was made of morocco leather and had as high an opinion of herself as an elegant lady, refused even to reply to such a suggestion.

The next day the little boy who owned the toys came in. He painted the top red and yellow and pounded a brass tack into the middle of it. The top looked quite magnificent when it spun around.

"Look at me!" the top said to the ball. "What do you say now? Shouldn't we be sweethearts? We suit each other so well. You leap and I dance. No one could be happier than the two of us."

"Oh, is that what you think?" said the ball. "You don't seem to realize that my father and mother were morocco-leather slippers or that I have a cork in my middle!"

"Yes, but I'm made of mahogany," said the top. "And the judge himself made me. He has his own lathe, and he did it with the greatest of pleasure."

"Am I really supposed to believe that?" said the ball.

"May I never be spun again if I'm lying!" replied the top.

"You present yourself well," said the ball. "But even so, I can't. I'm almost as good as engaged to a swallow. Every time I fly up in the air, he sticks his head out of the nest and says, 'Will you?' And now I've inwardly said yes, and that's almost as good as an engagement. But I promise that I'll never forget you."

"Well, that's a big help!" said the top, and then they said no more to each other.

The next day the ball was taken out. The top watched as she

flew high up in the air, just like a bird, until she was out of sight. Each time she came back down, but she always made a big leap when she touched ground. And that was either from longing or because she had a cork in her middle. The ninth time the ball disappeared and didn't come back. The boy looked and looked, but the ball was gone.

"I know where she probably is," sighed the top. "She's in the swallow's nest and is married to the swallow."

The more the top thought about it, the more entranced he became with the ball, precisely because he couldn't have her. That's why his love kept growing. The fact that she had taken another was the strange thing about it. And the top danced and spun around, but he was always thinking about the ball, who in his thoughts grew more and more beautiful. Many years passed in this fashion. And by then it had become an old love.

And the top was no longer young. But then one day he was gilded all over; he had never looked so splendid. He was now a golden top, and he leaped until he hummed. Oh yes, he was quite something! But with one leap he went too high and . . . he was gone!

They looked and looked, even down in the cellar, but the top was nowhere to be found.

Where was he?

He had jumped into the trash bin, where all sorts of things lay: cabbage stalks, sweepings, and rubble that had fallen from the eaves.

"Well, this is certainly a fine place to be! The gilding will soon come right off me! And what sort of riffraff have I landed among?" Then he cast a sidelong glance at a long cabbage stalk that had been picked too clean and at a strange round object that looked like an old apple. But it wasn't an apple. It was an old ball that had lain for many years up in the eaves with water seeping through it.

"Thank God that someone my equal has finally arrived, someone I can talk to!" said the ball, looking at the gilded top. "I'm actually made of morocco leather, stitched together by maiden hands, and I have a cork in my middle, but no one would know that by looking at me. I was just about to celebrate my wedding to a swallow, but then I landed in the eaves, and that's where I've been for five years, seeping water. That's a long time, let me tell you, for a young lady!"

But the top didn't say a word. He was thinking about his old sweetheart. And the more he listened, the more he felt sure that this ball was his sweetheart.

Then the maid came to empty the trash. "Hey, here's the golden top!" she said.

And the top was brought back to the parlor with great ceremony, but nothing was heard of the ball. And the top never said another word about his old love, which fades when your sweetheart has lain in the eaves for five years, seeping water. Why, you wouldn't even recognize her if you met her in the trash bin.

The Ugly Duckling

I t was so lovely out in the country. It was summer. The rye was yellow, the oats green, the hay had been gathered in stacks down in the green meadows. That's where the stork was walking around on his long red legs, speaking Egyptian, because that was the language he had learned from his mother. Surrounding the fields and meadows were great forests, and in the middle of the forests were deep lakes. Oh yes, it was truly lovely out in the country! In the midst of the sunshine stood an old estate with a deep moat all around. From the walls and down to the water grew huge dock leaves that were so tall that little children could stand upright under the largest of them. It was just as wild in there as in the thickest forest, and this was where a duck was sitting on her nest. She had to sit there to hatch her little ducklings, but now she was getting tired of it all because it was taking such a long time, and she rarely had visitors. The other ducks were more fond of swimming around in the moat than running over to sit under a dock leaf to chat with her.

Finally one egg cracked open after the other. "Peep! Peep!" they said. All the egg yolks had come alive and were sticking out their heads.

"Quack! Quack!" she said, and they all rushed out as fast as they could and looked all around under the green leaves. Their mother let them look as much as they liked, because green is good for the eyes.

"How big the world is!" said all the youngsters, because now they had quite a bit more room than when they were lying inside the eggs.

"You think this is the whole world?" said their mother. "It

stretches far away to the other side of the garden, all the way to the pastor's field, although I've never been that far. But you're all here now, aren't you?" And then she got up. "No, I don't have all of you. The biggest egg is still lying here. How long is it going to take? I'm getting very tired of this!" And then she sat down again.

"So, how's it going?" said an old duck who came to visit.

"One egg is taking such a long time," said the duck on the nest. "It won't crack open. But take a look at the others. They're the loveliest ducklings I've ever seen! They all look like their father, that rogue who never comes to see me."

"Let me look at the egg that won't crack open," said the old duck. "I'll bet it's a turkey egg! I was once fooled like that myself, and I had my share of troubles with those youngsters, because they're afraid of the water, let me tell you. I couldn't get them to go in. I quacked and snapped, but it did no good. Let me see that egg. It's a turkey egg, all right! Just leave it here and go teach the other children to swim."

"I think I'll sit on it for a while longer," said the duck. "I've been sitting here this long, I might as well sit here the rest of the summer."

"Be my guest," said the old duck, and then she left.

Finally the big egg cracked open. "Peep! Peep!" said the youngster and tumbled out. He was so big and hideous. The duck looked at him. "That's certainly an awfully big duckling," she said. "None of the others look like that. He couldn't be a turkey chick, could he? Well, we shall soon see! Into the water he goes, even if I have to kick him in myself."

The next day the weather was gloriously beautiful. The sun shone on all the green dock plants. The mother duck and her whole family went down to the moat. Splash! She jumped into the water. "Quack! Quack!" she said, and one duckling after the other plopped in. The water washed over their heads, but they popped up at once and floated around so beautifully. Their legs moved on their own, and all of them were in the water; even the hideous gray youngster was swimming along.

"No, he's not a turkey," she said. "Look how beautifully he uses his legs, how erect he holds himself! That's my child! Actually he's quite handsome if you take a good look. Quack! Quack! Come along with me, and I'll take you out into the world and introduce you to the duck yard. But stay close to me so that no one steps on you, and watch out for the cats."

And then they went into the duck yard. There was a terrible ruckus going on because two families were fighting over an eel head, and then the cat ended up getting it.

"See, that's how things go in the world," said the mother duck, licking her bill, because she too would have liked to have that eel head. "Use your legs now," she said. "See if you can't hurry it up, and dip your necks to the old duck over there. She's the most refined of anyone here. She has Spanish blood, that's why she's so fat. And see there: She has a red rag around her leg. That's a remarkably lovely thing and the highest honor any duck can be given. She's so important that they won't get rid of her, and both animals and humans must respect her. Hurry up! Don't put your legs together. A well-mannered duckling keeps his legs far apart, just like Father and Mother. Come on! Now dip your neck and say, 'Quack!'"

And that's what they did. But the other ducks standing around looked at them and said quite loudly, "Look at this! Now we've got to deal with that bunch too. As if there weren't enough of us already. And ugh, just take a look at that duckling! We're not going to put up with him!" And one of the ducks flew over and promptly bit him on the back of the neck.

"Leave him alone!" said the mother. "He's not hurting anyone!"

"Yes, but he's too big and too odd looking," said the duck who had bitten him. "So he's going to be pushed around."

"What handsome children that mother has!" said the old duck with the rag around her leg. "All of them so handsome except for one; that one certainly didn't turn out too well. I wish she could hatch that one over again."

"That's not possible, Your Grace," said the mother duck. "He may not be handsome, but he has a genuinely good nature, and he swims as beautifully as any of the others; yes, I'd venture to say even a little better. I think he'll be handsome when he grows up, or with time he might get a little smaller. He was too long in the egg, and that's why he isn't the right shape." Then she plucked at the back of his neck and smoothed out his feathers. "Besides, he's a drake," she said, "so it doesn't matter as much. I think he'll turn out to be strong, and I'm sure he'll win a place for himself."

"The other ducklings are so charming," said the old duck. "Make yourselves at home, and if you happen to find an eel head, you can bring it to me."

And so they made themselves at home.

But the poor duckling who was the last to come out of his egg and looked so horrid was bitten, shoved, and teased by both the ducks and the hens. "He's too big," they all said. And the tom turkey, who was born with spurs, which made him think he was an emperor, puffed himself up like a ship at full sail, walked right over to him, and started gobbling until he turned bright red in the face. The poor duckling had no idea which way to turn. He was very sad because he looked so hideous and was ridiculed by the whole duck yard.

That's how it went on the first day, and afterward it got worse and worse. The poor duckling was chased by everyone. Even his siblings were mean to him, and they always said, "If only the cat would get you! What a horrid troublemaker you are!" And his mother said, "If only you were far away!" The ducks bit him, and the hens pecked at him, and the maid who was supposed to feed the animals gave him a kick with her foot.

Then he took off running and flew over the hedge. The little birds in the bushes darted up into the air out of fright. "It's because I'm so hideous," thought the duckling and closed his eyes but still kept on running. Then he reached the great marsh where the wild ducks lived. There he lay all night, he was so tired and sad.

In the morning the wild ducks flew up, and they looked at their new companion. "Who on earth are you?" they asked, and the duckling turned this way and that, greeting them as best he could.

"You're awfully hideous," said the wild ducks. "But that doesn't matter to us, provided you don't marry anyone in our family." The poor thing! He had no intention of getting married, as long as he was allowed to sit among the reeds and drink a little marsh water.

There he stayed for two whole days. Then two wild geese came along, or rather two wild ganders, because they were males. It wasn't long ago that they had come out of their eggs, and that's why they were so brash.

"Listen here, my friend," they said. "You're so hideous that we actually like you! Want to come along and be a migrating bird? Nearby, in another marsh, there are some heavenly sweet wild geese, all of them young ladies who could say, 'Quack!' You're in a position to be a success, because you're so hideous."

"Bang! Boom!" they suddenly heard overhead. Both the wild geese fell dead into the reeds, and the water turned blood-red. Bang! Boom! was heard again, and entire flocks of wild geese rose up from the reeds. Then shots rang out again. A great hunt was under way. The hunters lay all around the marsh. Some were even up in the tree branches that stretched far out over the reeds. Blue smoke drifted like clouds among the dark trees and hovered far out over the water. Through the mud came the hunting dogs. Splash! Splash! Reeds and rushes swayed on all sides. What a horror it was for the poor duckling! He turned his head to tuck it under his wing, but just at that moment a huge terrifying dog stopped right next to him, his long tongue hanging out of his mouth and his eyes shining horridly. He lowered his jaws toward the duckling, showed his sharp teeth and . . . Splash! Splash! He left without taking him.

"Oh, thank God," sighed the duckling. "I'm so hideous that not even the dog wanted to bite me."

And he lay very still as the bullets whistled through the reeds, with one shot exploding after the other.

Not until late in the day was it quiet, but the poor youngster still didn't dare stand up. He waited another few hours before he looked around and then hurried away from the marsh as fast as he could, racing over field and meadow. There was a strong wind, so he had a hard time making headway.

Toward evening he reached a poor little farmhouse. It was so wretched that it couldn't make up its mind which way to fall, and that's why it was still standing. The wind was blowing so hard against the duckling that he had to sit on his tail to hold his ground, and it got worse and worse. Then he noticed that the door had come loose from one of its hinges and was hanging so crookedly that he could slip through the crack into the house, and that's what he did.

Inside lived an old woman with her cat and her hen. The cat, who was called Sonny, could arch his back and purr. He could even throw off sparks, but for that you had to stroke his fur the wrong way. The hen had very short little legs, and that's why she was called "Henny Shortlegs." She was good at laying eggs, and the woman was as fond of her as her own child.

In the morning they noticed at once the strange duckling. The cat started purring and the hen began to cluck.

"What's this?" said the woman, looking all around, but she couldn't see well, and that's why she thought the duckling was a plump duck that had gone astray. "What a nice find," she said. "Now I can have duck eggs, if only it's not a drake. We'll have to give it a try."

And so the duckling was accepted on a trial basis for three weeks, but no eggs appeared. The cat was master of the house, and the hen was the mistress. They both kept on saying, "*We* and the rest of the world," because they thought they were half of it, and the better half at that. The duckling thought it might be possible to have another opinion, but the hen wouldn't stand for it.

"Can you lay eggs?" she asked.

"No."

"Well then, you'd better keep your mouth shut!"

And the cat said, "Can you arch your back, purr, and throw sparks?"

"No."

"Well then, we don't want to hear from you when sensible people are talking!"

And the duckling sat in the corner, in a bad temper. Then he happened to think about the fresh air and sunshine. He had such a strange desire to float on the water that at last he couldn't resist, he had to tell the hen.

"What's come over you?" she asked. "You don't have anything to do, that's why you get such ideas into your head. Lay eggs or purr, and it will pass."

"But it's so lovely to float on the water," said the duckling. "So lovely to dip your head under water and dive down to the bottom."

"Oh, that's a great pleasure, all right!" said the hen. "You must be crazy! Ask the cat—and he's the smartest one I know—whether he likes floating on the water or diving underneath. I won't even talk about myself. Or you can ask our mistress, the old woman.

There's no one wiser than her in the whole world. Do you think she wants to float and get water on her head?"

"You don't understand me," said the duckling.

"Well, if we don't understand you, then who does? You'll never be smarter than the cat or the old woman, not to mention myself. Stop making a fuss, child! And thank your Creator for all the kindness that has been shown to you. Haven't you ended up in a warm house, with companions that you can learn something from? But you're a fool, and it's not amusing to be around you. Believe me, it's for your own good that I'm telling you these unpleasant things. That's how you know who your true friends are. So see to it that you lay eggs and learn to purr and throw sparks."

"I think I'll go out into the wide world," said the duckling.

"Well, go ahead!" said the hen.

And so the duckling left. He floated on the water, then dove down, but all the animals ignored him because he was ugly.

Then autumn came, the leaves in the forest turned brown and yellow, the wind seized hold of them so they danced around, and the sky looked cold. The clouds hung heavy with hail and snowflakes, and on the fence stood a raven, shrieking "Ow! Ow!" from sheer cold. Yes, you could end up freezing just by thinking about it. Things certainly weren't going well for the poor duckling.

One evening as the sun was setting gloriously, a whole flock of lovely big birds came out of the thickets. The duckling had never seen anything so beautiful. They were a dazzling white, with long supple necks. They were swans. They uttered quite a wondrous sound, spread out their magnificent long wings, and flew away from the cold regions to the warmer countries, to open waters. They climbed so high, so high, and the little ugly duckling felt quite strange. He spun around in the water like a wheel, stretching his neck high up into the air after them, uttering a cry so loud and strange that it scared even him. Oh, he couldn't forget those lovely birds, those happy birds. As soon as he lost sight of them, he dove straight down to the bottom, and when he came back up, he was practically beside himself. He didn't know what those birds were called or where they were flying, but he loved them as he had never loved anyone else. He didn't envy them in the least; how could he even think of wishing for such loveliness? He would have been happy if the ducks had merely allowed him to stay among them. The poor ugly creature!

And the winter was so cold, so cold. The duckling had to swim around in the water to keep it from freezing over. But every night the hole in which he was swimming grew smaller and smaller. It froze so hard that the icy crust crackled. The duckling had to keep moving his legs or the water would close up. At last he grew so weak that he lay quite still and then was frozen into the ice.

Early in the morning a farmer appeared. He saw the duckling, went out, smashed the ice to bits with his wooden clog, and carried the bird home to his wife. There the duckling was revived.

The children wanted to play with him, but the duckling thought they were trying to hurt him and flew in terror right into the milk basin so the milk splashed all over the room. The farmer's wife screamed and flapped her hands in the air. Then the duckling flew into the trough of butter and then into the flour barrel and out again. What a sight he was! The farmer's wife screamed and swung at him with the hearth tongs, and the children tumbled all over each other to catch the duckling, as they laughed and shrieked. It was a good thing that the door stood open. Out he rushed into the bushes in the newly fallen snow. There he lay, as if in a daze.

But it would be much too sad to recount all the suffering and misery he had to endure that harsh winter. He was lying in the marsh among the rushes when the sunshine once again began to feel warm. The larks sang. It was lovely springtime.

Then all of a sudden he lifted his wings; they flapped stronger than before and powerfully carried him away. And before he even knew it, he was in a great garden where the apple trees stood in bloom, where the lilacs hung fragrantly on their long green boughs all the way down to the winding waterways. Oh, it was so lovely there, so springtime fresh! And right in front of him, out of the thickets, came three lovely white swans. They ruffled their feathers and floated so lightly on the water. The duckling recognized the magnificent creatures and was stirred by a strange sadness.

"I'll fly over to them, those royal birds. And they'll peck me to death because someone like me, who is so hideous, dares approach them. But it doesn't matter! Better to be killed by them than to be nipped by the ducks, pecked by the hens, kicked by the maid who tends the chicken coops, and to suffer so terribly all winter." And he flew out into the water and swam over to the magnificent swans. They saw him and came gliding toward him with ruffled feathers. "Go ahead and kill me!" said the poor bird, and he bent his head down to the surface of the water and waited for death. But what did he see in the clear water? He saw beneath him his own image, and he was no longer a clumsy, grayish-black bird, horrid and hideous. He was a swan!

It doesn't matter if you're born in a duck yard when you've been lying inside a swan's egg.

He actually felt glad about all the suffering and hardships he had endured. Now he could appreciate his happiness and all the loveliness that awaited him. And the great swans swam all around him, stroking him with their bills.

Several little children came into the garden. They threw bread and grain into the water, and the youngest of them cried, "There's a new one!"

And the other children also shouted joyfully, "Yes, a new one has arrived!" And they clapped their hands and danced around. They ran to find Father and Mother. Bread and cakes were tossed into the water, and they all said, "The new one is the most beautiful of all! So young and so lovely!" And the old swans bowed to him.

Then he felt quite bashful and tucked his head behind his wings. He didn't know what to make of it. He was much too happy, but not the least bit proud, because a good heart is never proud. He thought about how he had been badgered and scorned, and now he heard everyone say that he was the loveliest of all the lovely birds. The lilacs dipped their boughs all the way down to him in the water, and the sun shone so warm and so fine. Then he ruffled his feathers, raised his slender neck, and rejoiced with all his heart. "I never dreamed of so much happiness when I was the ugly duckling!"

The Fir Tree

Out in the forest stood such a charming fir tree. It was in a good spot where it could get sunshine and there was plenty of air. All around grew scores of bigger companions, both firs and pines, but the little fir tree was so eager to grow up that it didn't think about the warm sun or the fresh air. It didn't pay any attention to the farm children who walked past, chattering, whenever they were out gathering strawberries or raspberries. Often they would come by with a whole pitcher full or they would have strawberries threaded on a piece of straw. Then they would sit down near the little tree and say, "Oh, how charming and little it is!" That's not at all what the tree wanted to hear.

The following year it was a full length taller, and the year after that yet another. On a fir tree you can always tell how many years it has been growing by how many layers of branches it has.

"Oh, if only I were a big tree like the others," sighed the little tree. "Then I could spread out my branches all around and from the top I could gaze out on the wide world. The birds would build nests in my branches, and when the wind blew, I could nod so grandly, like all the others."

The tree took no pleasure in the sunshine, in the birds, or in the crimson clouds that sailed overhead both morning and evening.

When it was winter, and the snow lay all around, glittering white, a hare often came bounding along and sprang right over the little tree. Oh, how annoying that was! But two winters passed and by the third the tree was so tall that the hare had to go around it. "Oh, to grow and grow, to get bigger and older. That is the only lovely thing in this world," thought the tree.

In the autumn the woodcutters would always appear to chop

down some of the biggest trees. It happened every year, and the young fir tree, which was now quite grown-up, would start trembling because the tall, magnificent trees would topple to the ground with a groan and a crash. Their branches would be cut off, and they looked so naked, tall and slender. They were almost beyond recognition. But then they were loaded onto wagons, and horses carried them away, out of the forest.

Where were they going? What was in store for them?

In the spring, when the swallow and stork appeared, the tree asked them: "Do you know where they were taken? Have you seen them?"

The swallows didn't know anything, but the stork looked thoughtful, nodded his head, and said, "Oh, yes, I think so. I met many new ships as I flew here from Egypt. On the ships were magnificent mast trees, and I'd venture to say they were yours. They smelled of fir. I bring you many greetings. How they swaggered and swayed!"

"Oh, if only I too were big enough to fly across the sea! What is the sea like, anyway? How does it look?"

"Well, it's much too complicated to describe," said the stork and flew off.

"Enjoy your youth!" said the rays of sunlight. "Enjoy your fresh growth and the young life inside you!"

The wind kissed the tree, and the dew shed tears over it, but the fir tree did not understand.

When Christmastime came, quite young trees were felled, trees that were often not even as tall or as old as the fir tree, which could never find any peace but was always eager to be off. These young trees, and they were the most beautiful of all, always kept their branches. They were loaded onto wagons, and horses carried them away, out of the forest.

"Where are they going?" asked the fir tree. "They're no bigger than I am. There was even one that was much smaller. Why do they keep all their branches? Where are they being taken?"

"We know! We know!" chirped the sparrows. "In town we've looked in the windows. We know where they're being taken. Oh, they end up in the greatest splendor and glory you could ever imagine. We've looked in the windows and seen them being planted in the middle of the warm parlor and decorated with the loveliest things: gilded apples, gingerbread, toys, and hundreds of candles!"

"And then?" asked the fir tree, all its branches aquiver. "And then? What happens next?"

"Well, that's all we saw. But nothing could match it."

"Maybe I was meant to take this glorious path," rejoiced the fir tree. "That's even better than going across the sea. What an agony of longing! If only it were Christmas. Now I'm as tall and broad as the others that were carried off last year. Oh, if only I were on that wagon right now. If only I were in the warm parlor with all that splendor and glory! And then . . . ? Well, then something even better is bound to happen, something even more wonderful, or why would they decorate me like that? Something even grander, even more glorious is bound to happen. But what? Oh, how I'm suffering! Oh, how I yearn! I just don't know what's come over me."

"Take pleasure in us!" said the air and the sunlight. "Take pleasure in your fresh youth out in the open!"

But the fir tree felt no pleasure at all. It grew and grew. Both winter and summer it was green; dark green it stood there. Everyone who saw it said, "That's a lovely tree!" And at Christmas, it was the very first to be cut down. The ax bit deep into its marrow, and the tree fell to the ground with a sigh. It felt a pain, a weakness, it couldn't even think about happiness. It was sad to part with its home, with the spot where it had sprouted up, for the tree realized that it would never see its dear old companions again: the small shrubs and flowers all around, maybe not even the birds. Leaving was certainly not pleasant.

The tree didn't recover until it was unloaded in a courtyard with all the other trees and it heard a man say, "That one is magnificent. That's the one we want."

Then two servants in fine livery came and carried the fir tree into an enormous, beautiful room. Portraits hung on all the walls, and next to the large woodstove stood big Chinese vases with lions on the lids. There were rocking chairs, silk-covered sofas, big tables covered with picture books, and toys worth a hundred times a hundred *rigsdaler*—at least that's what the children said. And the fir tree was set in a large wooden tub filled with sand, but no one could tell that it was a wooden tub because green fabric was wrapped all around it, and the tub stood on top of a big, colorful carpet. Oh, how the tree trembled! What was going to happen next? Then the servants and the maids proceeded to decorate the tree. On one branch they hung little woven baskets cut out of colored paper; each basket was filled with sweets. Gilded apples and walnuts hung on the tree as if they had grown there, and more than a hundred little candles, red and blue and white, were fastened to the branches. Dolls that looked as lifelike as human beings swayed in the boughs. The tree had never seen anything like it before. And at the very top they put a big star made from shiny gold paper. It was magnificent, quite incomparably magnificent.

"Tonight," they all said, "tonight the tree will shine!"

"Oh," thought the tree. "If only it were evening. If only they'd light the candles soon. And what will happen after that? Will trees come from the forest to look at me? Will the sparrows fly past the window? Will I take root and stand here, decorated like this, all winter and summer long?"

Oh yes, the tree thought it knew all about it. But it had a terrible bark-ache from sheer yearning, and bark-aches are just as bad for trees as headaches are for the rest of us.

Finally the candles were lit. What splendor, what magnificence! Every branch of the tree trembled so much that one of the candles set fire to a bough. How it stung!

"God help us!" shrieked the maids, and hastily put out the fire.

Now the tree didn't even dare tremble. Oh, how awful! It was so afraid of losing any of its finery. It was quite bedazzled by all the splendor. And then the double doors flew open, and a crowd of children rushed in, as if they were about to topple the whole tree. The grown-ups followed more sedately. The children stood in utter silence, but only for a moment. Then they began shouting again so their voices echoed through the room. They danced around the tree, and one present after the other was plucked from the branches.

"What are they doing?" thought the tree. "What's going to happen?" And the candles burned all the way down to the boughs, and as they burned down, they were put out, and then the children were allowed to plunder the tree. Oh, how they rushed at it, making all the branches groan. If the tree hadn't been tied to the ceiling by its top and the gold star, it would have toppled right over.

The children danced around with their splendid toys. No one paid any attention to the tree except for the old nursemaid, who walked around it, peering in among the branches. But she was only checking to see that not a fig or apple had been overlooked.

"A story! A story!" shouted the children, pulling a stout little man over to the tree, and he sat down right underneath it. "Because we're out in the forest," he told them, "and it may do the tree some good to listen along! But I'm only going to tell you one story. Do you want to hear the one about Ickety-Ackety or the one about Clumpa-Dumpa, who fell down the stairs but still ended up on the throne and won the hand of the princess?"

"Ickety-Ackety!" cried some of the children. "Clumpa-Dumpa!" cried the others. They shouted and shrieked, and only the fir tree stood in silence and thought, "Won't I get to take part? Won't I get to do anything?" It had been part of the celebration, after all; it had done what it was supposed to do.

And then the man told the story of Clumpa-Dumpa, who fell down the stairs but still ended up on the throne and won the hand of the princess. And the children clapped their hands and shouted, "Tell us more, tell us more!" They wanted to hear the one about 'Ickety-Ackety' too, but he would only tell them the story about Clumpa-Dumpa. The fir tree stood quite still and pensive. The birds in the forest had never mentioned anything like this. "Clumpa-Dumpa fell down the stairs, and yet won the hand of the princess. Well, well, so that's the way the things are out in the world," thought the fir tree, believing that it was all true because such a nice man had told the story. "Well, well! Who knows, maybe I too will fall down the stairs and win the princess." And the fir tree looked forward to the next day when it would be adorned with candles and toys, gold and fruit.

"Tomorrow I won't tremble," it thought. "I will fully enjoy all my glory. Tomorrow I'll hear the story about Clumpa-Dumpa again, and maybe the one about Ickety-Ackety too." And the tree stood still and pensive all night long.

In the morning a servant and a maid came into the room.

"Now the finery is going to start again!" thought the tree. But they dragged it out of the parlor and up the stairs to the attic. And there, in a dark corner where no daylight shone, they left it. "What does this mean?" thought the tree. "I wonder what I'm supposed to do here? I wonder what I'm going to hear now?" It leaned against the wall and stood there thinking and thinking. And it had plenty of time for that, because day after day and night after night went by. No one came up to the attic, and when someone finally did, it was only to put some large boxes in the corner. The tree stood quite hidden; you would almost think it had been completely forgotten.

"Now it's winter outside," thought the tree. "The ground is hard and covered with snow. The people wouldn't be able to plant me. No doubt that's why I'm standing here, safe indoors until springtime. What a good plan! How kind the people are! If only it wasn't so dark in here and so terribly lonely. There's not even a little hare. It was so nice out there in the forest when the snow lay on the ground and the hare came running past. Yes, even when it leaped right over me, although I didn't like it much at the time. But up here it's terribly lonely."

"Squeak, squeak!" said a little mouse at that very moment and came scurrying. And then another little mouse appeared. They sniffed at the fir tree and scurried in and out of its branches.

"It's awfully cold," said the little mice. "But otherwise it's quite blissful to be here. Don't you agree, you old fir tree?"

"I'm not old at all!" said the fir tree. "There are plenty of trees that are much older than I am!"

"Where did you come from?" asked the mice. "And what do you know?" They were awfully curious. "Tell us about the loveliest place on earth! Have you ever been there? Have you been in the pantry where cheeses are lined up on the shelves and hams hang from the ceiling? Where you can dance on tallow candles? Where you go in skinny but come out fat?"

"I don't know that place," said the tree. "But I do know the forest, where the sun shines and the birds sing." And then the tree told them all about its youth, and the little mice had never heard anything like that before. They listened closely and said, "Oh, you've seen so much! How happy you've been!"

"Me?" said the fir tree, thinking about everything it had just described. "Why yes, I suppose those were quite delightful days, after all." But then the tree told them about Christmas Eve, when it was decorated with cakes and candles.

"Oh!" said the little mice. "How happy you've been, you old fir tree!"

"I'm not old at all!" said the tree. "It was only this winter that I came here from the forest. I'm in the prime of my life, I've just stopped growing."

"How wonderfully you describe things!" said the little mice, and the following night they brought along four other little mice who wanted to hear what the tree had to tell. And the more the tree told them, the more clearly it remembered everything and thought, "Those actually were quite enjoyable days. But they can come again, they can come again! Clumpa-Dumpa fell down the stairs, yet he won the hand of the princess. Maybe I too can win a princess." And then the fir tree thought about a charming little birch tree that grew out in the forest. For the fir tree, the birch was a real and lovely princess.

"Who's Clumpa-Dumpa?" asked the little mice. And then the fir tree told them the whole story; it could remember every single word. And the little mice were ready to run all the way to the top of the tree out of sheer glee. The next night many more mice came, and on Sunday there were even two rats. But they said the story wasn't amusing, and that made the little mice sad, because then they thought less of the story themselves.

"Is that the only story you know?" asked the rats.

"The only one," replied the tree. "I heard it on the happiest evening of my life, but back then I didn't realize how happy I was!"

"It's an exceptionally tedious story. Don't you know any about bacon and tallow candles? Any pantry stories?"

"No," said the tree.

"Well, thanks for nothing!" replied the rats, and they went back home.

Eventually the little mice disappeared too, and then the tree sighed, "It was so nice having those nimble little mice sitting around me and listening to what I told them. Now that too is over. But I'm going to remember to enjoy myself when they finally take me out of here."

But when would that happen?

Well, one day in the early morning, servants came up to the attic and started rummaging around. The boxes were moved aside, and the tree was pulled out. Now, it's true that they threw it to the floor rather hard, but then a man dragged it at once toward the stairs, where daylight was shining.

"Now life will begin again!" thought the tree. It could feel the fresh air, the first rays of sun. And then it was out in the courtyard. Everything happened so fast that the tree forgot all about taking a look at itself. There was so much to see all around. The courtyard was next to a garden, and everything was in bloom. The roses hung so fresh and fragrant over the little fence, the linden trees were blossoming, and the swallows flew about, saying, "Kirra-virra-vit, my husband has arrived!" But it wasn't the fir tree they meant.

"Now I'm going to live!" rejoiced the tree, spreading its branches wide. But alas, its boughs were all withered and yellow. In the corner among the weeds and nettles was where the tree came to rest. The star made from gold paper was still on its top, shimmering in the bright sunshine.

In the courtyard several of the lively children were playing who had danced around the tree at Christmastime, taking such delight in it. One of the youngest children came over and tore off the golden star.

"Look what's still sitting on the horrid old Christmas tree!" he said, stomping on the branches so they groaned under his boots.

And the tree looked at all that floral splendor and freshness in the garden. Then it looked at itself and wished that it had stayed in the dark corner of the attic. The tree thought about its fresh youth in the forest, about the joyous Christmas Eve, and about the little mice who had listened so happily to the story about Clumpa-Dumpa.

"It's over, it's over!" said the poor tree. "If only I had enjoyed it while I could. It's over, it's over!"

And the hired man came over and chopped the tree into little pieces; it made a whole stack. How lovely the tree flared up under the big copper cauldron. And it sighed so deeply; each sigh was like the sound of a little shot. That's why the children who were playing came running over and sat down in front of the fire, staring into the flames and shouting, "Bang, snap!" But with each sharp crack, which was a deep sigh, the tree thought about a summer day in the forest, or about a winter night out there, when the stars were shining. It thought about Christmas Eve and about Clumpa-Dumpa, the only story it had ever heard and knew how to tell. And before long the tree had burned up.

The boys played in the courtyard, and on his chest the youngest one had the gold star that the tree had worn on its happiest evening. Now it was over, and the tree was gone, along with the story. It was over, over, and that's what happens to every story!

The Snow Queen

A Tale in Seven Stories

FIRST STORY
WHICH IS ABOUT THE MIRROR AND ITS PIECES

All right! Now let's begin. When we reach the end of the story, we'll know more than we know now, because there was an evil troll. He was one of the very worst; he was the Devil! One day he was in a truly good mood, because he had created a mirror that had the power to make everything good and beautiful that was reflected in it shrink to almost nothing, while whatever was worthless and loathsome would stand out clearly and look even worse. In the mirror the loveliest landscape looked like boiled spinach, and the best people turned beastly or stood on their heads with no stomachs. Their faces became so distorted that they were beyond recognition, and if you had a freckle, you could be sure that it would spread over your nose and mouth. That was excellent fun, said the Devil. If a good, pious thought passed through someone's mind, a smirk would appear in the mirror, and the troll-demon would have to laugh at his ingenious invention. Everyone who attended troll school—because he ran a troll school—told everyone else that a miracle had occurred. For the first time, they said, it was possible to see how the world and human beings actually looked. They ran around with the mirror, and in the end there wasn't a country or a person that hadn't been distorted by it. Then they even wanted to fly up to Heaven itself to ridicule the angels and Our Lord. The higher they flew with the mirror, the more it smirked. They could hardly hold onto it. Higher and higher they flew, closer to God and the angels. Then the mirror began trembling so terribly as it smirked that it flew out of their hands and plummeted to earth, where it broke into a hundred million billion pieces and more. And that was precisely the reason why it did even more harm than before, because some of the pieces were hardly bigger than a grain of sand. They flew around in the wide world, and whenever they landed in someone's eye, that's where they would stay. Then those people would see everything wrong, or only have eyes for what was bad in something, since every little speck of mirror had kept the same powers that the whole mirror possessed. Some people even got a little piece of mirror in their heart, and then it was quite dreadful. The heart would turn into a lump of ice. Some pieces of mirror were so big that they were used for windowpanes, but it wasn't worth looking through those panes to see your friends. Other pieces ended up in eyeglasses, and then things would go badly when people put on the glasses to see properly and fairly. The Evil One laughed until his belly split, it tickled him so splendidly. But outside, little pieces of glass were still flying around in the air. Now let's hear what happened!

SECOND STORY
A LITTLE BOY AND A LITTLE GIRL

In the big city, where there are so many buildings and people that there isn't enough room for everyone to have a little garden, and where most people have to be content with flowers in pots, there were two poor children who did have a garden that was slightly bigger than a flowerpot. They were not brother and sister, yet they were as fond of each other as if they had been. Their families lived right next door to each other; they lived in two garret rooms. At the place where the roof of one building touched the roof of the other and the gutter ran along the eaves, a little window jutted out from each building. All you had to do was step over the gutter to go from one window to the other.

Outside, each family had a big wooden box, and in it grew herbs for cooking and a little rosebush. There was one in each box; they grew so wondrously. Then their parents decided to set the boxes atop the gutter so they almost reached from one window to the other and looked exactly like two flower beds. Pea vines hung down the sides of the boxes, and the rosebushes sprouted long branches that twined around the windows and bent toward each other. It was almost like a triumphal arch of greenery and blossoms.

Since the boxes were quite high and the children knew that they weren't supposed to crawl out, they were often allowed to climb out the windows to each other and sit on their little stools beneath the roses. That's where they played so happily.

In the winter, of course, that amusement would come to an end. The windows were often completely frosted over, but then they would heat up copper *skillings* on the stove, place the hot *skillings* on the frozen windowpane, and then a lovely peephole would appear, so round, so round. Through it a blessed, gentle eye would peek, one in each window—it was the little boy and the little girl. His name was Kai and hers was Gerda. In the summer they could reach each other with a single bound. In the winter they first had to go down all those stairs and then up all those other stairs. Outside the snow swirled in drifts.

"The white bees are swarming," said old Grandmother.

"Do they have a queen bee too?" asked the little boy, because he knew that real bees had one.

"Yes, they do," said Grandmother. "She flies in the thick of the swarm. She's the biggest of them all, and she never rests on the ground. She flies up at once inside the black cloud. Many a winter night she flies through the city streets, peering in the windows, and then they frost over so strangely, looking like flowers."

"Oh yes, we've seen that!" said both children, so they knew it must be true.

"Can the Snow Queen come inside?" asked the little girl.

"Just let her come," said the boy, "and I'll put her on the hot stove and then she'll melt."

But Grandmother stroked his hair and told them other stories.

One evening when little Kai was home and almost undressed, he climbed up onto the chair by the window and peeked out the little hole. A few snowflakes were falling outside, and one of them, the biggest of all, remained lying on the edge of one of the flower boxes. The snowflake grew bigger and bigger until it became at last a whole woman, dressed in the sheerest white gossamer, which looked as if it were made of millions of starlike flakes. She was so beautiful and elegant but made of ice, dazzling, glittering ice, and yet she was alive. Her eyes stared like two bright stars, but there was nothing calm or peaceful about them. She nodded at the window and waved her hand. The little boy was terrified and jumped down from the chair. Then it seemed as if a huge bird flew past the window outside.

The next day was bright and cold. And then came spring. The sun shone, green sprouts appeared, the swallows built their nests, the windows were flung open, and the little children once again sat in their tiny garden high up in the eaves, at the very top of the buildings.

That summer the roses bloomed so marvelously. The little girl had learned a hymn that spoke of roses, and those roses made her think of her own. She sang it for the little boy, and he sang along:

"In the valley where roses grow wild,
There we will speak to the Christ child!"

And the children held each other's hands, kissed the roses, and looked into God's bright sunshine, speaking to it as if the Christ child were there. How lovely the summer days were, how heavenly to be outside near the fresh rosebushes that never seemed to stop blooming.

Kai and Gerda sat looking at a picture book with animals and birds. That was when—just as the clock struck five on the big church tower—Kai said, "Ow! Something stabbed me in the heart! And now I have something in my eye!"

The little girl put her arm around his neck. He blinked his eyes. No, there was nothing to be seen.

"I think it's gone," he said, but it was not gone. It was one of those specks of glass that came from the mirror, the troll mirror. Of course we remember it, the horrid glass that made everything great and good that was reflected in it become small and hideous, while the evil and wicked appeared quite clearly, and every fault that anything possessed was noticed at once. Poor Kai, he had also gotten a speck right in the heart, which would soon turn into a lump of ice. At the moment it didn't hurt, but it was there.

"Why are you crying?" he asked. "It makes you look so horrid. There's nothing wrong with me. Ugh!" he suddenly shouted. "That rose over there has been gnawed by a worm. And look, that one is completely crooked. These roses are actually quite disgusting.

They look like the boxes they're standing in." And then he kicked the box hard with his foot and tore off two of the roses.

"Kai, what are you doing!" cried the little girl. And when he saw her horror, he tore off another rose and then dashed through his window, away from blessed little Gerda.

Later, when she brought out the picture book, he said that it was for babies, and if Grandmother told them stories, he would always come with some objection. Whenever he had the chance he would walk behind her, putting on glasses, and talking the way she did. It was a perfect likeness, and then people would laugh at him. Soon he could walk and talk like everyone on the whole street. Everything that was odd about them and unattractive, Kai could imitate. Then people said, "He certainly has a clever head on his shoulders, that boy!" But it was the glass that had landed in his eye and the glass that sat in his heart; they were the reason he teased even little Gerda, who loved him with all her soul.

The games he played were now very different from before; they were so logical. One winter day, as the snowflakes swirled in drifts, he brought out a big magnifying glass, held out a corner of his blue coat, and let the flakes land on it.

"Look into the glass, Gerda," he said, and every snowflake grew much bigger, looking like a magnificent flower or a ten-pointed star. It was lovely to see.

"Do you see how ingenious they are?" said Kai. "They're much more interesting than real flowers. And none of them has a single flaw, they're quite perfect, as long as they don't melt!"

A little while later Kai appeared wearing big gloves and carrying his sled on his back. He shouted right into Gerda's ear, "I have permission to go sledding at the big square where the others are playing!" And off he went.

Over in the square the most daring of the boys would often tie their sleds to the farmer's wagon and then they would ride along for a good stretch down the road. They were having a merry time. In the midst of their games, a huge sleigh appeared. It was painted all white, and in it sat someone swathed in a shaggy white fur and wearing a shaggy white cap. The sleigh circled the square twice, and Kai quickly tied his little sled to it, and then he was riding along. The sleigh went faster and faster, right into the next street.

The person who was driving turned around and nodded in such a friendly way at Kai, as if they knew each other. Each time Kai tried to untie his little sled, the person would nod again, and then Kai stayed where he was. They drove right out through the city gates. Then the snow began to come down so heavily that the little boy couldn't even see his hand in front of him, but he kept racing along. He hastily let go of the rope to get away from the huge sleigh, but it did no good. His little sled hung on, moving with the speed of the wind. Then he shouted quite loudly, but no one heard him. The snow swirled in drifts, and the sleigh sped along. Once in a while it would give a hop, as if flying over ditches and fences. Kai was quite terrified. He wanted to say the Lord's Prayer but all he could remember was his multiplication tables.

The snowflakes grew bigger and bigger, until at last they looked like big white hens. Suddenly they leaped aside, the huge sleigh came to a halt, and the person who was driving it stood up. The fur coat and cap were nothing but snow. It was a woman, standing so tall and straight, so shimmering white. It was the Snow Queen.

"We've made good progress!" she said. "But aren't you freezing? Crawl in under my bearskin." And she set him in the sleigh beside her, wrapping the bearskin around him. He felt as if he were sinking into a snowdrift.

"Are you still freezing?" she asked, and then she kissed him on the forehead. Ooh! It was colder than ice; it went right to his heart, which was already half ice. He felt as if he would die, but only for a moment, and then he felt fine. He no longer noticed the cold all around him.

"My sled! Don't forget my sled!" That was the first thing he thought of, and so it was tied onto one of the white hens, which flew along behind with the sled on its back. The Snow Queen kissed Kai again, and then he forgot all about little Gerda and Grandmother and everyone else back home.

"No more kisses for you," she said. "Or I might kiss you to death!"

Kai looked at her. She was so beautiful; he couldn't imagine a wiser or lovelier face. She no longer seemed made of ice, as she had when she sat outside the window and beckoned to him. To his eyes she now seemed perfect. He was not the least bit afraid. He told her that he could do his figures in his head, even with fractions, or how many square miles each country had, and "how many inhabitants," and she kept on smiling. Then he thought that what he knew was not nearly enough. He looked up at the vast, vast sky, and she flew along with him, flew high up into the black cloud, and the storm rumbled and roared, as if it were singing ancient ballads. They flew over forests and lakes, over sea and land. Beneath them rushed the cold wind. The wolves howled, the snow sparkled, and over it flew shrieking black crows. But up above, the moon glowed big and bright, and Kai gazed at it all night—that long, long winter night. In the daytime he slept at the Snow Queen's feet.

THIRD STORY
THE FLOWER GARDEN OF THE WOMAN
WHO KNEW MAGIC

But how did little Gerda feel when Kai didn't come back? Where was he? No one knew, no one could tell her. The boys said only that they had seen him tie his little sled to a magnificent huge sleigh that drove down the street and out the city gates. No one knew where he was; many tears fell. Little Gerda wept so hard and so long. Then they said that he was dead; he had drowned in the river that ran close to the city. Oh, those were such long and dark winter days.

Then came spring with warmer sunshine.

"Kai is dead and gone!" said little Gerda.

"I don't believe it," said the sunshine.

"He's dead and gone!" she told the swallows.

"We don't believe it," they replied, and in the end Gerda didn't believe it either.

"I'll put on my new red shoes," she said one morning. "Kai has never seen them, and then I'll go down to the river and ask about him."

It was very early. She kissed old Grandmother who was sleeping, put on her red shoes, and walked all alone out the gates to the river.

"Is it true that you've taken my little playmate? I'll give you my red shoes if you'll give him back to me."

And it seemed to her that the waves nodded quite strangely. Then she picked up her red shoes, her dearest possessions, and threw both of them into the river. But they fell close to shore, and the little waves promptly brought them back to her on land, as if the river didn't want to take her dearest possessions since it didn't have little Kai. But she thought that she hadn't thrown them far enough, and so she climbed into a boat that was floating among the reeds. She went all the way out to the farthest end and threw the shoes, but the boat wasn't tied securely, and with her movement, it glided away from land. She noticed this and hurried to get out, but before she could make her way back, the boat was more than two feet from shore, and it began to slip away even faster.

Then little Gerda grew quite frightened and started to cry, but no one heard her except the sparrows. They couldn't carry her back to land, but they flew along the shore and sang, as if to comfort her, "Here we are! Here we are!" The boat drifted with the current, and little Gerda sat quite still in her stocking feet. Her little red shoes floated along behind, but they couldn't reach the boat. It was picking up speed.

It was beautiful on both banks, with lovely flowers, old trees, and sheep and cows on the slopes, but not a person in sight.

"Maybe the river will take me to little Kai," thought Gerda, and then her spirits rose. She stood up and for many hours looked at the beautiful green banks. Then she came to a big cherry orchard. There stood a little house that had strange red and blue windows, as well as a thatched roof. Outside stood two wooden soldiers who presented arms for all who sailed past.

Gerda called to them. She thought they were alive, but of course they didn't answer. She came quite close to them, and the river lifted the boat toward land.

Gerda shouted even louder, and then out of the house came an old, old woman leaning on a crooked stick. She was wearing a big sun hat that was painted with the loveliest flowers.

"You poor little child!" said the old woman. "How did you end up in the big strong current, drifting far out in the wide world?" And then the old woman came right out into the water, hooked her crooked stick on the boat, pulled it ashore, and lifted out little Gerda.

Gerda was glad to be on dry land, yet she was a little afraid of the strange old woman.

"Come here and tell me who you are and how you happened to get here," she said.

Gerda told her everything, and the old woman shook her head and said, "My, my!" After Gerda had told her everything and asked whether she had seen little Kai, the woman said that he had not come past but no doubt he would. She shouldn't be so sad, but have a taste of her cherries and look at her flowers. They were more beautiful than any picture book; each of them could tell a whole story. Then she took Gerda by the hand. They went inside the little house, and the old woman locked the door.

The windows were high up with panes that were red, blue, and yellow. The daylight shone so strangely inside, from all those colors. On the table were the loveliest cherries, and Gerda ate as many as she liked, because she was no longer afraid. While she ate, the old woman combed her hair with a golden comb, and her hair curled and gleamed such a lovely yellow all around her cheerful little face, which was so round and looked like a rose.

"Oh, how I've longed for such a sweet little girl," said the old woman. "Now you'll see how well the two of us will get along!" And as she combed little Gerda's hair, Gerda forgot more and more about Kai, who was like a brother, because the old woman knew magic, although she was not a bad witch. She merely did a little conjuring for her own amusement, and now she wanted to keep little Gerda. That's why she went into the garden, stretched out her crooked stick toward all the rosebushes, and no matter how lovely their blossoms, every one of them sank into the black earth. It was impossible to tell where they had stood. The old woman was afraid that when Gerda saw the roses, she would think about her own, remember little Kai, and run off.

Then she led Gerda out to the flower garden.

Oh, what a fragrance, what loveliness there was! Every imaginable flower, from every season of the year, stood there in full bloom. No picture book could be more colorful or beautiful. Gerda jumped for joy and played until the sun went down behind the tall cherry trees. Then she was given a lovely bed with red silk comforters filled with blue violets, and she slept and dreamed as blissfully as any queen on her wedding day.

The next day she played again with the flowers in the warm sunshine. In that manner many days passed. Gerda knew every flower, but no matter how many there were, she still thought that one must be missing, though she didn't know which it might be. Then one day she was sitting and looking at the old woman's sun hat with the painted flowers, and the most beautiful of all was a rose. The old woman had forgotten to remove it from her hat when she put the others into the ground. That's what happens when you don't have your wits about you. "What!" said Gerda. "Aren't there any roses here?" And she leaped among the flower beds, searching and searching, but there was not one to be found. Then she sat down and wept, but her hot tears fell on the very spot where a rosebush had vanished. When the hot tears watered the earth, the bush suddenly shot up, as full of blossoms as when it sank. Gerda embraced the bush, kissed the roses, and thought about the lovely roses back home, and then about little Kai.

"Oh, how long I've lingered!" said the little girl. "I was supposed to find Kai!"

"Do any of you know where he is?" she asked the roses. "Do you think he's dead and gone?"

"Well, he's not dead," said the roses. "We've been in the ground where all the dead are, but Kai wasn't there."

"Oh, thank you!" said little Gerda, and she went over to the other flowers and looked inside their chalices and asked, "Do you know where little Kai is?"

But each flower stood in the sun dreaming of its own tale or story. Little Gerda heard so many of them, but no one knew anything about Kai.

What did the fire lily say?

"Do you hear the drum? Bam! Bam! It has only two beats, always Bam! Bam! Listen to the women's mournful song. Listen to the shouts of the priests. In her long red gown the Hindu woman stands on the pyre. The flames leap up around her and her dead husband. But the Hindu woman is thinking of the man who is alive here in the crowd, the man whose eyes burn hotter than flames, the man whose fiery eyes reach deeper into her heart than the blaze that will soon burn her body to ashes. Can the flame of the heart die in the flames of the pyre?"

"I don't understand that at all!" said little Gerda.

"That's my tale," said the fire lily.

What does the morning glory say?

"Above the narrow mountain road perches an old baronial castle. The dense periwinkles twine around the ancient red walls, leaf upon leaf, over to the balcony. That's where a lovely girl stands. She is bending over the railing and gazing down the road. No rose hangs fresher from its branch than she. No apple blossom, when the wind lifts it from the tree, floats lighter than she. How her magnificent silk gown rustles! 'Will he never come?'"

"Is Kai the one you mean?" asked little Gerda.

"I'm only telling you my tale, my dream," replied the morning glory.

What does the little snowdrop say?

"Between the trees a long board hangs from ropes. It's a swing. Two charming little girls—their dresses as white as snow, long green silk ribbons fluttering from their hats—are sitting there, swinging. Their brother, who is bigger than they are, is standing on the swing. He has one arm hooked around the rope to hold on, because in one hand he has a little bowl, in the other a clay pipe. He's blowing soap bubbles. The swing sways, the bubbles fly with lovely, shifting colors. The last one is still clinging to the stem of the pipe, quivering in the wind. The swing sways. The little black dog, as light as the bubbles, stands on his hind legs to get up on the swing. The swing flies. The dog falls, barking and angry. They're teasing him, the bubbles burst. A swinging board, a leaping froth picture, that is my song!"

"Your story may well be a beautiful one, but you tell it so mournfully, and you don't mention Kai at all. What do the hyacinths say?"

"There were three lovely sisters, so transparent and delicate. The gown of one sister was red, the second sister's was blue, and the third sister's was pure white. Hand in hand they danced by the quiet lake in the bright moonlight. They were not elf girls, they were human children. There was such a sweet fragrance, and the girls disappeared into the forest. The fragrance grew stronger. Three coffins, in which the lovely girls lay, glided from the depths of the forest out across the lake. Shimmering fireflies flitted around like tiny hovering lights. Are the dancing girls asleep or are they dead? The fragrance of flowers says that they are corpses. The evening bell tolls for the dead!"

"You make me sad," said little Gerda. "Your fragrance is so strong that it makes me think of the dead girls. Oh, is little Kai dead after all? The roses were inside the earth, and they say no."

"Ding, dong!" rang the bells of the hyacinths. "We're not ringing for little Kai, we don't know him at all. We're just singing our song, the only one we know."

And Gerda went over to the buttercup, which shone among the glistening green leaves.

"You're a bright little sun!" said Gerda. "Tell me if you know where I can find my playmate."

And the buttercup shone so beautifully and looked back at Gerda. What song would the buttercup sing? But it was not about Kai either.

"In a little courtyard shone Our Lord's sun, so warm on the first day of spring. Its rays slid down the white wall of the neighbor's house. Close by grew the first yellow flowers, gleaming gold in the warm sunshine. The old grandmother was sitting outside in her chair. Her granddaughter, the poor, enchanting servant girl, had come home for a short visit. She kissed her grandmother. There was gold, the heart's gold, in that blessed kiss. Gold on her lips, gold in the ground, gold up above in the morning hour. See, that's my little story!" said the buttercup.

"Poor old Grandmother!" sighed Gerda. "Oh, she must miss me, she must be grieving for me, just as she did for little Kai. But I'll soon go back home, and I'll bring Kai with me. It's no use asking the flowers, they only know their own songs, they can't tell me anything." Then she tucked up her little dress so she could run faster, but the narcissus struck her across the leg as she jumped over it. She stopped, looked at the tall yellow flower, and asked, "Do you happen to know anything?" She bent all the way down to the narcissus. And what did it say?

"I can see myself! I can see myself!" said the narcissus. "Oh, oh, how fragrant I am! Up in the tiny garret room stands a little dancer, half dressed. She stands first on one leg, then on two. She kicks at the whole world. She's just an illusion. She pours water from the teapot onto a piece of cloth she's holding—it's a corset. Cleanliness is a good thing! The white dress hangs on a hook. It too has been washed in the teapot and dried on the roof. She puts it on, and the saffron-yellow scarf around her neck makes the dress shine even whiter. Her leg in the air! See how proudly she sways on one stalk! I can see myself! I can see myself!"

"I don't like that one bit!" said Gerda. "What kind of a story is that?" And she ran to the edge of the garden.

The door was closed but she wiggled the rusty latch until it came loose and the door flew open. Then little Gerda ran barefoot out into the wide world. She looked back three times, but no one came after her. At last she could run no farther and sat down on a big rock. When she looked around, summer was over; it was late autumn. She hadn't noticed this at all inside the lovely garden, where the sun always shone and there were flowers from every season of the year.

"Dear God! How long I have lingered!" said little Gerda. "It's already fall. This is no time to rest!" And she stood up to go.

Oh, how tender and sore were her little feet, and everything around her looked cold and raw. The long willow leaves had turned quite yellow, and drops of fog dripped from them. One leaf fell after another. Only the blackthorn still bore fruit, tart enough to pucker your lips. Oh, how gray and dreary it was in the wide world.

FOURTH STORY
THE PRINCE AND PRINCESS

Gerda had to rest again. Then right across from where she was sitting, a big crow landed in the snow. He had been sitting and watching her for a long time, wagging his head. Now he said, "Caw! Caw! Go daw! Go daw!" He couldn't say "good day" any better than that, but he meant the little girl well and asked her where she was going, all alone out in the wide world. The word *alone* was something that Gerda understood quite well, and had felt what it meant firsthand. So she told the crow all about her life and asked him whether he had seen Kai.

The crow nodded rather thoughtfully and said, "That could be! That could be!"

"What? Have you really?" cried the little girl, and practically crushed the crow to death, she kissed him so hard.

"Be sensible, be sensible!" said the crow. "I think I know. I think it might be little Kai. But now he seems to have forgotten you in favor of the princess."

"Does he live with a princess?" asked Gerda.

"Just listen!" said the crow. "But it's hard for me to speak your language. If you understand crow-speak I can explain things much better."

"No, I never learned it," said Gerda. "But Grandmother can speak it, and she knows P-talk too. If only I had learned it!"

"Doesn't matter," said the crow. "I'll try to tell you as best I can, but I'm still going to do a poor job of it." And then he told her what he knew.

"In the kingdom where we now find ourselves, there lives a princess who is terribly clever. She has read all the newspapers that exist in the world and forgotten them again, that's how clever she is. The other day she was sitting on the throne—and they say that's not especially amusing—and she happened to hum a song, the one that goes: Why shouldn't I marry? 'You know, there's something to that,' she said, and then she decided to get married. But she wants a husband who knows how to respond when spoken to, someone who won't just stand there looking elegant, because that's much too boring. So she gathered all her ladies-in-waiting, and when they heard what she had in mind, they were quite pleased. 'We like that!' they said. 'We were thinking about that very thing the other day.' You can trust me that every word I say is true," said the crow. "I have a tame sweetheart who is allowed to move freely through the palace, and she has told me everything."

Of course his sweetheart was also a crow, for crows seek their equals, and they are always crows.

"The newspapers were printed at once with a border of hearts and the monogram of the princess. There you could read that any good-looking young man was welcome to come up to the palace and speak with the princess. The one who spoke so it was clear that he felt at home, the man who spoke the best, was the one the princess would take as her husband. Oh yes!" said the crow. "You can believe what I tell you. It's as true as I'm sitting here. Men came swarming, there was a great hubbub and commotion, but with no success, either on the first day or the second. They could all speak well when they were out on the street, but as soon as they entered the palace gates and saw the Royal Guards dressed in silver, and the footmen dressed in gold standing along the stairs, and the great illuminated halls, then they were struck dumb. And if they stood in front of the throne where the princess sat, they couldn't think of a thing to say except for the last word she had uttered, and she didn't care to hear herself repeated. It was as if the men's bellies had been filled with snuff inside the palace, and they fell into a daze until they came back out to the street. Then they had no trouble talking. A line stretched from the city gates all the way to the palace. I went there to see it myself!" said the crow. "They grew hungry and thirsty, but from the palace they received not so much as a glass of lukewarm water. Some of the cleverest did bring sandwiches along, but they refused to share with their neighbor. They thought: 'Let him look hungry, then the princess won't choose him!'"

"But what about Kai, little Kai?" asked Gerda. "When did he arrive? Was he there in the crowd?"

"Give me time! Give me time! I'm just getting to him! It was on the third day that a little man arrived, without a horse or carriage, and marched quite boldly right up to the palace. His eyes shone like yours, he had lovely long hair, but his clothes were in tatters."

"That was Kai!" Gerda rejoiced. "Oh, at last I've found him!" And she clapped her hands.

"He had a little knapsack on his back," said the crow.

"No, that must have been his sled," said Gerda, "because he left with his sled."

"That could be," said the crow. "I didn't look very closely. But I know from my tame sweetheart that when he went through the palace gates and saw the Royal Guards dressed in silver, and the footmen dressed in gold standing along the stairs, he wasn't the least bit daunted. He nodded and said to them, 'It must be boring to stand on the stairs. I'd much rather go inside.' There the halls were ablaze with light. There the Privy Councilors and Excellencies walked around barefoot, carrying gold platters. It was enough to intimidate anyone! The creaking of his boots was terribly loud, and yet he wasn't afraid."

"It must have been Kai!" said Gerda. "I know that he had new boots. I've heard them creak in Grandmother's parlor."

"And creak they did!" said the crow. "He boldly walked right up to the princess who was sitting on a pearl as big as a spinning wheel. Grouped all around were the ladies-in-waiting with their maids and the maids of their maids, and all the chamberlains with their servants and the servants of their servants, who all have pages. And the closer they stood to the door, the more haughty they looked. The page of the servants' servants, who always wears slippers, was almost unbearable to look at, so haughty did he seem, standing in the doorway."

"That must have been terrible!" said little Gerda. "And yet Kai won the princess."

"If I weren't a crow, I would have won her myself, even though I'm engaged. He supposedly spoke as well as I do when I speak crow-speak. That's what my tame sweetheart told me. He was bold and charming. He hadn't come as a suitor but simply to listen to the wisdom of the princess, which he found to his liking, and she in turn found him to her liking."

"I'm sure of it! That was Kai!" said Gerda. "He was so clever. He could do his figures in his head, even with fractions. Oh, won't you take me inside the palace?"

"Well, that's easy enough for you to say," said the crow. "But how are we going to do that? I'll have to talk to my tame sweetheart about it; surely she can advise us. Because I must tell you that a little girl like you will never be granted permission to enter in the usual manner."

"Oh yes, I will," said Gerda. "When Kai finds out that I'm here, he'll come out at once to get me."

"Wait for me by the stile over there," said the crow as he wagged his head and then flew off.

It was after dark before the crow came back. "Caw, caw!" he said. "I bring you many greetings from my sweetheart. And here's a scrap of bread for you; she took it from the kitchen. There's plenty of bread, and you must be hungry. It's not possible for you to enter the palace. You're barefoot, after all. The guards dressed in silver and the footmen dressed in gold would never permit it. But don't cry, we'll find a way to get you in. My sweetheart knows of a little back stairway that leads to the bedchamber, and she knows where to find the key."

So they went into the garden, along the great promenade, where one leaf fell after another. And when the lights in the palace were put out, one after another, the crow led little Gerda over to a back door that stood ajar.

Oh, how Gerda's heart was pounding with fear and longing! She felt as if she were about to do something wrong, but all she wanted was to find out whether it was little Kai. Oh yes, it had to be him. She could see so vividly his clever eyes, his long hair. She could see so clearly the way he smiled when they sat under the roses back home. Surely he would be glad to see her, to hear what a long way she had come for his sake, to know how sad they all were at home when he didn't come back. Oh, she felt both fear and joy.

Then they were on the stairs. A little lamp was burning atop a cupboard. In the middle of the room stood the tame crow, turning her head to all sides and looking at Gerda, who curtsied as Grandmother had taught her.

"My fiancé has spoken so highly of you, my dear," said the tame crow. "Your life story, your vita, as it's called, is also most touching. If you take the lamp, I will lead the way. We're taking the direct route because then we won't meet anyone."

"I think someone is coming right behind us," said Gerda, as

something rushed past her. The shadows on the walls looked like horses with flowing manes and slender legs, hunter boys, and gentlemen and ladies on horseback.

"Those are just dreams," said the crow. "They've come to gather the thoughts of the royal personages for the hunt. All the better, because now you can observe them in bed. But if you win honor and nobility, I expect you to show a grateful heart."

"That's no way to talk!" said the crow from the forest.

Then they entered the first hall. Its walls were adorned with rose-colored satin and artificial flowers. Here the dreams had already rushed past them, but they moved so fast that Gerda had no chance to see the royal personages. One hall was more magnificent than the other. Oh yes, it could be quite intimidating! And then they were in the bedchamber. The ceiling looked like an enormous palm tree with fronds of glass, precious glass. In the center of the room, hanging from a thick stalk of gold, were two beds, each of which looked like a lily. One was white, and in it lay the princess. The other was red, and that was the one in which Gerda was to look for little Kai. She bent back one of the red leaves and then she saw the nape of a brown neck. Oh, it was Kai! She called his name quite loudly, holding the lamp over him. The dreams came rushing back on horseback, returning to the room. He awoke, turned his head . . . It was not little Kai.

The prince looked like Kai only from the back of his neck, but young and handsome he certainly was. And from the white lily-bed the princess peeked out and asked what was going on. Then little Gerda began to weep and told them the whole story and about everything the crows had done for her.

"You poor little thing!" said the prince and princess, and they praised the crows and said that they weren't the least bit angry with them, although they should never do it again. This time, however, they would be given a reward.

"Do you want to fly away free?" asked the princess. "Or would you like a permanent position as the court crows, and be welcome to all the scraps in the kitchen?"

And both crows curtsied and asked for a permanent position, because they were thinking of their old age and said, "It would be good to have something for our golden years," as they put it.

And the prince climbed out of his bed to let Gerda sleep in it, because that was the least he could do. She folded her little hands and thought: "How good the people and animals are." Then she closed her eyes and slept blissfully. All the dreams came flying back, and this time they looked like God's angels. They were pulling a little sled, and on it sat Kai, nodding. But it was only a dream, and that's why it vanished as soon as she awoke.

The next day she was dressed from head to toe in silk and velvet. She was invited to stay at the palace and live comfortably, but she wanted only a little carriage with a horse, and a pair of little boots. Then she would be off again into the wide world to look for Kai.

And she was given both the boots and a muff. She was dressed exquisitely, and when she was ready to leave, a new carriage made of pure gold was waiting at the door. It bore the coat of arms of the prince and princess, shining like a star. The coachman, footmen, and postilions—there were postilions too—wore gold crowns. The prince and princess helped her into the carriage and wished her the best of luck. The forest crow, who was now married, accompanied her for the first fifteen miles. He sat beside her because he couldn't bear to ride backward. The other crow stood at the gate and flapped her wings. She wasn't coming along because she had been suffering from headaches ever since she had been given a permanent position and had too much to eat. The inside of the coach was lined with sugar pastries and on the seat were fruits and gingersnaps.

"Farewell! Farewell!" called the prince and princess, and little Gerda wept and the crow wept. That's how the first miles passed. Then the crow also bid her farewell, and that was the saddest leave-taking of all. He flew up into a tree and flapped his black wings as long as he could see the carriage, which gleamed like the bright sun.

FIFTH STORY
THE LITTLE ROBBER GIRL

They drove through the dark forest, but the coach shone like a torch. It dazzled the eyes of the robbers, and that was something they couldn't abide.

"It's gold! It's gold!" they shouted as they rushed forward, seized hold of the horses, killed the little postilions, the coachman, and the footmen and then yanked little Gerda out of the carriage.

"She's plump, she's charming, she's been fattened up on nut-meats!" said the old robber hag, who had a long bristly beard and eyebrows that hung down into her eyes. "She's as nice as a fat little lamb! Oh, how delicious she's going to taste!" And then she pulled out her gleaming knife, which shone so brightly that it was terrifying.

"Ow!" said the hag all at once. She had been bitten on the ear by her own little daughter, who was hanging on her back and was so wild and naughty that it was sheer delight. "You odious child!" said the mother, and then she didn't have time to slaughter Gerda.

"I want her to play with me," said the little robber girl. "She has to give me her muff and her beautiful dress and sleep with me in my bed." Then she bit her mother again so the robber hag leaped into the air and spun around, and all the robbers laughed and said, "Look how she's dancing with her brat!"

"I want to ride in the carriage," said the little robber girl, and she insisted on having her way, because she was so spoiled and stubborn. She and Gerda got into the carriage and then they drove over stumps and thickets, deeper into the forest. The little robber girl was as big as Gerda, but stronger, with wide shoulders and a dark complexion. Her eyes were quite black; they looked almost sad. She put her arm around little Gerda's waist and said, "I won't let them slaughter you as long as you don't make me angry! You're a princess, aren't you?"

"No," said little Gerda and told her all about what she had been through and how much she loved little Kai.

The robber girl gave her a somber look, nodded her head slightly, and said, "I won't let them slaughter you even if you do make me angry; I'll do it myself!" And then she dried Gerda's eyes and tucked both of her hands into the beautiful muff, which was so soft and so warm.

Then the carriage came to a halt. They were in the middle of the courtyard at the robbers' castle. It was cracked from top to bottom. Ravens and crows were flying out of the open crevices, and huge bulldogs, each of which looked as if it could swallow a person whole, were leaping high into the air. But they didn't bark, because that was forbidden.

Inside the vast, ancient, soot-filled hall a great fire was blazing in the middle of the stone floor. Smoke drifted along the ceiling, trying to find its way out. Soup was cooking in a big copper kettle, and hares and rabbits were turning on spits.

"Tonight you'll sleep here with me and all my little animals," said the robber girl. They ate and drank and then went over to a corner where hay and blankets had been spread out. Overhead on lathes and beams sat almost a hundred doves that all seemed to be asleep, although they stirred a bit when the little girls approached.

"They're all mine," said the little robber girl as she grabbed the nearest one, held it by its legs, and shook it so it flapped its wings. "Kiss it!" she cried and fluttered it in Gerda's face. "There sit my wood rascals!" she went on, pointing to a hole high up on the wall that had several bars fastened over it. "They're wood rascals, those two doves! They'd fly off in an instant if they weren't kept properly locked up. And here's my old sweetheart Bey!" She tugged on the antler of a reindeer who was tethered with a copper ring around his neck. "We have to keep him penned up too or he'd run away. Every single evening I tickle him on the neck with my sharp knife. He's so scared of it!" And the little girl pulled a long knife out of a crack in the wall and let it slide along the reindeer's throat. The poor animal kicked his legs, and the robber girl laughed. Then she pulled Gerda along to bed.

"Do you take your knife to bed with you?" asked Gerda, giving it a rather frightened look.

"I always sleep with a knife," said the little robber girl. "You never know what might come along. But tell me again what you told me before about little Kai and why you've gone out into the wide world." And Gerda told her everything from the beginning, and the wood doves cooed up above in their cage, while the other doves slept. The little robber girl put one arm around Gerda's neck, held the knife in her other hand, and slept so noisily that you could clearly hear her. But Gerda couldn't sleep a wink; she didn't know whether she was going to live or die. The robbers sat around the fire, singing and drinking, and the robber hag was turning somersaults. Oh, what an awful sight that was for the little girl!

Then the wood doves said, "Coo, coo! we've seen little Kai. A white hen was carrying his sled. He was sitting in the Snow Queen's carriage, which raced low over the forest when we lay in our nest. She blew on all the fledglings, and they all died except the two of us. Coo, coo!"

"What's that you're saying up there?" called Gerda. "Where did the Snow Queen go? Do you know anything about it?"

"She must have gone to Lapland, where there's always snow and ice. Just ask the reindeer who's tethered to the rope."

"There's ice and snow, it's so blissful and grand!" said the reindeer. "There you can bound freely through the great sparkling valleys! That's where the Snow Queen has her summer tent, but her permanent castle is up near the North Pole, on the island called Spitsbergen."

"Oh Kai, little Kai," sighed Gerda.

"You'd better lie still now," said the robber girl. "Or I'll stick my knife in your belly!"

In the morning Gerda told her everything that the wood doves had said. The little robber girl gave her a somber look but nodded her head and said, "Never mind! Never mind! Do you know where Lapland is?" she asked the reindeer.

"Who would know better than I?" said the animal, and his eyes sparkled. "That's where I was born and raised, that's where I bounded through the snowfields."

"Listen to me!" said the robber girl to Gerda. "You can see that all our menfolk are gone, but Mother is still here, and she's going to stay. But later in the morning she'll take a drink from that big bottle and then have herself a little nap. That's when I'm going to do something for you." And she jumped out of bed, threw her arms around her mother's neck, tugged on her beard, and said, "My own sweet goat, good morning!" And her mother pinched her nose until it turned red and blue, but it was all done with affection.

When her mother had taken a drink from her bottle and lain down for a little nap, the robber girl went over to the reindeer and said, "I have a great urge to tickle you many more times with my sharp knife, because you're so amusing when I do that, but never mind. I'm going to untie your rope and help you outside so you can run off to Lapland. But you must be quick about it and take this little girl to the Snow Queen's castle, where her playmate is. I'm sure you've heard her story. She talked loud enough, and you're always eavesdropping!"

The reindeer leaped for joy. The robber girl picked up little Gerda and took the precaution of tying her on. She even gave her a little cushion to sit on. "Never mind," she said. "Here are your fur boots, because it will be cold. I'm keeping the muff; it's much too charming! But you're not going to freeze. Here are my mother's big knitted mittens. They'll reach all the way up to your elbows. Stick your hands in! Now your hands look just like my hideous mother's!"

And Gerda wept with joy.

"I don't like your sniveling!" said the little robber girl. "Try and look pleased. And here are two loaves of bread and a ham so you won't starve." Everything was tied onto the reindeer's back. The little robber girl opened the door and lured all the big dogs inside. Then she sliced through the rope with her knife and said to the reindeer, "Run! But take good care of the little girl!"

And Gerda stretched out her hands in the big knitted mittens toward the robber girl to bid her farewell. Then the reindeer flew off over thickets and stumps, through the great forest, over marshes and steppes, as fast as he could go. The wolves howled and the ravens shrieked. "Crackle! Crackle!" said the sky. It looked as if it had a nosebleed.

"Those are my old Northern lights," said the reindeer. "Look how they shine!" And then he kept on running, night and day. The loaves of bread were eaten, the ham was too, and then they were in Lapland.

SIXTH STORY
THE LAPP WOMAN AND THE FINN WOMAN

They stopped at a little house. It was a pitiful hovel. The roof reached all the way to the ground, and the door was so low that the family had to crawl on their bellies to go in or out. No one was home except an old Lapp woman who was frying fish over a whale-oil lamp. And the reindeer told her Gerda's whole story, but first he told his own, because he thought it was much more important, and Gerda was so worn out from the cold that she couldn't even speak.

"Oh, you poor things!" said the Lapp woman. "And you still have a long way to go. You have to travel hundreds of miles through Finnmark, because that's where the Snow Queen lives, out in the country, burning blue lights every single evening. I'm going to write a few words on a dried cod, because I have no paper, and then I'll give it to you to take along to the Finn woman up there. She can give you better directions than I can."

After Gerda had warmed up and was given something to eat and drink, the Lapp woman wrote a few words on a dried cod, told Gerda to take good care of it, tied her firmly to the reindeer again, and off he went. "Crackle! Crackle!" it said up in the sky. All night long the loveliest blue Northern lights blazed, and then they arrived in Finnmark and knocked on the Finn woman's chimney because she had no door.

It was so hot inside that even the Finn woman walked around almost naked. She was short and quite grimy-looking. She un-buttoned little Gerda's clothes at once and pulled off her knitted mittens and boots, because otherwise she would have been too hot. She put a piece of ice on top of the reindeer's head and then read what was written on the dried cod. She read it three times until she knew it by heart and then put the fish into her cooking pot since it was edible, after all, and she never wasted anything.

The reindeer told first his own story and then little Gerda's, and the Finn woman blinked her wise eyes but didn't say a word.

"You're so clever," said the reindeer. "I know that you can tie up all the winds of the earth with a thread. When the skipper loosens one knot he has a good wind; if he loosens another, a sharp wind blows; and if he loosens the third and fourth, then a storm rages so fiercely that the forests topple. Won't you give this little girl a potion to lend her the strength of twelve men so she can vanquish the Snow Queen?"

"The strength of twelve men," said the Finn woman. "Yes, that should be enough." And then she went over to a shelf, took down a big rolled-up hide, and spread it out. Strange-looking letters were printed on it, and the Finn woman began reading so intently that sweat poured down her forehead.

But the reindeer again pleaded earnestly for little Gerda. And Gerda, her eyes full of tears, gave the Finn woman such an imploring look that the woman began blinking once more and drew the reindeer over to a corner to whisper to him as she put fresh ice on his head.

"It's true that little Kai is with the Snow Queen. He thinks everything there is to his taste and liking, and he believes that it's the best place in the world, but that's because he has a splinter of glass in his heart and a tiny speck of glass in his eye. They have to be taken out, otherwise he will never be a human being, and the Snow Queen will keep her hold over him."

"But can't you give little Gerda a potion to drink so she will gain power over all that?"

"I can't give her any greater power than she already has. Don't you see how great it is? Don't you see how people and animals want to serve her, how she has come so far in the world in her bare feet? She must not learn of her power from us. It resides in her heart, it lies in the fact that she is a sweet and innocent child. If she can't reach the Snow Queen on her own and remove the glass from little Kai, there's nothing we can do to help her. Ten miles from here is the edge of the Snow Queen's garden. You can carry the little girl that far. Set her down near the big bush with the red berries in the snow. Don't chitter-chatter for long, and hurry back here!" Then the Finn woman lifted little Gerda onto the reindeer's back, who set off as fast as he could.

"Oh, I forgot my boots! I forgot my knitted mittens!" cried little Gerda. She could feel the sting of the cold, but the reindeer didn't dare stop. He ran until he came to the big bush with the red berries. That's where he set Gerda down and kissed her on the lips, and big shiny tears ran down the animal's cheeks. Then he ran back as fast as he could. There stood poor Gerda, with no shoes, with no gloves, in the middle of the terrible, ice-cold Finnmark.

She set off as fast as she could. Then a whole regiment of snowflakes appeared, but they didn't fall from the sky, which was quite clear and glowing with the Northern lights. The snowflakes were running along the ground, and the closer they came, the bigger they grew. Gerda remembered well how big and artful they had seemed when she looked at the snowflakes through the magnifying glass, but this time they were truly enormous and terrifying. They were alive. They were the Snow Queen's advance troops. They had the strangest shapes. Some looked like big horrid porcupines, others like giant knots of snakes with writhing heads; still others looked like fat little bears with their fur sticking out all over. All of them were dazzling white, all of them were living snowflakes.

Then little Gerda said the Lord's Prayer, and the cold was so great that she could see her own breath. It came out of her mouth like a cloud of smoke. Her breath got thicker and thicker, forming into bright little angels that grew bigger and bigger as they touched the ground. All of them wore helmets on their heads and carried spears and shields in their hands. There were more and more of them, and by the time Gerda had finished saying the Lord's Prayer, there was an entire legion around her. They thrust their spears at the fearsome snowflakes, which shattered into hundreds of pieces, and little Gerda continued on, quite safe and undaunted. The angels patted her feet and hands, and then she didn't feel the cold as much. She walked briskly toward the Snow Queen's castle.

But first we must see how Kai is doing. It's true that he wasn't thinking about little Gerda, and least of all that she might be standing outside the castle.

THE SEVENTH STORY
WHAT HAPPENED AT THE SNOW QUEEN'S
CASTLE AND WHAT HAPPENED AFTERWARD

The castle walls were made of drifting snow and the windows and doors of razor-sharp winds. There were over a hundred halls, all of them shaped by the drifting snow. The largest stretched for many miles. All of them were lit by the bright Northern lights, and they were so vast, so empty, so icy cold, and so glittering. Never was there any merriment, not so much as a little bear-dance when a gale blew in and the polar bears would walk on their hind legs to show off their elegant manners. Never a little card party with snout-slapping and paw-tugging. Never a little coffee klatsch held by the white fox ladies. Empty, vast, and cold were the halls of the Snow Queen. The Northern lights flared so precisely that it was possible to count when they would be at their height and when they were at their lowest. In the middle of the endless, empty snow hall was a frozen lake. It was cracked into thousands of pieces, but each piece was exactly like all the others, and that was quite a feat. In the center sat the Snow Queen whenever she was home, and then she would say that she was sitting on the Mirror of Reason, that it was one of a kind and the best thing in the world.

Little Kai was quite blue with cold; in fact, he was almost black, yet he didn't notice because she had kissed the shivers out of him, and his heart was practically a lump of ice. He was dragging around several sharp, flat pieces of ice, which he placed in every imaginable way, trying to make a pattern out of them. It was just like when the rest of us take little wooden tiles and put them together to make shapes, called the Chinese puzzle game. Kai was also making shapes, the most ingenious of all. It was the Ice Game of Reason. To his eyes the shapes were quite splendid and of the utmost importance— that was the work of the speck of glass in his eye! He created whole shapes that formed words, but he never could figure out how to form the one word he was looking for, the word *eternity*. And the Snow Queen had said, "If you can create that shape for me, then you will be your own master, and I will give you the whole world and a pair of new skates." But he couldn't do it.

"Now I've got to dash off to the warm countries," said the Snow Queen. "I want to go out and peer into the black cauldrons." She meant the fire-spurting mountains of Etna and Vesuvius, as they're called. "I need to whitewash them a bit. It's only proper; it would look so good on top of all those lemons and grapes!" And then the Snow Queen flew off, and Kai was left all alone in the vast, empty ice hall that went on for miles. He looked at the pieces of ice and thought and thought so hard that his mind groaned. So stiff and still did he sit that you'd almost think he had frozen to death.

That's when little Gerda entered the castle through the huge portal, which was made of razor-sharp winds. But she said an evening prayer, and then the winds died down as if they wanted to sleep, and she stepped inside the vast, empty, cold halls. Then she

saw Kai. She recognized him, she threw her arms around his neck,
holding him tight and crying, "Kai! Sweet little Kai! I've found
you at last!"

But he sat there quite motionless, stiff and cold. Then little Gerda
wept hot tears. They fell on his breast, they seeped into his heart,
they thawed out the lump of ice and dissolved the little shard of
mirror inside. He looked at her, and she sang the hymn:

> "In the valley where roses grow wild,
> There we will speak to the Christ child!"

Then Kai burst into tears. He wept so hard that the speck of mirror
rolled out of his eye. He recognized her and rejoiced. "Gerda!
Sweet little Gerda! Where have you been all this time? And where
have I been?" He looked all around. "How cold it is here! How
empty and vast it is here!" He hugged Gerda tight, and she laughed
and cried with joy. It was so blissful that even the pieces of ice
began to dance around them with joy. When the pieces grew tired
and lay down to rest, they were lying in precisely the shape of the
letters the Snow Queen had told Kai to create so that he would be
his own master and she would give him the whole world and a
new pair of skates.

Gerda kissed his cheeks, and they bloomed. She kissed his eyes,
and they shone like her own. She kissed his hands and feet, and he
grew strong and healthy. The Snow Queen was welcome to come
home: His release lay spelled out before them in glittering pieces
of ice.

And they took each other by the hand and wandered out of the
enormous castle. They talked about Grandmother and about the
roses up on the roof, and wherever they went, the winds lay
perfectly still and the sun broke through. When they reached the
bush with the red berries, the reindeer stood there, waiting. He
had brought along another young reindeer whose udder was full,
and she gave the children her warm milk and kissed them on the
lips. Then they carried Kai and Gerda first to the Finn woman's
house, where they warmed themselves in the hot room and received
directions for their homeward journey; then on to the Lapp woman,
who had sewn new clothes for them and made ready her sleigh.

And the reindeer and his young companion ran alongside and accompanied them to the very border of the country, where the first green sprouts were peeking out. That's where they bid farewell to the reindeer and the Lapp woman. "Farewell!" they all said. And the first little birds began to chirp, the forest had green buds, and out of the woods, riding a magnificent horse that Gerda recognized (it had been harnessed to the golden carriage), came a young girl with a shimmering red cap on her head and pistols in front. It was the little robber girl who had grown tired of staying home and was now on her way north, though later, if it didn't please her, she might head for other parts. She recognized Gerda at once, Gerda recognized her, and they both rejoiced.

"You're a strange fellow, the way you tramp around," she said to little Kai. "I wonder if you really deserve to have someone running to the ends of the earth for your sake!"

But Gerda patted her on the cheek and asked about the prince and princess.

"They've gone off to foreign lands," said the robber girl.

"What about the crow?" asked little Gerda.

"Oh, the crow is dead," she replied. "His tame sweetheart is a widow now, and she walks around with a scrap of black woolen yarn on her leg. She moans so pitifully, and it's all nonsense! But tell me how things have gone for you, and how you managed to find him."

So Gerda and Kai both told her the story.

"Well, snip-snap-snurra-bassalurra!" said the robber girl, and she took them both by the hand and promised that if she ever passed through their city, she would come to visit them. Then she rode off into the wide world, but Kai and Gerda walked hand in hand. And as they walked, a lovely spring arrived with flowers and greenery. The church bells chimed, and they recognized the tall towers and the big city. This was where they lived. They walked through the city and over to Grandmother's door, up the stairs, into the room, where everything stood exactly as it had before. And the clock went, "Tick, tick!" and its hands were moving. But as they stepped through the door, they noticed that they had grown up. The roses on the eaves of the roof were blossoming in the open windows, and there stood their little childhood stools. Kai and

Gerda sat down on them and held each other's hands. They had forgotten all about the cold, empty splendor of the Snow Queen's castle as if it had been a bad dream. Grandmother was sitting in God's bright sunshine and reading aloud from the Bible: "Unless you become as little children, you shall not enter the kingdom of Heaven."

And Kai and Gerda looked into each other's eyes, and all of a sudden they understood the old hymn:

> "In the valley where roses grow wild,
> There we will speak to the Christ child!"

There they sat, two grown-ups, and yet they were children—children at heart—and it was summer. Warm, blissful summer.

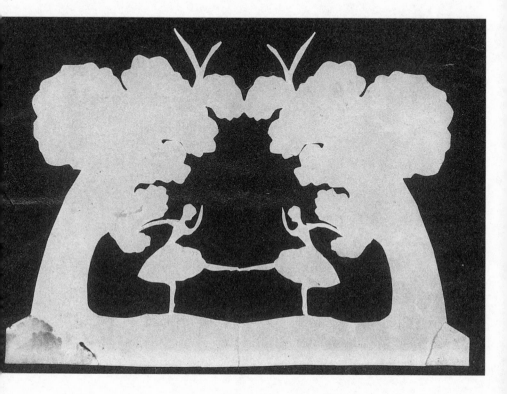

The Red Shoes

There was a little girl who was so delicate and charming, but in the summer she always had to go barefoot because she was poor. In the winter she wore big wooden clogs that made her little ankles turn quite red, and that was awful.

In the middle of the village lived old Mother Shoemaker. She sat and sewed as best she could, using old strips of red cloth to make a little pair of shoes. Quite clumsy they were, but well-intended, and the little girl was to have them. The little girl's name was Karen.

On the very day that her mother was buried, Karen was given the red shoes, and she wore them for the first time. Now, it's true that they weren't the proper shoes for mourning, but she didn't have any others, and so she wore them on her bare feet, walking behind the humble coffin made of straw.

All at once a grand old carriage appeared, and inside sat a grand old woman. She looked at the little girl and felt sorry for her. Then she said to the pastor, "Listen here, give me that little girl and I will be kind to her!"

Karen thought she said this because of her red shoes, but the old woman said they were awful, and they were burned, while Karen was dressed in nice, clean clothes. She had to learn to read and sew, and people said that she was charming, but the mirror said, "You are much more than charming, you're lovely!"

Then the queen happened to travel through the land, and she brought along her little daughter, who was a princess. People came flocking to the palace, and Karen was there too. The little princess stood in a window for all to see dressed in fine white clothes. She wore neither a train nor a golden crown, but she had lovely, red kidskin shoes. Of course they were much prettier than the ones that Mother Shoemaker had sewn for little Karen. But nothing in the world could compare with red shoes!

Then Karen was old enough to be confirmed. She was given new clothes and she was also to have new shoes. The rich shoemaker in town measured her little foot. This was at home in his own parlor, where big glass cupboards stood filled with elegant shoes and shiny boots. Everything looked charming, but the old woman didn't see well, so it gave her no pleasure. In the midst of all the shoes stood a pair of red ones just like the ones the princess had worn. How beautiful they were! The shoemaker said they had been sewn for the child of a count, but they didn't fit properly.

"They must be made of the finest leather," said the old woman. "How they shine!"

"Yes, how they shine!" said Karen. And they fit, so they were bought. But the old woman didn't know that they were red, because she would never have allowed Karen to be confirmed wearing red shoes, and yet she did.

Everyone looked at her feet. When she walked up the church aisle toward the chancel doorway, she thought even the old paintings on the crypts, those portraits of pastors and their wives wearing stiff collars and long black gowns, had fixed their eyes on her red shoes. And that was all she could think of when the pastor placed his hand on her head and spoke of the holy baptism, of the pact with God, and the fact that she should now be a good Christian. The organ played so solemnly, the children sang so beautifully, and the old cantor sang too, but Karen thought only of her red shoes.

By that afternoon the old woman had heard from everyone that the shoes were red, and she said how dreadful that was. It wasn't the least bit proper. From that day on, whenever Karen went to church, she would always wear black shoes, even if they were old.

The following Sunday was her first communion, and Karen looked at the black shoes, she looked at the red ones—and then she looked at the red ones again and put them on.

It was lovely sunny weather. Karen and the old woman walked along the path through the grain fields where it was rather dusty.

At the church door stood an old soldier with a crutch and a long, odd-looking beard that was more red than white; in fact, it was red. He bowed all the way to the ground and asked the old woman whether he might wipe off her shoes. Karen stretched out her little foot too. "Oh look, what lovely dancing shoes!" said the soldier. "Stay on tight when you dance!" Then he slapped his hand on the soles.

The old woman gave the soldier a little *skilling* and then went with Karen into the church.

Everyone inside looked at Karen's red shoes; all the paintings looked at them too. And when Karen knelt before the altar and put the golden chalice to her lips, she thought only of the red shoes. They seemed to be swimming around in the chalice before her, and she forgot to sing the hymn, she forgot to say the Lord's Prayer.

Then everyone left the church, and the old woman climbed into her carriage. As Karen lifted her foot to climb in after her, the old soldier who was standing close by said, "Oh look, what lovely dancing shoes!" And Karen couldn't help herself, she had to take a few dance steps. As soon as she started, her feet kept on dancing. It was as if the shoes had taken control. She danced around the corner of the church, she couldn't stop herself. The coachman had to run after and grab her, and he lifted her into the carriage, but her feet kept on dancing and she kicked hard at the kind old woman. Finally they managed to take off the shoes, and her feet stopped moving.

At home the shoes were put in a cupboard, but Karen couldn't help looking at them.

Then the old woman fell ill, and they said she wouldn't live long. She needed someone to nurse and tend her, and who should do it but Karen? But over in town there was to be a great ball, and Karen was invited. She looked at the old woman, who didn't have long to live, after all. She looked at the red shoes, and she didn't think there was any sin in that. She put on the red shoes. Why shouldn't she? And then she went to the ball and began to dance.

But when she wanted to turn right, the shoes danced to the left, and when she wanted to move up the floor, the shoes danced down the floor, down the stairs, along the street, and out the town gate. Dance she did, and dance she must, right out into the dark forest.

Then she saw a light overhead among the trees, and she thought it must be the moon, because it had a face, but it was the old soldier with the red beard. He sat there nodding and said, "Oh look, what lovely dancing shoes!"

Then Karen was horrified and tried to take off the red shoes, but they wouldn't come off. She tore off her stockings, but the shoes had grown onto her feet; dance she did and dance she must, over field and meadow, in rain and in sunshine, night and day, but nighttime was the most terrible of all.

She danced into the open churchyard, but the dead weren't dancing. They had better things to do than dance. She wanted to sit down on the pauper's grave where bitter tansy grew, but for her there was no peace or rest. And when she danced toward the open church door, she saw an angel there in long white robes, with wings that reached from his shoulders to the ground. His face was stern and solemn, and in his hand he held a sword, gleaming and wide.

"Dance you shall!" he said. "Dance in your red shoes until you turn pale and cold! Until your skin shrivels up like a mummy's! Dance from door to door. And wherever proud and vain children live, you will knock so they hear and fear you! Dance you shall, dance—!"

"Have mercy!" cried Karen. But she didn't hear what the angel replied, because her shoes carried her through the gate, out to the field, across the road, and along the path, and always she had to keep dancing.

Early one morning she danced past a door she knew quite well. Inside a hymn could be heard, and they carried out a coffin that was adorned with flowers. Then she knew that the old woman was dead, and she felt as if she had now been forsaken by everyone and cursed by the angel of God.

Dance she did, and dance she must, dance into the dark night. Her shoes carried her over thickets and stumps, her feet were worn bloody. She danced across the heath to a lonely little house. She knew that this was where the executioner lived. She tapped her finger on the windowpane and said, "Come out! Come out! I can't come inside, because I'm dancing!"

And the executioner said, "Don't you know who I am? I chop off the heads of evil people, and I can feel my ax is trembling!"

"Don't chop off my head," said Karen. "Because then I won't be able to repent my sin. But chop off my feet with the red shoes!"

Then she confessed to her sin, and the executioner chopped off her feet with the red shoes. But the shoes kept dancing with the little feet across the fields and into the deep forest.

And he carved wooden feet and crutches for her, taught her a hymn that sinners always sing, and she kissed the hand that had wielded the ax and set out across the heath.

"Now I've suffered enough for those red shoes," she said. "Now I'm going to church so they can see me." And she walked as fast as she could toward the church door, but when she got there, the red shoes were dancing in front of her. She was horrified and turned away.

All week long she was sad and wept many bitter tears, but when Sunday came, she said, "All right! Now I've suffered and struggled enough! I should think that I'm just as good as many of those people sitting so proudly inside the church." Then she set off quite boldly, but she got no farther than to the gate when she saw the red shoes dancing in front of her. She was horrified and turned away, repenting her sin with all her heart.

She went over to the parsonage and asked if she might be taken into service there. She would work hard and do everything she could. She had no wish for wages; all she asked for was a roof over her head and permission to stay with good people. The pastor's wife felt sorry for her and gave her a position. And she was hardworking and thoughtful. Quietly she would sit and listen when the pastor read aloud from the Bible in the evening. All the children were very fond of her, but whenever they spoke of adornments and finery and being as lovely as a queen, she would shake her head.

The next Sunday they all went to church and they asked if she would like to come along, but with tears in her eyes she looked sadly at her crutches. Then the others went to hear God's Word while she went alone into her tiny room. It was only big enough for a bed and a chair. There she sat with her hymnbook. As she began reading with a pious heart, the wind carried the tones of the organ from the church to her. She raised her tear-stained face and said, "Oh, help me, God!"

Then the sun shone so bright, and right in front of her stood the angel of God in the white robes, the one she had seen that night at the church door. He was no longer holding a sharp sword but a lovely green bough that was covered with roses. He touched it to the ceiling, which raised up high, and at the spot he had touched shone a golden star. He touched the walls and they moved outward. She saw the organ that was playing; she saw the old paintings of the pastors and their wives. The congregation was sitting in the carved pews and singing from their hymnals.

The church itself had come home to the poor girl in the tiny, cramped room, or perhaps she had gone to the church. She was sitting in a pew with the others from the parsonage. When they finished the hymn and looked up, they nodded and said, "It was right for you to come, Karen."

"It was God's mercy," she said.

The organ soared, and the children's voices in the choir sounded gentle and lovely. The bright, warm sunshine streamed through the window, reaching the church pew where Karen sat. Her heart was so filled with sunlight, with peace and joy, that it burst. Her soul flew on the sunlight to God, and no one asked about the red shoes.

The Shepherdess and the Chimney Sweep

Have you ever seen a very old wooden cupboard, all black with age and carved with curlicues and foliage? That's exactly the kind that stood in the parlor. It was inherited from Great-Grandmother and carved with roses and tulips from top to bottom. It had the strangest curlicues and in among them poked out tiny stag heads with jagged antlers, but in the middle of the cupboard a whole man had been carved. He was certainly ridiculous to look at, and smirk he certainly did; you couldn't call it laughing. He had goat legs, tiny horns on his forehead, and a long beard. The children in the parlor always called him Billygoat-Leg-Field-Marshal-Brigadier-General-Commander-Sergeant, because it was a hard name to say, and there aren't many who have such a title. And to carve him like that was certainly a feat. Yet there he was! He was always looking at the table under the mirror, because that's where an elegant little shepherdess made of porcelain stood. Her shoes were gilded, her gown charmingly tucked up with a red rose, and she also had a golden hat and shepherd's crook. She was lovely. Right next to her stood a little chimney sweep, as black as coal, yet also made of porcelain. He was just as clean and handsome as anyone else. He was just pretending to be a chimney sweep. The porcelain-maker could just as well have made him a prince, because it made no difference!

There he stood, holding his ladder in such a charming manner, and with a face as pink and white as a girl's. That was actually a mistake because he should have been at least a little sooty. He stood quite close to the shepherdess. They had both been set where they stood, and since they had been placed there, they had become engaged. They suited each other, after all. They were young, they were made of the same porcelain, and they were both equally fragile.

Close to them stood another doll who was three times as big; it was an old Chinese man who could nod. He was also made of porcelain and said that he was grandfather to the little shepherdess, although he couldn't prove it. He claimed to have authority over her, and that's why he was nodding to Billygoat-Leg-Field-Marshal-Brigadier-General-Commander-Sergeant, who had asked for the hand of the little shepherdess.

"Now there's a husband for you," said the old Chinese man. "A husband that I think might well be made of mahogany. He can make you Mrs. Billygoat-Leg-Field-Marshal-Brigadier-General-Commander-Sergeant. He has a whole cupboard full of silverware, not to mention what he keeps in the secret cubbyholes."

"I don't want to live inside the dark cupboard," said the little shepherdess. "People say he has eleven porcelain wives in there."

"Then you can be the twelfth," said the Chinese man. "Tonight, as soon as the old cupboard starts to creak, you will be married, as surely as I'm Chinese!" Then he nodded his head and fell asleep.

But the little shepherdess wept and looked at her heart's beloved, the porcelain chimney sweep.

"I think I have to ask you to go with me out into the wide world," she said, "because we can't stay here."

"I'll do anything you like," said the little chimney sweep. "Let's leave right now. I feel certain I can support you with my profession."

"If only we could get down from this table," she said. "I won't be happy until we're out in the wide world."

And he reassured her and showed her where to put her little foot on the carved edges and the gilded foliage around the table leg. He also used his ladder, and then they reached the floor. But when they looked over at the old cupboard, there was such a commotion going on. All the carved deer were sticking their heads farther out, lifting their antlers, and turning their heads. Billygoat-Leg-Field-Marshal-Brigadier-General-Commander-Sergeant leaped high into the air and shouted to the old Chinese man, "They're running away! They're running away!"

Then they were both quite frightened and quickly jumped into the drawer beneath the window seat.

Inside lay three or four incomplete decks of cards and a little puppet theater that had been cobbled together. A play was being performed, and all the queens, both diamonds and hearts, clubs and spades, sat in the front row, fanning themselves with their tulips. Behind them stood all the jacks, displaying their heads both up and down, the way cards do. The play was about two lovers who couldn't be together, and the shepherdess cried because it was just like her own story.

"I can't stand any more of this!" she said. "I have to get out of this drawer!" But when they came out onto the floor and looked up at the table, the old Chinese man was awake and his body was wobbling all over, because his lower half was all of one piece.

"Here comes the old Chinese man!" shrieked the little shepherdess, and then she fell to her porcelain knees, she was in such despair.

"I have an idea," said the chimney sweep. "Why don't we crawl into the big potpourri jar that's standing in the corner? We can lie there with the roses and lavender and throw salt in his eyes when he comes near."

"I wouldn't recommend it," she said. "And besides, I happen to know that the Chinese man and the potpourri jar were once engaged, and a little affection always remains when you've been in love like that. No, we have no choice but to go out into the wide world!"

"Are you sure you have the courage to go with me out into the wide world?" asked the chimney sweep. "Have you considered how big it is, and that we'd never be able to come back here?"

"Yes, I have," she said.

The chimney sweep stared at her hard, and then he said, "My path goes through the chimney. Are you sure you have the courage to crawl with me through the woodstove, through both the belly and the pipe? Then we'll be into the chimney, and that's where I know how to use my skills. We'll climb so high that they won't be able to reach us, and at the very top is an opening that leads out to the wide world."

And he led her over to the door of the stove.

"How black it looks in there!" she said, but she followed him, both through the belly and through the pipe, where it was pitch-black night.

"Now we're inside the chimney," he said. "And look! Look! Up above the loveliest star is shining!"

It was a real star in the sky that was shining down on them, as if to show them the way. And they crawled and climbed. It was an awfully long way—higher and higher—but he lifted and helped her, he held on to her and showed her the best places to set her little porcelain feet. Then they reached all the way up to the very edge of the chimney and sat down on it, because they were tired, of course, and they had every right to be.

The sky and all its stars were overhead; all the rooftops in town were below them. They looked all around, far out into the world. The poor shepherdess had never dreamed it would be like this. She leaned her little head against the chimney sweep, and then she wept so hard that the gold came off her sash.

"It's too much," she said. "I can't stand it! The world is much too big. If only I were back on the little table under the mirror! I'll never be happy until I'm back there again. I've followed you out into the wide world, so now you can follow me home, if you're the least bit fond of me."

And the chimney sweep spoke sensibly to her, talking about the Chinese man and Billygoat-Leg-Field-Marshal-Brigadier-General-Commander-Sergeant, but she sobbed even harder and kissed her little chimney sweep. So he had no choice but to give in, even though it was a mistake.

And so they crawled with great difficulty back down the chimney; they crept through the pipe and the belly of the stove. It wasn't at all pleasant. Then they stood inside the dark stove. There they waited behind the door to find out what was going on in the room. It was very quiet. They peeked out. Oh, there in the middle of the floor lay the old Chinese man! He had fallen off the table when he tried to come after them, and now he was broken in three pieces. His whole back had come off in one piece, and his head had rolled into a corner. Billygoat-Leg-Field-Marshal-Brigadier-General-Commander-Sergeant stood where he always stood, thinking things over.

"How awful!" said the little shepherdess. "Old Grandfather has been smashed to bits, and it's all our fault. I'll never be able to endure it." And she started wringing her tiny little hands.

"He can still be mended," said the chimney sweep. "He can easily be mended. Don't take it so hard! When they glue on his back and put a strong rivet in his neck, he'll be as good as new and able to say many more unpleasant things to us."

"Do you think so?" she said. And then they climbed back up onto the table where they had stood before.

"Well, look how far we got!" said the chimney sweep. "We could have saved ourselves all that trouble."

"If only we had old Grandfather mended," said the shepherdess. "Do you think it's expensive?"

And mended he was. The family had his back glued on, and a strong rivet was put in the nape of his neck. He was as good as new, though he could no longer nod.

"You've certainly grown haughty since you were smashed to pieces!" said Billygoat-Leg-Field-Marshal-Brigadier-General-Commander-Sergeant. "But I don't think that's anything to brag about! Is she going to be mine or isn't she?"

The chimney sweep and the little shepherdess gave the old Chinese man such pleading looks. They were so afraid that he would nod, but he couldn't. And he felt uncomfortable telling a stranger that he had a permanent rivet in the nape of his neck. So the porcelain couple stayed together, and they blessed Grandfather's rivet and loved each other until they broke.

The Shadow

I n the hot countries the sun is certainly scorching! People turn as brown as mahogany. Why, in the hottest countries of all, they're even baked black. But it was to one of the moderately hot countries that a learned man had come from the cold lands. There he thought he could run around just as he did back home, but he soon discovered otherwise. He and all sensible people had to stay indoors. The shutters and doors stayed closed all day long. The whole building seemed to be asleep, or else no one was home. The narrow street with the tall buildings where he lived was also laid out so that it was flooded with sunlight from morning to evening. It was truly quite unbearable! The learned man from the cold countries—he was a young man, a clever man—felt like he was sitting in a blazing oven. It took a toll on him; he grew quite thin, and even his shadow shrank. It was smaller than it was back home; the sun took a toll on it too. Neither of them livened up until evening, when the sun went down.

That was a real pleasure to see. As soon as a candle was brought into the room, the shadow would stretch all the way up the wall. Why, it would even go along the ceiling, it made itself so long. It had to stretch out to regain its strength. The learned man would go out onto the balcony to stretch himself there, and as the stars appeared in the lovely clear sky, he seemed to come back to life. On all the balconies along the street—and in the warm countries every window has a balcony—people appeared, because they had to have air, even if they were used to being mahogany! Everything grew quite lively, both upstairs and down. Shoemakers and tailors, everybody moved out into the street. Tables and chairs appeared, and candles burned. Over a thousand candles were burning, and one person would talk while another sang. People strolled, carriages rolled past, mules walked along with a cling-a-ling because they were wearing bells. Bodies were buried with hymns, street urchins set off firecrackers, and the church bells rang. Oh yes, it was very lively down in the street. Only in one building, which stood right across from where the learned stranger was staying, was it completely silent. Yet someone did live there, because there were flowers on the balcony. They grew so wondrously in the heat of the sun, and that would be impossible unless they were watered, and someone must have watered them. People had to be living there. The door across the way also stood ajar in the evening, but it was dark inside, at least in the front room. From farther inside came the sound of music. The learned stranger thought the music was quite marvelous, but it could also be that he was imagining things, because he found everything in the warm countries to be marvelous. If only there weren't so much sun. The stranger's landlord said he didn't know who had rented the neighbor's house. He hadn't seen anyone, after all, and as for the music, he thought it was awfully dreary. "It sounds like someone is sitting there practicing a piece that he can't figure out. Always the same tune. 'I'm going to get it right!' he's probably saying, but he never does, no matter how much he plays."

One night the stranger awoke as he slept in front of the open balcony door. The drapes lifted with the wind, and he thought a peculiar glow was coming from the neighbor's balcony. All the flowers were gleaming like flames in the loveliest colors. In the midst of the flowers stood a slender, enchanting maiden, and she seemed to be glowing too. It actually hurt his eyes. Now he opened them as wide as he possibly could and roused himself from sleep. In a single bound he was on the floor. Very quietly he moved behind the drapes, but the maiden was gone and the glow was too. The flowers weren't shining at all but just stood there as nicely as they always did. The door was ajar, and from far inside came the sound of music so gentle and lovely that it prompted the sweetest of thoughts. Yet it was like a spell, and who lived there? Where was the real entrance? The whole ground floor was one shop after another, and people couldn't be constantly running through them.

One evening the stranger was sitting out on his balcony. In the room behind him a candle burned, so it was quite natural for his shadow to go over to the neighbor's wall. Yes, there it sat across the way, amid the flowers on the balcony. And whenever the stranger moved, the shadow moved too, because that's what a shadow does.

"I think my shadow is the only living thing to be seen over there!" said the learned man. "Look how nicely it's sitting among the flowers. The door is ajar. If only my shadow would be clever enough to go inside, take a look around, and then come and tell me what it saw. Yes, you'd be doing me a service," he said in jest. "Please step inside. Are you going or not?" Then he nodded to his shadow, and the shadow nodded back. "All right, go on, but don't get lost!" The stranger stood up, and over on the neighbor's balcony his shadow stood up too. The stranger turned, and his shadow turned too. Why, if anyone had been paying proper attention, he would have clearly seen the shadow go inside the half-open balcony door at the neighbor's house, just as the stranger went inside his own room, letting the long drapes fall behind him.

The next morning the learned man went out to drink his coffee and read the papers. "What's this?" he said as he stepped out into the sunshine. "I don't have any shadow! So it really must have gone over there last night, and it hasn't come back. How tedious that is!"

He was annoyed, not so much because the shadow was gone but because he knew there was another story about a man without a shadow. Everyone back home in the cold countries knew about it, and if the learned man now came and told his own story, they would say that he was just copying the other one and he shouldn't bother. So he decided not to say anything about it, and that was sensible.

In the evening he went back out onto his balcony. He had placed the candle quite rightly behind him, for he knew that a shadow always wants to have its master as a screen, but he couldn't lure it out. He made himself small, he made himself big, but there was no shadow. None appeared. He said, "Ahem, ahem!" but it did no good.

It was annoying, but in the warm countries everything grows very quickly. After a week had passed he noticed, to his great delight, that a new shadow had begun to grow outward from his feet whenever he was out in the sun. The roots must have stayed with him. After three weeks he had quite an acceptable shadow, which, when he set off for home in the northern countries, grew bigger and bigger during the journey, until at last it was twice as big and twice as long as it should be.

Then the learned man arrived home. He wrote books about what was true in the world, and about what was good and what was beautiful, and days passed into years. Many years passed.

Then one evening he was sitting in his parlor and he heard a faint knock on the door.

"Come in," he said, but no one did. Then he opened the door and before him stood such an exceedingly thin person that he was quite taken aback. And incidentally, the person was so remarkably well dressed that he had to be a distinguished man.

"With whom do I have the honor of speaking?" asked the learned man.

"Oh, I thought as much," said the elegant man. "You don't recognize me! I've become so solid that I've acquired real flesh and clothing. You probably never thought you'd see me in such top form. Don't you even recognize your old shadow? Well, I suppose you thought I'd never come back. Things have gone exceptionally well for me since I was last with you. I've become quite a wealthy man, in every respect. If I have to buy my freedom from service, I can!" And then he jingled a whole bundle of precious seals that hung from his watch, and he stuck his hand under the thick gold chain that he wore around his neck. Oh, how all his fingers glittered with diamond rings! And everything was genuine.

"I can't believe my eyes!" said the learned man. "What is all this?"

"Well, it's definitely not something ordinary!" said the shadow. "But then you're not an ordinary man, and as you know, I've been following in your footsteps ever since childhood. As soon as you found that I was mature enough to go out into the world alone, I went my own way. And now I find myself in the most splendid of circumstances, but a sense of longing came over me to see you again before you die. You *are* going to die, you know! I also wanted to see these regions again because a person is always fond of his homeland. I know that you have a new shadow. Do I owe anything to it or to you? Please tell me if I do."

"Oh, is it really you?" said the learned man. "This is highly unusual! I never would have believed that a person's old shadow could come back as a human being!"

"Tell me what I have to pay you," said the shadow. "Because I don't want to be indebted to you in any way."

"How can you say that?" said the learned man. "What kind of debt are you talking about? You're as free as anyone! I'm extremely happy about your good fortune! Sit down, old friend, and just tell me a little about how all this happened and what you saw over at the neighbor's house, back in the warm countries."

"All right, I'll tell you," said the shadow, sitting down. "But then you have to promise me that you'll never tell anyone here in town, no matter where you meet me, that I was once your shadow. I'm thinking about getting engaged. I'm able to support more than one family!"

"Never fear," said the learned man. "I won't tell anyone who you really are. Here is my hand. I promise, and a man is true to his word."

"A word is true to its shadow," said the shadow, and of course that was the way it had to talk.

Yet it was quite remarkable how much of a human being it had become. The shadow was dressed all in black, made from the finest of black cloth, with patent-leather boots, and a top hat that could be snapped closed so only the crown and the brim remained. To say nothing of what we already know he was wearing: seals, a gold chain, and diamond rings. Oh yes, the shadow was exceptionally well dressed, and that was exactly what made him a human being.

"Well, let me tell you!" said the shadow, setting his feet in the patent-leather boots as hard as he could on the sleeve of the learned man's new shadow, which lay like a poodle at his feet. He did this either out of haughtiness or perhaps to make it stick to him. But the shadow on the floor kept motionless and calm in order to listen. No doubt it wanted to find out how it too could win its freedom and become its own master.

"Do you know who was living in the neighbor's house?" said the shadow. "It was the most lovely creature of all—it was Poetry! I was there for three weeks, and that had as great an effect as if I had lived three thousand years and read everything that was ever composed or written. That's what I'm telling you, and it's all true. I've seen everything, and I know everything!"

"Poetry!" cried the learned man. "Oh yes, yes—she's often a recluse in the big cities. Poetry! Yes, I saw her for one brief moment, but I had sleep in my eyes. She was standing on the balcony, shimmering like the Northern lights. So tell me, tell me! You were on the balcony, you went through the door, and then—?"

"Then I was in the antechamber," said the shadow. "It was the antechamber you were always sitting there looking at. There were no candles, it was in a kind of twilight, but one door after another stood open to a long row of rooms and halls. And all of them were brightly lit. I would have been killed by light if I had gone right in to see the maiden. But I was level-headed, I took my time, and that's what you have to do."

"And what did you see?" asked the learned man.

"I saw everything, and I'll tell you all about it, but . . . It's not a matter of pride, but . . . as a free man, and considering the talents that I possess, not to mention my good position, my admirable circumstances . . . I would appreciate it if you would address me in the formal manner."

"I beg your pardon," said the learned man. "It's an old habit that's hard to change. You're perfectly right, and I won't forget. But now, sir, tell me everything you saw."

"Everything!" said the shadow. "Because I saw everything and I know everything!"

"What did it look like in the innermost halls?" asked the learned man. "Was it like in a green forest? Was it like in a holy sanctuary? Were the halls like the starry sky when you stand atop the high mountains?"

"Everything was there!" said the shadow. "I didn't go all the way inside, of course. I stayed in the front room in the twilight, but that was an excellent place to be. I saw everything and I know everything! I've been to Poetry's court, in the antechamber."

"But what did you see? Were all the ancient gods walking through the great halls? Were the ancient heroes fighting? Were sweet children playing and talking about their dreams?"

"I tell you, I was there and you must realize that. I saw everything there was to see. If you had come over there, you would not have become a man, but I did! And on top of that I learned to see my innermost nature, what I was born with, the kinship that I have with Poetry. Well, back when I was living with you, I never thought about it, but as you know, whenever the sun came up or the sun went down, I would grow so astoundingly big. In the moonlight I was almost more distinct than you were. Back then I didn't understand my nature; in the antechamber it all became clear to me. I became a human being! I came back out a mature man, but you were no longer in the warm countries. As a human being I was ashamed to walk around like that. I needed boots, clothing, the whole human facade that makes a person recognizable. I made my way . . . well, I'll tell you, since you're not going to put it in any book, after all. I made my way under the skirts of the cake-wife; that's where I hid. The woman had no idea how much she was hiding. Not until evening did I go out. I ran through the streets in the moonlight. I stretched myself up a wall; it tickles the back so wonderfully! I ran up and I ran down, looking into the highest windows, into parlors and garret rooms. I looked where no one else can look, and I saw what no one else can see, what no one ought to see. What an ignoble world it really is! I wouldn't even want to be a man except that being human is considered worthwhile. I saw the most unthinkable things among women, among men, among parents, and among the sweet, marvelous children. I saw," said the shadow, "what no person should know, but what everyone would like to know: bad things about their neighbors. If I had written something for a newspaper, people would have read it! Instead I wrote directly to the person involved, and terror overcame all the towns that I visited. They were so afraid of me! They were also enormously fond of me. The professors made me a professor, the tailors gave me new clothes. I'm very well outfitted. The master of the mint made coins for me, and women told me I was quite handsome! That's how I became the man that I am! And now I'll say farewell. Here's my card. I live on the sunny side, and I'm always home when it rains." And then the shadow left.

"How strange that was!" said the learned man.

Days and years passed, and then the shadow came back.

"How's it going?" the shadow asked.

"Oh my!" said the learned man. "I write about the true and the good and the beautiful, but no one wants to hear about such things. I'm in utter despair, because I take it all to heart."

"But I don't," said the shadow. "I'm getting fat, and that's what a person should be. Well, you just don't understand the world. It's making you ill. You have to travel! I'm taking a trip this summer. Would you like to come with me? I wouldn't mind having a traveling companion. Would you like to come along, as my shadow? It would be a great pleasure to take you with me, and I'll pay for the trip."

"That's going a bit far," said the learned man.

"It all depends on how you look at it," said the shadow. "It would do you a world of good to travel. If you'll be my shadow, everything on the trip will be free."

"This has gone far enough," said the learned man.

"But that's how the world is," said the shadow. "And that's how it will always be." Then the shadow left.

Things were not going well for the learned man. Sorrow and torment plagued him, and what he said about the true and the good and the beautiful was for most people like tossing roses to a cow. In the end he was quite ill.

"You look like a shadow of yourself," people told him, and the learned man would shiver, because it made him think.

"You should go to a spa," said the shadow, who had come to visit him. "There's no other choice! I'll take you along for old time's sake. I'll pay for the trip, and you can write up an account and entertain me a bit along the way. I want to go to a spa too. My beard isn't growing out the way it should. That's also an affliction; a man has to have a beard! Now be sensible and accept the offer. We'll travel together as friends."

And so they departed. The shadow was the master, and the master was the shadow. They drove together, they rode and walked together, side by side, in front or in back, depending on where the sun stood. The shadow made sure to keep himself in the master's position, and the learned man didn't think much about it. He was such a good-hearted person, and exceedingly gentle and kind. Then one day he said to the shadow, "Now that we've become traveling companions, as we have, and since we've also grown up together since childhood, shouldn't we drink a toast and call each other by our first names? That would be much more friendly."

"There's something in what you say," said the shadow, who was now the real master. "That's very straightforward and well-meaning of you. So allow me to be just as well-meaning and straightforward. You, as a learned man, undoubtedly know how strange nature can be. Some people can't stand to touch newsprint without falling ill. Others feel a pain in all their limbs if a nail is scraped against a windowpane. I get the same feeling when I hear you using my first name. I feel as if I were being pressed to the ground in my former position with you. As you can see, it's a feeling, not a matter of pride. I can't allow you to use my first name, but I will be happy to address you in that manner, to meet you halfway."

And so the shadow called his former master by his first name.

"Things have certainly gone too far," the learned man thought, "when I have to use his last name while he calls me by my first." But he had to put up with it.

Then they arrived at a spa where many foreigners were staying, including a lovely king's daughter, who was suffering from the illness of being able to see too much, and that was quite worrisome.

She noticed at once that the man who had arrived was a very different sort of person from all the rest. "They say he's here to make his beard grow, but I can see the real reason: He's not able to cast a shadow."

She grew curious, and so she set off for a stroll and began conversing at once with the foreign gentleman. As the daughter of a king, she could come straight to the point, and so she said, "Your illness is that you're not able to cast a shadow."

"Your Royal Highness must be improving greatly!" said the shadow. "I know that your complaint is that you see much too well, but your sight has weakened, so you must be cured. I have quite a remarkable shadow. Don't you see that man who's always accompanying me? Other people have an ordinary shadow, but I'm not fond of the ordinary. People often give their servants finer livery than they wear themselves, and in the same fashion I've dressed up my shadow as a human being! As you can see, I've even given him his own shadow. It's very expensive, but I like having something unique!"

"What?" thought the princess. "Is it true that I've actually recovered? This spa is the best of them all! These days the waters have such wondrous powers. But I'm not going to leave, because things are so amusing here right now. This stranger is very much to my liking. If only his beard won't start growing, because then he'll leave."

That evening in the grand ballroom, the king's daughter danced with the shadow. She was light on her feet, but he was even lighter. She had never had such a dance partner before. She told him what country she came from, and he knew that country. He had been there, but back then she hadn't been at home. He had peeked in the windows upstairs and down, he had seen both one thing and another, and so he could reply to the king's daughter and drop hints that made her quite amazed. He must be the wisest man in the whole world! Her respect for his knowledge grew, and when they started dancing again, she fell in love. The shadow was well aware of this, because she was practically looking straight through him. Then they danced again, and she was just about to speak of it, but she was level-headed. She thought about her country and kingdom and about all the people she would rule. "He's certainly a wise man," she said to herself. "That's good. And a lovely dancer. That's good too. But I wonder if he has deeper knowledge; that's just as important. He will have to be questioned." And so, little by little, she began to ask him about the most difficult things, questions that she herself could never have answered. And the shadow gave her a peculiar look.

"So you can't answer my questions?" said the king's daughter.

"They belong to my childhood lessons," said the shadow. "I think even my shadow over there by the door could answer them."

"Your shadow?" said the king's daughter. "That would be highly unusual!"

"Well, I'm not saying that he definitely could," said the shadow. "But I think he can. He's been accompanying me for so many years, and listening, so I think he can. But if Your Royal Highness will permit, I must bring it to your attention that he is so proud of passing for a human being that if he's going to be in a good mood, and he will have to be in order to answer properly, then he has to be treated like a person."

"Oh, I like that!" said the king's daughter.

And so she went over to the learned man near the door. She talked to him about the sun and the moon, and about people both outwardly and inwardly, and he replied both wisely and well.

"What a man he must be to have such a wise shadow," she thought. "It would be a sheer blessing for my people and my kingdom if I chose him as my consort. And that's what I'm going to do!"

They soon came to an agreement, the king's daughter and the shadow, but no one was to know about it until she returned home to her own kingdom.

"No one, not even my shadow," said the shadow, and of course he had his own reasons for that.

Then they came to the country where the king's daughter ruled whenever she was home.

"Listen here, my good friend," said the shadow to the learned man. "Now that I've become as happy and powerful as anyone can be, I want to do something special for you. You will live with me in the palace, drive with me in my royal carriage, and have a hundred thousand *rigsdaler* a year. But you must let everyone call you shadow, you mustn't say that you've ever been a human being, and once a year, when I'm sitting on the balcony in the sunshine holding an audience, you must lie at my feet as a shadow should. I have to tell you that I'm marrying the king's daughter. Tonight the wedding takes place."

"No, now things have gone much too far!" said the learned man. "I refuse, I refuse to do it! That would mean betraying the whole country and the king's daughter too. I'm going to tell the whole story. That I'm a human being, and you're the shadow. That you're just masquerading!"

"No one will believe you," said the shadow. "Be sensible, or I'll call the guard."

"I'm going straight to the king's daughter," said the learned man.

"But I'm going first," said the shadow. "And you're going to jail!" And that's what happened, because the sentries obeyed the man who was to be the husband of the king's daughter.

"You're shaking," said the king's daughter when the shadow

came to her. "Has something happened? You mustn't be ill this evening, now that we're going to celebrate our wedding."

"I've been through the most horrible experience anyone could have!" said the shadow. "Imagine . . . Well, I suppose a poor shadow brain can't stand very much. Imagine . . . my shadow has gone mad. He thinks he's a human being and that I—just imagine—that I'm his shadow!"

"How horrible!" said the princess. "He's locked up, isn't he?"

"Yes, he is. I'm afraid he'll never come to his senses."

"Poor shadow!" said the princess. "How unhappy he is. It would be true kindness to free him from the meager life he has left. Now that I think about it, I believe it's going to be necessary to do away with him in all secrecy."

"How painful that is!" said the shadow. "After all, he was a loyal servant." And then he uttered what sounded like a sigh.

"What a noble character you have," said the king's daughter.

That evening the whole city was lit up. The cannons were fired, boom! and the soldiers presented arms. Now that was a wedding! The king's daughter and the shadow came out onto the balcony to be seen by all, and receive another round of hurrahs.

The learned man heard none of it, because by then they had taken his life.

The Old House

On the street stood an old, old house. It was almost three hundred years old. You could read this for yourself on the beam where the year had been carved along with tulips and hops vines. An entire verse was spelled out like in the old days, and in the beam above each window a grimacing face had been carved. The second story jutted far out over the first, and right under the eaves was a leaden drain pipe with a dragon head. The rainwater was supposed to run out of its mouth, but it ran out of the stomach instead, because there was a hole in the pipe.

All the other houses on the street were so new and so nice, with big windowpanes and smooth walls. It was easy to see that they wanted nothing to do with the old house. They were probably thinking, "How long is that eyesore going to stand here on the street looking ridiculous? The bay window sticks out so far that we can't see from our windows what's happening over there. The staircase is as wide as a castle's and as steep as a church tower's. The iron railing looks like the entrance to an old tomb, and it even has brass knobs. How tasteless!"

Right across the street stood nice, new houses, and they thought the same as all the rest. But at a window sat a little boy with fresh red cheeks and bright, shining eyes, and he liked the old house best of all, both in the sunshine and in the moonlight. If he looked across at the wall where the plaster had worn off, he could sit there and see the most wondrous pictures, imagining exactly how the street had looked in the past, with stairs and bay windows and peaked gables. He could see soldiers with halberds, and roof eaves that ended in dragons and serpents. That certainly was a house worth looking at! And in it lived an old man who wore thick woolen trousers, a dress coat with big brass buttons, and a wig that you could tell was a real wig. Every morning an old servant would come to clean for him and run errands. Otherwise the old man in the thick woolen trousers was all alone in the old house. Occasionally he would come over to the window and look out, and the little boy would nod to him, and the old man would nod back. In that way they became acquaintances and then they were friends, although they had never spoken to each other, but that didn't really matter.

The little boy heard his parents say, "The old man over there lives quite comfortably, but he's so terribly lonely."

The following Sunday the little boy wrapped something in a piece of paper, went down to the gate, and when the servant who ran errands came past, he said to him, "Listen here! Would you take this for me to the old man across the street? I have two tin soldiers, and this is one of them. It's for him, because I know he's so terribly lonely."

The old servant looked quite amused, nodded, and carried the tin soldier over to the old house. Later a message arrived asking whether the little boy might like to come over for a visit. His parents gave him permission, and so he went over to the old house.

The brass knobs on the stairway railing gleamed much brighter than usual; you would think they had been polished in honor of his visit. And it looked as if the carved trumpeters—for there were trumpeters carved on the door, standing amid the tulips—were blowing with all their might. Their cheeks looked much plumper than they had before. Oh yes, they blew: "Dut-ta-tada! The little boy is coming! Dut-ta-tada!" And then the door opened. The entire hallway was lined with old portraits: knights in armor and ladies in silk gowns. And the armor clattered and the silk gowns rustled! Then there was a stairway that led upward for a long way and downward for a short way—and then he came out onto a balcony that certainly was quite rickety, with big holes and long cracks in it, but grass and leaves were growing out of all of them. The whole balcony outside, the yard and outer wall, was covered with so much greenery that it looked like a garden, though it was only a balcony. Here stood old flowerpots with faces and donkey ears. The flowers now grew as if they were wild. One pot was completely overflowing with carnations, or rather with green stalks, shoot upon shoot, and quite clearly it said, "The air has caressed me, the sun has kissed me and promised me a little flower on Sunday, a little flower on Sunday!"

Then they entered a room where the walls were covered with pigskin and printed with golden blossoms.

> "Gilding wears thin
> But never pigskin!"

said the walls.

And there stood leather chairs with very high backs, carved all over, and with arms on either side. "Sit down! Sit down!" they said. "Oh, how I creak! I'm probably going to get rheumatism just like the old cupboard. Rheumatism in my back, oh!"

And so the little boy stepped inside the parlor, which was where the bay window was and where the old man was sitting.

"Thank you for the tin soldier, my little friend!" said the old man. "And thank you for coming to see me."

"Thanks! Thanks!" or "Creak! Creak!" said all the pieces of furniture; there were so many of them that they practically fell over each other trying to see the little boy.

In the middle of the wall hung a painting of a lovely lady, so young, so happy, but dressed in a fashion from olden days, with powder in her hair and clothes that stood out stiffly. She said neither "thanks" nor "creak" but gazed with her gentle eyes at the little boy, who asked the old man at once, "Where did you get her from?"

"From the junk dealer around the corner," said the old man. "He has so many portraits. No one knows those people or cares about them, because they've all gone to their graves, but in the old days I knew her, and now she's been dead and gone for fifty years."

Under the painting, behind glass, hung a bouquet of withered flowers. They too must have been fifty years old; that's how old they looked. And the pendulum on the big clock swung back and forth, and the hands moved, and everything in the parlor grew even older, though they didn't notice.

"Back home they say you're so terribly lonely," said the little boy.

"Oh," he said, "old memories and all they bring with them come to visit me, and now you've come too. I'm doing just fine."

And then he took from the shelf a book with pictures in it. There were long processions, the most wondrous carriages that you don't see anymore today, soldiers like the jack of clubs, and tradesmen with fluttering banners. On the tailors' banner there were scissors held by two lions. And on the shoemakers' instead of a boot there was an eagle with two heads, because shoemakers always have to be able to say about everything: "It's a pair." Oh yes, that was quite a picture book!

The old man went into the other room to get jam and apples and nuts. Things certainly were blissful in that old house.

"I can't bear it!" said the tin soldier, who was standing on top of the chest of drawers. "It's so lonely here and so sad. No, when you've been part of a family, you can't get used to this. I can't bear it! The days are long and the evenings are even longer. It's not at all the same over here as it was at your house where your father and mother talked so pleasantly, and where you and all the other sweet children made such a lovely commotion. Oh, how lonely it is over here with the old man! Do you think anyone gives him kisses? Do you think anyone gives him gentle looks or Christmas trees? He'll get nothing but a funeral. I can't bear it!"

"You mustn't be so sad about it," said the little boy. "I think it's quite lovely, and all the old memories, and all they bring with them, come to visit."

"Well, I can't see them, and I don't know them," said the tin soldier. "I can't bear it!"

"You must," said the little boy.

And the old man appeared with the most pleased expression on his face, the loveliest jam, apples, and nuts, and then the little boy thought no more about the tin soldier.

Happy and pleased, the little boy went back home. Days passed and weeks passed, and nods were given to the old house and received from the old house, and then the little boy went back there again.

And the carved trumpeters blew: "Dut-ta-tada! Here's the little boy! Dut-ta-tada!" The swords and armor in the knight paintings clattered and the silk gowns rustled. The pigskin spoke, and the old chairs had rheumatism in their backs: "Ow!" It was exactly like the first time, because over there a day or an hour was just like any other.

"I can't bear it!" said the tin soldier. "I've been weeping tin! It's much too sad over here. I'd rather go to war and lose my arms and legs! At least that would be a change. I can't bear it! Now I know what it means to have a visit from your old memories, and all they bring with them. I've had visits from mine, and I can tell you that in the long run there's no pleasure in it. Finally I was just about to jump off the chest of drawers. I saw all of you over at your house quite clearly, as if you were actually here. It was once again that Sunday morning, as you well remember. All of you children were standing in front of the table and singing your hymns, the way you sing them every morning. You stood there so devoutly with folded hands, and Father and Mother were just as solemn. Then the door opened and your little sister Maria, who's not yet two and who always dances whenever she hears music or song, no matter what kind, was brought in. She shouldn't have done it but she began to dance. She couldn't find the rhythm because the tempo was so slow. She stood first on one leg and bowed her head all the way down, and then on the other leg and bowed her head all the way down, but it didn't quite work. The rest of you stood there, looking very serious, all of you, although it must have been hard. But I was laughing inside, and that's why I fell off the table and got a dent that I still have today, because it wasn't proper for me to laugh. But the whole scene was now replayed inside me, and everything else that I've experienced. Those must be the old memories and all they bring with them! Tell me, do you still sing on Sunday? Tell me something about little Maria. And how is my friend, the other tin soldier? Oh, he must be happy! I can't bear it!"

"But I gave you away," said the little boy. "You have to stay here. Can't you understand that?"

And the old man brought out a drawer that held many things to look at: a tin coin holder and a metal perfume box, and old playing cards, big and gilded, the kind that are never seen anymore. And more drawers were opened. The piano was opened too. It had a landscape painted on the inside of the lid, and it was quite hoarse when the old man played it. Then he hummed a tune.

"Oh, how she could sing that song!" he said. Then he nodded at the portrait that he had bought from the junk shop, and the old man's eyes shone so bright.

"I want to go to war! I want to go to war!" shouted the tin soldier as loud as he could and plummeted right down to the floor.

Well, where did he go? The old man looked, the little boy looked. He was gone, and gone he stayed. "I'm sure I'll find him," said the old man, but he never did. The floor was much too open and full of holes. The tin soldier had fallen through a crack and that's where he lay, as if in an open grave.

The day was over, and the little boy went home. That week passed and more weeks passed. The windows were quite frozen. The little boy had to sit and breathe on them to make a peephole to see the old house, and over there the snow had drifted into all the curlicues and inscriptions. It covered the whole stairway, as if no one was home and, in fact, no one was home. The old man was dead!

In the evening a hearse stood outside, and into it they placed him lying in his coffin. He was going to rest in his grave out in the country. That's where they drove him now, but no one accompanied him, since all his friends were dead. And the little boy blew kisses after the coffin as it drove away.

Several days later there was an auction at the old house, and the little boy saw from his window what was being carried off: the old knights and the old ladies, the flowerpots with the long ears, the old chairs and the old cupboards. One item went to one place, another somewhere else. The portrait of the woman that was found at the junk shop went back to the junk shop, and that's where it stayed, because no one knew her anymore. No one cared about that old painting.

In the spring they tore the house down, because it was nothing but an eyesore, people said. You could look from the street right into the parlor at the pigskin wall covering, which was ripped and torn. And the greenery on the balcony was draped wildly around the toppled timbers. And then it was all cleared away.

"That's better!" said the neighboring houses.

And a lovely house was built with big windows and smooth white walls. But in front, on the spot where the old house had actually stood, a little garden was planted, and up along the neighbors' walls grew wild vines. In front of the garden was placed a big iron fence with an iron gate. It looked so elegant that people stopped to peer inside. And the sparrows clung by the score to the vines, chattering all at once as best they could, but they weren't talking about the old house, because they didn't remember it. So many years had passed that the little boy had grown up to be a man; yes, a fine young man who brought his parents much joy. He had just married, and with his little wife he had moved into this house with the garden. He stood there with her as she planted a meadow flower, which she thought was so enchanting. She planted it with her little hand and patted the earth with her fingers. "Ow! What's that?" She had jabbed herself. Something sharp was sticking up from the soft earth.

It was . . . Why, just imagine! It was the tin soldier, the one who had disappeared up in the old man's parlor. It had tumbled and rolled between the timbers and rubble and finally had lain for many years in the earth.

The young wife wiped off the soldier, first with a green leaf and then with her own fine handkerchief, which had such a lovely scent. For the tin soldier it was like awakening from a trance.

"Let me see him," said the young man, laughing and shaking his head. "Oh, it can't possibly be him, but he reminds me of a story about a tin soldier that I had when I was a little boy." And then he told his wife about the old house and the old man and about the tin soldier that he had sent over to him because he was so terribly lonely. He told the story in such detail that the young wife had tears in her eyes over the old house and the old man.

"But it's possible it could be the same tin soldier," she said. "I'm going to keep him and remember everything you told me. But you have to show me the old man's grave."

"Oh, I don't know where it is," he said. "No one knows. All his friends were dead, there was no one to take care of it, and I was just a little boy."

"How terribly lonely he must have been!" she said.

"Terribly lonely," said the tin soldier. "But how lovely it is not to be forgotten."

"Lovely!" cried something close by, but no one except the tin soldier noticed that it was a scrap of the pigskin wall covering that had lost all its gilding. It looked like wet earth, but it had something to say, and it did:

> "Gilding wears thin,
> But never pigskin!"

Although the tin soldier found that hard to believe.

The Little Match Girl

It was so horribly cold. It was snowing and it was beginning to get dark. It was also the last evening of the year, New Year's Eve. In the cold and the dark a poor little girl was walking along the street, bareheaded and barefoot. Now, it's true that she was wearing slippers when she left home, but what good did that do? The slippers were much too big. Her mother had worn them last, that's how big they were. And the little girl lost them when she dashed across the street as two carriages raced by terribly fast. One slipper was nowhere to be found, and a boy ran off with the other one. He said he could use it as a cradle when he had children of his own.

So there walked the little girl with her bare little feet that were red and blue from the cold. In an old apron she carried some matches, and a few she held in her hand. No one had bought any from her all day long. No one had given her so much as a little *skilling*. Hungry and cold she walked along, looking so miserable, that poor little thing! Snowflakes fell on her long blond hair that curled beautifully at the nape of her neck, but she had no thought for such finery. Lights glowed in all the windows, and the street smelled wonderfully of roast goose. It was New Year's Eve, after all. Yes, that's what she was thinking.

Over in a niche between two houses, where one jutted out a little farther into the street than the other, that's where she sat down and curled up. She tucked her little feet under her, but she froze even more. She didn't dare go home because she hadn't sold any matches and didn't have a single *skilling*. Her father would beat her, and it was cold at home too. They barely had a roof over their heads, and the wind whistled right through, even though they had stuffed straw and rags into the biggest cracks. Her little hands were almost dead from the cold. Oh, how warm a little match would feel. If only she dared take just one from the bundle, strike it against the wall, and warm her fingers. She pulled one out. Scritch! How it sparked, how it burned! It was a warm, bright flame, like a tiny candle when she cupped her hand around it. What an odd candle! The little girl thought she was sitting in front of a big cast-iron stove with shiny brass knobs and a brass belly. The fire burned so blissfully and felt so warm! Oh, what was that? The little girl had just stretched out her feet to warm them too when . . . the flame went out, the cast-iron stove vanished. She was sitting with the little stub of the burned-out match in her hand.

She struck another. It burned, it glowed, and at the spot where the light touched the wall it became transparent, like a veil. She was looking right into a room where the table was set with a dazzling white cloth and fine porcelain. The roast goose was steaming wonderfully, stuffed with prunes and apples. And what was even more amazing, the goose leaped up from the platter and waddled across the floor with a knife and fork in its back. Right over to the poor girl it came. Then the match went out, and she could see nothing but the thick, cold wall.

She lit another. Then she was sitting under the loveliest Christmas tree. It was even bigger and more richly decorated than the one she had seen through the glass door of the rich merchant's house at Christmas. A thousand candles were burning on the green boughs, and colorful pictures like the ones that adorned the shop windows looked down at her. The little girl stretched both hands into the air . . . and then the match went out. All the Christmas candles rose higher and higher; she saw that they had now become the bright stars. One of them fell, leaving a long fiery path in the sky.

"Someone is dying now," said the little girl, because her old grandmother, the only person who had ever been kind to her but who was now dead, had told her: When a star falls, a soul rises up to God.

She struck another match against the wall. It lit up everything around her, and in the radiance stood her old grandmother, so bright, so glittering, so gentle and blessed.

"Grandmother!" cried the child. "Oh, take me with you! I know you'll be gone when the match goes out. Gone just like the warm cast-iron stove, the lovely roast goose, and the big, heavenly Christmas tree!" Quickly she struck all the other matches in the bundle. She wanted so much to hold on to her grandmother, and the matches burned with such a radiance that it was brighter than the light of day. Grandmother had never before looked so beautiful or so grand. She lifted the little girl into her arms, and they flew in radiance and joy, so high, so high. And there was no cold, no hunger, no fear. They were with God!

But in the niche of the house, in the cold early morning, the little girl sat with red cheeks and a smile on her lips. Dead, frozen to death on the last evening of the old year. The morning of the new year rose up over the little body sitting there holding all those matches, with one bundle almost completely charred. She had tried to warm herself, they said. No one knew what beauty she had seen, or with what radiance she and her old grandmother had passed into the joy of the New Year.

The Story of a Mother

A mother was sitting beside her little child. She was so sad, so afraid that he would die. He was very pale, and his little eyes were closed. He was breathing faintly, and once in a while he took a deep breath, as if he were sighing, and the mother would gaze even more sorrowfully at the little soul.

Then there was a knock on the door and in came a poor old man wrapped in what looked like a big horse blanket, because it was warm, and that's what he needed. It was a cold winter, after all. Everything outside was covered with ice and snow, and the wind was blowing so hard that it stung your face.

Since the old man was shaking with cold and the little child was sleeping for a moment, the mother went over to put a little pot of beer on the stove, to warm it up for him. The old man sat and rocked while the mother sat down on a chair close by. She looked at her sick child who was breathing hard and lifted the little hand.

"You think I'll be allowed to keep him, don't you?" she said. "Surely Our Lord wouldn't take him from me!"

And the old man, who was Death himself, nodded so strangely; it could just as well mean yes as no. The mother looked down at her lap and the tears ran down her cheeks. Her head grew heavy. For three nights and days she hadn't closed her eyes, and now she fell asleep, but only for a moment. Then she gave a start and shivered with cold. "What's this?" she said and looked all around. But the old man was gone and her little child was gone too. He had taken the child with him, and over in the corner the old clock was whirring and whirring. The big lead weight plunged all the way down to the floor: Bam! And the clock too stood still.

But the poor mother ran out of the house, calling for her child.

Outside in the midst of the snow sat a woman wearing long black robes, and she said, "Death has been in your house. I saw him rush off with your little child. He moves faster than the wind, and he never brings back what he takes."

"Just tell me which way he went," said the mother. "Tell me which way and I'll find him!"

"I know which way," said the woman in the black robes. "But before I tell you, you will have to sing for me all the songs you've ever sung for your child. I'm fond of them, I've heard them before. I am the Night. I saw your tears when you sang them."

"I'll sing them all, every one of them," said the mother. "But don't stop me from reaching him, from finding my child!"

But the Night sat mute and motionless. Then the mother wrung her hands as she sang and wept, and there were many songs, but even more tears. Then the Night said, "Go to the right, into the dark pine forest. That's where I saw Death headed with your little child."

Deep inside the forest the paths crossed, and she no longer knew which way to go. That's where a hawthorn bush stood. It had neither leaves nor flowers. It was cold wintertime, after all, and frost hung from the branches.

"Have you seen Death go past with my little child?"

"Oh yes!" said the hawthorn bush. "But I won't tell you which way he went unless you first warm me up at your heart. I'm freezing to death. I'm becoming nothing but ice!"

And she pressed the hawthorn bush tightly to her breast so it would warm up properly. The thorns went right into her flesh, and her blood flowed in big drops. But the hawthorn bush shot out fresh green leaves, and flowers appeared on it in the cold winter night, so warm did it feel at the heart of a sorrowful mother. And the hawthorn bush told her which way she should go.

Then she came to a great lake, where there were neither ships nor boats. The lake was not frozen enough to bear her, or open and shallow enough for her to be able to wade through it, yet she had to cross it if she wanted to find her child. So she lay down to drink all the water from the lake, although of course this was impossible for a human to do. But the sorrowful mother thought that even so, maybe a miracle would occur.

"No, it will never work!" said the lake. "Why don't the two of us come to an agreement instead. I'm fond of collecting pearls, and your eyes are the clearest ones I've ever seen. If you will cry them out for me, then I will carry you across to the great hothouse where Death lives, tending the flowers and trees. Each of them is a human life."

"Oh, I would give anything to reach my child!" said the weeping mother, and she cried even harder. Her eyes sank to the bottom of the lake and turned into two precious pearls. Then the lake lifted her up as if she were sitting on a swing, and she flew in a great arc to the shore on the other side where a strange house stood, stretching for miles. It was impossible to tell whether it was a mountain with forests and caves or whether it had been hammered together, though the poor mother couldn't see it, because she had cried her eyes out.

"Where can I find Death, who took my little child?" she said.

"He hasn't arrived yet," said the old woman who tended the graves and was supposed to take care of Death's great hothouse. "How did you manage to find your way here, and who helped you?"

"Our Lord helped me," she said. "He is merciful, and you will be too. Where can I find my little child?"

"Well, I don't know your child," said the woman. "And you can't see. Many flowers and trees have withered in the night. Death will soon come to replant them. I suppose you know that everyone has his tree or flower of life, depending on what kind of person he is. They look just like other plants, but they have hearts that beat. A child's heart beats too. Listen for it, and maybe you can recognize your child's. But what will you give me if I tell you what else you have to do?"

"I have nothing to give," said the sorrowful mother. "But I will go to the ends of the earth for you."

"Well, there's nothing there that I want," said the woman. "But you can give me your long black hair. I'm sure you know how beautiful it is, and it's to my liking. I will give you my white hair in return, at least that's something."

"Is that all you ask?" she said. "I will gladly give it to you!" And she gave away her beautiful hair and received the old woman's snow-white hair in return.

Then they went into Death's great hothouse, where flowers and trees grew in wondrous profusion. There were delicate hyacinths under glass bells, and big, hardy peonies. Water plants grew there, some quite healthy, others sickly. Water snakes rested on them, and black crabs were clamped onto their stalks. There were lovely palms, oaks, and plane trees, parsley and flowering thyme. Each tree and each flower had its own name; each was a human life. The person was still alive: one in China, one in Greenland, all around the world. There were big trees in small pots, making them look so miserable and ready to burst the pots. And in many places dreary little flowers stood in rich soil with moss all around, coddled and well tended. The sorrowful mother bent over all the smallest plants and listened to the human hearts beating inside them, and among the millions she recognized her own child's.

"Here it is!" she cried, and stretched her hand over a little blue crocus drooping wretchedly to one side.

"Don't touch the flower!" said the old woman. "Stand over here, and when Death arrives—I'm expecting him any minute— don't let him pull up the plant. If you threaten to do the same with other flowers, then he'll be frightened! He has to answer to Our Lord for them; none can be pulled up until He gives permission."

All of a sudden an ice-cold wind rushed through the hall, and the blind mother could tell that Death had arrived.

"How did you manage to find your way here?" he asked. "How could you get here faster than I did?"

"I'm a mother," she said.

And Death stretched out his long hand toward the delicate little flower, but she cupped her hands firmly around it, very tightly, and yet afraid that she might touch one of its petals. Then Death blew on her hands, and it felt colder than the cold wind, and her hands fell weakly away.

"There's nothing you can do to me," said Death.

"But Our Lord can," she said.

"I merely do His will," said Death. "I am His gardener. I take all His flowers and trees and plant them in the great garden of Paradise in the unknown land. But how well they thrive or what it's like there, I can't tell you."

"Give me my child back!" said the mother, and she wept and

pleaded. Suddenly she grabbed hold of two beautiful flowers nearby, one in each hand, and shouted at Death, "I'll tear up all your flowers, because I'm in such despair!"

"Don't touch them!" said Death. "You say you're so unhappy, and now you want to make another mother just as unhappy."

"Another mother!" said the poor woman and let go of both flowers at once.

"Here are your eyes," said Death. "I fished them out of the lake, they were shining so brightly. I didn't know they were yours. Take them back, they're even clearer than before. Then look down into this deep well right here. I'll tell you the names of the two flowers you wanted to tear up, and you'll see their whole future, their entire human life. You'll see what you wanted to disturb and destroy!"

She looked down into the well, and it was sheer bliss to see how one of them became a blessing for the world, to see how much joy and happiness spread all around. And she looked at the other life, and it was sorrow and suffering, horror and misery.

"Both are God's will," said Death.

"Which of them is the flower of unhappiness and which is the blessed one?" she asked.

"I won't tell you," said Death. "But I will tell you this: One flower belongs to your own child. It was your child's fate that you saw, your own child's future."

Then the mother screamed in terror, "Which of them is my child? Tell me! Save the innocent one! Save my child from all that misery! Better to take him away. Take him to God's kingdom. Forget my tears, forget my pleas and everything I've said and done."

"I don't understand you," said Death. "Do you want your child back, or should I take him inside, to the place that you cannot know?"

Then the mother wrung her hands, fell to her knees, and prayed to Our Lord, "Don't listen when I plead against Your will, for Your will is best! Don't listen to me! Don't listen to me!"

She bowed her head to her lap.

And Death took her child into the unknown land.

The Collar

Once upon a time there was an elegant gentleman whose only possessions were a bootjack and a comb, but he had the loveliest collar in the world. And the story we're going to hear is about that collar.

The collar had now reached the age when he was thinking about getting married, and he happened to land in the wash along with a garter.

"Oh!" said the collar. "I've never met anyone so slender or so elegant before, so soft and so dainty. May I ask you your name?"

"I won't tell you," said the garter.

"Where do you belong?" asked the collar.

But the garter was quite modest and thought that was a strange thing to ask.

"You must be a waistband," said the collar. "The kind of waistband worn on the inside. I can tell that you're both useful and decorative, little maiden."

"You mustn't speak to me," said the garter. "I don't think I've given you any cause to do so."

"Oh yes, when someone is as lovely as you are," said the collar, "that's reason enough."

"Stop acting so familiar," said the garter. "You look so masculine."

"I'm an elegant gentleman," said the collar. "I have a bootjack and a comb." But that, of course, wasn't true. It was his master who owned these things, but he was boasting.

"Don't be so familiar," said the garter. "I'm not used to that."

"What a prude!" said the collar, and then he was taken out of the wash. He was starched, hung on a chair in the sunshine, and then placed on the ironing board. There came the hot iron.

"Madam!" said the collar. "Little widow! I'm getting quite hot! I'm turning into someone else, I'm losing all my creases, you're burning a hole in me! Ooh! I must propose to you!"

"Scrap!" said the iron and slid haughtily over the collar, because she was imagining that she was a steam engine going out to the railway to pull railcars.

"Scrap!" she said.

The collar was a bit frayed around the edges, and the scissors came to snip off the frayed part.

"Oh," said the collar. "You must be the prima ballerina. How you can stretch your legs! That's the most enchanting thing I've ever seen. No human being could possibly match you."

"I know," said the scissors.

"You deserve to be a countess," said the collar. "All I have is an elegant gentleman, a bootjack, and a comb. If only I had the title of count!"

"Is he proposing?" said the scissors. Then she grew angry and gave the collar a proper snip, so he ended up being thrown away.

"I suppose I should propose to the comb. It's remarkable how you manage to keep all your teeth, little miss!" said the collar. "Have you ever thought about getting engaged?"

"Oh yes, I most certainly have," said the comb. "I'm engaged to the bootjack."

"Engaged?" said the collar. Now there was no one left to propose to, and so he felt only contempt for the idea.

A long time passed, and the collar ended up in a bin at the paper mill. There was a big rag-party, with the fine scraps in one group and the rough in another, just as it should be. They all had plenty to say, but the collar most of all. He was a regular braggart.

"I've had terribly many sweethearts," said the collar. "I couldn't get any peace! But then I was an elegant gentleman and well starched! I had both a bootjack and a comb that I never used. You should have seen me back then, seen me lying on my side. I'll never forget my first sweetheart. She was a waistband, so elegant, so soft, and so charming. She threw herself into a washbasin for my sake! There was also a widow who was piping hot, but I left her standing there, turning black. Then there was the prima ballerina. She gave me the rip that I now bear. She was so fierce! My own comb was in love with me. She lost all her teeth from lovesickness. Yes, I've seen plenty of that sort of thing! But I feel worst about the garter— I mean the waistband that went into the washbasin. I have a lot on my conscience. It's about time I was turned into white paper."

And that's what happened. All the rags were turned into white paper, but the collar turned into this very piece of white paper that we're looking at now, the one on which this story is printed. That's because he boasted so terribly afterward about things that had never happened. That's something we should remember, so we don't behave the same way, because we never can tell whether we too might one day end up in the rag bin and be turned into white paper and have our whole story printed on it, even our innermost secrets, and then have to run around talking about them, just like the collar.

The Bell

In the evening in the narrow streets of the big city, when the sun went down and the clouds shone like gold up among the chimney tops, first one person and then another would often hear an odd sound, like the chiming of a church bell. But it was heard for only a moment, because there was such a rumbling of wagons and such shouting, and that was quite distracting. "Now the evening bell is ringing," people would say. "Now the sun is going down."

Those who were walking outside the city, where the houses stood far apart, with gardens and small fields, saw an even more splendid evening sky and heard the bell chime much louder. The sound seemed to come from a church deep inside the silent, fragrant forest, and people would look in that direction and grow quite solemn.

Many years passed, and one person began saying to another, "I wonder if there's a church out there in the forest? That bell has a strange, lovely ring to it. Let's go out and take a closer look." And the rich people drove while the poor walked, but the road seemed exceptionally long. When they reached a grove of willow trees that grew at the edge of the forest, they sat down and looked up at the long branches and thought they were truly out in nature. A pastry chef from the city went out and pitched his tent, and then another pastry chef came along, and he hung a bell right over his tent, but it was the kind of bell that had been tarred to withstand the rain, and the clapper was missing. When people returned home, they said it had been so romantic, and that went far beyond tea-party chatter. Three people claimed to have gone all the way through the forest to the other side, and they had heard the strange bell ringing the whole time, but it seemed to them that the sound was coming from the city. One of them wrote an entire ballad about it and said that the bell rang like a mother's voice singing to a beloved child. No melody was lovelier than the chiming of that bell.

The Emperor of the country had also taken notice and promised that whoever could discover where the sound was coming from would win the title of World Bell-Ringer, even if it turned out not to be a bell.

Now many people went to the forest in the hope of acquiring that excellent position, but there was only one who came home with any sort of explanation. No one had gone far enough inside, not even this man, and yet he said that the bell sound came from an enormous owl inside a hollow tree. It was some kind of owl of wisdom who was constantly knocking its head against the tree, but whether the sound came from its head or from the hollow trunk, he couldn't yet say for certain. Then he was appointed World Bell-Ringer and each year he wrote a short dissertation about the owl. But no one was any the wiser.

Then confirmation day came around, and the pastor spoke so beautifully and fervently. Those who were to be confirmed were very moved. It was an important day for them; they had suddenly turned from children into grown-ups. Their childish souls now seemed to pass into more sensible adults. The sunshine was at its loveliest. The children who had been confirmed walked out of the city, and from the forest the great unknown bell chimed, wondrous and loud. They suddenly had such a desire to go to the forest, all but three of them. The first had to go home to try on her ball gown, because that gown and that ball were the reasons why she had been confirmed right now; otherwise she wouldn't have been invited. The second was a poor boy who had borrowed his confirmation jacket and boots from the landlord's son, and they had to be returned at a certain time. The third said that he didn't go to strange places unless his parents went along, and he had always been a well-behaved child; that's what he would continue to be now, even after being confirmed. There was no need to make fun of him, but they did.

So three of them stayed behind as the others set off. The sun shone and the birds sang and the children sang too, holding each other's hands, because they had not yet found work and were all newly confirmed before Our Lord.

But soon two of the youngest grew tired and headed back to the city. Two other girls sat down to make wreaths, so they didn't go along either. When the rest reached the willow trees and the pastry chef's tent, they said, "Look, here we are! The bell doesn't exist at all. It's just something people have imagined."

At that very moment, from deep in the forest, the bell rang so sweetly and solemnly that four or five of the children decided to go farther into the forest. It was so dense, so laden with leaves that it was quite difficult to make any headway. Woodruff and windflowers seemed to grow much too high. Flowering convolvulus and blackberry vines hung in long garlands from tree to tree where the nightingale sang and the rays of sun played. Oh, it was so blissful, but there was no pathway for the girls to follow. Their clothes would have been torn to shreds. There were huge boulders covered with moss of all different colors. Fresh spring water was trickling out and saying, quite strangely, "Glug, glug!"

"That couldn't be the bell, could it?" said one of the boys as he lay down to listen. "We're going to have to study this." Then he stayed behind and let the others continue on.

They came to a house made of bark and branches. A huge tree with wild apples was bending over it, as if to shake all its blessings onto the roof, which was covered with rose blossoms. The long branches wound around the whole gable, and from the gable hung a little bell. Could that be the one they had heard? Yes, they all thought it was, except for one boy. He said the bell was too small and delicate to be heard as far away as they had heard it, and that its tones were quite different from those that could move a human heart. The boy who spoke was a king's son, and so the others said, "Someone like that always wants to seem more clever."

Then they let him continue on alone, and as he walked his chest became more and more filled with forest-loneliness. But he could still hear the little bell that had pleased the others, and sometimes, when the wind came from the direction of the pastry tent, he could also hear people singing as they drank tea. But the deep peals of the bell grew even louder; it soon sounded as if an organ were playing along. The sound came from the left, from the side of the heart.

Then there was a rustling in the thicket and a little boy stood in front of the king's son, a boy wearing wooden clogs and a jacket so short that it was quite clear what long wrists he had. They recognized each other. He was the boy who couldn't come along because he had to go home and return his jacket and boots to the landlord's son. That's what he had done, and then, wearing wooden clogs and his own ragged clothes, he had set off alone, because the ringing of the bell was so loud and deep that he had to find it.

"We could go together," said the king's son. But the poor boy with the wooden clogs was quite bashful. He tugged at the short sleeves of his jacket and said he was afraid he wouldn't be able to walk fast enough. And besides, he thought they should look for the bell on the right, because that's where everything grand and glorious could be found.

"Well, then our paths won't cross," said the king's son and nodded to the poor boy, who headed for the darkest and thickest part of the forest, where the thorns tore his poor clothes to shreds and bloodied his face, hands, and feet. The king's son also had a few deep scratches, but the sun shone on his path, and he's the one we're going to follow, because he was a spirited lad.

"I will and I must find that bell," he said. "Even if I have to go to the ends of the earth."

Horrid monkeys sat high in the trees, gaping with all their teeth bared. "Should we pelt him?" they said. "Should we pelt him? He's a king's son!"

But he walked undisturbed deeper and deeper into the forest, where the most wondrous flowers grew. There were white paradise lilies with blood-red filaments, sky-blue tulips that flashed in the wind, and apple trees with apples that looked exactly like huge, shimmering soap bubbles. Just imagine how those trees shone in the sunlight! Stags and does played in the grass in the loveliest green meadows where magnificent oaks and beech trees grew. If one of the trees had a split in the bark, grass and long vines grew from the crevice. There were also enormous stretches of forest with quiet lakes where white swans swam and flapped their wings. The king's son often stopped to listen, and many times he thought that the ringing of the bell was coming to him from one of these deep lakes. But then he realized that it wasn't coming from there at all. It was from even deeper in the forest that the bell was ringing.

Then the sun began to set. The air blazed red, like fire. It grew so quiet, so quiet inside the forest. He sank to his knees, sang his evening hymn, and said, "Will I never find what I'm looking for? Now the sun is setting, now night is coming, dark night. Yet maybe I could see the round, red sun one more time before it sinks completely behind the earth. I'll climb up on the rocks over there. They're as high as the tallest trees."

He grabbed hold of vines and roots, climbing up the wet rocks where water snakes were coiled, where toads seemed to be barking at him. But he reached the top before the sun had set completely, seen from that height. Oh, what splendor! The sea, the great glorious sea, tumbled its long waves against the shore and stretched out before him, with the sun floating like a great gleaming altar out where the sea and sky met. Everything merged into blazing colors. The forest sang and the sea sang and his heart sang too. All of nature was one great holy cathedral in which the trees and drifting clouds were the pillars, the flowers and grass the woven velvet cloth, and the sky itself the enormous dome. Up there the red colors were extinguished as the sun vanished, but millions of stars were lit, millions of diamond lamps glittered. And the king's son spread out his arms toward the sky, toward the sea and the forest.

At that moment, from the aisle on the right, appeared the poor boy with the short sleeves and the wooden clogs. He had arrived at the same time, taking his own path. The two boys ran to each other and held hands in the great cathedral of nature and poetry. Above them rang the invisible sacred bell, and blessed spirits hovered and danced around them to a jubilant "Hallelujah!"

The Marsh King's Daughter

S torks tell their children so many tales, all of them about the swamp and bog. They're usually tailored to suit the age and level of understanding. The youngest children are amused if someone says "tickle prickle, grumble mumble!" For them, that's fine, but the older ones want a deeper meaning, or at least something about their own family. Of the two oldest and longest tales that have been passed down by the storks, we all know one of them, the one about Moses who was set in the waters of the Nile by his mother. He was found by a king's daughter, was brought up well, and became a great man, but afterward no one knew where he was buried. That's quite well known!

The other tale is still little known, maybe because they've kept it to themselves in Denmark. This tale has passed from stork mother to stork mother for more than a thousand years, and each of them has told it better and better, but now we will tell it best of all.

The first stork couple who told the story and actually took part in it had their summer residence on top of the Viking's timbered house up near Wild Bog in Vendsyssel. That's in Hjørring County, far to the north, up toward Skagen in Jutland, if we're going to be precise about it. It's still an enormously large bog that you can read about in the official description of the county. It was once on the ocean floor, but it rose up, as the book says. It stretches for miles, surrounded on all sides by wet meadows and shifting marshlands, with peat bogs, cloudberries, and scraggly trees. Fog is almost always hovering above it, and seventy years ago there were still wolves. It can truly be called Wild Bog, and you can imagine what a wilderness it was, how many swamps and lakes there were a thousand years ago. Well, back then the details were the same as you see now: the reeds were the same height, with the same kind of long leaves and violet-brown feathery flowers that they now bear. The birches stood there with their white bark and delicate, drooping leaves, just as they do today. And as for the living creatures that came here, well, the fly wore its gauzy garments in the same style as now. The stork's natural color was white, with black and red stockings. At that time the humans, on the other hand, wore a different style of dress than today, but to all of them, whether thrall or hunter, to anyone who stepped into the quagmire, the same thing happened a thousand years ago that still happens today to those who come here: they fell in and sank down to the Marsh King, as they called him, who ruled the great Bog Kingdom. He could also be called the Quagmire King, but we prefer to say Marsh King, and the storks called him that too. Very little is known about his rule, but maybe that's for the best.

Close to the bog, right near Limfjord, stood the Viking's timbered house with a stone-lined cellar, a tower, and three floors. High atop the roof the stork had built his nest. Stork Mother sat on the eggs, certain that they would all turn out just fine.

One evening Stork Father was gone a rather long time, and when he returned home, he looked rumpled and harried.

"I have something quite dreadful to tell you!" he said to Stork Mother.

"Don't tell me!" she said. "Keep in mind that I'm sitting on eggs. You might upset me, and then it might affect the eggs."

"I have to tell you!" he said. "She came here, the daughter of our landlord in Egypt. She dared to make the journey up here. And now she has disappeared!"

"The one who's kin to the fairies? Oh, tell me! You know I can't stand to wait when I'm sitting on eggs!"

"Well, you see, Mother, she believed what the doctor said, just like you told me. She believed that the white water lily up here could help her sick father, and she took to the air wearing a skin of feathers with two other feather-clad princesses who come north every year to bathe and be rejuvenated. She came, and now she has disappeared."

"You're being so long-winded," said Stork Mother. "The eggs might catch cold. I can't stand to be kept in suspense!"

"I've been keeping an eye out," said Stork Father. "And this evening I was walking among the reeds, where the quagmire can bear my weight, when three swans appeared. There was something about the way they moved that said to me: Watch out, they're not all swan, they're just swan skins! You know the feeling, Mother. You know, as I do, what the real thing is."

"Of course," she said. "But tell me about the princess. I'm bored hearing about swan skins."

"In the middle of the bog, as you know, there's a kind of lake," said Stork Father. "You can see a bit of it if you raise yourself up. Over there near the reeds and the green quagmire lay a big alder log. That's where the three swans landed, flapping their wings and looking all around. One of them threw off her swan skin, and I recognized her: our princess from home in Egypt. She sat there, wearing no cloak other than her long black hair. I heard her ask the two others to take good care of her swan skin while she dove underwater to pick the flower she thought she could see. They nodded and took flight, lifting up the limp feather gown. 'I wonder what they're going to do with it,' I thought, and apparently she asked them the same question, and their answer she could see for herself: They flew off with her swan skin. 'Go ahead and dive down!' they shouted. 'Never again will you fly wearing a swan skin, never again will you see the land of Egypt! Stay here in Wild Bog!' And then they tore her feather skin into a hundred pieces so the feathers flew all around, like a snowstorm. And off they flew, those two wretched princesses."

"That's horrible!" said Stork Mother. "I can't stand to hear about this. So tell me what happened next!"

"The princess wailed and wept. Tears rolled down onto the alder log, and then it started to move, because it was the Marsh King himself, the one who lives in the bog. I saw the log turn over and then it was no longer a log. Long, mud-covered branches were sticking up like arms. Then the poor child grew frightened and ran off, onto the shifting quagmire, but at that spot it can't even bear my weight, let alone hers. She sank at once, and the alder log went down with her. He was the one who dragged her in. Big black bubbles rose up, and then not a trace remained. Now she's buried in Wild Bog. She will never take the flower to the land of Egypt. You wouldn't have been able to stand watching it, Mother!"

"You shouldn't tell me things like that right now. It might affect the eggs! I'm sure the princess can take care of herself. She's bound to get help. If it had been you or me, or one of ours, it would be all over."

"Still, I'm going to take a look every day," said Stork Father, and he did.

A long time passed.

Then one day he saw that from deep down on the bottom a green stalk was shooting up, and when it reached the surface of the water, a leaf grew out of it, getting wider and wider. Not long after, a bud appeared, and early one morning when the stork flew over it, the strong sunlight made the flower bud open. In the middle lay a lovely child, a little girl, as if she had just stepped out of the bath. She looked so much like the princess from Egypt that at first the stork thought it was her, grown small, but after he thought about things, it seemed more reasonable that she was the child of the princess and the Marsh King. That's why she was lying inside a water lily.

"But she can't stay here," thought the stork. "And it's already so crowded in my nest. But I have an idea. The Viking woman has no children, though she has often wished for one, and I'm always blamed for bringing babies, so for once I'm going to prove them right! I'll fly to the Viking woman with the child. What joy there will be!"

And the stork picked up the little girl, flew over to the timbered house, and with his beak pecked a hole in the windowpane made from a pig's bladder. He placed the child in the arms of the Viking woman and then flew back to Stork Mother and told her all about it while the youngsters listened—they were old enough to understand.

"You see, the princess isn't dead! She sent her child up here, and now I've found a place for her."

"That's what I've said all along," said Stork Mother. "Pay a little attention to your own children now. It will soon be traveling time; I'm starting to feel a tickle under my wings. The cuckoo and the nightingale have already left, and I've heard the quails saying that we'll soon have good tailwinds. Our youngsters will know how to do us proud on the maneuvers, if I know them right!"

Oh, how happy the Viking woman was when she woke in the morning to find the lovely little child in her arms. She kissed and caressed her, but the child screamed terribly, flailing her arms and legs. She didn't seem the least bit pleased. Finally she cried herself to sleep, and as the child lay there like that, she was one of the loveliest creatures ever seen. The Viking woman was so happy, so light in body and soul. She now had a feeling that her husband and all his men might arrive just as unexpectedly as the little girl had, so she and the entire household set to work putting everything in order. The long, colorful tapestries that she and the maids had woven with images of their gods—Odin, Thor, and Freya, as they were called—were hung on the walls. The thralls polished the old shields that were on display, cushions were placed on the benches, and dry firewood was put on the hearth in the middle of the hall so the fire could be lit at once. The Viking woman joined in the work, and by evening she was very tired and slept well.

But when she awoke toward morning, she was terribly frightened, because the little child had vanished. She sat up, lit a pine splinter, and looked all around, and at the spot where she had stretched out her feet in bed lay not the little child but a big, hideous frog. She was quite disgusted by it, picked up a heavy stick, and would have killed the frog, but it looked at her with such strange, sad eyes that she couldn't strike it. Once again she looked all around. The frog uttered a faint, pitiful croak. She gave a start and sprang out of bed over to the shuttered window, which she threw open. At that very moment the sun appeared, casting its rays on the bed and the big frog. Suddenly the beast's wide lips seemed to shrink and became little and pink; its limbs stretched out to become the most charming figure. It was her own lovely little child lying there, and not a hideous frog.

"What's this?" she said. "Was I having a bad dream? It's my own enchanting fairy child lying here!" And she kissed the girl and pressed her to her heart, but the child scratched and bit as if she were a wild kitten.

Not that day nor the next did the Viking lord arrive. He was on his way, but the wind was against him; it was blowing south for the storks. Tailwind for one and headwind for another.

In a couple of days and nights it became clear to the Viking woman what was wrong with her little child. A terrible spell had been cast over her. By day she was as lovely as a sylph, but she had a mean and wild nature. At night, on the other hand, she was a hideous frog, quietly whimpering, with sorrowful eyes. Two temperaments that switched back and forth, both outwardly and inwardly. This was because the little girl who had been brought by the stork possessed in the daytime her real mother's looks but had her father's disposition. At night, on the other hand, her kinship to him became visible in the shape of her body, while from inside radiated her mother's character and heart. Who could break the power of this black magic? It caused the Viking woman both alarm and sorrow, and yet her heart clung to the poor creature, whose condition she didn't dare mention to her husband when he returned home. Then he would certainly put the poor child out on the road, as was the custom, and anyone who wished could take her. The gentle Viking woman didn't have the heart to do that. He would only be allowed to see the child in the light of day.

Early one morning there was the rush of stork wings above the roof. That's where more than a hundred stork pairs had rested during the night after the great maneuvers. Now they were taking flight to head south.

"Every man ready!" came the order. "Women and children too!"

"We feel so light," said the stork fledglings. "It's tickling and prickling all the way to our feet, as if we were filled with live frogs. How lovely it is to be traveling abroad!"

"Stay with the flock!" said Father and Mother. "And stop clacking your beaks so much, it's not good for your lungs!"

And off they flew.

At the same moment the *lur* horn sounded over the heath. The Viking had landed with all his men. They were returning home with rich bounty from the Gallic coast, where people in terror sang as they had in Bretland:

"Free us from the wild Norsemen!"

Oh, what fun and merriment there was in the Viking stronghold near Wild Bog. The mead cask was brought into the hall, the fire was lit, and horses were slaughtered; a proper feast was being prepared. The priest splashed warm horse blood on the thralls as consecration. The fire crackled, smoke drifted along the ceiling, and soot dripped from the timbers, but they were used to it. Guests were invited and were given fine gifts; forgotten were schemes and falsehoods. They drank and drank, tossing gnawed bones at each other's face; that was a sign of good humor. The *skald*—he was a kind of musician but also a warrior, and since he had been with them he knew what he was singing about—presented them with a ballad that recounted all their war exploits and deeds. Every verse was followed by the same refrain: "Fortunes die, kinsmen die, every man must die, but never will die a glorious name!" And then they all struck their shields and pounded the table with their knives or a bone, making a tremendous noise.

The Viking woman sat on the cross bench in the vast banquet hall. She was wearing a silk gown, gold bracelets, and big amber beads; she had on all her finery. The *skald* mentioned her too in his song, speaking of the golden treasure that she had brought her rich husband, and he was truly pleased with the lovely child. He had seen her only in the daytime in all her loveliness. He approved of the wild nature she possessed; he said she could become a formidable warrior maiden who would slay her foe. She wouldn't blink an eye if a practiced hand, in jest, should slice off her eyebrows with a sharp sword.

The mead cask was emptied, a new one was brought up, yes, drink there was in abundance. These were men who could hold a great deal. Back then there was a proverb: "Cattle know when to start home from grazing, but unwise men never know the measure of their bellies." Well, they knew, of course, but it's one thing to know and another to act. They also knew that "Love turns to hate if he stays too long in another man's house." Yet there they stayed. Meat and mead are good things. They had a merry time, and at night the thralls slept in the warm ashes, dipping their fingers in the greasy soot and licking them. What a splendid time!

Once again that year the Viking set off on a raid, paying no heed to the autumn storms that were brewing. With his men he headed for the coast of Bretland. It was, after all, "just across the water," as he said. His wife stayed behind with the little girl, and it's true that the foster mother soon grew more fond of the poor frog with the pious eyes and the deep sighs than of the lovely girl who bit and scratched everyone.

The raw, wet autumn fog, called "Mouthless," which gnaws off the leaves, hovered over forest and heath. "Featherless Bird," as they called the snowflakes, flew thick and fast. Winter was on its way. The sparrows took over the stork nest, arguing in their own fashion about the absent master and mistress. And the stork couple with their youngsters? Where were they now?

The storks were in the land of Egypt, where the warm sun shone as it does for us on a lovely summer day. The tamarinds and acacias were blooming all around, Muhammad's crescent was shining brightly from the domes of the mosques. Many a stork pair sat on the slender towers, resting after their long journey. Great flocks had nest after nest atop the mighty pillars and crumbled arches of temples and abandoned sites. The date palm lifted its canopy high overhead, as if it wanted to be a parasol. The grayish-white pyramids stood like silhouettes against the clear air of the desert, where the ostrich showed how it could use its legs, and the lion sat with great wise eyes, gazing at the marble sphinx that lay half buried in sand. The waters of the Nile had retreated, the whole riverbed was swarming with frogs, and for the stork family that was the loveliest sight in the land. The children thought they were seeing things, so marvelous did they find it all.

"That's how things are here, that's how they always are for us in our warm country," said Stork Mother, and the youngsters felt a tickling in their bellies.

"Is there more for us to see?" they said. "Are we going much, much farther into the country?"

"There's nothing more to see," said Stork Mother. "In the lush region there's nothing but wild forest where the trees grow close together, tangled up with spiny, twining plants. Only the elephant with his plump legs can make a path. The snakes are too big for us, and the lizards too quick. If you go out in the desert, you'll get sand in your eyes if the weather is fine, and if it's not, you'll end up in a dust devil. No, this is the best place. This is where the frogs and grasshoppers are. This is where I'm staying, and so are you."

And stay they did. The older storks sat in their nests on the slender minarets, resting and yet busy smoothing out their feathers and rubbing their beaks on their red stockings. Then they would stretch out their necks, nod gravely, and raise their heads with the high foreheads and the elegant smooth feathers, their brown eyes shining so wisely. The girl fledglings walked gravely around among the lush reeds, stealing glances at the other stork youngsters and making friends. Every third step they would swallow a frog, or they would walk along dangling a little snake—they thought it made them look quite nice, and it tasted good too. The boy fledglings quarreled, flapping their wings at each other, pecking with their beaks, yes, even drawing blood. And then one after the other they got engaged, boy fledglings and girl fledglings; that was what they lived for, after all. And they built nests and then started quarreling all over again, because in the hot countries everyone has such a temper. Yet it was pleasant, and a particularly great joy for the old storks: Their children could do no wrong! Every day the sun shone, every day was filled with eating; their only thought was pleasure.

But inside the lavish palace of their Egyptian landlord, as they called him, there was no pleasure to be found.

The rich, mighty lord lay on a divan, all his limbs rigid, stretched out like a mummy in the middle of the great hall with the colorfully painted walls. It was as if he were lying inside a tulip. Kinsmen and servants stood around him. He wasn't dead, but neither could he be called properly alive. The healing white water lily from the northern countries, the one that was going to be found and plucked by the person who loved him most, would never arrive. His lovely young daughter who, wearing a swan skin, had flown over sea and land, far to the north, would never come back. "She is dead and gone!" the two swan maidens had reported when they returned. Together they had made up a whole story about it, and here's what they said:

"All three of us were flying high in the air when a hunter saw us and fired his arrow. It struck our young friend and, slowly singing her farewell, she sank like a dying swan into the middle of the forest lake. There on the shore beneath a fragrant weeping birch we buried her. Yet we took our revenge. We tied a torch beneath the wings of the swallow who was nesting under the hunter's thatched roof. The eaves caught fire, the house went up in flames, and he was burned to death inside. The glow reached across the lake to the drooping birch where she is now earth in the earth. She will never return to the land of Egypt."

And then they both wept, and Stork Father, when he heard about it, clacked his beak so hard that it rattled.

"Lies and deception!" he said. "I have an urge to jab my beak right through them."

"And snap it off," said Stork Mother. "Then you'd certainly look good! Think first about yourself and then about your family; nothing else matters."

"Well, I'm still going to perch on the rim of the open dome tomorrow, when all the learned and wise men gather to talk about the sick man. Maybe then they'll get a little closer to the truth."

And the learned and wise men gathered and talked a great deal, and at length, but the stork could make no sense of it. The ill man had no benefit from it either, nor did his daughter in Wild Bog. Yet we might as well listen in for a while; people have to listen to so much.

But it would be best to hear and know what came before, so we can better follow the story, at least as well as Stork Father did.

"Love nourishes life. The greatest love nourishes the greatest life. Only through love can he win the salvation of life." This is what was said, and it was exceptionally wise and well put, claimed the learned men.

"What an enchanting idea," said Stork Father at once.

"I don't really understand it," said Stork Mother. "And it's not my fault, it's the idea's fault. But that doesn't matter, I have other things to think about."

Then the learned men had talked about love between this and that, the difference that existed between the love that sweethearts felt and the love between parents and children, between the light and the plants, the way the rays of the sun kissed the marsh and the sprout that resulted. It was all presented in such a long-winded and learned fashion that it was impossible for Stork Father to follow, never mind repeat. He grew quite thoughtful, closed his eyes halfway, and stood on one leg the whole next day. Learning was so hard for him to bear.

Yet this much Stork Father had understood: He had heard both the common folk and the highest nobles say from their hearts that it was a great misfortune for many thousands and for the country itself that the man lay ill and could not get well. What a joy and a blessing it would be if he regained his health. "But where does the flower grow that can give him health?" They had asked everyone, searched the learned writings, searched the gleaming stars, searched the weather and wind, searched along all the pathways they could find, and finally the learned and the wise, as we mentioned, decided this: "Love nourishes life, life for the father," and in this way they said more than they knew. They repeated it and wrote it down as a precept: "Love nourishes life." But as to how everything might follow this precept, well, they didn't get any farther. At last they agreed that help must come from the princess, who with all her soul and heart loved her father. They finally also decided how this might be done. Yes, it was more than a year and a day ago that she was sent out at night, just as the bright new moon set once more. She headed for the marble sphinx in the desert, tossed aside the sand from the base of the door, and then walked through the long passageway that led into the center of the great pyramids. There, one of the mighty ancient kings lay in his mummy case, surrounded by splendor and glory. Here she was to lower her head to the dead, and then it would be revealed to her how to win life and salvation for her father.

All this she had done, and in her dreams she learned that from the deep bog up in the land of Denmark—the place was described in great detail—she was to bring home the lotus blossom that touched her breast in the water's deep. Then he would be saved.

And that's why she flew in a swan's skin from the land of Egypt up to Wild Bog. See, Stork Father and Stork Mother knew all this, and now we understand it more clearly than we did before. We know that the Marsh King pulled her down, we know that for those back home she was dead and gone. Only the wisest among them continued to say, as Stork Mother did: "She'll take care of herself!" And that's what they were counting on, because they couldn't think of anything better.

"I think I'm going to steal the swan skins from those two wretched princesses," said Stork Father. "Then they won't be able to go to Wild Bog and do any more harm. I'll hide the swan skins up there until they're needed."

"Where are you going to hide them up there?" asked Stork Mother.

"In our nest at Wild Bog," he said. "Our youngest fledglings and I can help each other carry them, and if they get too heavy for us, then there are places along the way to hide them until the next migration. I suppose one swan skin would be enough for her, but two would be better. It's always good to have a lot of traveling clothes in a northern country."

"Nobody's going to thank you for this," said Stork Mother. "But you're the boss. I have nothing to say except during brooding season."

In the Viking stronghold at Wild Bog, which is where the storks flew in the spring, the little girl had been given a name. They called her Helga, but that name was much too gentle for the kind of temperament possessed by the loveliest of all creatures. Month by month this became more apparent. Over the years, as the storks made the same journey—in the autumn to the Nile, in the spring to Wild Bog—the little child grew up. And before anyone had time to think about it, she had become the loveliest maiden, in her sixteenth year. Lovely on the outside, but harsh and rough at the core, wilder than most in those harsh, dark times.

She found it amusing to splash her white hands with the steaming blood of the horses slaughtered as offerings. She savagely bit in half the neck of the black rooster that the priest was about to sacrifice, and to her foster father she said in all seriousness:

"If your enemy came and threw a rope around the timber heads on the roof, if it flew off your bedchamber while you slept, I wouldn't wake you even if I could. I wouldn't be able to hear it, so loud does the blood still buzz in the ear that you once boxed years ago. I haven't forgotten."

But the Viking didn't believe what she said. Like the others, he was deceived by her loveliness; nor did he know how spirit and hide could change in little Helga. Without a saddle she would ride her horse as if one with it, racing off at full gallop, and she refused to jump off if it began fighting with other mean-spirited steeds. Wearing all her clothes she would often fling herself from the slope into the strong current of the fjord and swim out to meet the Viking when his boat was headed for land. She cut the longest lock from her lovely long hair and plaited it into a string for her bow.

"Self-made is well-made!" she said.

As was the custom at the time, the Viking woman was strong in will and temper, but toward her daughter she seemed gentle and fearful because she knew, after all, that a spell had been cast over the terrible child.

Whenever her mother stood on the gallery or stepped out into the courtyard, Helga, seemingly out of spiteful pleasure, all too often would climb up onto the edge of the well, throw out her arms and legs, and then plummet into the narrow, deep hole. Frog that she was, she would dive down and then resurface, then crawl up like a cat and come back to the great hall soaking wet, making the green leaves spread on the floor swirl around in the wet stream.

Yet there was one bond that held little Helga, and that was the twilight. Then she would grow quiet and almost pensive, allowing herself to be called and led. Then some sort of inner sense would draw her to her mother. When the sun set and the transformation took place, both inside and out, she would sit there, quiet, sorrow-ful, shriveled up in the shape of a frog, her body hardly bigger than such an animal's, and for that very reason all the more hideous. She looked like a pitiful dwarf with a frog's head and webbing between her fingers. There was something so sad about the look in her eyes. She had no voice, only a hollow croak, just like a child who sobs in her dreams. Then the Viking woman would lift Helga onto her lap. She forgot about her horrid shape, seeing only the sad eyes, and said more than once:

"I almost wish that you were always my mute frog child. You're more terrible to look at when the loveliness is on the outside."

And she drew runes against sorcery and sickness, casting them over the miserable child, but there was no improvement.

"You'd never think she was once so small that she could lie inside a water lily," said Stork Father. "Now she's all grown-up and the spitting image of her Egyptian mother, whom we've never seen again. She didn't take care of herself, like you and the learned men thought. Year in and year out I've flown back and forth over Wild Bog, but she has never given any sign. Yes, I may as well tell you that during all these years when I've come up here ahead of you so I could repair the nest and get things ready, I've spent whole nights flying steadily across the open water, like an owl or a bat, but it did no good. Nor have we had any use for the two swan skins that the children and I dragged up here from the land of the Nile. And it wasn't easy. It took us three trips to carry them. Now they've lain for many years in the bottom of the nest, and if a fire ever broke out here and the timbered house burned down, they'd be gone."

"And our good nest would be gone too," said Stork Mother. "You think less about that than about those feather robes and your bog princess. Maybe you should go down there and stay with her in the marsh! You're a bad father to your own children, that's what I've said ever since I sat on the very first egg. I only hope that we and the children won't take an arrow in the wing from that crazy Viking girl. She has no idea what she's doing. And we've been here a little longer than she has, after all; she should bear that in mind. We never forget our obligations, and we pay our rent every year: a feather, an egg, and a fledgling, as is proper. When she's outdoors do you think I feel like going down there the way I did in the past and the way I do in Egypt? There I'm practically friends with everyone, without forgetting my place, and I can peek into vessels and pots. No, I sit up here, annoyed with her—that girl! And I'm annoyed with you too! You should have left her in the water lily, then she would be long gone!"

"You're much more respectful than your words," said Stork Father. "I know you better than you know yourself."

And then he leaped up, twice flapped his wings hard, stretched out his legs behind, and flew off, sailing without moving his wings. He was a good distance away when he took another powerful stroke. The sun shone on his white feathers, his neck and his head stretched out in front. He flew with speed and style.

"He's still the handsomest of them all," said Stork Mother. "But I'm not going to tell him that."

★

In early autumn the Viking came home with plunder and prisoners. Among them was a young Christian priest, one of the men who persecuted the gods of the Nordic countries. Recently there had been much talk in the hall and the women's house about the new faith that was spreading widely in all the lands to the south. Yes, the holy Ansgar had even reached as far as Hedeby on the Schlei. Even little Helga had heard about the faith in the white Christ, who out of love for human beings had given his life to save them. For her it went in one ear and out the other, as they say. The word *love* seemed to mean something to her only when she was huddled inside the pitiful frog shape in the locked chamber. But the Viking woman had listened and felt strangely gripped by the legends and sagas told about the son of the one true God.

When the men returned home from the raid, they told stories about the magnificent temples of precious hewn stones that had been built for the one whose message was love. A pair of heavy golden vessels, artfully carved and made entirely of pure gold, had been carried home. Both of them had an odd spicy scent. They were incense vessels that the Christian priests swung in front of the altar where blood never flowed, but wine and the consecrated bread became the blood of the one who had given his life for generations not yet born.

The captured young Christian priest was taken to the depths of the stone-lined cellar of the timbered house. Ropes of bast were tied around his feet and hands. Lovely he was, "Like Balder to look at!" said the Viking woman, and she was touched by his suffering. But young Helga suggested that a rope be looped behind his knees and tied to the tails of wild oxen.

"Then I'll let the dogs loose. Ooh! Across bogs and watery meadows, off to the heath! That will be a merry sight, even merrier to follow along after him."

Yet that was not the death the Viking intended him to suffer. Instead, as one who had denied and persecuted the high gods, he was to be killed the following morning on the sacrificial stone in the grove. It would be the first time that a human being was sacrificed there.

Young Helga begged to be allowed to splash his blood on the idols and the people. She sharpened her gleaming knife. When one of the big fierce dogs, of which there were plenty on the estate, ran across her feet, she stuck the knife into his side. "That was just to try it out," she said. The Viking woman looked sadly at the wild, mean-spirited girl, and when night came and the shape of beauty in her daughter's body and soul changed places, she spoke to her warm words of sadness, from a sorrowful soul.

The ugly frog with the monstrous body stood in front of her, fixing those sorrowful brown eyes on her, listening and seeming to understand human words.

"Never, even to my husband, has it ever crossed my lips how doubly I suffer over you," said the Viking woman. "There is more pain in my heart over you than even I could imagine. Great is a mother's love. But never has love appeared in your spirit. Your heart is like a cold lump of marsh clay. How did you ever end up in my house?"

Then the pitiful creature began trembling strangely, as if the words had touched an invisible bond between body and soul. Big tears appeared in her eyes.

"Hard times will come to you someday," said the Viking woman. "And it will be terrible for me as well. It might have been better if you had been set out on the road as a child, and the cold of night had lulled you to death." And the Viking woman wept bitter tears as she left, angry and sad, going behind the hide coverlet that hung from a beam to divide the room.

Alone in the corner sat the shriveled frog. She didn't make a sound, but after a brief interval a half-stifled sigh rose inside her, as if, in pain, a life were born deep inside her heart. She took a step forward, listened, took another step, and then grabbed with her clumsy hands the heavy bolt on the door. Gently she slid it back, quietly she pulled out the peg that had been put in the latch. She grabbed the lighted lamp that stood in the front room. A strong will seemed to give her strength. She pulled the iron peg out of the locked trap door and crept down to the prisoner. He was asleep. She touched him with her cold, clammy hand. When he awoke and saw the hideous creature, he shivered as if before an evil vision. She pulled out her knife, cut off his bonds, and beckoned him to follow her.

He uttered sacred names, made the sign of the Cross, and when the creature stood there unchanged, he said these words from the Bible:

"'Blessed is he that considereth the poor: the Lord will deliver him in time of trouble.' Who are you? How is it that you have the appearance of a beast and yet are filled with deeds of mercy?"

The frog creature beckoned and led him behind the tapestry dividers, along a lonely passageway and out to the stables, where she pointed to a horse. He swung himself up onto its back; then she climbed up in front of him and held on to the animal's mane. The prisoner understood, and at a fast trot they took a road that he never would have found, heading for the open heath.

He forgot about her hideous shape. He realized the Lord's grace and mercy were at work through this monster. He said pious prayers and sang sacred songs. Then she began to tremble, as if the power of the prayers and songs were at work, or was it a shiver of cold at the morning that would soon arrive? What was it that she felt? She lifted herself high in the air, wanting to stop the horse and jump down. But the Christian priest held her tight with all his strength, loudly singing a hymn, as if it had the power to break the spell that held her in the hideous frog form. And the horse ran even more wildly. The sky turned red, the first rays of sunlight broke through the clouds, and with the clear flood of light came the transformation: She became the lovely young girl with the demonic, evil heart. The priest was holding the most beautiful young woman in his arms, and he was horrified. He leaped down from the horse and stopped the animal, believing that he was confronting another fiendish spell. But young Helga had leaped to the ground at the same instant. The short child's gown reached only to her knees. She tore the sharp knife from her belt and rushed at the astonished man.

"Let me at you!" she cried. "Let me at you, and the knife will bury itself inside you! You're as pale as straw. Thrall! Beardless one!"

She rushed at him and they fought a hard battle, but an invisible power seemed to give the Christian man strength. He held her tight, and the old oak tree nearby seemed to come to his aid by using its roots, half freed from the earth, to bind her feet, which had slipped underneath. Close by trickled a spring. He splashed the fresh water over her breast and face, asking the impure spirit to leave and blessing her in the Christian fashion. But the waters of baptism have no power when the flood of faith does not stream from within.

Yet in this he was also the stronger one. Yes, more than a man's strength against the warring evil power lay in his actions. It seemed to captivate her. She lowered her arms, looking with astonished eyes and pale cheeks at this man who appeared to be a mighty sorcerer, strong in black magic and the secret arts. They were dark runes he spoke, magic runes he sketched in the air! She would not have blinked at a gleaming ax or sharp knife if he had swung one at her eyes, but she blinked when he made the sign of the Cross on her forehead and breast. And now she sat like a tame bird, her head bowed to her breast.

Then he gently spoke to her of the deed of love she had performed for him during the night when she had come to him in a hideous frog skin to untie his bonds and lead him out to light and life. She too was bound, bound with tighter bonds than he. But he said that she too, with his help, would come to light and life. To Hedeby, to the holy Ansgar, he would bring her. There, in the Christian city, the enchantment would be broken. But he didn't dare allow her to sit in front of him on the horse, even though she would have willingly sat there.

"Behind me on the horse you must sit, not in front! The beauty of your spell has a power that comes from the Evil One. I fear it; yet the victory is mine in Christ."

He fell to his knees, praying so piously and fervently. It was as if nature in the silent forest then became consecrated as a holy church. The birds began to sing as if they belonged to the new congregation, the wild mint plants gave off a fragrance as if they wanted to replace ambergris and incense. Loudly he proclaimed the words from the scriptures:

" 'To give light to them that sit in darkness and in the shadow of death, to guide our feet into the way of peace.' "

And he spoke of the renewal of nature, and as he talked the horse, which had carried them in their wild flight, stood still and shook the great blackberry vines so the ripe, juicy berries fell into little Helga's hand, offering her refreshment.

Patiently she allowed herself to be lifted onto the back of the horse, sitting there like a sleepwalker who is not awake and yet cannot wander. The Christian man tied together two branches with a rope of bast to form a Cross, which he held high in his hand. Then they rode through the forest, which grew thicker as the road went deeper, until there was no road at all. The blackthorn stood like a road barrier, and they had to ride around it. The spring became not a trickling stream but a stagnant bog, and they had to ride around it. There was strength and refreshment in the fresh forest air. There was no less power in the words of gentleness resounding in faith and Christian love, in the fervent desire to lead the spellbound child to light and life.

People say, of course, that the raindrop hollows out the hard stone, and over time the waves of the sea round the jagged rocks torn from the cliffs. The dew of mercy that had appeared to little Helga hollowed out what was hard and rounded off what was sharp, although this was not something noticeable; she didn't know it herself. How can the sprout in the earth know that the refreshing rain and the warm rays of sunlight will bring forth the plant and blossom it has concealed within?

Just as the mother's song imperceptibly becomes fixed in the mind of her child who, babbling, repeats individual words without understanding them, and later these words form into ideas and over time become clearer—that was how the Word was at work here, with the power to create.

They rode out of the forest, across the heath, and once again through trackless forests. Then toward evening they encountered robbers.

"Where did you steal that lovely lass from?" they shouted as they stopped the horse and pulled the two riders down, because the robbers were many in number. The priest had no weapon other than the knife he had taken from little Helga. He thrust it in every direction. One of the robbers swung his ax, but the young Christian man made a fortunate leap aside, otherwise he would have been hit. Then the blade of the ax struck deep into the neck of the horse so the blood gushed out and the animal toppled to the ground. Little Helga, who awoke from her long, deep trance, rushed over and threw herself at the gasping animal. The Christian priest stood in front to shield and protect her, but one of the robbers swung his heavy iron hammer at the priest's forehead, crushing it, and blood and brains sprayed all around. He fell to the ground, dead.

The robbers seized little Helga by her white arms, but at that very moment the sun went down. The last ray of light was extinguished, and she was changed into a hideous frog. Her greenish-white lips stretched over half her face, her arms were thin and slimy, a wide hand with webbing spread out like a fan. In horror the robbers released her. She stood as a hideous monster among them, and in accordance with her frog nature, she leaped into the air, higher than she was tall, and disappeared into the thicket. Then the robbers sensed that this must be Loki's evil cunning or some secret black magic and, terrified, they fled.

The full moon had risen; soon it was glowing and bright. Out of the thicket, in the pitiful skin of a frog, crept little Helga. She paused at the body of the Christian priest and at her murdered steed. She looked at them with eyes that seemed to weep; the frog head gave a croak like a child bursting into tears. She flung herself first at one, then at the other. She scooped up water in her hand, which had grown bigger with its webbing and more hollow, and she poured the water over them. Dead they were, and dead they would remain. She understood this. Soon the wild animals would come and devour their bodies. No, that must not happen! That's why she dug in the earth as deep as she could. She wanted to open up a grave for them, but the only thing she had to dig with was a hard tree branch and her own hands. Between her fingers the webbing cracked and blood flowed. She realized that she wouldn't be able to accomplish the task. Then she took some water and washed the face of the dead man. She covered it with fresh green leaves, brought over big boughs and placed them over him, shaking foliage in between. She took the heaviest stones she could carry, placed them on top of the dead bodies, and stuffed the crevices with moss. At last she thought the grave was big enough and protected, but during this heavy toil the night had passed. The sun broke forth . . . and little Helga stood there in all her loveliness, with bleeding hands, and for the first time with tears on her blushing maiden's cheeks.

In that transformation it was as if two temperaments began

warring inside her. She trembled and looked around, as if awaking from a fearful dream. Then she rushed over to the slender beech tree and clung to it to find support of some kind. Suddenly, in a flash, she clambered like a cat up to the treetop and held on. She sat there like a frightened squirrel, sat there all day long in the deep forest-loneliness, where everything is quiet and dead, or so people say. Dead? Yes, well, a couple of butterflies flitted around each other, either playing or squabbling. Nearby were several anthills, each with hundreds of tiny creatures busily racing back and forth. In the air danced countless gnats, swarm upon swarm. Hosts of buzzing flies sped past, along with ladybugs, dragonflies, and other winged insects. Earthworms crawled out of the wet ground, and moles pushed their way up. Otherwise it was quiet and dead all around—dead, as they say with all sincerity. No one took any notice of little Helga except for the jays that flew shrieking around the treetop where she sat. They hopped along the boughs toward her with bold curiosity. A wink of her eye was the wink that chased them off. But they were none the wiser about her, nor was she.

When evening approached and the sun began to set, the transformation prompted her to move again. She slid down from the tree, and as the last ray of sun was put out, she stood there in the shriveled frog form, with the torn webbing on her hands. But her eyes now shone with a glowing beauty that they had scarcely possessed in her lovely form. They were the eyes of a gentle, pious girl shining behind the frog mask. They bore witness to her deep spirit, her human heart. And the eyes of beauty dissolved in tears, the heart wept heavy tears of relief.

Still lying near the grave mound was the Cross made from branches bound together with a rope of bast, which was the last work of the man who was now dead and gone. Little Helga picked it up; the idea came all on its own. She planted it among the stones covering him and the murdered horse. The sadness of the memory brought tears, and in this sorrowful state she scratched the same symbol in the earth around the grave, making such a decorative boundary around it. As she drew the sign of the Cross with both hands, the webbing fell away like torn gloves. When she washed herself in the gushing spring and marveled at her fine white hands,

she again made the sign of the Cross in the air between herself and
the dead man. Then her lips quivered, her tongue moved, and the
name she had heard sung and spoken so often on their ride through
the forest, issued from her lips. She said: "Jesus Christus."

Then the frog skin fell away, and she was the lovely young girl.
Yet her head bowed forward in weariness, her limbs needed rest.
She slept.

But her slumber was very brief. At midnight she was awakened.
In front of her stood the dead horse, so radiant and full of life, with
light shining from its eyes and from the wounded neck. Close by
appeared the murdered Christian priest—"More beautiful than
Balder!" the Viking woman would have said—and yet he appeared
in flames of fire.

There was a solemnity in his big, gentle eyes, a pronouncement
of justice, a look so penetrating that it seemed to shine straight
into the corners of the heart of the one on trial. Little Helga
trembled at the sight, and her memory awoke with the force of
Judgment Day. Everything good that had been granted to her,
every loving word that had been said to her, seemed to come alive.
She understood that it was love that had kept her going during
those days of trial, in which the offspring of soul and marsh was
fermenting and struggling. She acknowledged that she had merely
followed the urgings of her moods and had done nothing on her
own. Everything had been given to her, everything had been
guided. She bowed, meek, humble, ashamed before the One who
had the power to read every fold of her heart. And at that moment
she sensed, like a lightning flash from the purifying fire, the flame
of the Holy Spirit.

"You daughter of the marsh," said the Christian priest. "From
the marsh, from the earth have you come. From the earth shall you
rise once more. The ray of sunlight in you, conscious of its body,
will return to its source—the ray that is not from the sun's body,
but the ray from God. No soul shall perish, but long is the temporal
life, which leads to the eternal. I come from the land of the dead.
You too shall one day travel through the deep valleys into the
radiant mountains where mercy and perfection dwell. I cannot lead
you to Hedeby for a Christian baptism. First you must shatter the
watery shield over the deep quagmire, pull out the living root of

your life and your cradle. You must perform your deed before consecration can occur."

And he lifted her up onto the horse, handing her a golden incense vessel like the one she had seen before in the Viking stronghold. From it came a scent, sweet and strong. The open wound in the forehead of the murdered man shone like a radiant diadem. He took the Cross from the grave and raised it high in the air. Then they raced off through the sky, above the rustling forest, above the mounds where the warriors were buried, seated on their slaughtered steeds. And the mighty figures rose up, came riding out, and halted atop the burial mounds. In the moonlight the broad gold circlets with the golden nodes glittered around their foreheads; their cloaks fluttered in the wind. The serpent who brooded over the treasure raised its head and looked at them. The dwarf folk peeked out from mounds and plowed furrows; they teemed with red, blue, and green lights, a swarm to behold, like sparks in the ashes of burned paper.

Over forest and heath, rivers and watery meadows they flew, up toward Wild Bog; above it they hovered in great circles. The Christian priest raised the Cross high. It gleamed like gold, and from his lips sounded the chanting of the mass. Little Helga sang along, the way a child sings to her mother's song. She swung the incense vessel, making an altar scent appear, so strong, so miraculous that the reeds and rushes of the bog began to bloom. All the sprouts shot up from the deep bottom, everything alive rose up. A profusion of water lilies spread all around, like a woven carpet of flowers, and on it lay a sleeping woman, young and lovely. Little Helga thought she was looking at herself, her mirror image in the still water. But it was her mother she saw, the Marsh King's wife, the princess from the waters of the Nile.

The dead Christian priest commanded the slumbering woman to be lifted onto the horse, but the animal sank under the burden as if its body were merely a shroud flying in the wind. Yet the sign of the Cross made the phantom of the air strong, and all three of them rode to dry land.

Then the rooster crowed in the Viking's stronghold, and the visions dissolved in the fog that vanished in the wind. Facing each other stood the mother and daughter.

"Is it myself that I see in the deep water?" said the mother.

"Is it myself that I see in the gleaming shield?" exclaimed the daughter, and they drew close to each other, breast against breast, embracing each other. The mother's heart beat more strongly, and she understood.

"My child! Flower of my own heart! My lotus from the deep waters!"

And she embraced her child and wept. Her tears were a new life, the baptism of love for little Helga.

"In a swan skin I came here, casting it aside," said the mother. "I sank through the shifting flood, deep down in the marshy bog, which closed like a wall around me. But soon I felt a fresher current; a force kept driving me deeper, ever deeper. I felt sleep pressing on my eyelids, I fell asleep, I dreamed. I thought I was once again lying inside the pyramid of Egypt, but in front of me still lay the rocking alder log that had frightened me on the surface of the bog. I looked at the cracks in the bark, and they glowed with colors and became hieroglyphics. It was the mummy's shroud I was looking at. It burst, and out stepped the thousand-year-old king, the mummy figure, black as pitch, gleaming black like a forest snail or the oily black marsh. The Marsh King or the pyramid's mummy, I didn't know which. He wrapped his arms around me, and I felt as if I would die. I didn't sense life again until my breast grew warm from a little bird flapping its wings inside, chirping and singing. The bird flew from my breast, high up toward the dark, heavy surface, but a long green ribbon still tied it to me. I heard its yearning cries and understood: Freedom! Sunshine! To Father! Then I thought about my father back home in the sunlit land, my life, my love! And I released the ribbon, let it fly away. Home to Father! Ever since that moment I have not dreamed. I slept a sleep that was certainly deep and long, until this hour when sounds and scents lifted and released me."

The green ribbon from the mother's heart to the bird's wings— where was it fluttering now, where had it been tossed? Only the stork had seen it. The ribbon was the green stalk, the bow the gleaming flower, the cradle for the child who had now grown so lovely and once again rested at her mother's heart.

And while they stood there, embracing each other, Stork Father flew in circles around them. Then he raced off to his nest and there found the feather skins, hidden for years. He threw one over each of them. The skins closed around them, lifting them up from the ground as two white swans.

"Let's have a talk," said Stork Father, "now that we can understand each other's language, even though the beak may be cut differently on one bird than on the other. How fortunate it is that you came here tonight. Tomorrow we'll be gone: Mother, myself, and the children. We're flying south. Well, just take a look at me! I'm an old friend from the land of the Nile, and Mother is too, though more in her heart than in her beak. She always believed that the princess would take care of herself. The children and I carried the swan skins up here. Oh, how happy I am! And what good luck that I'm still here. When dawn comes, we'll be off. A big flock of storks, and we'll be flying in the lead. Just fly behind us and you won't lose your way. The children and I will keep an eye on you."

"And I must bring the lotus blossom," said the Egyptian princess. "It will fly at my side, wearing a swan skin. I have the flower of my heart with me; that's how things have turned out. And so the riddle has been solved. Homeward, homeward!"

But Helga said that she couldn't leave the Danish land until she once again had seen her foster mother, the loving Viking woman. In Helga's mind appeared every beautiful memory, every loving word, every tear her foster mother had wept, and at that moment it was almost as if she loved this mother more dearly than any other.

"Yes, we must go to the Viking manor," said Stork Father. "That's where Mother and the children are waiting. How they will stare and clack their beaks! Well, Mother doesn't say much. She's curt and to the point, but she has good intentions. I'll start clacking at once so they can hear we're coming."

Then Stork Father began clacking his beak, and the swans flew off to the Viking stronghold.

Inside everyone was still sleeping soundly. Not until late at night had the Viking woman fallen asleep. She lay there, fearing for little Helga who had been missing for three whole days along with the Christian priest. She must have helped him escape; it was her horse that was gone from the stables. By what power had all of this taken place? The Viking woman thought about the miracles they had heard were performed by the white Christ and by those who believed in him and followed him. All these thoughts took shape in the realm of her dreams. It seemed to her that she was still awake, thinking in her bed, with the darkness brooding outside. A storm came. She heard the rolling of the sea to the west and the east, from the North Sea and the waters of the Kattegat. The monstrous serpent that encircled the earth in the depths of the sea was shaking with convulsions. The Twilight of the Gods was approaching: Ragnarok, as the heathen folk called the final hour when everything would perish, even the high gods themselves. The Gjallarhorn sounded, and over the rainbow rode the gods, clad in steel, to fight the last battle. Ahead of them flew the winged Valkyries, and behind them came the figures of dead warriors. The entire sky was lit up around them with the glow of Northern lights, but darkness was the victor. It was a terrible hour.

And on the floor, next to the terrified Viking woman, stood little Helga in the frog's hideous form. She too was shaking, and she pressed close to her foster mother, who took the child onto her lap and lovingly held her tight, no matter how hideous the frog skin looked. The sky resounded with the blows of swords and clubs, with the rush of arrows, as if a raging hailstorm were passing overhead. The hour had come when heaven and earth would explode, the stars would fall, everything would be consumed in the fire of Surt. Yet she knew that a new earth and heaven would come. Grain would billow where the sea now rolled across the golden sandy bottom. The unnameable god would rule, and up to him would rise Balder, gentle and loving, released from the realm of the dead. He was coming. The Viking woman saw him; she recognized his face. It was the captured Christian priest. "White Christ!" she called aloud, and as she spoke his name, she pressed a kiss to the forehead of the hideous frog child. Then the frog skin fell away, and little Helga stood there in all her loveliness, more gentle than ever before and with shining eyes. She kissed her foster mother's hands, blessing her for all the care and love the woman had given her during those days of trial and need, thanking her for the thoughts she had impressed upon and awakened in her, thanking her for speaking the name, which she repeated: White

Christ! And little Helga rose up as a mighty swan, spreading her wings out wide with the rushing sound made by flocks of migratory birds flying off.

With that, the Viking woman awoke, and from outside she could still hear the same great flapping of wings. She knew it was time for the storks to leave; it was them she heard. She wanted to see them one more time before they departed, to bid them farewell. She stood up and went out onto the gallery. Then she saw on the roof of the outbuilding stork after stork. All around the manor, above the tall trees, flew flocks in great circles. But right in front of her, on the edge of the well where little Helga had so often sat and screamed at her in her wildness, two swans now sat, looking at her with wise eyes. And she remembered her dream; it still filled her mind whole, as if it were quite real. She thought about little Helga in the swan form, she thought about the Christian priest, and suddenly she felt a wondrous joy in her heart.

The swans flapped their wings, bowed their heads, as if they too wanted to send a greeting. And the Viking woman stretched out her arms toward them, as if she understood, smiling amid tears and all her whirling thoughts.

Then with a great flapping of wings and clacking beaks, all the storks rose up and started on their journey south.

"We're not waiting for the swans," said Stork Mother. "If they want to go with us, they'll just have to come. We can't stay here until the plovers leave. There's something so charming about traveling as a family, after all, not like the chaffinches or reeves, where the males fly in one group and the females in another—properly speaking, it's not decent! And what kind of way is that to flap your wings, what the swans are doing?"

"Everyone has his own way of flying," said Stork Father. "The swans fly on the diagonal, the cranes in a triangle, and the plovers like a snake, in single file."

"Don't mention snakes when we're flying up here," said Stork Mother. "It will make the children want things they can't have."

"Are those the high mountains down there that I've heard about?" asked Helga in her swan skin.

"They're thunderclouds, drifting below us," said her mother.

"What are those white clouds rising so high up?" asked Helga.

"Those are the eternally snowcapped mountains that you're looking at," said her mother, and they flew over the Alps, heading south toward the blue Mediterranean Sea.

"The lands of Africa! The shores of Egypt!" rejoiced the daughter of the Nile, now in swan form, from high in the air as she glimpsed her homeland, like a wavy yellowish-white stripe.

The birds too looked down and hastened their flight.

"I can smell the Nile marsh and the wet frogs," said Stork Mother. "I feel a tickling inside me! Oh yes, now you're going to have tasty things to eat, and you'll see the marabou, the ibis, and the cranes. They're all related to our family, though not nearly as handsome as we are. They put on such airs, especially the ibis. He's been so pampered by the Egyptians. They make him into mummies, stuffing him with aromatic herbs. I'd rather be stuffed with live frogs, and you would too, and you will! Better to have something in your craw while you're alive than be put on display when you're dead! That's my opinion, and I'm always right."

"The storks have arrived," people said in the great house on the banks of the Nile. In the open hall on soft cushions covered with leopard skin, the royal lord lay stretched out, neither alive nor dead, hoping for the lotus blossom from the deep bog in the North. Kinsmen and servants stood around him.

Into the hall flew two magnificent white swans; they had come with the storks. They threw off their dazzling feather skins and there stood two lovely women, looking as much alike as two drops of dew. They bent over the pale, withered old man. They tossed their long hair back. And as little Helga leaned over her grandfather, his cheeks flushed, his eyes grew bright, and life returned to his rigid limbs. The old man sat up, healthy and rejuvenated. Daughter and granddaughter took him in their arms as if giving him a joyous morning greeting after a long, melancholy dream.

And there was joy everywhere on the estate and in the stork nest too, although there the greatest joy was over the good food: the swarms of frogs. And while the learned men in all haste wrote down a rough account of the story about the two princesses and the flower of health, which was a great event and a blessing for home and country, the stork parents spoke of it in their own way to their families, though not until they had all eaten their fill. They had other things to do, after all, than listen to stories.

"Now I'm sure you'll be given a title," whispered Stork Mother. "It's only reasonable."

"Oh, and what exactly would that be?" said Stork Father. "And what have I done? Nothing!"

"You've done more than all the others. Without you and the children the two princesses would never have seen Egypt again or made the old man well. You'll get a title. I'm sure you'll be given the title of doctor, and then our children will inherit it, and their children after them. You already look like an Egyptian doctor—at least in my eyes!"

The learned and wise formulated the basic principle, as they called it, that underlay the whole event: "Love nourishes life!" They explained this in several ways: "The warm ray of sun was the Egyptian princess. She went down to the Marsh King, and from their encounter sprang the flower."

"I can't repeat their words exactly," said Stork Father, who had listened from the rooftop and was trying to tell his family about it in the nest. "What they said was so complicated and so wise that they were at once given presents and promotions in rank. Even the royal chef was given a grand medal of distinction—that was probably for the soup!"

"And what did you get?" asked Stork Mother. "They can't forget the most important one of all, and that's you! The learned men just clacked their beaks over the whole thing. But I'm sure your turn will come."

Late at night, when the peace of slumber rested over the great, happy house, there was one person still awake, and it wasn't Stork Father, in spite of the fact that he was standing on one leg in the nest, a sleeping sentry. No, little Helga was awake, leaning over the balcony and gazing at the clear sky with the great, sparkling stars, bigger and purer in luster than she had ever seen them in the North, and yet the same. She thought about the Viking woman at Wild Bog, about her foster mother's gentle eyes, about the tears she had wept over the poor frog child, who now stood in the brilliant, starry splendor near the waters of the Nile in the lovely spring air. She thought about the love in the heathen woman's breast, the love she had shown to the pitiful creature who in human guise was an evil animal and in animal skin too beastly to look at or touch. She gazed at the glittering stars and remembered the glow from the dead man's brow when they flew over forest and bog. His voice resounded in her memory, words she had heard spoken as they rode along and she sat like someone bewitched, words about the great source of love, the highest love, that encompassed all creatures.

Oh, what had not been given, won, achieved! Little Helga's thoughts dwelled, by night and by day, on the vast sum of her happiness and were mesmerized by it like the child who turns swiftly from giver to what is given—to all those lovely gifts. She seemed caught up in the rising bliss that might come, would come. She was borne through miracles to ever higher joy and happiness, and one day she lost herself so much in this that she gave no more thought to the giver. It was the rashness of youthful audacity making its impetuous move! And it made her eyes light up, but she was suddenly torn away by a great commotion in the courtyard below. There she saw two mighty ostriches swiftly racing around in tight circles. Never before had she seen such an animal, such a huge bird, so plump and heavy. Its wings looked as if they had been clipped, the bird itself as if it had been harmed. She asked what had happened to it, and for the first time she heard the legend the Egyptians tell about the ostrich.

How lovely its kind had once been, its wings big and strong. Then one evening the forest's mighty birds said to it, "Brother! Should we, God willing, fly to the river tomorrow to drink?" And the ostrich replied, "I'm willing!" When day came, they flew off, heading first high up toward the sun, God's eye, ever higher and higher, with the ostrich far ahead of all the others. It flew with pride toward the light. It put its trust in its own powers and not in the giver. It did not say, "God willing!" Then the avenging angel drew aside the veil from the flaming radiance, and at that instant the bird's wings were singed. Miserable, it sank to earth. The ostrich and its kin can never again rise up. It flees in terror, rushing around in circles in the narrow space, a reminder to us humans that in our thoughts, with every deed, we should say, "God willing!"

Helga thoughtfully bowed her head. She gazed at the racing ostrich, saw its fear, saw its foolish joy at the sight of its own huge shadow on the white sunlit wall. And in her mind, somber thoughts planted deep roots. A life so rich, moving toward happiness, had been given, won. What would happen, what was yet to come? The best, "God willing!"

In early spring when the storks once again headed north, little Helga took off her gold bracelet, scratched her name on it, and beckoned to Stork Father. She put the gold bracelet around his neck and asked him to take it to the Viking woman, who would then understand that her foster daughter still lived, was happy, and had not forgotten her.

"This is hard to carry," said the stork when the bracelet was put around his neck. "But you don't throw gold and honor into the road. They'll realize up there that good fortune comes with the stork."

"You lay gold and I lay eggs," said Stork Mother. "But you lay only once, and I've been doing it all these years. Yet neither of us gets any appreciation. It's an outrage!"

"We have our good conscience, Mother," said Stork Father.

"You can't wear that around your neck," said Stork Mother. "It doesn't bring good winds or food."

And off they flew.

The little nightingale who sang in the tamarind bush would soon be heading north too. Little Helga had often heard it singing up there at Wild Bog. She would give it a message to take along. She knew the language of the birds from the time she flew in a swan skin. Since then she had often talked to the stork and swallow. The nightingale would understand her. And she asked it to fly to the beech forest on the Jutland peninsula where she had made the grave of stones and boughs. She told it to ask all the little birds to protect the grave and to sing a song and then another.

Off flew the nightingale. And time flew, too!

The eagle stood on the pyramid and saw in the autumn a stately caravan with richly laden camels. Armed men wearing costly attire rode snorting Arabian horses, shining white as silver and with quivering red nostrils. Their manes, thick and long, hung down around their elegant legs. Rich guests and a royal prince from the land of Arabia, handsome as a prince should be, entered the proud house where the stork's nest now stood empty. The birds who lived in it were in a northern country, of course, but soon they would return.

They arrived on the day that was filled with the greatest joy and merriment. Wedding splendor everywhere, and little Helga was the bride, dressed in silks and jewels. The bridegroom was the young prince from the land of Arabia. They sat at the head of the table between her mother and grandfather.

But she wasn't looking at the bridegroom's brown manly cheek where his black beard curled. She wasn't looking at his fiery dark eyes that were fixed on her. She was looking out, up at the glittering, sparkling star that shone down from the sky.

Then came the rustling sound of strong wings flapping in the air; the storks had come back. And the old stork couple, no matter how weary they were from the journey and in need of rest, flew at once down to the railing on the veranda. They knew all about the celebration. They had already heard at the border of the country that little Helga had ordered their likeness to be painted on the wall; they were part of her story.

"How very thoughtful that was," said Stork Father.

"How very paltry," said Stork Mother. "It was the very least she could do!"

When Helga saw them, she stood up and went out to them on the veranda, to stroke their backs. The old stork couple bowed their necks, as the youngest fledglings watched, feeling honored.

And Helga looked up at the glowing star that was shining brighter and brighter. Between her and the star a figure was moving, even purer than the air, and that's why it was visible. It hovered quite close to her; it was the dead Christian priest. He too had come to her celebration, come from the Kingdom of Heaven.

"There the radiance and glory surpass anything known on earth!" he said.

And little Helga prayed so tenderly, so fervently, as she had never prayed before, that for one single moment she might see inside, take one brief glance inside the Kingdom of Heaven, at the Father.

Then he lifted her up in radiance and glory, in a stream of melodies and thoughts; it glowed and resounded not just all around her but within her as well. Words cannot describe it.

"Now we must go back. You are missed!" he said.

"Just one more look," she begged. "Just one more brief moment."

"We must go back to earth, all the guests have gone."

"Just one more look. One last—!"

And little Helga once again stood on the veranda. But all the torches there had been put out, all the lights in the bridal hall were gone. The storks were gone, no guests were to be seen, and no bridegroom. Everything had vanished in three short minutes.

Then Helga grew frightened. She walked through the big, empty hall into the next room; there, foreign soldiers were sleeping. She opened the side door that led to her chambers, but when she thought she was standing inside, she was actually out in the garden. It was not like this before. The sky shone crimson. It was almost dawn.

Only three minutes in Heaven, and a whole night on earth had passed!

Then she saw the storks. She called to them, speaking their language, and Stork Father turned his head, listened, and came closer.

"You speak our language!" he said. "What is it you want? Why have you come here, strange woman?"

"But it's me! It's Helga! Don't you know me? Three minutes ago we were talking together, over there on the veranda."

"You must be mistaken," said the stork. "You must have dreamed the whole thing."

"No, no!" she said, and reminded him about the Viking stronghold and about Wild Bog and the journey they had made.

Then Stork Father blinked his eyes. "But that's an old story that I've heard from my great-great-great-grandmother's time! It's true that here in Egypt there was once such a princess from the land of

Denmark, but she disappeared on her wedding night many hundreds of years ago, and she never returned. You can read about it yourself here on this monument in the garden. Swans and storks are carved on it, and at the very top you're standing there yourself in the white marble!"

And what he said was true. Little Helga saw it, understood, and sank to her knees.

The sun broke through, and as in the past when its rays made the frog skin fall away and the lovely figure appear, now, at the baptism of light, a figure of beauty rose up, brighter and purer than air, a ray of light . . . to the Father.

Her body sank into dust. A withered lotus blossom lay where she had stood.

"That was a new ending to the story!" said Stork Father. "That's not what I expected at all. But I like it very much."

"What do you think the children will say about it?" asked Stork Mother.

"Well, of course that's what counts the most," said Stork Father.

The Wind Tells of Valdemar Daae and His Daughters

When the wind runs across the grass, the blades ripple like a pond; when it runs across the field, the grain billows like a lake. That's the dance of the wind. But listen to it speak: It sings the words out loud, and the sound is different in the trees of the forest than through the holes, cracks, and crevices of the wall. Can you see how the wind up there is chasing the clouds, as if they were a flock of sheep? Can you hear how the wind down here is sobbing through the open gate, as if it were a watchman blowing his horn? How odd the way it rushes down the chimney and into the stove. The fire flares up and sparks, shining far into the room. It's so warm and snug to sit here and listen to it. Just let the wind speak! It knows tales and stories, more than all the rest of us put together. Listen now, to the way it speaks:

"Hoo-ooh! Pass on!" That's the refrain to the song.

"Near the Great Belt there's an old manor house with thick red walls," says the wind. "I know every stone. I saw it in the past, when it was part of Marsk Stig's castle on the headland; it had to come down. The stones rose up again to become a new wall, a new estate in a different place; that was Borreby Manor, which stands there today.

"I've seen and known all the highborn gentlemen and ladies, the different families who have resided there. Now I'm going to tell you about Valdemar Daae and his daughters.

"He held his head so proudly; he was of royal lineage. He could do more than hunt a stag and empty a tankard. 'Everything will turn out fine,' he would say.

"His wife, straight-backed in a silk gown shot with gold threads, glided along her polished parquet floor. The tapestries were magnificent, the furniture costly and artfully carved. Silverware and gold she had brought to the house, German beer was stored in the cellar when there was beer to be had, and fiery black horses snorted in the stable. There were great riches at Borreby Manor, while the wealth lasted.

"And there were children: three elegant maidens—Ida, Johanna, and Anna Dorthea. I can still remember their names.

"They were wealthy people, refined people, born into glory and raised in it. Hoo-ooh! Pass on!" sang the wind and then resumed its story.

"There I never saw, as I did at the other old manors, the highborn mistress sitting in the great hall with her maids, turning the spinning wheel. She played the lilting lute and sang along, though not always the old Danish folk ballads, but rather songs in foreign tongues. The house was lively and festive. Distinguished guests came from far and near, music played, goblets clinked. I couldn't drown them out," said the wind. "There was an arrogance beyond all measure; noble folks, but not Our Lord.

"Then on the evening of May Day," said the wind, "I came from the west. I had seen ships smashed to wrecks on the west coast of Jutland, I had raced over the heath and the forest-green shore, across the island of Fyn, and then crossed the Great Belt, soaring and roaring.

"Then I lay down to rest on the coast of Sjælland, close to Borreby Manor where the forest still stood with glorious oaks.

"The young men from the region came there to gather boughs and branches, the biggest and driest they could find. They took them to town, placed them in a heap, and set fire to it. Then the girls and young men danced around the fire, singing.

"I lay still," said the wind, "but I gently moved one branch, the one that had been put there by the most handsome of the young men. His wood flared up, flared highest of all. He was the chosen one, awarded a title and proclaimed the May King. He chose from among the girls his little May Queen. There was joy and merriment greater than inside the rich Borreby Manor."

★

"And approaching the manor in a golden carriage drawn by six horses came the noble mistress and her three daughters, so elegant, so young; three enchanting flowers: rose, lily, and the pale hyacinth. Their mother was a resplendent tulip. Not one person in the whole crowd did she greet as they stopped their games to curtsy and bow. You'd almost think the mistress was brittle like a stalk.

"Rose, lily, and the pale hyacinth, yes, I saw all three! I thought to myself: Whose May Queen will they be someday? Their May King a proud knight, perhaps a prince? Hoo-ooh! Pass on! Pass on!

"Yes, the carriage rushed off with them, and the peasant folk rushed back to the dance. Preparations were made for summer in the town near Borreby, near Tjæreby, in all the surrounding towns.

"But that night when I rose up," said the wind, "the highborn mistress lay down, never to rise again. It came upon her as it comes upon all humans; it's nothing new. For a brief moment Valdemar Daae stood there, solemn and pensive. The proudest tree may be bowed but never broken, he heard a voice say inside him. His daughters wept, and at the manor everyone wiped their eyes, but Mistress Daae had passed on. And I passed on! Hoo-ooh!" said the wind.

"I went back, I went back often across the island of Fyn and the waters of the Great Belt. I sat down on Borreby Strand near the magnificent oak forest. There the osprey, the wood dove, the blue raven, and even the black stork built their nests. It was early in the year, some had eggs and some had fledglings. Oh, how they flew, how they shrieked. The crash of axes could be heard, blow after blow. The forest was going to be felled. Valdemar Daae wanted to build a costly ship, a man-of-war with three foredecks, which the king was certain to buy. That's why the forest had to fall, that landmark for the sailors, that home for the birds. The shrike flew off in terror; its nest was destroyed. The osprey and all the birds of the forest lost their homes. They flew around in confusion, shrieking in fear and anger. I understood them well. Crows and jackdaws jeered loudly: 'Gone the nest! Gone the nest! Gone! Gone!'

"And in the middle of the forest, near the crowd of workers,

stood Valdemar Daae and his three daughters. They were all laughing at the wild screams of the birds, but his youngest daughter,
Anna Dorthea, felt pity in her heart. They were also going to fell a
half-dead tree on whose bare branches the black stork had built its
nest, and the little fledglings were poking out their heads. She
pleaded for them, pleaded with tears in her eyes, and so the tree
was allowed to stay, keeping its nest for the black stork. It was a
mere trifle.

"They chopped and they sawed; a ship was built with three
foredecks. The master builder was of lowly lineage but of noble
countenance. His eyes and brow revealed how wise he was, and
Valdemar Daae liked to hear his stories, as did little Ida, the eldest
daughter, a girl of fifteen. And while he built the ship for her father,
he built for himself a dream castle in which he and little Ida lived
as man and wife. That might have happened if only the castle had
been made of mortared stone and ramparts and trenches, woods
and gardens. But for all his shrewdness, the master builder was still
an impoverished bird, and what place does a sparrow have in a
crane's mating dance? Hoo-ooh! I flew away and he flew away, for
he didn't dare stay, and little Ida recovered from it, because recover
she must."

"In the stable snorted the black horses—worth seeing, and seen
they were. The admiral was sent by the king himself to take a look
at the new man-of-war and discuss its purchase. He spoke in loud
admiration of the fiery horses. I heard it myself," said the wind. "I
followed the gentlemen through the open door and spread the
straw like rods of gold before their feet. Gold was what Valdemar
Daae wanted; the admiral wanted the black horses, for he praised
them so highly. But this was not understood, and so the ship was
never sold. It stood and gleamed at the shore, covered with planks,
a Noah's Ark that never entered the water. Hoo-ooh! Pass on! Pass
on! What a pity that was!

"In the wintertime, when the fields lay under snow, drift ice
filled the strait and I packed it against the shore," said the wind.
"Ravens and crows arrived, each one blacker than the last, in huge
flocks. They landed on that desolate, that dead, that lonely ship at
the shore and screamed their hoarse cries about the forest that was

gone, the many precious birds' nests that had been destroyed, the homeless old ones, the homeless young, and all for the sake of this great junk heap, this proud vessel that would never set sail.

"I whirled the snow into drifts. The snow lay like great swells rising high on all sides, rising over it. I let it hear my voice, what a storm has to say. I know I did my utmost to give it the knowledge a ship should have. Hoo-ooh! Pass on!

"And winter passed on, both winter and summer passed on. They race by and they pass on, just as I race by, just as the snow drifts, the apple blossom drifts, and the leaf falls. Pass on, pass on, pass on! So too must human beings.

"But the daughters were still young. Little Ida a rose as lovely to look at as when the shipbuilder saw her. Often I would seize hold of her long brown tresses when she stood in the garden near the apple tree, lost in thought, not noticing that I was sprinkling blossoms onto her hair, which had come undone. And she gazed at the red sun and the golden backdrop of sky between the dark shrubs and trees of the garden.

"Her sister was like a lily, shimmering and straight. Johanna, her bearing noble and erect, and like her mother a brittle stalk. She took pleasure in walking through the great hall where the ancestral portraits hung. The ladies were painted wearing velvet and silk with tiny pearl-studded caps on their plaited hair. What beautiful ladies! Their husbands wore steel or costly cloaks lined with squirrel skin with blue pleated ruffs. Their swords were fastened to their thigh and not to their waist. Where would Johanna's portrait one day hang on the wall? How would her noble husband look? Yes, that's what she thought about, that's what she chattered about; I heard it as I passed through the long corridor into the hall and then turned around.

"Anna Dorthea, the pale hyacinth, a mere child of fourteen, was quiet and pensive. Her big, pale blue eyes looked thoughtful, but a childish smile played on her lips. I could not blow it away, nor did I wish to.

"I met her in the garden, on the sunken road, and in the serf-tended fields. She was gathering herbs and flowers, the ones she knew that her father could use in the potions and tinctures he was distilling. Valdemar Daae was arrogant and proud, but also skillful and possessed of great knowledge. People had taken note of this, and there was much talk. The fire burned in his hearth even in summer; his chamber door was locked. This went on for days and nights, but he said very little about it. The forces of nature must be quietly explored. Soon he would discover the very best: red gold.

"That's why steam poured from the hearth, that's why it crackled and blazed. Oh yes, I was there," explained the wind. "'Let it go! Let it go!' I sang through the chimney. 'It will be nothing but smoke, soot, embers, and ashes! You'll burn yourself up!' Hoo-ooh! Pass on! Pass on! But Valdemar Daae did not let it go.

"The magnificent horses in the stable—what happened to them? What about the old silverware and gold in the cupboards and bowers, the cows in the fields, the lands and estate? Well, they could be melted! Melted in the gold crucible, and yet no gold appears.

"There was nothing left in the barn or storerooms, in the cellar or attic. Fewer servants, more mice. One windowpane shattered, another cracked; I no longer had to go through the door," said the wind. "When the chimney is smoking, a meal is cooking. And the chimney smoked, the one that devours all meals, for the sake of red gold.

"I blew through the castle gate, like a watchman blowing his horn, but there was no watchman," said the wind. "I spun the weathervane on the steeple; it creaked as if the watchman were snoring on the tower, but there was no watchman. There were rats and mice. Poverty set the table, poverty sat in the wardrobe and in the pantry. The door came off its hinges, cracks and crevices appeared. I went out and I went in," said the wind. "That's why I know all about it.

"In smoke and ashes, in sorrow and sleepless nights the hair in his beard and on his brow turned gray, his skin grimy and yellow, his eyes so greedy for gold, the long-awaited gold.

"I blew smoke and ashes into his face and beard. Debts appeared instead of gold. I sang through the broken panes and open cracks, blew at his daughters' sleeping benches where their clothes lay faded and threadbare, because they had to last forever. That song was not sung at the cradle of these children. The noble life became a wretched life. I was the only one who sang aloud in the castle," said the wind. "I snowed them in, because that's said to bring warmth. They had no firewood. The forest, where they should have found wood, had been felled. It was a bitter frost. I swung through sound holes and corridors, over gables and walls to keep myself brisk. Inside they lay in their beds because of the cold, those noble daughters. Their father crept under the hide coverlet. Nothing to bite and nothing to burn, that's the noble life! Hoo-ooh! Pass on! But Sir Daae could not.

"'After winter comes spring,' he said. 'After bad times come good. But they're long overdue, long overdue. Now the manor has been mortgaged. Now is the time of our greatest need—and so the gold will come. At Easter!'

"I heard him muttering to the spider's web, 'You clever little weaver! You've taught me to keep going. If your web is torn apart, you start over and complete it. Torn apart again—and undismayed you set to work, from the beginning. The beginning! That's what a person has to do. And he will be rewarded.'

"It was Easter morning. The bells chimed, the sun played in the sky. Burning with fever he had kept vigil, boiling and cooling, mixing and distilling. I heard him sigh like a desperate soul, I heard him pray, I could sense that he was holding his breath. The lamp had gone out, he didn't notice. I blew on the charcoal embers, they shone on his chalk-white face, it took on a tinge of color. His eyes were squinting in their deep sockets, but now they grew bigger, bigger—as if they would burst.

"Look at that alchemical flask! Something is shining inside! It's gleaming, pure and heavy! He lifted it up with a trembling hand, he shouted with a trembling tongue, 'Gold! Gold!' And with that he grew faint, I could have blown him over," said the wind. "But I merely blew on the glowing coals and followed him through the door to where his daughters sat freezing. His coat was covered with ashes, they hung in his beard and in his tangled hair. He drew himself up tall, lifted his precious treasure in the fragile flask. 'Discovered! Recovered! Gold!' he cried, holding high the flask, which sparkled in the sunlight. But his hand shook and the flask dropped to the floor and shattered into a thousand pieces. Burst was the last bubble of his well-being. Hoo-ooh! Pass on! And I rushed from the alchemist's manor.

"Late in the year, when the days are short up here, when the fog arrives with its dishrag and wrings wet drops onto the red berries and the leafless branches, I arrived in a cheerful mood to air things out. I blew the air clean and snapped off rotten branches, and that's not a huge task, but it has to be done. Things were swept clean in another way at Borreby Manor, the home of Valdemar Daae. His enemy, Ove Ramel from Basnæs, had come with the purchased mortgage deed in hand for the estate and all its contents. I drummed on the broken windowpanes, slammed the ramshackle doors, whistled through the cracks and crevices: Hoo-ee! Sir Ove would have no desire to stay there. Ida and Anna Dorthea wept brave tears. Johanna stood straight-backed and pale, chewing her thumb until it bled. What good would that do? Ove Ramel granted Sir Daae permission to stay at the manor for the rest of his life, but he won no thanks for his offer. I was listening. I saw the landless gentleman raise his head even prouder, giving it a toss, and I blew a gust at the estate and the old linden trees, breaking the thickest branch in half, though it wasn't even rotten. It lay in front of the gate, like a broom, if anyone wanted to do any sweeping. And sweep they did. I thought as much!

"It was a hard day, a bitter hour to endure, but the will was stubborn, the neck was stiff.

"Not a thing did they possess but the clothes on their backs. Oh yes, the alchemical flask that had been recently purchased and filled with scrapings from what had spilled on the floor; the promised treasure that had failed to last. Valdemar Daae hid it inside his waistcoat, then took his stick in hand, and the once rich gentleman and his three daughters left Borreby Manor. I blew cold air on his hot cheeks, I caressed his gray beard and his long white hair, I sang the only way I know how: Hoo-ooh! Pass on! Pass on! That was the end of their rich splendor.

"Ida and Anna Dorthea walked on either side of him. Johanna turned around at the gate. What good was that? Their fortunes were not about to turn. She looked at the red stones in the wall that came from Marsk Stig's castle, she thought about his daughters:

'The eldest took the youngest's hand,
And they set off into the wide world!'

"She thought about that song. Here were the three of them; their father was with them too. They were walking along the road they once had traveled in a carriage. They were setting off as beggars with their father for Smidstrup Field, to the mud-and-wattle hovel they had leased for ten marks a year, their new manor house with empty walls and empty vessels. Crows and jackdaws flew above them, screeching as if in spite, 'Gone the nest! Gone the nest! Gone! Gone!' just as the birds had screeched in Borreby Forest when the trees were felled.

"Sir Daae and his daughters certainly heard it. But I blew hard at their ears; it wasn't worth hearing.

"Then they went inside the mud-and-wattle hovel at Smidstrup Field. And I rushed across bog and field, through naked hedges and plucked forests, to open waters, other lands. Hoo-ooh! Pass on! Pass on! And keep on for years and years!"

What happened to Valdemar Daae? What happened to his daughters? The wind says:

"The last I saw of them, yes, the very last, it was Anna Dorthea, the pale hyacinth. By then she was old and bowed, it was half a century later. She had lived the longest, she knew the whole story.

"Over there on the heath near the town of Viborg stood the dean's stately new manor with red stones and a stepped gable. Thick smoke rose from the chimney. The gentle mistress and her fair daughters sat in the bay window and gazed out over the garden's drooping boxthorn, out toward the brown heath. What were they looking for? They were looking for the stork's nest out there on the tumbledown house. The roof was covered with moss and houseleeks—what was left of the roof. It was the stork's nest that provided the most cover, and it was the only thing that had been mended; the stork kept it in good repair.

"It was a house to be looked at but not touched. I had to move cautiously," said the wind. "For the sake of the stork's nest the house was allowed to stand, otherwise it was an eyesore on the heath. But the dean didn't want to chase the stork away, so the hovel was allowed to remain, and the poor person inside was permitted to live there. For that she could thank the Egyptian bird. Or was it gratitude because she had once pleaded for the nest of his wild black brother in Borreby Forest? Back then the poor thing was a young girl, an elegant pale hyacinth in the noble garden. She remembered it all: Anna Dorthea.

"'Oh! Oh!' Yes, human beings can sigh just like the wind does through the reeds and rushes. 'Oh! No bells tolled over your grave, Valdemar Daae. The poor schoolboys did not sing when the former lord of Borreby was laid in the earth. Oh! Everything comes to an end, even misery. Sister Ida became a peasant's wife. That was the harshest trial for our father. His daughter's husband a wretched thrall subject to the master's punishment to ride the wooden horse. Surely by now he must be in his grave? And you as well? Ida! Oh yes! Oh yes! It is not yet over, old wretch that I am. Poor wretch that I am! Release me, mighty Christ!'

"That was Anna Dorthea's prayer in the pitiful hovel that was allowed to stand for the sake of the stork.

"The most spirited sister I took care of myself," said the wind. "She had clothes made to match the spirit that was hers at birth. She appeared as a poor lad and hired on with a ship's captain. Few in words, sullen in looks, but willing to do her job, although she could not climb. Then I blew her overboard before anyone found out that she was a woman. What a good thing I did!" said the wind.

"It was Easter morning, just like the time when Valdemar Daae thought he had discovered red gold, when I heard beneath the stork's nest between the flimsy walls, a hymn, Anna Dorthea's last song.

"There was no windowpane, there was merely a hole in the wall. The sun appeared, like a lump of gold, and settled there. How it glowed! Her eyes burst, her heart burst. They would have done so even if the sun had not shone on her that morning.

"The stork gave her a roof over her head until her death. I sang at her grave," said the wind. "I sang at her father's grave. I know where it is and where hers is too, but no one else knows.

"New times, other times! Old thoroughfares lead to fenced fields, hallowed graves become frequented highways. And soon the steam engine will come with its strings of cars and roar over the graves, forgotten just like the names. Hoo-ooh! Pass on!

"That's the story of Valdemar Daae and his daughters. Go ahead and tell it better, the rest of you—if you can!" said the wind, and turned away.

It was gone.

The Snowman

"I'm creaking all over, it's so wondrously cold," said the snowman. "The wind can certainly bite life into a person! And how that glowering creature over there is glaring!" It was the sun he meant; it was just about to go down. "She's not going to make me blink, I know how to hold on to my tiles!"

He had two big triangular roof tiles for his eyes. His mouth was part of an old rake, and that's why he had teeth.

He was born to the boys' shouts of hurrah, greeted with the clanging of bells and the crack of whips from the sleighs.

The sun went down, the full moon rose, big and round, bright and lovely in the blue sky.

"There we have her again from a different direction," said the snowman. He thought it was the sun that had reappeared. "I've taught her not to glare. Now she can hang there and shine so I can see myself. If only I knew what to do so I could move. I would dearly like to move. If I could do that, I would go down and slide around on the ice, the way the boys were doing. But I don't know how to run."

"Gone, gone!" barked the old watchdog. He was rather hoarse and had been that way ever since he was the house pet and lay under the stove. "The sun will surely teach you to run. I saw that happen to your predecessor last year and to his predecessor too. Gone, gone! Every one of them gone!"

"I don't understand what you're saying, my friend," said the snowman. "Is that thing up there supposed to teach me to run?" He meant the moon. "Well, it's true that she ran off before when I gave her a stern look. Now she's sneaking up from a different direction."

"You don't know a thing!" said the watchdog. "But then, you've only recently been patted together. What you're looking at is called the moon; the one that left is the sun. She'll be back in the morning, and she'll teach you to run down to the moat. We'll soon have a change in the weather, I can feel it in my left hind leg; I've got a shooting pain in it. We're due for a change in the weather."

"I don't understand him," said the snowman. "But I have the feeling that he's telling me something unpleasant. The one that was shining and went down, the one he calls the sun . . . I have a feeling that she's not my friend either."

"Gone, gone!" barked the watchdog as he spun around three times and then lay down inside his house to sleep.

A change in weather truly did come. A fog, thick and damp, spread in the early morning hour over the entire region. At dawn came a light breeze. The wind was so icy that the frost took a firm grip, but what a sight there was when the sun came up! All the trees and shrubs were covered with rime; it looked like an entire forest of white corals, as if all the branches were heaped with dazzling white flowers. The infinitely numerous and delicate network of branches, which is impossible to see in the summer because of all the leaves, now appeared, every single twig. It was a lacework, and so glittering white, as if a white glow were streaming from every branch. The weeping birch stirred in the wind; there was life in it, like in the trees during the summer. It was lovely beyond compare! And when the sun shone, oh, how everything sparkled, as if powdered with diamond dust, and all across the snow on the ground glittered huge diamonds, or you might also think that countless tiny little candles were burning, even whiter than the white snow.

"It *is* lovely beyond compare!" said the young girl who had come into the garden with a young man and stopped right next to the snowman to look at the glittering trees. "There's no sight as lovely as this in the summertime," she said, and her eyes shone.

"And a lad like that we wouldn't find at all," said the young man, pointing at the snowman. "He's splendid!"

The young girl laughed, nodded at the snowman, and then danced with her friend across the snow, which creaked under them as if they were treading on starch.

"Who are those two?" the snowman asked the watchdog. "You've been on the manor longer than I have; do you know them?"

"Yes, I do," said the watchdog. "She once petted me, and he once gave me a meat bone. Those two I wouldn't bite!"

"But what are they doing here?" asked the snowman.

"Sweeeeeeeeet-hearts!" said the watchdog. "They're going to move into a doghouse together and gnaw on bones. Gone, gone!"

"Are those two just as important as you and I?" asked the snowman.

"They belong to the master's family, of course!" said the watchdog. "How little a person knows when he's born yesterday! I can see that about you. I have age and knowledge, I know everyone here on the manor. And I've known a time when I didn't have to stand out here in the cold on a chain. Gone, gone!"

"The cold is lovely," said the snowman. "Tell me more, tell me more. But you mustn't rattle your chain, because it makes me creak inside."

"Gone, gone!" barked the watchdog. "A pup I once was; little and charming, they said. Back then I lay on the velvet chair inside the manor, lay on the laps of the whole family. They kissed me on the snout and wiped my paws with embroidered handkerchiefs. I was called 'the loveliest' and 'little doggie.' But then I got too big for them, so they gave me to the housekeeper. I wound up in the cellar. You can look down into it from where you're standing. You can look right into the room where I was the master because I was living with the housekeeper. It was a more modest place than upstairs, I suppose, but more comfortable. I wasn't hugged and hauled around by the children, the way I was upstairs. The food was just as good as before, and there was more of it. I had my own pillow, and there was a stove. At this time of year that's the loveliest thing in the world. I crept all the way under it so I was completely out of sight. Oh, I still dream about that stove. Gone, gone!"

"Does a stove look so lovely?" said the snowman. "Does it look like me?"

"It's just the opposite of you! It's coal-black, with a long neck and a brass belly. It devours wood so that fire pours out of its mouth. You have to keep to one side of it, very close, right underneath. Oh, such boundless comfort! You should be able to see it through the window from where you're standing."

And the snowman looked, and he actually saw a black, polished object with a brass belly. Fire was glowing inside it down below. A strange feeling came over the snowman; he couldn't explain it. Something came over him that he didn't recognize but that all humans recognize, as long as they're not snowmen.

"And why did you leave her?" said the snowman. He felt that the stove had to be a female creature. "How could you ever leave such a place?"

"Well, I was forced to," said the watchdog. "They threw me outside and put me here on a chain. I bit the youngest squire on the leg because he kicked away the leg bone I was gnawing on; and a leg for a leg, in my mind! But they didn't take it well, and from that day on I've stood out here, chained up, and I've lost my clear voice. Just listen to how hoarse I am: Gone, gone! And that was the end of that!"

The snowman wasn't listening anymore. He was still looking inside the housekeeper's cellar quarters, peering down into her room where the stove stood on its four cast-iron legs and looked to be about the same size as the snowman himself.

"It's creaking so strangely inside of me!" he said. "Will I never be allowed inside there? It's a harmless wish, and surely our harmless wishes should be fulfilled. It's my greatest wish, my only wish, and it would be practically an injustice if it weren't granted. I must go inside, I must lean against her, even if I have to break the window!"

"You'll never get inside there," said the watchdog. "And if you reached the stove, then you'd be gone. Gone!"

"I'm already as good as gone," said the snowman. "I think I'm breaking in half!"

All day long the snowman stood there looking in the window. At dusk the room became even more inviting. From the stove came such a gentle light, not like the glow of the moon or the sun, no, but only the way a stove can glow when there's something inside it. When the door opened, flames would shoot out, as they usually did. The snowman's white face flared bright red; he was red all down his chest.

"I can't bear it!" he said. "How becoming she looks when she sticks out her tongue!"

The night was very long, but not for the snowman. He stood lost in his own lovely thoughts and they froze so they creaked.

In the early morning hour the cellar windows were frosted over; they bore the loveliest ice blossoms that any snowman could ask for, but they hid the stove. The windowpanes refused to thaw out. He couldn't see her. There was a creaking and crunching—it was exactly the kind of frosty weather that should please a snowman, but he was not pleased. He could and should have felt so happy, but he was not happy; he was suffering from stove-longing.

"That's a bad sickness for a snowman," said the watchdog. "I too have suffered from that sickness, but I got over it. Gone, gone! Now we're going to have a change in the weather."

And the change in weather arrived. The frost turned to thaw.

The thaw grew stronger, the snowman grew weaker. He didn't say a word, he never complained, and that's a sure sign.

One morning he toppled over. Something that looked like a broomstick was poking up in the air where he had stood; that's what the boys had built him around.

"Now I can better understand his longing," said the watchdog. "The snowman had a stove poker inside his body. That's what was stirring inside him. Now that's over. Gone, gone!"

And soon winter was over too.

"Gone, gone!" barked the watchdog. But the little girls on the manor sang:

> 'Sprout forth, woodruff! Fresh and fair,
> Hang down, willow, your mitten pair!
> Come, cuckoo, come lark! Let's sing!
> In February we're having spring!
> I'll sing along, Chirp-chirp! Cuckoo!
> Come, dear sun, come often too!'

And no one gave another thought to the snowman.

The Ice Maiden

L et's pay a visit to Switzerland, let's take a look around in the
glorious mountain landscape where the forests grow on the
steep rock faces. Let's climb up to the dazzling snowfields
and then walk back to the green meadows where the rivers and
streams rush along as if afraid they might not reach the sea in time
and disappear. The sun is blazing in the deep valley. It's blazing on
the heavy snow masses high above, making them melt together
over the years into gleaming blocks of ice, to become cascading
avalanches and towering glaciers. Two of them lie in the wide
ravines beneath Schreckhorn and Wetterhorn, near the little mountain village of Grindelwald. They are peculiar sights, and that's
why, in the summer, many strangers come here from all countries
of the world. They come over the high, snow-covered mountains;
they come from below, in the deep valleys. For hours they have to
climb, and as they climb, the valley sinks farther behind. They look
down into it as if they were peering from a balloon. Clouds often
hover overhead like thick, heavy curtains of smoke around the
mountain peaks, while down in the valley, where scores of brown
wooden houses are scattered about, a ray of sun still glitters, lighting
up a patch in radiant green, as if it were transparent. The water
rushes, drones, and roars below, the water trickles and murmurs
above, looking like fluttering ribbons of silver along the rock face.

On both sides of the road leading up the slope stand half-timbered
houses, each with its own little potato patch, which is a necessity
since inside there are many mouths to feed. This place is brimming
with children, and they certainly have big appetites. From all the
houses they tumble out, crowding around the travelers, whether
they arrive on foot or by coach. All the children are engaged in

trade. The little ones offer for sale exquisitely carved wooden houses that look like the ones built in these mountains. Rain or shine, the swarms of children appear with their wares.

Twenty-odd years ago, a little boy would stand here from time to time, but always slightly apart from the other children, wanting to sell something too. He stood with such a serious expression and with both hands holding tight to his splint-wood box, as if he didn't want to part with it after all. But it was precisely because of this earnestness and the fact that the lad was so young that people noticed him, yes, even singled him out, and he often made the best sales, though he couldn't have said why. Higher up the mountain lived his maternal grandfather, who carved the exquisite, splendid houses, and up there in one room stood an old cupboard filled with all kinds of carvings. There were nutcrackers, knives, forks, and boxes with lovely foliage and leaping chamois; everything that might please a child's eye. But the little boy, whose name was Rudy, looked with greater desire and longing at the old rifle up in the rafters. His grandfather had said that one day it would be his, but first he had to grow strong and big enough to use it.

Even though the boy was young, he was put in charge of watching the goats. If being able to clamber around with them was the sign of a good herder, then Rudy was a good herder. He climbed even a bit higher than they did because he was fond of looking for birds' nests high up in the trees. He was daring and bold, but no one ever saw him smile except when he stood near the rushing waterfall or when he heard the rumble of an avalanche. He never played with the other children. He joined them only when his grandfather sent him down to sell his wares, and Rudy didn't care much for that. He preferred to scamper around on the slopes alone or sit with his grandfather and listen to him talk about the old days and the people in nearby Meiringen, where he was from. The people hadn't been there since the beginning of the world, he said, but had migrated there. They had come from the far north, and that's where their ancestors lived, known as "Swedes." It took great wisdom to learn this, and Rudy had learned it, but he gained even more wisdom from spending time with the other occupants of the house, those belonging to the race of animals. They had a big dog named Ajola that Rudy had inherited from his father, and they had a tomcat. It was this cat, in particular, who came to mean a great deal to Rudy. The cat taught him how to climb.

"Come out on the roof with me!" the cat had said, quite clearly and intelligibly, because when you're a child and can't yet talk, you understand perfectly the hens and ducks, cats and dogs. They speak to us just as clearly as Father and Mother speak; you just have to be very young. Even Grandfather's cane can whinny and turn into a horse, with head, legs, and tail. For some children the ability to understand fades later than for others, and people say they are slow and remain children for far too long. But people say so many things!

"Come with me, little Rudy, out onto the roof!" That was one of the first things the cat said, and Rudy understood. "People just imagine that they're going to fall. You won't fall if you're not afraid. Come on, put one paw here, the other over there. Feel your way with your front paws. Keep your eyes alert, and your limbs nimble. If there's a gap, then jump over it, and hold on tight, that's what I do."

And that's what Rudy did too. That's why he sat so often up on the ridgepole with the cat. He also sat with him in the treetops, and he even sat high up on rocky precipices where the cat never went.

"Higher! Higher!" said the trees and shrubs. "Do you see how high we climb? Look how high we reach, where we cling so tightly, even to the very tip of the narrow rock ledge."

And Rudy would make his way to the top of the mountain, often before the sun had reached it, and take his morning drink: the fresh, invigorating mountain air, the drink that only Our Lord can prepare, although humans can read the recipe. It says: fresh fragrance of mountain herbs, mint from the valley, and thyme. Everything that is oppressive the hovering clouds absorb, and then the winds card them through the spruce forests like wool. The breath of fragrance turns to air, light and fresh, always fresher. That was Rudy's morning drink.

The sunbeams, daughters of the sun, brought their blessings and kissed his cheeks, while Vertigo stood nearby, lurking but not daring to approach. And the swallows from Grandfather's house— never fewer than seven nests—flew up to him and the goats, singing: "You and us! Us and you!" They brought greetings from home, even from the two hens, the only birds allowed inside the house, though Rudy never spoke to them.

In spite of his young age, he had traveled quite a bit, and over considerable distances for such a small lad. He was born in Canton Valais and was carried here over the mountains. Recently he had gone on foot to visit nearby Staubbach waterfall, which billows like a silver veil in the air before the snow-covered, dazzling white Jungfrau. And he had been to Grindelwald to see the great glacier, but that was a sad story; that was where his mother had met her death. "That's where all childish merriment was swept out of little Rudy," his grandfather said. "Before the child was a year old he laughed more than he cried," his mother had written. But ever since he landed in the ice crevasse, quite a different temperament had taken hold of him. Grandfather rarely spoke of this, but everyone on the mountain knew what had happened.

Rudy's father, as we know, had been the mail-coach driver. The big dog at home had always accompanied him on his route over the Simplon Pass and down to Lake Geneva. Rudy's relatives on his father's side still lived in the valley of the Rhône in Canton Valais. His uncle was a skilled chamois hunter and a well-known guide. Rudy was only a year old when he lost his father, and his mother decided to take her little child home to her family in the Berner Oberland. Her father lived several hours' journey from Grindelwald. He was a woodcarver and earned enough to live comfortably. In June she left, carrying her infant, in the company of two chamois hunters, heading home across the Gemmi Pass to reach Grindelwald. Most of the journey was behind them when they came across the ridge to the snowfield and caught sight of her home valley, with its familiar wooden houses scattered about. All that remained was the difficult task of walking across the highest part of one of the great glaciers. The newly fallen snow hid a chasm, which did not reach down to the very bottom where the water roared, but it was still deeper than a man's height. The young woman carrying her child slipped, fell through, and was gone. No one heard a scream or a sigh, but they heard a little child crying. More than an hour passed before her two companions managed to bring ropes and poles from the nearest house below, hoping they might help. After great difficulty they pulled from the icy crevasse two bodies, or so it seemed. Using every means possible they succeeded in calling the child back to life, but not the mother. And so the old grandfather received in his house not his daughter but his daughter's son, the child who laughed more often than he cried, though that habit now seemed to have been broken. The change no doubt occurred inside the glacier cleft, inside the strange, cold world of ice where the souls of the condemned are locked inside until Judgment Day, as the Swiss peasants believe.

Not unlike a rushing stream, frozen and pressed into green blocks of glass, the glacier lies there, with one immense block of ice heaped on top of another. In the depths below thunders the roiling current of melted snow and ice. Deep caves and mighty chasms tower up inside. It's a wondrous glass palace, and inside lives the Ice Maiden, the glacier queen. She who kills and crushes is partly a child of the air, partly the mighty ruler of the river. That's why she has the power to ascend with the speed of a chamois up to the very peak of the snowy mountain where the most daring of mountain climbers have to chop footholds in the ice. She sails on a slender spruce bough along the speeding river, leaps from boulder to boulder, with her long snow-white hair fluttering around her and her blue-green gown glistening like water in the deep Swiss lakes.

"Crush, hold tight! The power is mine!" she says. "A lovely boy they stole from me, a boy I had kissed, but not kissed to death. He is once again among humans. He is herding goats on the mountain, clambering up, always upward, away from the others, but not from me. He's mine, and I shall take him!"

And she told Vertigo to carry out her orders. In the summertime it was too sultry for the Ice Maiden out in the open where the mint plants thrive. So Vertigo rose up and dove down; one appeared, then three. Vertigo has many sisters, a whole flock of them. And the Ice Maiden chose the strongest among them who rule both indoors and out. They sit on banisters and on tower railings, they run like squirrels along mountain ledges, they leap outdoors and tread air the way swimmers tread water, luring their victims out and down into the abyss. Vertigo and the Ice Maiden both seize hold of humans the way the polyp grabs everything that comes near. Vertigo would seize hold of Rudy.

"You want me to grab him," said Vertigo. "But I can't do it! The cat, that scoundrel, has taught the boy his tricks. That child has a special power that chases me away. I can't reach that little lad when he's hanging from a branch over the abyss, no matter how I'd like to tickle the soles of his feet or give him a shove into the air. I can't do it!"

"We can do it!" said the Ice Maiden. "You or I! I! I!"

"No, no!" they heard as if the mountain were echoing the ringing of the church bells, but it was a song, it was a voice, it was a merging choir from other spirits of nature, gentle, loving, and good: the sunbeams' daughters. Each evening they settle down in a circle on the mountain peaks, spreading out their rose-colored wings, which, as the sun sinks, blaze redder and redder, making the towering Alps glow. People call it the "alpenglow." Then, after the sun goes down, they retreat inside the summits, into the white snow, sleeping there until the sun comes up, when they once again emerge. They especially love flowers, butterflies, and human beings, and little Rudy was their favorite.

"You'll never catch him. You'll never keep him," they said.

"Bigger and stronger ones have I caught and kept," said the Ice Maiden.

Then the daughters of the sun sang a song about the wanderer from whom the whirling wind tore his cloak and carried it off at a raging speed. The wind took the mortal husk but not the man. "You children of force might seize him but you can never hold him. He is stronger, he is more ethereal than we are! He climbs higher than our mother, the sun! He knows the secret word that binds the wind and water so they must serve and obey him. If you loosen the heavy, oppressive weight, he will rise up even higher."

How lovely was the choir, ringing like church bells.

And every morning the rays of the sun shone through the one little window in Grandfather's house, to reach the silent child. The sunbeams' daughters wanted to thaw out, warm up, take away once and for all the ice-kisses that the royal maiden of the glacier had given him when he lay in the arms of his dead mother inside the deep ice crevasse from which he was rescued, as if by a miracle.

II.
JOURNEY TO THE NEW HOME

Rudy was now eight years old. His uncle in the Rhône Valley, on the other side of the mountains, wanted the boy to come stay with him; there he could be given better training and have more of a future. His grandfather realized this and agreed to let him go.

So Rudy would soon be leaving. There were many others besides his grandfather from whom he needed to take leave. First there was Ajola, the old dog.

"Your father drove the mail coach, and I was the mail-coach dog," said Ajola. "We traveled up and down; I know all the dogs and people, even on the other side of the mountains. I've never been one to say much, but now that we don't have much longer to talk, I want to say a bit more than I usually do. I want to tell you a story that I've been brooding about for a long time. I don't understand it, and you won't either, but that doesn't matter because what it taught me is that things aren't fairly divided up in the world, either for dogs or for humans. Not everyone was born to lie on a lap or to slurp up milk. It's not something I've ever been accustomed to, but I've seen a puppy riding along in the mail coach, sitting where a person should sit. The lady who was his mistress, or for whom he was the master, had brought along a milk bottle and was feeding the puppy with it. She offered him bread sprinkled with sugar, but he didn't even deign to eat it, just sniffed at it, and then she ate it herself. I ran through the mud alongside the coach, as hungry as a dog can be. I was chewing on my own thoughts; things were not as they should be, but no doubt plenty of things are not. I hope you're allowed to ride inside a carriage, and ride in luxury, but that's not something you can bring about on your own. I've never been able to do it, either by barking or baying."

That was Ajola's speech, and Rudy threw his arms around the dog's neck and kissed him right on his wet snout. Then he picked up the cat, who tried to twist out of his grasp.

"You're getting too strong for me, and I don't want to use my claws on you! Go ahead and clamber over the mountains. I taught you how to climb. Don't ever believe that you're going to fall, and then you'll do just fine!" Then the cat ran off because he didn't want Rudy to see the sorrow shining in his eyes.

The hens scurried around on the floor. One of them had lost her tail. A traveler who wanted to be a hunter had shot off her tail, because the man mistook the hen for a bird of prey.

"Rudy is going over the mountains," said one of the hens.

"He's always in a hurry," said the other. "And I don't like farewells." Then both of them trotted off.

He also said goodbye to the goats, and they shouted, "Back! Back! Ba-aaa!" And it was very sad.

Among the people of the district there were two clever guides who were about to set off over the mountains. They were heading down the other side toward Gemmi Pass, and Rudy went along with them, on foot. It was a difficult hike for such a young lad, but he was strong, and his courage never flagged.

The swallows flew along part of the way. "You and us! And us and you!" they sang. The path led over the tumbling Lütschine, which, in scores of little streams, rushes out of the black chasm of the Grindelwald glacier. Drifting tree trunks and fallen boulders served as a bridge. Then they reached the alder thickets and started to ascend the mountain, close to the place where the glacier had broken loose from the slope. They were walking on the glacier, across the blocks of ice and around them. Rudy had to crawl for a bit, then walk for a bit. His eyes were shining with sheer enjoyment, and he set down his iron-clad mountaineering boots very firmly, as if he wanted to mark his passage. The black sediment that the mountain stream had poured over the glacier gave it a singed appearance, yet the blue-green, glassy ice shone through. They had to go around the little ponds, rimmed by upthrust blocks of ice, and on this detour they came past a great boulder teetering on the edge of a crevasse. The boulder lost its balance, toppled over, and tumbled down, its echo resounding far below, from the deep, hollow passageways of the glacier.

Upward, ever upward they went. The glacier loomed above, like a river of wildly towering ice masses, squeezed between steep cliffs. For a moment Rudy thought about what he had heard, that he and his mother had fallen into one of these cold-breathing chasms, but such thoughts quickly passed; it merely seemed to him like one of the many stories he had heard. Occasionally, when the men thought the path was a bit too difficult for the little fellow to climb, they reached out their hands to him, but he was never tired, and on the slippery path he stood as steady as a chamois. Sometimes they walked across rocky ground, then between rocks with no trace of moss, then among low spruce trees, only to emerge once more onto the green pastures, ever changing, ever new. All around loomed the snowcapped peaks, the ones he, like every child here, knew by name: Jungfrau, Mönch, and Eiger. Rudy had never before climbed so high, never before set foot on the spreading sea of snow. There it lay with its motionless waves of snow from which the wind had blown little tufts the way it blows foam from the swells of the sea. Glacier after glacier, holding each other by the hand, if you can say such a thing; each is a glass palace for the Ice Maiden, whose power and intent is to capture and to bury. The sun blazed hot, and the snow was so dazzling, as if strewn with pale blue, sparkling glints of diamond. Countless insects, especially butterflies and bees, lay piled dead in the snow; they had ventured too high, or the wind had carried them until they breathed their last in this cold. Around Wetterhorn a finely carded wisp of wool seemed to hover, a threatening cloud. It dropped lower, billowing with what it concealed inside: a *Föhn*. Its power would be deadly when it broke loose. Impressions of the entire trek became unforgettably fixed in Rudy's memory: making camp for the night on the slope, the path onward, the deep mountain clefts where the water, for a dizzying length of time, had sawed through the stone.

An abandoned stone hut on the other side of the snow sea provided shelter for the night; here they found charcoal and spruce boughs. They soon lit a fire, and made their beds for the night as best they could. The men sat around the fire smoking tobacco and drinking the warm spiced drink they had made for themselves. Rudy was given his share. And they talked about the mysterious creatures of the Alps: about the strange huge serpents in the deep lakes; about the night folk, the ghostly army that carried sleepers through the air to the wondrous floating city of Venice; and about the wild herdsman who drove his black sheep across the pastures. Although they had never been seen, people had heard the sound of their bells, heard the flock's eerie bellowing. Rudy listened with curiosity but no fear, which was something unknown to him, and as he listened he thought he sensed a ghostly, hollow roar. Yes! It grew more and more distinct. The men heard it too, stopped their talking, listened, and told Rudy that he must not fall asleep.

It was a *Föhn* blowing, that violent windstorm that hurls itself down from the mountains to the valley and in its ferocity breaks trees as if they were reeds, shoves half-timbered houses from one bank of the river to the other, the way we move chess pieces on the board.

An hour had passed when they told Rudy that now it was over, now he could go to sleep; exhausted from the hike, he fell asleep as if on command.

Early the next morning they departed. On that day the sun lit up for Rudy new mountains, new glaciers and snowfields. They had entered Canton Valais and were on the slope of the ridge that could be seen from Grindelwald but still far from his new home. Other mountain clefts, other pastures, forests, and pathways appeared; other houses, other people emerged. But who were these people he saw? How monstrous they looked, forbidding and obese, with sallow faces and necks of heavy, disgusting flesh that hungIn great pouches. They were cretins, miserably dragging themselves around and staring with dull eyes at the strangers who had arrived. The women were the worst looking of all. Were these the people of his new home?

III.
HIS UNCLE

When Rudy reached his uncle's house the people looked the way he was used to seeing them, thank the Lord. Only one cretin lived there, a poor dim-witted lad, one of those poor creatures who in their poverty and desolation have always been taken in by families in Canton Valais, staying a few months at each home in turn. Poor Saperli happened to be staying there when Rudy arrived.

His uncle was still a strong hunter, but he was also a skilled cooper. His wife was a small, lively woman with a face like a bird, eyes like an eagle, and a long neck covered with down.

Everything was new for Rudy: the clothing, customs, even the language, but his child's ear would quickly learn to understand it. Everything looked so prosperous compared to his grandfather's home. The house they lived in was bigger, the walls adorned with chamois horns and gleaming, polished rifles. Above the door hung a painting of the Virgin Mary with fresh Alpine roses and a glowing lamp standing in front.

His uncle was known as one of the region's most skillful chamois hunters, as well as the best and most experienced guide. Rudy was now to be the house pet, although it's true that they already had a pet: an old, blind, and deaf hunting dog who could no longer be of service, though he once had been. They remembered the animal's skill in earlier times, and that's why he was now a member of the family, living out his days in comfort. Rudy patted him, but the dog didn't care much for strangers, and Rudy was still a stranger, although not for long. He soon took root in their home and their hearts.

"Things aren't so bad here in Canton Valais," said his uncle. "We have plenty of chamois, and they won't die out soon, like the Alpine ibex. Things are much better now than in the old days. No matter how much the past is praised, the present is better. A hole has been punched in the bag and fresh air has come to our isolated valley. Something better always emerges when antiquated ways are discarded," he said. And when his uncle was in a talkative mood, he would tell about his childhood years, back when his father was in his prime and Valais was a closed bag, as he called it, with far too many ill people, wretched cretins. "But the French soldiers came. They were the true doctors; they killed off both the disease and the people. Those Frenchmen knew how to strike. They could strike in many ways, and the girls could strike too!" And with that his uncle nodded to his French-born wife and laughed. "The French could strike rocks so they gave way! They carved the Simplon Pass out of the cliffs, carved a road so that I can now say to a three-year-old child: Walk down to Italy. Just follow the highway. And the child will find his way south to Italy if he keeps to the highway."

And then his uncle sang a French song and gave a cheer for Napoleon Bonaparte.

That was the first time Rudy heard about France, about Lyon, the great city on the Rhône River, which his uncle had visited.

It wouldn't take many years for Rudy to become a skilled chamois hunter. He had a talent for it, said his uncle, and he taught the boy to hold a rifle, to aim and fire it. During hunting season he took Rudy along to the mountains, letting him drink the warm chamois blood, which would cure a hunter of vertigo. He taught the boy to recognize the times when, on various mountain slopes, avalanches would roll, at noon or in the evening, all depending on how the sun cast its rays. He taught him to pay careful attention to the chamois and learn from their leaping, so that he would land on his feet and stand firm. And if there was no foothold in the mountain cleft, then he would have to use his elbows for support; hold tight, using the muscles in his thighs and calves; even the back of his neck could catch hold if necessary. The chamois were clever, sending out their scouts, but the hunter had to be even more clever, tracking them downwind. He could fool them by hanging his coat and hat on an alpenstock, and the chamois would mistake the coat for the man. Rudy's uncle tried this trick one day when they were out hunting together.

The mountain path was narrow; in fact, there was very little left of it, only a thin ledge close to the gaping abyss. The snow was partially thawed, and the rock crumbled when they stepped on it, so his uncle lay down, stretching out as far as he could, and crawled forward. Every stone that broke off would fall, strike the slope, bounce, and keep on rolling, leaping from one rock face to another before it came to rest in the black depths. A hundred paces behind his uncle stood Rudy on the very last solid heap of rock, and in the air he saw approaching, hovering over his uncle, a mighty bearded vulture, beating his wings and about to toss the creeping snake over the precipice to turn it into carrion. His uncle had eyes only for the chamois and its young kid that were visible across the chasm. Rudy fixed his eyes on the bird, understanding its intent, and that's why he put his hand on his rifle to shoot. Then the chamois set off running up the slope. His uncle fired, and the animal was struck by the lethal bullet, but its kid escaped, as if it had spent a lifetime fleeing from danger. The enormous bird of prey also sped away, frightened by the shot. His uncle never realized his peril, but heard of it first from Rudy.

Now, as they headed home in the best of moods and his uncle whistled a tune from his youth, they suddenly heard a strange sound, not far away. They looked to both sides, they looked up, and there at the top of the steep mountain ridge the snow cover rose up, rippling the way a spreading piece of linen does when the wind rushes underneath. The waves on the crest broke as if they were marble slabs bursting and then set free in foaming, gushing water, booming like a muted peal of thunder. It was an avalanche that came crashing down, not on top of Rudy and his uncle, but close, much too close to them.

"Hold on tight, Rudy!" he shouted. "Hold on with all your might!"

And Rudy grabbed hold of the nearest tree trunk. His uncle climbed up into the branches of the tree above and held on tight as the avalanche rolled past, many yards away from them, but the draft of the wind, the gales in its wake, broke and crushed trees and bushes all around as if they were dry reeds and then tossed them aside. Rudy lay pressed to the ground. The tree trunk he had been clinging to looked as if it had been sawed in half, and the crown had been flung far away. There, among the shattered branches, lay his uncle with his head smashed in. His hand was still warm, but his face was beyond recognition. Rudy stood there, pale and trembling. It was the first time he felt fear in his life, the first moment of terror he had ever known.

Carrying his message of death he returned late that evening to the home that was now a house of sorrow. His uncle's wife stood without uttering a word, without shedding a tear, and only when the body was brought did her grief give voice. The poor cretin crept into his bed and was not seen all the next day. Toward evening he came to Rudy.

"Write a letter for me. Saperli can't write. Saperli can take the letter to the post office."

"A letter from you?" said Rudy. "Who is it to?"

"To Master Christ."

"Who do you mean by that?"

The dim-witted lad, as they called the cretin, looked at Rudy with pitiful eyes, clasped his hands, and said in a somber and pious voice:

"Jesus Christ. Saperli wants to send him a letter, to beg him to let Saperli die instead of the master of this house."

Rudy took Saperli's hand in his. "That letter will never reach its destination. That letter won't bring him back."

Rudy found it difficult to explain to him how impossible that was.

"Now you're the sole support of this household," said his foster mother. And that's what Rudy became.

IV.

BABETTE

Who is the best shot in Canton Valais? Oh yes, the chamois knew. "Watch out for Rudy!" they might say. Who is the most handsome hunter? "Why, Rudy is!" said the girls, but they didn't say: "Watch out for Rudy!" Not even their somber mothers said that, because he nodded just as politely to them as to the young girls. He was so lively and cheerful; his cheeks were tan, his teeth a fresh white, and his eyes shone coal-black. A handsome fellow he was, and only twenty years old. The icy water never bit his flesh when he swam. He could wriggle through the water like a fish, climb like no one else, cling to the rock face like a snail. Strong muscles and sinews he possessed. This was also apparent in the way he leaped; the cat was the first to teach him how, and later the chamois. The best guide to entrust yourself to was Rudy. He could have made a fortune doing that. He had no thoughts for the cooper trade, which his uncle had also taught him. His sole desire was to shoot chamois, and that's what brought in the money. Rudy was a good match, as they said, if only he wouldn't look beyond his social station. As a dancer he was what girls dreamed of, and a few of them walked around, wide awake, thinking about him.

"He kissed me at the dance," said the schoolmaster's Annette to her dearest friend, but she shouldn't have mentioned it, even to her dearest friend. That sort of news is hard to keep secret; it's like sand in a bag full of holes—it runs out. Soon, no matter how proper and respectable Rudy might be, everyone knew that he kissed the girls at the dances. And yet he had never kissed the one he wanted most to kiss.

"He's no fool," said an old hunter. "He kissed Annette. He started with 'A' and will probably kiss his way through the whole alphabet."

One kiss at a dance was all the gossips could say about Rudy so far, but he did kiss Annette, yet she was not in the least the true flower of his heart.

Down near Bex, among the great walnut trees, close to a small, rushing mountain stream, lived the wealthy miller. His residence was a large, three-story building with little towers covered with wooden shingles and trimmed with tin-plate that gleamed in the sunshine and moonlight. Atop the largest tower was a weather vane with a glittering arrow piercing an apple; it was supposed to signify Wilhelm Tell's arrow shot. The mill looked both prosperous and elegant, easily sketched or described in writing. But the miller's daughter was not so easily sketched or described. At least that's what Rudy would have said, and yet she stood etched in his heart, where her eyes shone bright enough to start a fire. The blaze had appeared suddenly, just as fires do, and the strangest thing was that the miller's daughter, the charming Babette, was unaware of it. She and Rudy had never spoken so much as two words to each other.

The miller was rich, and his wealth meant that Babette's social standing was quite high. But nothing is so high, said Rudy to himself, that it can't be reached. You simply have to climb, and you won't fall if you believe that you won't. That was the rule he had learned at home.

Now, it so happened that Rudy had business in Bex, and it was quite a journey to get there. The railroad had not yet come to those parts. From the Rhône Glacier, along the base of the Simplon Range, between scores of shifting mountain ridges, stretches the wide valley of Valais with its mighty Rhône River, which often overflows and floods the fields and roads, destroying everything. Between the towns of Sion and St-Maurice, the valley curves, bending like an elbow, becoming so narrow below St-Maurice that there is only room for the riverbed and a narrow lane. Canton Valais ends here, and an old tower stands sentry, perched on the slope, looking out across the stone bridge to the tollbooth on the other side, where Canton Vaud begins. Not far from there is the nearest town of Bex. Along the way, with each step forward, everything swells with richness and abundance, as if you were in a grove of chestnut and walnut trees. Here and there cypresses and pomegranate blossoms peer out. There is a southern warmth, as if you had come to Italy.

Rudy reached Bex, took care of his business, and had a look around, but not a single worker did he see from the mill, let alone Babette. Things were not as he had wished.

Evening came, and the air was filled with a fragrance from the wild thyme and the flowering lindens. A glittering sky-blue veil seemed to hover over the forest-green mountains. Silence enveloped them. It was not the silence of sleep or of death; no, it was as if all of nature were holding its breath, standing still so its photograph could be taken against the backdrop of blue sky. Here and there among the trees and across the green fields stood poles holding the telegraph wires that stretched along the quiet valley. Leaning against one of these poles was a figure so motionless that you might think it was a dead tree trunk, but it was Rudy who stood there, as silent as everything else around him at that moment. He was not asleep, nor was he dead. But just as great events of the world so often fly through the telegraph wires—moments in life that are important to some individual—although no sign of this is indicated by the slightest trembling or sound from the wire, so did there pass through Rudy's mind his life's happiness, mighty, overwhelming, his *constant thought* from that moment on. His eyes were fixed on one spot among the leaves: a light from the parlor in the miller's house, where Babette lived. Rudy stood there so quietly that you might think he was aiming at a chamois. But at that moment he was himself like a chamois who for minutes at a time can stand as if chiseled out of the mountain; then suddenly, at the sound of a stone rolling, it makes a leap and races off. And that's precisely what Rudy did. A thought rolled.

"Never give up!" he said. "Pay a visit to the mill. Say good evening to the miller, good evening to Babette. You won't fall if you believe you won't. Babette must have a look at me sooner or later if I'm to be her husband."

And Rudy laughed and headed for the mill in good spirits. He knew what he wanted. He wanted Babette.

The river with its pale yellow water roared past, the willows and linden trees leaned over the rushing water. Rudy walked along the path, and as it says in the old children's song:

> "... there was no one home at the miller's house
> But a little cat and a little mouse!"

The parlor cat stood on the steps, arching her back, and said, "Meow!" But Rudy paid no attention to what she was saying. He knocked. No one heard him, no one opened the door. "Meow!" said the cat. If Rudy had been younger, he would have understood the cat's language and heard her say, "Nobody's home!" As it was he had to go over to the mill to inquire. There he learned that the master of the house was traveling; he had gone far away to the city of Interlaken—"inter lacus," meaning between the lakes, as the schoolmaster, Annette's father, in his wisdom had explained. There, far away, was the miller and Babette too. A great shooting competition would begin the next day and last for a whole week. Swiss from all the German cantons were in attendance.

Poor Rudy, you might say. This was not the most fortunate time for him to come to Bex. He might as well go back home, and he did, taking the road via St-Maurice and Sion, back to his own valley, his own mountains, but he was not downhearted. By the time the sun came up the next morning, his spirits had been up for a long time; in fact, they had never been down.

"Babette is in Interlaken, many days' journey from here," he said to himself. "It's a long trek if you take the regular highway, but it's not very far if you head across the mountains, and that's the route for a chamois hunter to take. I've taken that path before; that's where my home district lies, where I lived with my grandfather as a child. And they're having a shooting competition in Interlaken. I'll be the winner there, and I'll also win Babette, as soon as I make her acquaintance."

With a light knapsack to carry his Sunday clothes, his rifle, and his hunter's bag, Rudy set off up the mountain, taking the short route, which was still long enough, but the shooting match had only just begun that day and would last through the week. They had told him that during that time the miller and Babette would be staying with their relatives in Interlaken. Rudy headed across the Gemmi Pass; he wanted to go by way of Grindelwald.

Briskly and joyously he strode along, heading upward in the fresh, light, invigorating mountain air. The valley dropped farther behind, his field of vision expanded. Here a snowy peak, there a snowy peak, and soon the gleaming white of the Alpine range. Rudy knew each snowcapped mountain. He headed toward the Schreckhorn, which thrust its white-powdered stone finger high in the blue air.

Finally he crossed the ridge, and the pastures sloped down toward his home valley. The air was light; his spirit was light too. The mountains and valley were covered with flowers and greenery, and his heart was brimming with the youthful thought: I will never grow old, I will never die. Live, prevail, enjoy! Free as a bird, light as a bird was he. And the swallows flew past, singing as they had in his childhood: "You and us! And us and you!" Everything was soaring and joyous.

Below lay the velvet-green meadow, scattered with brown wooden houses; the Lütschine River thundered and roared. He saw the glacier with its glass-green edges in the grimy snow and its deep fissures; he saw both the upper and lower glacier. The ringing bells in the church reached out to him, as if they wanted to chime a welcome home. His heart beat faster, swelling so much that for a moment Babette vanished from inside it, so big did his heart grow, so filled with memories.

Once again he walked along the road where as a little boy he had stood with the other children in the ditch, selling carved wooden houses. Up there beyond the spruce trees his grandfather's house still stood. Strangers lived there now. Children came running along the road, wanting to sell him something. One of them held out an Alpine rose. Rudy took this as a good sign and thought of Babette. Soon he crossed the bridge where the two forks of the Lütschine merge. More leafy trees grew there, the walnut trees giving shade. Now he could see flags waving, the white cross on the red background, found on both Swiss and Danish flags. And before him lay Interlaken.

It was certainly a magnificent city. Like no other, thought Rudy. A Swiss city dressed in its Sunday best. It was not like the other provincial towns with a crowd of massive stone buildings, ponderous, foreign-looking, and imposing. No, here it looked as if the wooden houses from up on the slopes had come running down into the green valley next to the clear, swiftly moving river and had lined up in a row, a bit unevenly, to form a street. And the most splendid street of all, well, it had certainly sprung up since Rudy was last here, as a child. It seemed to have been created when all the charming wooden houses that his grandfather had carved and that filled the cupboard back home had taken up position and grown in size, just like the old, the most ancient of chestnut trees. Every building was a hotel, as they were called, with carved wooden trim around the windows and balconies and their roofs jutting out, so decorative and dainty. And in front of each building was a complete flower garden, stretching out to the wide paved road. Along the road stood the buildings, but only on one side; otherwise they would have hidden the fresh green meadow on the other side where the cows ambled with their bells ringing as they did in the high Alpine pastures. The meadow was surrounded by tall mountains, which seemed to part right down the middle so you had a good view of the gleaming snowcapped peak of the Jungfrau, the loveliest of all the Swiss mountains.

What a throng of festively dressed gentlemen and ladies from foreign lands, what a swarm of country people from the various cantons! Marksmen wore on their hats little rosettes with the number of their position in the shooting match. There was music and singing, barrel organs and wind instruments, shouting and commotion. The buildings and bridges were decorated with verses and emblems, flags and banners fluttered, and rifles fired shot after shot. That was the best music to Rudy's ears, making him completely forget about Babette, who was the reason he had come.

The marksmen made their way to target practice. Rudy quickly joined them, and he was the most skilled, the happiest of all. Each time he hit the bull's-eye.

"Who is that stranger, that very young hunter?" people asked.

"He speaks French the way it's spoken in Canton Valais. But he can also make himself understood quite well in our German language," said others. "As a child he lived here in the region, near Grindelwald," one of them explained.

He was a spirited fellow. His eyes shone, his gaze and arm were steady; that's why he hit his mark. Joy prompts courage, and courage was what Rudy had always possessed. Quickly he attracted a whole circle of friends around him. He was hailed and praised, and Babette had nearly vanished from his thoughts. Then a heavy hand fell on his shoulder, and a rough voice addressed him in French.

"You're from Canton Valais?"

Rudy turned around and saw a ruddy, pleased face, a stout man; it was the rich miller from Bex. Hidden behind his portly body was the delicate, dainty Babette, who soon peeked out with those sparkling dark eyes of hers. The rich miller was making much of the fact that a hunter from his canton was taking the best shots and winning acclaim. Rudy was certainly a child of fortune. What he had come to find, but here had nearly forgotten, had now found him instead.

When you're far from home and meet people from your own district, you behave as old friends, you talk to each other. At the shooting competition Rudy was the best shot, just as the miller back home in Bex was the best with his money and his fine mill. And so the two men shook hands, something they had never done before. Babette too clasped Rudy's hand sincerely, and he clasped hers in return and looked at her; he looked at her so she flushed bright red.

The miller spoke of the long route that had brought them there, the many great cities they had seen. It had been a proper journey: They had sailed by lake steamer and traveled by rail and by coach.

"I took a shorter route," said Rudy. "I came over the mountains. No path is so high that it can't be traveled."

"But you could also break your neck," said the miller. "And you look like the sort who *will* break your neck one day, as daring as you are."

"You won't fall if you believe that you won't," said Rudy.

And the miller's relatives in Interlaken, with whom the miller and Babette were staying, invited Rudy to visit them since he was from the same canton as their family. That was a welcome invitation for Rudy. Fortune was with him, as it always is with the person who believes in himself and remembers that "Our Lord may provide the nuts, but He does not crack them open!"

Rudy was treated like one of the family by the miller's relatives, and they drank a toast to the best marksman. Babette clinked glasses too, and Rudy thanked them for the toast.

Toward evening they all strolled along the beautiful road past the festive-looking hotels beneath the old walnut trees. There was such a crowd, such jostling, that Rudy had to offer Babette his arm. He was so happy that he had met people from Vaud, he said. Vaud and Valais were good neighbors. He expressed his joy with such fervor that Babette felt compelled to clasp his hand. They walked along almost like old friends, and she was so amusing, that petite, charming girl. It was quite enchanting, thought Rudy, the way she would point out what was ridiculous and affected about the way the foreign ladies were dressed and the way they walked, although she didn't mean to make fun of them, because they might very well be quite respectable people. Oh yes, Babette knew all about that, since she had a godmother who was such an elegant English lady. Eighteen years ago, when Babette was baptized, she had come to Bex; she had given Babette the precious brooch that she wore on her bodice. Twice her godmother had sent a letter, and this year she was supposed to meet Babette here in Interlaken along with her daughters, who were old maids, close to thirty, said Babette. She herself was only eighteen.

Her sweet little lips never paused even for a moment, and everything Babette said sounded to Rudy's ears as if it were of the utmost importance. He told her in turn whatever he could think of to tell: how often he had been to Bex, how well he knew the mill, and how often he had seen Babette, though she probably had never noticed him. And when he last paid a visit to the mill, his head filled with thoughts that he could not mention, she and her father were gone, far away. But the distance didn't stop him from clambering over the barrier that made the road so long.

Yes, that much he did say, along with a great many other things. He told her how fond he was of her—and that it was for her sake and not because of the shooting competition that he had come.

Babette fell silent; it was almost too much, all that he had confided in her at once.

And as they walked, the sun sank behind the towering wall of mountains. The Jungfrau stood there in all its splendor and glory, surrounded by the forest-green wreath of nearby slopes. The whole crowd stood still and looked in that direction. Rudy and Babette also gazed at all that magnificence.

"Nowhere is lovelier than here!" said Babette.

"Nowhere!" said Rudy, looking at Babette.

"Tomorrow I must leave," he said after a moment.

"Come visit us in Bex," whispered Babette. "It would please my father."

V.

ON THE JOURNEY HOME

Oh, how much Rudy had to carry when he headed home across the mountains on the following day. Yes, he had three silver cups, two excellent rifles, and a coffeepot made of silver, which could be put to good use when he had a home of his own. Yet this was not the most important thing. There was something much more important, much more powerful that he carried, or rather that carried him home across the high mountains. But the weather was raw, gray, rainy, and dreary. The clouds were draped like funeral crepe over the heights, shrouding the gleaming mountain peaks. From the forest floor rang the last blows of the ax, and down the slope rolled the tree trunks, looking like kindling from above, but close up they were trees as heavy as masts. The Lütschine roared its monotonous tone, the wind howled, the clouds sailed by. Suddenly a young girl was walking beside Rudy. He hadn't noticed her until she was quite close. She too was headed over the mountain. Her eyes had a peculiar power, compelling him to look into them; they were so strangely crystal-clear, so deep and fathomless.

"Do you have a sweetheart?" asked Rudy. All his thoughts were filled with having a sweetheart.

"No, I do not!" she said and laughed, but it sounded as if she were lying. "Let's not take the long way around," she went on. "We should head more to the left, it's shorter."

"Yes, if you want to fall into a crevasse!" said Rudy. "You should know the way better if you're going to be the guide."

"But I do know the way," she said. "And I have my wits about me. Yours are down there in the valley. Up here you have to think about the Ice Maiden. She's not kind to human beings, they say."

"I'm not afraid of her," said Rudy. "She was forced to let me go when I was a child. I'm sure I can escape her now that I've grown up."

And it grew darker. Rain fell, snow came, glittering, blinding.

"Give me your hand and I'll help you climb," said the girl, and she touched him with ice-cold fingers.

"You help me?" said Rudy. "I don't yet need the help of a girl to climb." And he walked faster, away from her. The blizzard closed around him like a curtain, the wind whistled, and behind him he heard the girl laughing and singing. It sounded very strange. She must be some kind of troll in the service of the Ice Maiden; Rudy had heard about such things when he was a child and spent the night up here on his trek through the mountains.

The snowfall eased up, the clouds lay beneath him. He looked back. There was no one in sight, but he heard laughter and yodeling, and it didn't sound as if they came from a human being.

When Rudy finally reached the mountaintop where the path headed down toward the valley of the Rhône, he saw in the clear blue strip of sky off toward Chamonix two gleaming stars. They were sparkling so brightly, and he thought about Babette, about himself and his good fortune, and the thoughts warmed his heart.

VI.
THE VISIT TO THE MILL

"What grand trophies you've brought home!" said Rudy's old foster mother, and her strange eagle-eyes flashed as she moved her scrawny neck even faster in odd twisting circles. "Good fortune is with you, Rudy. Let me kiss you, my dear boy!"

And Rudy allowed her to kiss him, but his face showed that he was merely tolerating the situation, all these minor household ordeals. "How handsome you are, Rudy!" said the old woman.

"Don't try to flatter me," said Rudy and laughed, but he was pleased.

"I'll say it again," said the old woman. "Good fortune is with you."

"Yes, that much I do believe," he said, thinking of Babette.

Never before had he longed as he did now for the deep valley.

"They must have come home by now," he said to himself. "It's already two days past the time when they planned to return. I have to go to Bex."

So Rudy went to Bex, and the miller and his daughter were home. He was warmly welcomed, and they brought him greetings from their family in Interlaken. Babette said very little. She had grown so silent, but her eyes spoke, and that was quite enough for Rudy. The miller usually liked to do the talking—he was used to having people laugh at his jests and puns since he was the rich miller, after all. But he seemed to prefer listening to Rudy tell hunting tales about the hardships and dangers that chamois hunters encountered on the high mountain summits: how they had to crawl their way along the unstable snowy cornices that were plastered to the slopes by wind and storms, how they crawled over the precarious bridges the snowstorms dumped across the deep ravines. Rudy looked so lively, and his eyes shone as he talked about the hunter's life, about the clever chamois and their daring leaps, about the mighty *Föhn* and the rumbling avalanches. He was quite aware that with each new description he was winning over the miller more and more, and that what especially appealed to the man was his account of the bearded vulture and the bold golden eagles.

Not far from there, in Canton Valais, there was an eagle's nest, ingeniously built under an overhanging mountain ledge. There was an eaglet in the nest, but it was impossible to reach. Only a few days ago an Englishman had offered Rudy a whole fistful of gold if he would bring the bird back alive. "But there's a limit to everything," he said. "That eaglet is impossible to reach, it would be madness even to try."

And the wine flowed, and the words flowed with it, but the

evening was much too short, thought Rudy, and yet it was past midnight when he ended his first visit at the mill.

The lights glittered a little while longer from the window and through the green boughs. Out of the open hatch in the roof came the parlor cat and along the eaves came the kitchen cat.

"Is there any news from the mill?" said the parlor cat. "Here in the house a secret engagement has taken place. The father doesn't yet know about it. Rudy and Babette have been stepping on each other's paws all evening under the table. They stepped on me twice, but I didn't meow because that would have attracted attention."

"Well, I would have meowed," said the kitchen cat.

"What's proper in the kitchen is not proper in the parlor," said the parlor cat. "I wonder what the miller will say when he hears about the engagement."

Yes, what would the miller say? Rudy wondered the same thing, and he couldn't wait long to find out. And so only a few days later, when the omnibus rumbled across the Rhône Bridge between Valais and Vaud, Rudy was seated inside, in good spirits as usual, thinking lovely thoughts about hearing a "yes" that very evening.

And when evening arrived and the omnibus headed back in the other direction, Rudy was once again inside, going the same way back, while at the mill the parlor cat scurried to tell the news.

"You from the kitchen, have you heard? The miller now knows everything. It has all come to a fine end! Rudy arrived here toward evening, and he and Babette had a great deal to whisper about. They were standing in the corridor just outside the miller's room. I lay at their feet, but they had neither eyes nor thoughts for me.

" 'I'll go right in to see your father,' said Rudy. 'My purpose is honorable.'

" 'Should I go with you?' asked Babette. 'It might give you courage.'

" 'Oh, I have plenty of courage,' said Rudy. 'But if you come along, he'll have to be kind whether he wants to or not.'

"And then they went inside. Rudy stepped hard on my tail; Rudy is always so clumsy! I meowed, but neither he nor Babette had ears for me. They opened the door and went in together, with me leading the way. But I jumped up onto the back of a chair; I couldn't predict whether Rudy might start kicking. But the miller was the one who kicked. And it was a good kick! Out the door, up the mountain to the chamois! That's what Rudy can now aim for, and not our little Babette."

"But what did they say?" asked the kitchen cat.

"Say! They said all those things that are said when proposing: 'I love her and she loves me. And if there's milk in the basin for one, then there's enough milk in the basin for two.'

"'But her social standing is too high for you,' said the miller. 'She sits on grain, on golden grain, as you know. You can never reach her.'

"'Nothing sits too high. I can reach it if I want to,' said Rudy, because he's a spirited fellow.

"'But you said last time that you could never reach the eaglet. Babette sits even higher.'

"'I'll take them both,' said Rudy.

"'All right, I'll give her to you when you bring me the eaglet alive,' said the miller and laughed so hard that tears rolled down his face. 'But thank you for visiting us, Rudy. If you come back tomorrow, there won't be anyone home. Farewell, Rudy!'

"And Babette said farewell too, as pitifully as a little kitten who can't find her mother.

"'A promise is a promise, a man a man!' said Rudy. 'Don't cry, Babette, I'll bring back the eaglet.'

"'I hope you break your neck,' said the miller. 'Then we'll be spared all your visiting.' That's what I call a good kick! Now Rudy has gone off, and Babette is sitting there crying, but the miller is singing a song in German. He learned it on their travels. But I'm not going to worry about it; that won't help matters."

"But it would look good if you did," said the kitchen cat.

VII.

THE EAGLE'S NEST

From the mountain path sounded a yodel, so merry and loud, heralding good spirits and undaunted courage. It was Rudy. He was going to see his friend Vesinand.

"You must help me! We'll take Ragli along. I have to capture the eaglet up on the mountain ledge."

"How about capturing the dark side of the moon first, that's probably just as easy," said Vesinand. "You're certainly in good spirits."

"Yes, because I'm thinking about getting married. But in all seriousness, listen here, I need to tell you how matters stand with me."

And soon Vesinand and Ragli learned what Rudy intended.

"You're a daring lad," they said. "But it's impossible! You'll break your neck!"

"You won't fall if you think you won't," said Rudy.

At midnight they departed, carrying poles, ladders, and ropes. The path led through thickets and shrubbery, across scree, and upward, ever upward in the dark night. Water roared below, water trickled from above, sodden clouds drifted across the sky. The hunters reached the steep rock ledge. It grew darker there. The mountain walls almost met, and only high overhead in the narrow gap did the sky brighten. Close by, and below them, was a deep abyss with rushing water. All three of them sat still. They wanted to wait for daybreak when the eagle flew out. It had to be shot before they could even think of capturing the eaglet. Rudy squatted down, as motionless as if he were part of the rock where he was perched. He held his rifle out, ready to shoot, his eyes fixed on the uppermost cliff where the eagle's nest was hidden under the projecting ledge. The three hunters waited a long time.

Then high overhead they heard a crackling, whistling sound. A huge, hovering object darkened the sky. Two gun barrels took aim as the black eagle shape flew out of its nest. A shot rang out. For a moment the outspread wings moved, and then the bird slowly dropped, as if with its size and wingspan it might fill the whole ravine and in its fall carry the hunters down with it. The eagle sank into the depths. Tree branches groaned and shrubs broke under the bird's fall.

Then they got busy. Three of the longest ladders were tied together to reach all the way up. They were set on the farthest foothold at the edge of the ravine, but they didn't quite reach. And the cliff face stretched smooth as a wall quite a bit higher, where the nest was hidden in the shelter of the projecting rock. After some discussion, they agreed that there was no choice but to lower down into the ravine two ladders tied together and then attach them to the three others that were already in place below. With great difficulty they dragged the two ladders up to the top and tied the ropes tight. The ladders were shoved out over the projecting ledge and hung there, swinging freely above the abyss. Rudy was already sitting on the lowest rung. It was an ice-cold morning; clouds of fog were rising up from the black chasm. Rudy was sitting there like a fly perched on a swaying piece of straw that a nest-building bird had dropped on the edge of a tall factory chimney. But a fly can soar off if the straw comes loose; Rudy could only break his neck. The wind whistled around him, and down in the abyss the racing water roared from the thawing glacier, the Ice Maiden's palace.

Now he started the ladder swinging, like a spider trying to grab hold from his long, swaying thread. On the fourth try, when Rudy touched the tip of the ladders that were tied together and positioned below, he caught hold of them, and fastened them all together with a strong and steady hand, although they continued to wobble as if on worn hinges.

The five long ladders looked like a swaying reed reaching up toward the nest, leaning vertically against the rock face. Now came the most dangerous part, which required climbing like a cat climbs, but that was something Rudy could do; the cat had taught him how. He didn't notice Vertigo, who strode through the air behind him, stretching out her polyp arms toward him. Now Rudy was standing on the top rung of the ladder and realized that even at this height he was not high enough to see into the nest; only by using his hands could he reach it. He touched the thick, intertwining branches on the bottom of the nest to see how sturdy they were, and when he had found a thick and solid branch, he swung himself from the ladder up toward the branch and raised his head and chest over the side of the nest. Streaming toward him came a suffocating stench of carrion. Rotting lambs, chamois, and birds lay there, ripped to shreds. Vertigo, who was powerless to touch Rudy, blew the poisonous vapors into his face, trying to daze him. And down below in the gaping black depths on the racing water sat the Ice

Maiden herself, with her long, pale green hair, staring with deadly eyes like the barrels of a shotgun.

"Now I'm going to get you!"

In a corner of the eagle's nest Rudy saw a big, powerful eaglet that could not yet fly. He fixed his eyes on the bird, held on tight with one hand, and with the other flung a snare around the young eagle; it was captured alive, its legs caught in the tightening cord. Rudy tossed the snare holding the bird over his shoulder, making sure that the bird hung well below him as, with the help of a dangling rope, he held on until the tip of his foot once again reached the top rung of the ladder.

"Hold on! If you don't believe you're going to fall, you won't!" It was the old rule, which he followed, holding on tight as he crawled, certain that he would not fall, and he didn't.

Now came the sound of a yodel, so loud and joyous. Rudy was standing on solid ground with his eaglet.

VIII.
MORE NEWS FROM THE PARLOR CAT

"Here's what you demanded," said Rudy as he strode into the miller's house in Bex and set a big basket on the floor and removed the cloth. Two black-rimmed, yellow eyes glared, flashing and wild, ready to scorch and clamp onto whatever they looked at. The short, strong beak opened to bite, the neck was red and down-covered.

"The eaglet!" shouted the miller. Babette gave a shriek and jumped aside but could not take her eyes off either Rudy or the eaglet.

"You're not easily scared off," said the miller.

"And you always keep your word," said Rudy. "Each person has his trademark."

"But why didn't you break your neck?" asked the miller.

"Because I was holding on tight," replied Rudy. "And I still am. I'm holding tight to Babette."

"You'll have to wait until she's yours," said the miller, laughing, and Babette knew that was a good sign.

"Let's take the eaglet out of the basket. What awful glaring eyes it has! How did you manage to capture it?"

Then Rudy had to tell the story, and the miller looked at him with eyes that grew bigger and bigger.

"With your courage and your good fortune, you could support three wives!" said the miller.

"Thank you! Thank you!" cried Rudy.

"But you don't have Babette yet," said the miller, and playfully slapped the young Alpine hunter on the shoulder.

"Do you know the latest news at the mill?" the parlor cat asked the kitchen cat. "Rudy has brought us the eaglet and is going to take Babette in exchange. They kissed each other and let her father see them do it! They're as good as engaged. The old man didn't kick; he pulled in his claws, took an afternoon nap, and let those two sit and gush. They have so much to talk about that they won't be finished by Christmas!"

And it's true that they didn't finish by Christmastime. The wind whirled the brown leaves, and the snow filled the valley with drifts as it did on the high peaks. The Ice Maiden sat in her proud palace, which grew bigger in winter. The rock faces were covered with ice and icicles as thick as arms, as heavy as elephants, in the places where the mountain stream fluttered its veil of water in the summertime. Garlands of fantastic ice crystals shimmered above the snow-powdered spruce. The Ice Maiden rode on the howling wind across the deepest valleys. The blanket of snow spread all the way down to Bex. She could go and see Rudy, who was indoors more often than usual, sitting with Babette. In the summer they would be married. Their friends talked about them so much that their ears burned. The sun shone, the loveliest Alpine rose glowed: the lively, laughing Babette, who was as lovely as the spring that arrived, the spring that made all the birds sing of summer and of their wedding day.

"How those two can sit and hang on each other!" said the parlor cat. "I'm sick and tired of all that meowing."

IX.
THE ICE MAIDEN

Spring had unfurled its succulent green garland of walnut and chestnut trees that were most abundant from the bridge at St-Maurice to the shores of Lake Geneva along the Rhône, which with tremendous speed came rushing from its source beneath the green glacier, the ice palace, where the Ice Maiden lives. From there she let the fierce wind carry her up to the highest snowfields, and in the sharp sunlight she stretched out on the snowdrift cushions. There she sat and fixed her piercing gaze on the deep valley below, where people were busily moving about like ants over a sun-splotched stone.

"Powers of reason, as the children of the sun call you," said the Ice Maiden. "Vermin is what you are! Just one tumbling snowball and you and your houses and towns would be crushed and obliterated!" And she lifted her proud head higher and looked with deadly flashing eyes all around and far below. But from the valley came a rumbling sound, the shattering of rocks: human endeavors. Roads and tunnels were being constructed for the railroad.

"They're pretending to be moles," she said. "They're digging passageways, that's why I can hear sounds like gunfire. But when I move my palaces, the roar is louder than crashing thunder!"

From the valley a column of smoke rose up, moving forward like a fluttering veil; it was a drifting plume from the locomotive that was pulling a train along the newly opened railway, an undulating serpent whose joints were one car following another. Swiftly it sped forward.

"They're pretending to be gods down there, those powers of reason," said the Ice Maiden. "But the forces of nature are still in control." And she laughed, she sang, echoes filled the valley.

"That was an avalanche falling," said the people below.

But the sun's children sang even louder about human *intelligence* that prevails, that can harness the seas, move mountains, fill valleys; human intelligence, which is master of the forces of nature. At that very moment a party of travelers came across the snowfield where the Ice Maiden sat. They had tied themselves together with ropes to form one great body on the slippery ice surface near the deep crevasses.

"Vermin!" she said. "How can you be masters of the forces of nature?" And she turned away from them to cast a scornful glance at the valley far below, where the train was roaring past.

"There they sit, all those *ideas*! But they're caught in the grip of nature. I can see every one of them. One sits as proud as a king, all alone. Over there they're clustered together. And there half of them are asleep. When the steam dragon comes to a halt, they climb out and go on their way. Ideas going out into the world!" And she laughed.

"That was another avalanche!" said the people in the valley below.

"It won't reach us," said two people inside the steam dragon. "Two souls and one mind," as the saying goes. They were Rudy and Babette, and the miller was with them too.

"As baggage!" he said. "I've come along as one of the necessities!"

"There they sit, those two," said the Ice Maiden. "Scores of chamois have I crushed, millions of Alpine roses have I broken and shattered, with not a root remaining. I obliterate them all! Ideas! Powers of reason!" And she laughed.

"Yet another avalanche," they said down in the valley.

X.

BABETTE'S GODMOTHER

Staying in Montreux, one of the nearby cities which, along with Clarens, Vernex, and Crin, forms a garland around the northeastern end of Lake Geneva, were Babette's godmother—the elegant English lady—and her daughters, along with a young relative. They had only recently arrived, but the miller had already paid them a visit, announced Babette's engagement, and told them about Rudy and the eaglet, about his visit to Interlaken—in short, the entire story. It had amused them greatly and favorably disposed them to Rudy and Babette, and to the miller as well. All three of them had now been invited, and so they went. Babette would see her godmother, and her godmother would see Babette.

Near the little town of Villeneuve at the tip of Lake Geneva was a steamship which in half an hour's journey could reach Vernex, just below Montreux. This is a coast celebrated by poets. Here, under the walnut trees near the deep, blue-green lake, Byron sat and wrote his melodic verse about the prisoner in the gloomy Château de Chillon. There, where Clarens is reflected in the water along with the weeping willows, Rousseau wandered, dreaming of Heloïse. The Rhône River flows past beneath the towering, snow-capped mountains of the Savoy, and not far from its source in the lake is a little island. In fact, it's so small that from the shore it looks like a boat. It's a rocky crag. A hundred years ago a lady ordered it to be walled with stone, covered with earth, and then had three acacia trees planted there that now cast shadows over the whole island. Babette was simply delighted by this little spot; it was her favorite place on the entire voyage. She said they should go there, must go there; surely it would be incomparably lovely there, she thought. But the steamship continued past and pulled into harbor, as it should, at Vernex.

The little group then set off upward, between the white sunlit walls that surround the vineyards outside the small mountain town of Montreux. There fig trees offer shade in front of the farmhouses, and laurels and cypresses grow in the gardens. Halfway up stood the pension where Babette's godmother was staying.

They were warmly received. Her godmother was a large, friendly woman with a round, smiling face. As a child she must have looked much like one of Raphael's cherubs, but now she had the face of an older angel, with silvery-white hair curling all around. Her daughters were graceful, elegant, tall, and slender. The young cousin who was staying with them was dressed in white from head to toe, with golden hair and golden whiskers that were so plentiful they could have been divided up among three gentlemen. He promptly devoted the utmost attention to little Babette.

Lavishly bound books, sheet music, and drawings were spread across the big table. The balcony door stood open to the lovely expanse of lake, which was so sparkling and still that the Savoy Mountains with their villages, forests, and snowy peaks were reflected in it, upside down.

Rudy, who was usually so bold, lively, and undaunted, felt out of his element, as the expression goes. He walked about as if he were treading on peas across a slippery floor. How slowly the time passed; it was like a treadmill! And now they were going out for a stroll. That went just as slowly. Rudy would take two paces forward and one back to keep in step with the others. Down they went to Chillon, the gloomy old castle on the rocky island, to look at the torture stakes and dungeons, the rusty chains in the rock face, the stone benches for the condemned, the trap doors through which unfortunate prisoners were hurled below to land on iron spikes in the surf. That was what they called pleasurable sights! It was a place of execution, elevated through Byron's song to the world of poetry. Rudy sensed only the execution site. He leaned over the big stone window ledges and looked down into the deep, blue-green water and across to the lonely little island with the three acacia trees. That's where he yearned to be, away from all his chattering companions. But Babette was happy. She had enjoyed herself immensely, she later said. The cousin she thought quite perfect.

"Yes, a perfect gadabout!" said Rudy, and that was the first time Rudy had ever said anything that didn't please Babette. The Englishman had given her a little book as a souvenir of Chillon. It was Byron's poem "The Prisoner of Chillon" translated to French so that Babette could read it.

"It's all well and good with that book," said Rudy, "but the fine-combed fellow who gave it to you was certainly not to my liking."

"He looked like a flour sack without any flour!" said the miller and laughed at his own wit. Rudy laughed too and said that was very well put.

XI.
THE COUSIN

A couple of days later when Rudy paid a call at the mill, he found the young Englishman visiting. Babette had just placed in front of him several poached trout that she had garnished with parsley to make them look even finer. That was quite unnecessary. What did the Englishman want? Why had he come? To be waited on and coddled by Babette? Rudy was jealous, and that amused Babette. It pleased her to see all sides of his heart, both the strong and the weak. Love was still a game, and she was playing with Rudy's whole heart. Yet it should be said that he was her joy, her heart's desire, the best and most splendid in the world. But the gloomier he looked, the more her eyes sparkled. She would gladly have kissed the blond Englishman with the golden whiskers if it would have made Rudy dash away in fury, because it would show how much he loved her. That wasn't right, nor was it wise of little Babette, yet she was only nineteen years old. She didn't think much about it; she gave even less thought to how her behavior might be viewed by the young Englishman as merrier and more lighthearted than was proper for the respectable, newly engaged daughter of the miller.

At the place where the main road from Bex passes beneath the snowcapped peak, which in the Swiss language is called Les Diablerets, the mill stood quite close to a rushing mountain stream that was pale gray, like foaming soapy water. This stream did not drive the mill. The great mill wheel was turned by a smaller stream gushing down the cliff on the other side of the river and through a stone culvert under the road, its force and speed lifting it up to pour into an enclosed wooden basin, a wide flume across the racing river. The flume was filled with so much water that it overflowed, offering a wet, slippery path for anyone who might think of taking this route to reach the mill more quickly. That was exactly what the young man, the Englishman, had decided to do. White-clad like a millworker, he climbed along it in the evening, guided by the light that was shining from Babette's room. He had never learned to climb, and he narrowly missed ending up headfirst in the stream, but he escaped with wet sleeves and splashed trousers. Drenched and muddy he made his way to Babette's windows, where he clambered up the old linden tree and there hooted like an owl; it was the only bird he could imitate. Babette heard him and peeked through the thin curtains, but when she saw the white-clad man and realized who he was, her little heart began pounding with fear, but also anger. Hastily she put out the light, made sure that all the window hasps were fastened, and then left him to his hooting and howling.

How terrible it would be if Rudy were at the mill! But Rudy was not there; no, it was much worse than that. He was standing right below. Loud and angry words were spoken; a fight was about to ensue, maybe even a murder.

Babette opened her window in terror, calling Rudy's name, telling him to leave. She couldn't bear for him to stay, she said.

"You can't bear for me to stay?" he exclaimed. "So this was all arranged! You're expecting good friends, better than me! Shame on you, Babette!"

"You're despicable!" said Babette. "I hate you!" And now she was weeping. "Go! Go!"

"I don't deserve this!" he said, and he left. His cheeks were on fire, his heart was on fire.

Babette threw herself across the bed and wept.

"How I love you, Rudy! And yet you can think so badly of me!"

She was angry, very angry, and that was good for her because otherwise she would have been terribly sad. But now she could fall asleep and sleep the refreshing slumber of youth.

XII.
EVIL FORCES

Rudy left Bex, walking toward home, heading up into the mountains in the fresh, cool air where the snow lay, where the Ice Maiden ruled. The leafy trees stood far below, as if they were mere potato plants. The spruce trees and shrubbery became smaller, and Alpine roses grew along the snow that lay in scattered patches like linen spread out to bleach. There was a blue gentian growing there, and he crushed it with the butt of his rifle.

Higher up two chamois appeared. Rudy's eyes lit up, his thoughts took flight, but he wasn't close enough for a good shot. He climbed higher, where only scraggly grass grew between the boulders. The chamois walked calmly along the snowfield. He pushed on eagerly as the billowing fog sank down around him, and suddenly he was standing before the sheer rock face. Rain began pouring down.

He felt a burning thirst, heat in his head, cold in all his limbs. He reached for his hunter's flask, but it was empty; he hadn't given it a thought when he stormed up to the mountains. He had never been ill, but now he had a sense of what it must be like. He was tired, he felt the urge to throw himself to the ground and sleep, but water was streaming everywhere. He tried to pull himself together, but everything was shimmering strangely before his eyes. Suddenly he saw what he had never seen here before: a low hut, newly built, leaning against the rock face, and in the doorway stood a young girl. He thought she was the schoolmaster's Annette whom he had once kissed at a dance. But it was not Annette, and yet he had seen her before, perhaps near Grindelwald that evening when he headed home from the shooting competition in Interlaken.

"What are you doing here?" he asked.

"I live here," she said. "I'm taking care of my flock."

"Your flock? Where can it graze? There's nothing but snow and rocks here."

"You seem to know all about it," she said and laughed. "Just beyond and a little below here is a lovely grassy pasture. That's where my goats are. I take good care of them, and I never lose a single one. What's mine is always mine."

"How bold you are," said Rudy.

"You are, too," she replied.

"If you have any milk, give me some. I'm unbearably thirsty."

"I have something better than milk," she said. "And I'll give it to you. Yesterday some travelers came past with their guide. They left behind half a bottle of wine, better than any you've ever tasted. They won't be back for it, and I won't drink it, so you can have it."

She brought out the wine, poured it into a wooden bowl, and handed it to Rudy.

"That's good," he said. "I've never tasted wine so warm and so fiery." And his eyes shone. A liveliness, a glow came over him, as if all his sorrows and worries had evaporated. A sparkling, fresh sensation stirred inside him.

"But you *are* the schoolmaster's Annette, after all!" he exclaimed. "Give me a kiss!"

"I will if you give me the pretty ring you're wearing on your finger."

"My engagement ring?"

"That's the one!" said the girl, and she poured more wine into the bowl, then pressed it to his lips, and he drank. The joy of life coursed through his blood; the whole world was his, he thought, why should he worry? Everything exists for our pleasure and happiness. The stream of life is the stream of joy; to be caught up in it, to be carried off by it, that is happiness. He looked at the girl, who was Annette and yet not Annette, nor was she the troll phantom, as he had called the girl he had met near Grindelwald. This girl here on the mountain was as fresh as the new-fallen snow, as flourishing as an Alpine rose, and as nimble as a kid. Yet she was created from Adam's rib, as human as Rudy. And he flung his arms around her, and gazed into her wondrously clear eyes. It was only for a second, and yet . . . Yes, explain, recount, tell us in words: Was it the life of the spirit or of death that filled him? Was he lifted up or did he sink down into the deep, deadly ice abyss, deeper, ever deeper? He saw ice walls like blue-green glass. Bottomless chasms gaped all around and water dripped, ringing like a Glockenspiel and so crystal clear, gleaming in blue-white flames. The Ice Maiden gave him a kiss that froze right through his brow to his backbone. He screamed in pain, tore himself loose, toppled over and fell. Everything turned to night before his eyes, but he opened them again. Evil forces had made their play.

Gone was the Alpine girl, gone the mysterious hut. Water was running down the bare rock face, snow lay all around. Rudy was shivering with cold, drenched to the skin, and his ring was gone, the engagement ring that Babette had given him. His rifle lay in the snow at his feet; he picked it up and tried to shoot, but it misfired. Sodden clouds filled the crevasse like solid heaps of snow. Vertigo was sitting there, stalking her powerless prey, and from beneath her in the deep abyss came the sound of a boulder falling, crushing and tearing away everything that tried to break its fall.

But at the mill Babette sat and wept. Rudy had not come to visit for six days now. He was the one in the wrong; he was the one who should ask her forgiveness, for she loved him with all her heart.

XIII.
AT THE MILLER'S HOUSE

"What a terrible ruckus there is with those people!" said the parlor cat to the kitchen cat. "Now everything has fallen apart again between Babette and Rudy. She's crying, and he probably hasn't given her another thought."

"I don't like that," said the kitchen cat.

"I don't either," said the parlor cat. "But I'm not going to worry about it. Babette can go ahead and be sweethearts with red whiskers. Although he hasn't been back here either since he tried to climb onto the roof."

Evil forces make their play both outside of us and within; that's what Rudy had recognized and now pondered. What exactly had happened around him and inside him, high up on the mountain? Was it a vision or a feverish dream? Never before had he experienced fever or illness. But he had gained insight into himself even as he reproached Babette. He thought about the wild chase in his heart, the searing *Föhn* that had newly broken loose inside. Could he confess everything to Babette, every thought which, in that moment of temptation, could have made him act? He had lost her ring, but with its loss she had won him back. Would she confess to him? His heart felt as if it would split in half as he thought of her; so many memories rose up. He saw her before him, as large as life, laughing, a merry child. Many a loving word that she had spoken from the fullness of her heart flew like flashes of sunlight into his breast, and soon there was an entire sun inside him for Babette.

Surely she would be able to confess to him, and she must.

He went to the mill. There was a confession that began with a kiss and ended with Rudy as the sinner. *His* great error was in having doubted Babette's faithfulness, it was quite despicable of him! Such suspicion, such ferocity could make them both unhappy. Yes, it could! And that's why Babette held a little sermon for him; it amused her and made her look so lovely. Yet on one point Rudy had been right: Her godmother's relative was a gadabout! She was going to burn the book he gave her and not keep anything at all that might remind her of him.

"Well, now that's over!" said the parlor cat. "Rudy is back, they've come to an understanding, and that's the greatest joy of all, they say."

"Last night," said the kitchen cat, "I heard the rats say that the greatest joy is eating tallow candles and having a good supply of rancid pork. So who should we believe: the rats or the sweethearts?"

"None of them," said the parlor cat. "That's always the surest course."

The greatest joy for Rudy and Babette still lay ahead. The most beautiful of days, as it's called, was in the offing: their wedding day.

But the wedding would not take place in the church in Bex or in the miller's house. Babette's godmother wanted to host the wedding celebration, and the marriage ceremony itself would be held in the beautiful little church in Montreux. The miller insisted that her request be honored; he alone knew what the godmother had planned for the newlyweds. She was presenting them with a wedding gift that was certainly worth a minor concession. The date was set. The evening before, they would travel to Villeneuve and then in the morning continue by ship so as to arrive in Montreux in time for the godmother's daughters to help the bride dress.

"I suppose we'll at least have a celebration the day after the wedding here at home," said the parlor cat. "Otherwise I wouldn't give even a meow for the whole thing!"

"There's going to be a feast," said the kitchen cat. "Geese have been slaughtered, doves strangled, and a whole deer is hanging on the wall. My teeth itch at the mere sight of it! Tomorrow they begin their journey."

Yes, tomorrow! Tonight Rudy and Babette sat in the mill for the last time as an engaged couple.

Outside the Alps glowed, the evening bells chimed, the daughters of the sun sang: "Whatever is best will happen!"

XIV.
VISIONS IN THE NIGHT

The sun had gone down, the clouds were sinking over the valley of the Rhône between the towering mountains, the wind was blowing from the south, an African wind. Down over the high Alps came a *Föhn* that tore the clouds apart, and when the wind vanished, everything was quite still for a moment. The tattered clouds hung in fantastic shapes between the forest-covered slopes above the rushing Rhône River. They hung in shapes that looked like sea creatures from the primeval world, like hovering eagles from the sky, and like leaping frogs from the swamp. They sank down to the surging current, they sailed along it and yet were sailing in the air. The current carried with it a fir tree torn up by its roots, with the water making swirling eddies before it. That was Vertigo, with her sisters, spinning around in the rushing stream. The moon shone on the snowy peaks, on the dark forests and the strange white clouds: night visions, spirits of the forces of nature. The mountain farmer saw them through his windowpane; they were sailing below in hordes before the Ice Maiden. She had come from her glacier palace, she was sitting on the flimsy ship, an uprooted fir tree. The glacier water carried her along the river toward the open lake.

"The wedding guests are arriving!" the air and water whistled and sang.

Visions outside, visions within. Babette had a peculiar dream.

It seemed to her that she was married to Rudy, and had been for many years. He was now away hunting chamois, but she was at home, and sitting next to her was that young Englishman with the golden whiskers. His eyes were warm, his words exerted a magical power; he held out his hand and she had to follow him. They left the house. Kept going down and down! And Babette felt as if a burden were pressed to her heart, growing heavier and heavier; it was a sin against Rudy, a sin against God. Suddenly she was all alone, her clothes were ripped by the thorns, her hair was gray. In great pain she looked upward, and on the mountain crest she spotted Rudy. She stretched out her arms to him but didn't dare call out or pray, and neither would have done any good because she soon realized that it was not him at all, merely his hunting jacket and hat hanging from an alpenstock, the kind that hunters set up to fool the chamois. And in the utmost pain Babette lamented: "Oh, if only I had died on my wedding day, my happiest day! Lord, my God, that would have been merciful, my greatest joy! Then the best would have happened that could possibly happen for Rudy and me. No one knows the future." And in ungodly grief she threw herself into the deep mountain crevasse. A cord snapped, a funeral dirge sounded!

Babette awoke. The dream was over and erased, though she knew that she had dreamed something terrible. She had dreamed about the young Englishman whom she hadn't seen for months, hadn't given a thought. Was he in Montreux? Would she see him at the wedding? A tiny shadow slid across her delicate lips. Her brows knit together, but soon a smile and a sparkle returned to her eyes. The sun was shining so beautifully outside, and tomorrow was their wedding day, hers and Rudy's.

He was already in the parlor when she came downstairs, and soon they were off to Villeneuve. Both of them were so happy, and the miller was too. He laughed and beamed, in the best of moods; what a good father, an honest soul he was.

"Now we're the masters of the house!" said the parlor cat.

XV.
THE CONCLUSION

It was not yet evening when the three joyous people reached Villeneuve and ate their supper. The miller sat in the armchair with his pipe and took a little nap. The young couple walked arm in arm through the town and out along the road beneath the cliffs covered with brush, along the deep, blue-green lake. Gloomy Chillon with its gray walls and heavy towers was reflected in the clear water. The little island with the three acacias was even closer, looking like a bouquet on the lake.

"It must be lovely over there," said Babette. Once again she had the greatest desire to go there, and her wish could be fulfilled at once. A boat floated near the shore; the rope attached to it was easy to untie. There was no one around to ask for permission, so they simply took the boat. Rudy knew how to row.

The oars dipped like fish fins into the placid water, which was so supple and yet so strong, supporting like an entire back, swallowing like a whole mouth, gently smiling; softness itself and yet with a power terrifying and strong enough to destroy. A foaming wake appeared behind the boat, which in a few minutes carried the pair over to the island, where they stepped ashore. There was just enough room for the two of them to dance.

Rudy swung Babette around two or three times, and then they sat down on the little bench under the drooping acacias. They gazed into each other's eyes, held each other's hands, and everything around them glittered in the glow of the sinking sun. The spruce forests on the mountains were tinged red-violet just like flowering heather, and where the trees ended and the rock face emerged, the mountain glowed as if transparent. The clouds in the sky blazed like crimson fire, the whole lake was like a fresh, blushing rose petal. As the shadows climbed up the snow-covered slopes of the Savoy, the mountains turned blue-black, but the highest peak shone like red lava, displaying once again an instant from the creation of the mountains when these glowing masses rose up from the earth's womb, not yet extinguished. It was an alpenglow, the likes of which Rudy and Babette had never seen. The snow-covered Dents du Midi shimmered like the disk of a full moon as it rises on the horizon.

"So much loveliness! So much happiness!" they both said.

"The earth has no more to give me," said Rudy. "An evening hour like this is an entire lifetime. How often I've felt happy, the way I feel right now, and thought that even if everything should end right here, my life has been so happy. What a blessed world this is. And then the day would end but another would begin, and I thought *that* day was even more beautiful. Our Lord is infinitely good, Babette!"

"I'm so happy," she said.

"The earth has no more to give me!" exclaimed Rudy.

And the evening bells rang from the Savoy Mountains, from the Swiss mountains. Glowing like gold, the blue-black Jura rose up in the west.

"May God grant you all that is most splendid and best!" exclaimed Babette.

"And so He will," said Rudy. "Tomorrow it will be mine. Tomorrow you will be all mine. My own lovely little wife!"

"The boat!" cried Babette at the same instant.

The boat, which was to carry them back, had come loose and drifted away from the island.

"I'll get it!" said Rudy. He threw off his coat, tore off his boots, jumped into the lake, and swam briskly toward the boat.

Cold and deep was the clear, blue-green ice water from the mountain glacier. Rudy looked down into it, just one brief glance, and he seemed to see a gold ring tumbling, gleaming, sparkling. He thought about his lost engagement ring, and the ring grew bigger, expanding to a glittering circle, and inside of it shone the clear glacier. Infinitely deep chasms gaped all around, and the dripping water rang like a Glockenspiel, blazing with pale blue flames. In a mere second he saw what will take us many long words to describe. Young hunters and young girls, men and women who had once sunk into the glacier's crevasses stood there as large as life with open eyes and smiling lips, and from far below them came the echo of church bells from buried towns. The congregation knelt beneath the church dome, pieces of ice formed the organ pipes, the mountain stream played organ music. The Ice Maiden was sitting on the clear, transparent bottom. She rose up toward Rudy and kissed his feet. A deadly chill passed through his limbs, an electric shock—ice and fire. It was impossible to distinguish the difference in that brief touch.

"Mine! Mine!" echoed around him and inside him. "I kissed you when you were little. I kissed you on the lips. Now I'm kissing you on your toe and on your heel—you're all mine!"

And he vanished in the clear blue water.

Everything fell silent. The church bells stopped ringing, the last notes faded with the glow on the red clouds.

"You're mine!" echoed through the deep. "You're mine!" echoed on the heights, from eternity.

How lovely to fly from love to love, from earth to Heaven.

A cord snapped, a funeral dirge rang out, the icy kiss of death had conquered what was mortal. The prologue had ended before a life's drama could even begin, discord had dissolved into harmony. Would you call this a sad story?

Poor Babette! For her it was the hour of agony. The boat drifted farther and farther away. No one on land knew that the bridal couple had gone to the little island. The evening wore on, the clouds descended, darkness came. Alone, in despair, wailing, she stood there. A mighty storm hovered overhead. Lightning flashed above the Jura Mountains, over Switzerland, and over the Savoy. From all sides came flash after flash, thunder after thunder, rolling, one peal after the other, lasting for minutes at a time. The lightning bolts were as bright as the sun; every single vine could be seen as if it were noontime, and then everything was again pitch dark. The lightning formed ribbons, knots, zigzags, striking all around the lake, glittering from all sides, while the crashing thunder grew louder with the echoing roars. On land they pulled the boats up onto shore. Every living thing sought shelter. And then the rain came pouring down.

"I wonder where Rudy and Babette are in this terrible storm," said the miller.

Babette sat with her hands clasped, with her head bowed to her lap, mute from grieving, from screaming and wailing.

"In the deep water," she said to herself, "deep down, as if under the glacier, that's where he lies."

Into her mind came thoughts of what Rudy had told her about his mother's death, about his rescue when he was brought up from the glacier's crevasse as a corpse. "The Ice Maiden has taken him again!"

A lightning bolt flashed, as dazzling as sunlight on white snow. Babette sprang to her feet. The lake rose up suddenly, like a gleaming glacier. There stood the Ice Maiden, majestic, pale blue, shimmering, and at her feet lay Rudy's body. "Mine!" she cried and then all around there was darkness and torrents of water.

"How ghastly!" wailed Babette. "But why should he die just as our day of happiness had arrived? Dear God, enlighten me! Enlighten my heart. I don't understand Your ways. I am lost in Your power and wisdom."

And God enlightened her heart. A glimmer of memory, a merciful ray, her dream from the previous night, as large as life, flashed through her mind. She remembered the words she had spoken: her wish for the best for herself and for Rudy.

"Oh! Was it the fruit of sin in my heart? Was my dream a future life whose cord had to be cut for my own salvation? How miserable I am!"

Wailing, she sat there in the dark night. In the deep silence she thought she could still hear Rudy's words, the last thing he had said: "The earth has nothing more to give me!" His words resounded with the fullness of joy, repeated in the flood of grief.

A couple of years have passed. The lake smiles, the shores smile, the vines are heavy with grapes. Steamships with fluttering flags are racing past, pleasure boats with their billowing twin sails fly like white butterflies across the mirrored surface. The railway above Chillon has opened, leading deep into the valley of the Rhône. At every station strangers disembark. They arrive with their red-bound guidebooks and read about all the remarkable sights they will see. They visit Chillon, they notice out there in the lake the little island with the three acacias, and they read in their book about the bridal couple who, in the year 1856, sailed over there one evening; about the bridegroom's death, and "not until the next morning did anyone on shore hear the bride's despairing screams."

But the guidebook says nothing about Babette's quiet life with her father, not at the mill—strangers live there now—but in the beautiful house near the train station where, from the window on many an evening, she still gazes out across the chestnut trees toward the snowy mountains where Rudy once scampered. In the evening hour she sees the alpenglow. The children of the sun settle down up there and repeat the song about the wanderer whose cloak was torn away by the whirling wind and carried off: It took the mortal husk but not the man.

There is a rosy glow on the mountain snow. There is a rosy glow in every heart in which the thought resides: "May God let the best befall us!" But this is not always revealed to us as it was for Babette in her dream.

The Wood Nymph

A Tale from the 1867 Paris Exposition

W e're going to the exposition in Paris.
Now we're there! What speed, what haste, without
any kind of sorcery; we traveled by steam, on ships and
along railways.

Our time is the time of fairy tales.

We're in the center of Paris, in a grand hotel. Flowers adorn the
stairs all the way to the top, soft carpets cover the steps.

Our room is comfortable and the balcony door stands open,
facing a large square. Down below dwells the springtime. It was
brought to Paris, arriving at the same moment we did. It appeared
in the form of a big, young chestnut tree, with delicate newly
sprouted leaves. What springtime loveliness it wears compared to
the other trees on the square! One of them has passed completely
from the ranks of living trees and is lying down, pulled up by its
roots and tossed to the ground. In the spot where it once stood,
the fresh chestnut tree will be planted and grow.

For the moment the chestnut is still standing upright in the heavy
wagon that brought it to Paris this morning from many miles away
out in the country. There it stood for years, close to a mighty oak
tree. Under it the blessed old priest often sat, talking and telling
stories to the listening children. The young chestnut tree listened
too. The wood nymph inside it was still a child, after all. She could
remember back to the time when the tree was so small that it
reached only a little above the tall blades of grass and ferns. They
were then as big as they would ever be, but the tree grew bigger
and bigger each year, drinking in the air and sunshine, receiving
dew and rain, and inevitably being jostled and shaken by the strong
winds. That's all part of growing up.

The wood nymph was happy with her life, with the sunshine and the songs of the birds. Yet her greatest joy was in the human voice; she understood their language just as well as she understood the animals.

Butterflies, dragonflies, and houseflies, yes, everything that could fly paid a visit, and all of them gossiped. They talked about the village, the vineyards, the forest, the old castle and grounds with its moats and ponds. In the water dwelled living creatures that in their own way could fly from place to place underwater, creatures with knowledge and thoughts; they were so wise that they never said a word.

The swallow that had dipped down into the water spoke of the beautiful goldfish, about the fat bream, the plump tenches, and the old algae-covered carp. The swallow gave a very good description, but it's better to see for yourself, it said. Yet how could the wood nymph ever have a look at those creatures? She would have to make do with gazing out across the lovely landscape and sensing all the bustling human activity.

How lovely it was, but the loveliest of all was when the old priest stood under the oak and talked about France, about the great deeds of men and women whose names have been spoken with admiration down through the ages.

The wood nymph heard about the shepherdess Joan of Arc and about Charlotte Corday. She heard about the ancient times, about the days of Henri IV and Napoleon I, and about cleverness and greatness all the way up to the present. She heard names, each of which has resonated in the hearts of the people. France is the foremost country in the world, the seat of genius with the font of liberty.

The village children listened reverently, the wood nymph did no less; she was a pupil along with all the others. She saw in the shape of the sailing clouds image after image of what she was hearing.

The clouds in the sky were her picture book.

She felt so happy in beautiful France, and yet she had a feeling that the birds, in fact all the creatures that could fly, were much more blessed than she was. Even the housefly could look around, see far and wide, far beyond the wood nymph's horizon.

France was so vast and grand, but she saw only a small patch of it. The land stretched out into the world, with vineyards, forests, and great cities, and Paris was the grandest, the mightiest of all. The birds could fly there, but she never could.

Among the village children there was a little girl, so ragged, so poor, but lovely to look at; she was always singing and laughing, plaiting red flowers into her black hair.

"Don't go to Paris!" said the old priest. "You poor child, don't go there. It will be your ruin!"

And yet that's where she went.

The wood nymph often thought about her. They both shared the same desire and longing for the great city.

Spring came, then summer, autumn, winter. A couple of years passed.

The wood nymph's tree bore its first chestnut blossoms, and the birds chirped about it in the lovely sunshine. Then a stately coach came along the road carrying an elegant lady. She was driving the beautiful, prancing horses herself while a livery-clad little groom sat in back. The wood nymph recognized her. The old priest recognized her, shook his head, and said sadly:

"You went there and it was your ruin, poor Marie."

"How can he call her poor?" thought the wood nymph. "Oh, what a transformation! She's dressed like a duchess. That's what she became in the city of enchantment. Oh, if only I were there in all that radiance and splendor! At night the city illuminates the very clouds when I look toward the spot where I know it must be."

Yes, the wood nymph looked in that direction every evening, every night. She saw the glittering haze on the horizon. She missed it on the bright, moonlit nights; she missed the sailing clouds that showed her images from the city and from history.

A child reaches for her picture book; the wood nymph reached for the cloud world, her book of thoughts.

For her the summer-warm, cloudless sky was a blank page, and during the past few days she had seen nothing else.

Warm summertime had arrived, with sun-hot days and no breeze. Every leaf, every flower seemed in a stupor; the people did too.

Then clouds rose up, in the very direction where at night the glittering haze proclaimed: Here is Paris!

The clouds rose, forming an entire landscape of mountains, shooting through the air, out over the whole countryside, for as far as the wood nymph could see.

The clouds were piled like mighty blue-black boulders, layer upon layer, high in the air. Lightning bolts flashed from them. "They too are God's servants," the old priest had said. And then came a blinding, bluish flash, gleaming as if the sun itself had exploded the boulders. Lightning struck, smashing the mighty old oak tree to its roots. Its crown shattered, its trunk shattered. Split apart, it fell, as if spreading out to embrace the messenger of light.

No bronze cannons have ever boomed through the air and across the land at the birth of a royal child the way the thunder pealed at the passing of the old oak tree. The rain poured down, a refreshing wind blew, the storm had passed; it felt as solemn as a Sunday. The villagers gathered around the fallen old oak. The old priest spoke words of praise, and a painter sketched the tree itself as a lasting memorial.

"Everything passes on," said the wood nymph. "Passes on, like the clouds, never to come again."

The old priest came no more; the school roof had fallen in, his pulpit was gone. The children came no more, but autumn did return; winter came, but also spring. And during all these shifting seasons the wood nymph gazed in the direction where every evening and night, on the distant horizon, Paris gleamed like a radiant haze. Out of it flew locomotive after locomotive, one train after another, rushing, roaring, and at all hours. In the evening, at midnight, in the morning, and all day long the trains came, and crowding in and out of them were people from every country on earth. A new wonder of the world had summoned them to Paris.

How did this wonder manifest itself?

"A magnificent flower of art and industry," they said, "has sprung up from the barren sand of the Champ-de-Mars. A gigantic sunflower, from whose leaves you can learn geography and statistics, acquire the knowledge of a guild master, be uplifted by art and poetry, study the size and greatness of all the countries."

"A fairy-tale flower," others said, "a colorful lotus plant spreading its green leaves out across the sand like velvet carpets that burst forth in early spring. The summer will reveal all its glory, the autumn storms will blow it away, and not a leaf or root will remain."

Next to the École Militaire stretches the Champ-de-Mars in a time of peace, the field with neither grass nor straw, a patch of sandy steppe cut from the African desert, where Fata Morgana displays her mysterious air castles and hanging gardens. At the Champ-de-Mars they appeared even more magnificent, more wondrous, for ingenuity had made them real.

"A present-day Aladdin's palace is rising up!" people said. Day by day, hour by hour, it unfurls more and more of its rich splendors. The endless halls are resplendent with marble and colors. Here "Master Bloodless" is moving his steel and iron limbs in the great circular Palais des Machines. Works of art in metal, in stone, in textiles proclaim the spirit that is stirring in all the countries of the world. Halls of paintings, floral splendor, everything that spirit and hand can create in a craftsman's workshop is on display here. Even ancient relics from old castles and peat bogs have appeared.

This great, overwhelming, colorful show has to be diminished, reduced to a toy in order to be reproduced, comprehended, and seen in its entirety.

Like a Christmas banquet table, Champ-de-Mars presented an Aladdin's palace to industry and art, and surrounding it were trinkets from every country: trinkets of greatness. Each nation was given a memento of its homeland.

There stood the palace of Egypt, there the caravansary of the desert. The Bedouin on his camel, arriving from his land of sun, rushed past. There sprawled the Russian stables with magnificent, fiery horses from the steppes. The little Danish farmhouse with its thatched roof and its Dannebrog flag stood next to Gustav Vasa's house from Dalarna, carved so magnificently from wood. American cabins, English cottages, French pavilions, gazebos, churches, and theaters were wondrously scattered all around—and among them fresh green lawns, clear trickling water, flowering shrubs, rare trees, and hothouses that made you think you were in the tropical forests. Entire rose gardens, brought from Damascus, were resplendent beneath the rooftops. What colors, what fragrances!

Stalactite grottos, artificially constructed, surrounded pools of both fresh- and saltwater, offering a view of the marine realms; you could stand on the bottom among the fish and polyps.

All this, they said, is now presented and on exhibit at Champ-de-Mars. Across this enormous, richly set banquet table, like a swarm of busy ants, moves the whole crowd of people, on foot or conveyed in small carts, since not every pair of legs can tolerate such an exhausting trek.

From early morning until late in the evening they come. Steamship after steamship, packed with people, glides along the Seine. The onslaught of carriages keeps increasing; the crowds of people, both afoot and on horseback, swell constantly; the trams and omnibuses are crammed, stuffed, and bedecked with people. All these currents are moving toward one goal: The Paris Exposition! All the entrances are resplendent with the flag of France, while around the building that houses the bazaar of nations, banners flutter from every country. The Palais des Machines hums and buzzes, melodies chime from the bell towers, organs play inside the churches; hoarse, nasal songs blend together from the cafés of the East. It's like a kingdom of Babel, a babble of tongues, a Wonder of the World.

Assuredly that's the way it was; that's what all the reports said, and who hadn't heard them? The wood nymph knew everything that had been said about "the new Wonder" in the city of cities.

"Fly off, you birds! Fly off to have a look, then come back and tell me" was the wood nymph's plea.

Her longing swelled to a wish, became her life's desire.

And then . . . in the silent, still night, the full moon gleamed, and out of its disk the wood nymph saw a spark fly. It fell, glittering like a shooting star, and in front of the tree, whose branches shook as if pitched by a storm, stood a magnificent luminous figure. It spoke in tones as soft and strong as the trumpets on Judgment Day that will restore life with a kiss, summoning to judgment.

"You will go to the city of enchantment. There you will take root, sense the rushing currents, the air and sunlight. But your lifetime will be shortened; the number of years you could have expected out here in the open will be reduced to a paltry sum of years. You poor wood nymph, it will be your ruin! Your longing will grow, your craving, your demands become stronger. The tree itself will become a prison for you, you will abandon your husk, abandon your nature, to fly out and mix with the human beings. Then your years will dwindle to half the lifetime of a mayfly, to a single night. The flame of your life will be blown out, the tree's leaves will wither and vanish, never to come again."

That was its tune, that was its song, and the light disappeared, but the wood nymph's longing and desire did not. She trembled with anticipation, with the wild fever of intuition.

"I'm going to the city of cities!" she rejoiced. "Life is just beginning, billowing like a cloud. No one knows where it will lead."

At daybreak, when the moon turned pale and the clouds crimson, the hour of fulfillment arrived, the words of the promise were redeemed.

Men appeared with spades and poles. They dug around the roots of the tree, deep down and underneath. A cart drove up, pulled by horses. The tree's roots and the clump of earth that contained them were pulled up and wrapped in reed mats, almost like a warm foot muff. Then the tree was set on the cart and lashed tight. It was off on a journey, to *Paris*. It would remain there and grow in the great city of France, the city of cities.

The branches and leaves of the chestnut tree trembled as the cart began to move. The wood nymph trembled with the pleasure of anticipation.

"Away! Away!" sounded in every pulse. "Away! Away!" sounded in trembling, hovering words. The wood nymph forgot to say farewell to her home, to the swaying blades of grass and the innocent chamomile that had looked up to her as they would to a great lady in the garden of Our Lord, a young princess, playing shepherdess out here in the open country.

The chestnut tree was on the cart, nodding with its branches to say either "live well" or "away," the wood nymph wasn't sure which. She was thinking about, she was dreaming about, all that was so wondrously new and yet so familiar, all that was about to unfold. No child's heart full of innocent joy, no blood of passion, has ever begun a journey to Paris more filled with thoughts.

"Live well!" became "Away! Away!"

The wheels of the cart turned; what was distant became near, and then was left behind. The countryside changed as clouds change. New vineyards, forests, villages, houses, and gardens sprang up, approached, rolled past. The chestnut tree moved onward, the wood nymph moved with it. Locomotive after locomotive roared past each other, crisscrossing paths. The locomotives sent up clouds that formed shapes telling of Paris, which was where they came from and where the wood nymph was headed.

Surely everything around her knew and understood where she was going. She thought that every tree she passed was stretching out its branches toward her and pleading: "Take me along! Take me along!" Inside every tree lived another wood nymph, filled with yearning.

What changes! What speed! The buildings seemed to shoot up from the earth, more and more of them, closer and closer together. The chimneys rose up like flowerpots, stacked on top of each other and side by side along the rooftops. Enormous inscriptions composed of letters two feet high, and painted shapes that shone brightly, covered the walls from foundation to cornice.

"Where does Paris start, and when will I be there?" the wood nymph asked herself. The crowds of people swelled, the bustle and commotion grew, carriage followed carriage. There were people on foot and on horseback, and everywhere shop after shop, music, song, shrieks, and conversations.

The wood nymph in her tree was in the middle of Paris.

The big heavy cart came to a halt in a little square planted with trees and surrounded by tall buildings. Every window had its own balcony with people looking down at the young, fresh chestnut tree that came riding along and was now to be planted here in place of the dead, uprooted tree that lay stretched out on the ground. People on the square stopped and gazed with smiles and pleasure at the springtime greenery. The older trees, still in bud, rustled their branches in greeting: "Welcome! Welcome!" And the fountain, which tossed its jets of water into the air to make them splash into the wide basin, let the wind carry drops over to the newly arrived tree, as if offering a drink in welcome.

The wood nymph felt her tree being lifted out of the cart and placed at its future site. The tree's roots were covered with earth, fresh sod was laid on top. Blossoming shrubs and pots containing flowers were planted just like the tree. An entire garden plot was created in the middle of the square. The dead, uprooted tree, killed by gas fumes, cooking fumes, and the plant-suffocating city air, was put on the cart and driven away. The crowds of people watched. Children and old people sat on the benches outdoors and looked up through the tree's foliage. And we, who are telling this story, stood on the balcony, looking down at the young springtime from the fresh country air and said, as the old priest would have said, "You poor wood nymph!"

"How happy I am, how happy!" said the wood nymph. "And yet I can't quite grasp it, can't express what I feel. Everything is just as I imagined, and yet not as I imagined."

The buildings stood so tall, so close together. The sun shone directly on only one wall, which was pasted over with placards and posters. People stood in front, jostling each other. Wagons, both light and heavy, raced past. Omnibuses, those packed moving houses, sped by. Riders on horseback raced off; carts and carriages vied for the right of way. The wood nymph thought: If only the buildings, grown so tall and standing so close together, would start moving too, changing shape the way the clouds in the sky change, sliding aside so she would be able to see into Paris, look out over it. Notre Dame would appear, Place Vendôme, and the Wonder that had summoned and was still summoning all the foreigners here.

The buildings did not budge.

It was still daylight when the lamps were lit and the gaslight streamed from the shops, shining through the branches of the tree. It was like summer sunshine. The stars overhead appeared, the same ones the wood nymph had seen back home. She thought she could sense a breeze coming from there, pure and gentle. She felt uplifted, strengthened, and sensed a visual force penetrating every leaf of her tree, an awareness in the very tips of its roots. She found herself in the midst of the living world of humans, observed by gentle eyes. All around were sounds and commotion, colors and light.

From the side streets came the sound of wind instruments and the tunes of barrel organs made for dancing. Oh yes, for dancing, for dancing! For joy and pleasure they played.

It was music that would make people, horses, carriages, trees, and buildings dance if they could dance. An intoxicating joy rose inside the wood nymph's breast.

"How blissful and lovely!" she rejoiced. "I'm in Paris!"

The next day, the night that followed, and then another day offered the same sights, the same coming and going, the same life, changing and yet always the same.

"Now I know every tree, every flower on this square. I know every building, balcony, and shop where I've been placed in this cramped little corner that hides from me the magnificent, great city. Where is the Arc de Triomphe, the boulevards, and the Wonder of the World? I can see none of them. Imprisoned as if in a cage, I stand here among these tall buildings that I now have memorized with their inscriptions, placards, and signs, all the painted-on delicacies that no longer appeal to me. Where is everything I've heard about, known about, longed for, and the reason I wanted to come here? What have I won, gained, found? I yearn as I did before, I sense a life I must seize and embrace. I must join the ranks of the living! Cavort among them, fly like the birds, see and feel; actually become a human being and seize half a day of life in place of years of dwelling in the weariness and tedium of the ordinary, which will make me sicken and droop, sink like the meadow mist and vanish. I want to gleam like the cloud, gleam in the sun of life, gaze out across everything like the cloud, race off as it does, no one knows where."

This was the wood nymph's sigh, which rose up like a prayer.

"Take my years of life; give me half the life of a mayfly. Release me from my prison, give me a human life, human happiness for one brief moment, even a single night if that's all I can have, and then punish me only for my bold love of life, my longing for life. Obliterate me, let my husk, this fresh young tree, wither, fall, turn to ash, blow away on the wind."

The branches of the tree rustled, a tickling sensation arose, a trembling in all the leaves, as if a fire were coursing through them or shooting out of them. A stormy gust blew through the tree's crown, and in the midst of it a female shape rose up: the wood nymph. The next moment she was sitting under the gaslit, leafy branches, young and lovely, like poor Marie, to whom it was said: "The big city will be your ruin!"

The wood nymph sat at the foot of the tree, next to her house door, which she had closed and then thrown away the key. So young, so lovely! The stars looked at her, the stars winked; the gaslamps looked at her, glittered, blinked. How slender she was and yet so sturdy, a child and yet a full-grown maiden. Her clothing was silken, green as the fresh, unfurled leaves in the tree's crown. In her nut-brown hair hung a half-open chestnut blossom. She looked like the goddess of spring.

For only a brief moment did she sit there, motionless. Then she jumped up, and with the speed of a gazelle she raced off, around the corner. She ran, she leaped, like the flash in a mirror that is carried in the sun, the flash that with every movement is tossed first here, then there. If anyone had taken a close look and been able to see what there was to see, how wondrous it was! At every spot where she lingered for a moment her clothing changed, as did her shape, to match the character of that place, that building, and its lamp that shone upon her.

She reached the boulevard. There a sea of light streamed from the gas flames in the streetlamps, shops, and cafés. There the trees stood in rows, young and slender, each hiding its wood nymph from the rays of the artificial sunlight. The endlessly long sidewalk was like one huge banquet hall. Tables were set with all types of refreshments, from champagne and Chartreuse to coffee and beer. On display were flowers, pictures, statues, books, and colorful fabrics.

From amid the throngs beneath the tall buildings she looked out across the terrifying stream in the middle of the rows of trees. There surged a river of carriages, cabriolets, coaches, omnibuses, hansom cabs, gentlemen on horseback, and marching regiments. A person risked life and limb by crossing over to the opposite shore. Now a Bengal light flared, then the gaslight was even brighter. Suddenly a rocket shot skyward. Where did it come from, where was it going?

This was undoubtedly the great highway of the world's greatest city!

Here soft Italian melodies resounded, over there Spanish songs, accompanied by the clack of castanets. But loudest of all, drowning out everything else, were the music-box tunes of the day, the tingling cancan music that Orpheus never knew, nor was it ever heard by the beautiful Helen. Even the wheelbarrow would have danced on its wheel, if it could have managed to dance at all. The wood nymph danced, swayed, flew, her colors changing like a hummingbird in the sunlight, reflecting every building and the world inside.

Like the gleaming lotus blossom torn loose from its root and borne by the current and its eddies, she drifted away, and wherever she paused she would take on yet another shape. That's why no one was able to follow, recognize, or observe her.

Like cloud images, everything flew past her: face after face, but not one did she know, not a single figure from her home region did she see. In her mind two radiant eyes shone; she was thinking about Marie, poor Marie. That ragged, happy child with the red flower in her black hair. She was here in the great city, rich and radiant, like the time she drove past the priest's house, the wood nymph's tree, and the old oak.

She was most assuredly here, in the deafening din, perhaps having just alighted from that magnificent waiting coach. Splendid carriages were stopped here. The coachmen wore braided livery, the servants wore silk stockings. The noble passengers stepping out were all women, richly attired ladies. They walked through the open gates and up the steep, wide staircase that led to a building with marble-white pillars. Could this be the Wonder of the World? Marie must be here.

"*Sancta Maria!*" they sang inside. The fragrance of incense came billowing out from the high, painted, and gilded arches, where semidarkness dwelled.

It was the Madeleine Church.

Dressed in black attire, made from the costliest fabrics, tailored in the latest and highest fashion, the elegant feminine world glided across the polished floor. Their crests were engraved on the silver clasps of the velvet-bound prayer books and embroidered on the fine, strongly perfumed handkerchiefs trimmed with costly Brussels lace. Some of the women knelt in quiet prayer before the altars, others sought out the confessionals.

The wood nymph felt uneasy and alarmed, as if she had set foot in a place she should not enter. This was the home of silence, the great hall of secrets, where everything was whispered and soundlessly confided.

The wood nymph saw herself enshrouded in silk and a veil, her figure resembling that of the other wealthy, highborn women. Was each of them a child full of yearning like herself?

A sigh, so painfully deep, was heard. Did it come from the confessional corner or from the wood nymph's breast? She drew the veil more closely around her. She was breathing in the church incense, and not fresh air. This was not the place of her longing.

Away! Away! Flee without rest! The mayfly does not rest; her flight is her life.

She was once again outside beneath the glittering gas candelabras near the magnificent fountains. "Yet all the torrents of water do not have the power to rinse away the innocent blood shed here."

Those were the words that were spoken.

Foreigners stood there, conversing loudly and animatedly, the way no one had dared in the great hall of secrets that the wood nymph had just left.

A great stone slab was turned, lifted. She did not understand. She looked at the open stairs descending into the depths of the earth. They led downward, away from the starry-bright air, away from the sun-gleaming gas flames, away from the world of the living.

"I'm afraid," said one of the women standing there. "I don't dare go down inside. Nor do I care to see the splendor below. Stay here with me."

"And go back home?" said the man. "Leave Paris without seeing the most remarkable, the truest wonder of the day, created by the ingenuity and will of one man?"

"I'm not going down there" was the reply.

"The wonder of the day," he had said. The wood nymph heard it and understood. The goal of her greatest longing had been reached, and here was the entrance, down into the depths, beneath Paris. It was not as she had imagined, but she had heard him say that, had watched the strangers descend, and she followed them.

The stairs were made of cast iron, spiral-shaped, wide, and

comfortable. A single lamp was lit below, and another farther down.

They were standing in a labyrinth of endlessly long, intersecting halls and arched passageways. All the streets and lanes of Paris were here to see, as if in a dim mirror image. The names could be read, and each building above had its number below. Their roots shot out under the deserted asphalt pavements that squeezed along a wide canal with sludge gushing along. Higher up, fresh running water was conducted through an aqueduct, and above everything hung a network of gas pipes and telegraph wires. Lamps glowed in the distance, like reflections from the metropolis overhead. Now and then a great rumbling could be heard up above from heavy carts driving across the underground entrances.

Where was the wood nymph?

You've heard about the catacombs? They're nothing more than faint wisps compared to this new underground world, this modern-day wonder: the sewers of Paris. That was where the wood nymph now stood, and not at the world exposition at Champ-de-Mars.

Cries of amazement, admiration, and acknowledgment she heard.

"From down here," they said, "health and long years of life are now made possible for thousands upon thousands up above. Our age is the age of progress, with all its blessings."

That was the opinion of the humans, the words of the humans, but not of the creatures that had been born and lived down there: the rats. They were squeaking from the crevice in a section of old wall, so loud and clear that the wood nymph could understand them.

A big old male rat with a bitten-off tail piercingly screeched his fury, his worry, the one and only right opinion, and his family agreed with every word.

"I'm sickened by that meowing, that human meowing, that ignorant talk. Oh yes, things are certainly lovely down here with gas and petroleum! But that's not something I can eat. Everything has become so fine and so bright down here that it makes you sit around feeling ashamed without knowing why. If only we were living in the age of tallow candles. That wasn't so long ago. It was a romantic time, they say."

"What are you saying?" asked the wood nymph. "I didn't notice you before. What are you talking about?"

"About the good old days," said the rat. "Those gracious days of Great-Grandfather and Great-Grandmother Rat. Back then it was a grand occasion to come down here. It was a rats' nest beyond any in all of Paris! Mother Plague lived down here then. She killed human beings, but never rats. Thieves and smugglers breathed freely down here. It was a refuge for the most interesting characters, who are now seen only in the melodramas up above. The romantic age is over, even in our rats' nest. We now have fresh air down here, and petroleum."

That was what the rat was squeaking. He squeaked at the new age, and praised the past with its Mother Plague.

A cart was waiting, a kind of open omnibus, with small, lively horses harnessed in front. The group climbed in, to rush off along Boulevard Sebastopol, the underground one. Right overhead stretched the familiar one, crowded with people, up in Paris.

The cart vanished in the semidarkness, the wood nymph vanished, rising up in the glimmer of gas flames into the fresh air. Up there, and not down below among the intersecting vaults and their muffled air, would the Wonder be found, the Wonder of the World, the one she was seeking in her brief lifetime. Surely it would shine brighter than all the gas flames below, brighter than the moon that was now gliding into view.

Yes, of course! She saw it in the distance. It was shining before her, glinting, winking, like Venus in the sky.

She saw a radiant gate that stood open to a little garden filled with lights and dance melodies. The gaslights shone like borders of flowers around quiet little lakes and ponds where water plants, artificially made—cut from sheets of tin, then bent and painted— glittered in all that light, shooting two-foot-high jets of water from their chalices. Beautiful weeping willows, the real weeping willows of spring, lowered their fresh boughs like a green veil, transparent and yet concealing. Here among the shrubbery burned a bonfire, its red gleam casting light over the small, dim, silent arbors, pulsating with tunes; music that tickled the ear, enchanting, enticing, chasing the blood through people's limbs.

She saw young women, beautiful and festively dressed, with guileless smiles, and the light, laughing temperament of youth; a "Marie" with a rose in her hair, but without a carriage or groom. How they surged, how they whirled around in their wild dance! What was up, what was down? As if bitten by the tarantella, they leaped, they laughed, they smiled, blissfully happy to embrace the whole world.

The wood nymph felt herself swept up by the dance. Her elegant little feet wore silk slippers, chestnut-brown like the ribbon that fluttered from her hair over her bare shoulders. Her green silk gown billowed in great folds, but without hiding her beautifully shaped legs and exquisite feet that seemed to want to sketch magical circles in the air before the face of the dancing young man.

Was she in Armida's enchanted garden? What was this place called?

The name was lit up outside in the gas flames: MABILE.

Tunes and applause, rockets and trickling water, pierced by the pop of champagne corks. The wild dancing was bacchanalian, and over it all sailed the moon, its face a bit skewed. The sky without a cloud, clear and pure; it seemed possible to look straight into Heaven from Mabile.

A consuming, urgent joie de vivre shuddered through the wood nymph, like the intoxication of opium.

Her eyes spoke, her lips spoke, but the words were not heard above the clamor of flutes and violins. Her dancing partner whispered words in her ear that rippled in time with the cancan. She didn't understand them, we didn't understand them. He stretched out his arms toward her, around her, and embraced nothing but the transparent, gas-filled air.

The wood nymph was carried off by a current of air, the way the wind carries a rose petal. From high above she saw before her a flame, a flickering blaze high atop a tower. The fire gleamed from the object of her longing, gleamed from the red lighthouse on the Fata Morgana of Champ-de-Mars. That was where she was carried by the spring wind. She circled the tower, and the workers thought it was a butterfly they were watching descend, only to die, having arrived too soon.

★

The moon glittered, the gaslights and lanterns lit up the great buildings and the "Halls of Nations" scattered all around, illuminating the heights of the green lawns and the rocks so ingeniously man-made where waterfalls poured down under the power of "Master Bloodless." The caverns of the sea and the depths of the freshwater lakes, the realms of the fish, opened here. You were at the bottom of the deep ponds, you were under the sea in a glass diving bell. Water pressed against the thick glass walls on all sides and from above. Polyps, fathoms-long, slithery and wriggling like eels, alive and quivering, intestines and arms, seized hold, rose up, became rooted to the sea floor.

An enormous, wary flounder lay nearby, indolently, comfortably spreading itself out. Over it crawled a crab like a giant spider, while shrimp darted past with a speed and haste as if they were the moths and butterflies of the sea.

In the freshwater grew water lilies, reeds, and water gladioli. Goldfish were lined up like red cows in a field, all of them with their heads turned in the same direction so the current would enter their mouths. Thick, fat tenches stared at the glass walls with dull-witted eyes. They knew they were at the Paris Exposition. They knew that in barrels filled with water they had made the quite difficult journey to come here; they had been landsick on the train the way people become seasick on the ocean. They had come to see the exposition, and see it they did from their own freshwater or saltwater box seats, watching the throngs of people moving past, from morning to night. All the nations of the world had sent their humans for display so that the old tenches and bream, the nimble perch and algae-covered carp could see the humans and voice their opinion about such creatures.

"They're scale-fish," said a muddy little carp. "They change their scales two or three times a day and make mouth noises—speech, they call it. We don't change, and we make ourselves understood in a much easier way: by twitching our lips and staring with our eyes. We're much more advanced than human beings."

"Yet they have learned to swim," said a little freshwater fish. "I come from a big inland lake. During the hot days, humans come into the water, but first they take off their scales, then they swim. The frogs taught them how, by kicking their hind legs and stroking

with their front legs, though they can't do it for long. They want
to be like us, but that's impossible. Poor humans!"

And the fish stared. They thought the whole crowd of people
they had seen in the bright daylight was still moving about. Yes,
they were convinced they could still see the same figures that had
first struck their nerves of perception, so to speak.

A little perch, with beautiful tiger-striped skin and an enviably
rounded back, swore that the "human mire" was still there; he
could see it.

"I see it too, I see it quite clearly," said a jaundice-golden
tench. "I can clearly see the beautiful-shaped human form, the
'long-legged lady,' or whatever it was they called her. She had our
lips and staring eyes, two balloons behind and a closed parasol in
front, great duckweed appendages, and all sorts of baubles. She
should take everything off and move as we do, the way we were
created to move, then she would look like a respectable tench, as
much as a human being could."

"Where did he go? The one on the rope, the male human they
were pulling along?"

"He was riding in a wagon with a seat, sitting with a piece of
paper, pen and ink, writing everything up, writing everything
down. What was the meaning of that? They called him a writer."

"He's still riding along," said an algae-covered maidenly carp
who had the temptation of the world in her gullet; it had made her
hoarse. She had once swallowed a fishhook and was still patiently
swimming around with it in her throat.

"A writer," she said, "in fish terms, in understandable terms, is
a kind of octopus among humans."

That's how the fish talked. But in the midst of the artificially
constructed, water-bearing grotto, came the sound of hammering
and the songs of workers. They had to labor through the night in
order to finish it all on time. They were singing in the summer-night
dream of the wood nymph. She stood inside, soon to fly off and
vanish once more.

"Goldfish," she said, nodding to them. "So I managed to see
you after all. Yes, I know you. I've known you for a very long
time. The swallow told me all about you back home. How beautiful,
glittering, lovely you are! I could kiss each and every one of you. I

know the others too. That must be the fat bream, and that one the delectable brace, and here are the old algae-covered carp. I know you, but you don't know me."

The fish stared, not understanding a single word. They peered into the waning light.

The wood nymph was no longer there, she was standing outdoors where the world's "wonder-blossom" spread fragrances from the various lands: from the land of rye bread, the coast of dried cod, the realm of Russian leather, the riverbank of eau de cologne, and the Orient of rose oil.

After a night of dancing, we drive home half asleep, and in our ears echo the melodies that we heard, still so clear that we could sing each and every one of them. And just as in the eyes of a dead man the last sight he saw lingers for a time like a photograph, so did the tumult and glare of the day remain in the night; it had not slipped away, was not yet extinguished. The wood nymph could sense this, and she knew: It will still be rushing onward, even tomorrow.

The wood nymph stood among the fragrant roses, thinking she recognized them from her home. Roses from the castle grounds and from the priest's garden. The red pomegranate she saw here too, the kind that Marie had worn in her coal-black hair.

Memories from her childhood home out in the country flashed through her mind. She drank in the sights all around with greedy eyes as a feverish restlessness filled her, guiding her through the wondrous halls.

She felt tired, and her weariness grew. She felt an urge to rest on the soft Oriental cushions and carpets spread all around inside, or to lean like a weeping willow down toward the clear water and dive in.

But the mayfly never rests. The day would be over in minutes.

Her thoughts trembled, her limbs shook, she sank down onto the grass beside the trickling water.

"You leap from the earth with eternal life," she said. "Cool my tongue, give me refreshment!"

"I am not a living fount," replied the water. "A machine makes me leap."

"Green grass, give me some of your freshness," begged the wood nymph. "Give me one of your fragrant flowers!"

"We will die if you pull us out," replied the blades of grass and the flowers.

"Kiss me, you fresh gust of air! Just one kiss of life!"

"Soon the sun will kiss the clouds crimson," said the wind. "And then you will be among the dead, passing away as all the splendor here will pass away before the year is out. Then I can once again play with the light, loose sand on this site, blowing dust across the earth, dust through the air, dust! Nothing but dust!"

The wood nymph felt a sense of dread, like the woman who has slit her wrist in the bath and is bleeding, but as she bleeds wishes to go on living. She rose up, took a few steps forward, and then collapsed again before a little chapel. The door stood open, candles burned on the altar, the organ was playing.

What music! Such tones the wood nymph had never heard, and yet within them she seemed to hear familiar voices. They came from the depths of the heart of all creation. She thought she could sense the rustling of the old oak, she thought she could hear the old priest speaking about glorious deeds, about famous names, about what God's creation might offer as gifts to a future age, and must give to it in order to win eternal life.

The chords of the organ surged and resounded, saying in song:

"Your longing and desire tore you up by the roots from your God-given place. It was your ruin, you poor wood nymph!"

The tones of the organ, soft, gentle, and sounding like sobs, died out as sobs do.

In the sky the clouds gleamed crimson. The wind sighed and sang, "Away, dead ones, now the sun is rising."

The first ray fell on the wood nymph. Her figure shone with shimmering colors, like a soap bubble as it bursts, vanishes, and becomes a drop, a tear, that falls to the ground and disappears.

Poor wood nymph! A dew drop, nothing but a tear that was shed and then fled.

★

The sun shone over the Fata Morgana of Champ-de-Mars; it shone over great Paris, over the little square with the trees and the splashing fountain, between the tall buildings where the chestnut tree stood, but with drooping branches, withered leaves. The tree, which only yesterday stood as erect and full of life as spring itself. Now it had perished, they said. The wood nymph had perished, passed on like a cloud, and no one knew where.

On the ground lay a withered, tattered chestnut blossom. Not even the holy water of the church had the power to bring it back to life. A person's foot soon crushed it into the gravel.

All this happened and was witnessed.

We saw it ourselves, during the Exposition in Paris in 1867, during *our time*, the great, wondrous time of fairy tales.

The Most Incredible Thing

Whoever could present the most incredible thing would have the king's daughter and half the kingdom.

Those who were young, yes even the old, strained all their thoughts, sinews, and muscles. Two of them ate themselves to death and one died of drink while trying to do the most incredible thing, each according to his inclination. But that was not the way it should be done. Little street urchins practiced spitting on their own backs; that's what they thought was the most incredible of all.

On a certain day everything would be displayed, what each person had to show as the most incredible thing. Judges had been appointed, from three-year-old children to people as old as ninety. An entire array of incredible things was presented, but everyone quickly agreed that the most incredible of all was a large clock in a case, remarkably devised both inside and out. On the stroke of the hour living pictures would emerge to show what hour had struck. There were twelve images in all, with moving figures that sang and spoke.

"That is the most incredible thing!" everyone said.

The clock struck one, and Moses stood on the mountain and wrote on the law tablets the first commandment: "Thou shalt have no other gods before me."

The clock struck two, and the Garden of Eden appeared, where Adam and Eve met, both of them happy without owning so much as a clothes closet, nor did they need one.

At the stroke of three the Three Wise Men appeared. One of them was coal-black, but it wasn't his fault, because the sun had blackened him. They brought incense and precious treasures.

On the stroke of four the seasons of the year emerged: Spring with a cuckoo on a blossoming beech branch; Summer with a grasshopper on a ripe stalk of grain; Autumn with an empty stork's nest, since the bird had flown off; Winter with an old crow who could tell stories in the corner by the stove, old memories.

When the clock struck five, the five senses appeared. Sight came as an optician; Hearing as a coppersmith; Smell was selling violets and woodruff; Taste was a cook; and Feeling was an undertaker with mourning crepe all the way down to his heels.

The clock struck six, and there sat a gambler. He threw the die and it landed with the highest number up, and there it said six.

Then the seven days of the week appeared, or the seven deadly sins. People couldn't agree which they were, since they belonged together and weren't easy to tell apart.

Then came a choir of monks, singing the eight o'clock matins.

At the stroke of nine the nine muses appeared. One was occupied with astronomy, one with the historical archives, and the rest belonged to the theater.

At the stroke of ten Moses once again stepped forth with the law tablets on which stood the commandments of God, and there were ten.

The clock struck again, and little boys and girls jumped and leaped. They were playing a game and singing along: "Five-six-seven, the clock strikes eleven!" And that's what it had struck.

Now it struck twelve, and the watchman wearing a fur cap and carrying a morning star stepped forth. He was singing the old watchman song:

> It was at midnight
> That our Savior was born!

And as he sang, roses grew and turned into angel heads borne by rainbow-colored wings.

It was enchanting to hear, it was lovely to see. The whole thing was an incomparable work of art. It was the most incredible thing, said all the people.

The artist was a young man, tenderhearted, childishly happy, a loyal friend, and helpful to his impoverished parents. He deserved the princess and half the kingdom.

The day of decision arrived, the whole city was decorated, and the princess sat on the throne of the realm, which had been newly stuffed with horsehair, though that hadn't made it any more easing or pleasing. All the judges cast sly glances at the one who was to win, and there he stood, so confident and joyous. His happiness was assured. He had made the most incredible thing.

"No, I'm the one who's going to do it!" suddenly shouted a tall, strong, bony fellow. "I'm the man for the most incredible thing!" And then he swung a big ax at the work of art.

Crash! Bash! Smash! There the whole thing lay. Gears and springs rolled all around. It was all ruined!

"I'm the only one who could do it," said the man. "*My* deed has beaten his and beaten all of you. I have done the most incredible thing!"

"Destroying a work of art like that," said the judges. "Yes, that is the most incredible thing!"

Everyone said the same, and so he was to have the princess and half the kingdom, because a law is a law, even if it's the most incredible thing.

Trumpets blared from the ramparts and from all the city towers: "Let the wedding proceed!" The princess was not at all pleased, but she looked enchanting and she was pricelessly attired. The church glowed with candles. It was late in the evening, and that's when things look best. The city's noble maidens sang and led forth the bride. The knights sang and led forth the groom. He swaggered as if he could never be snapped in half.

Then the singing stopped. It was so quiet that you could have heard a pin hit the ground, but in the midst of the silence the great church door flew open with a crash and a thunder and . . . "Bam! Bam!" There came all the clockworks marching right down the church aisle, halting between the bride and groom. Dead people can't walk again—that's something we know for sure—but a work of art can. The body had been shattered but not the spirit. The spirit of art was levitating, though this was no matter for levity.

The work of art stood there as alive as when it was whole and untouched. It struck the hour, one after the other, all the way to twelve, and the figures came swarming out. First Moses. Flames of fire seemed to blaze from his forehead. He cast the heavy stone tablets of the law at the bridegroom's feet, pinning them to the church floor.

"I can't lift them up again," said Moses. "You've broken off my arms! Stay right where you're standing!"

Then came Adam and Eve, the Three Wise Men from the East, and the four seasons of the year. Each of them told him unpleasant truths. "Shame on you!"

But he was not ashamed.

All the figures that appeared at each stroke of the hour stepped out of the clock, and all of them grew to a terrifying size. There hardly seemed room left for the real people. And then, at the stroke of twelve, when the watchman emerged wearing his fur cap and carrying his morning star, a strange commotion ensued. The watchman went right up to the bridegroom and struck him on the forehead with the morning star.

"Lie there!" he said. "A blow for a blow! We are avenged and Master is too! Now we will go!"

And so the entire work of art disappeared. But the candles all around in the church became great flowers of light, and the gilded stars on the ceiling flashed long, clear rays. The organ began playing all on its own. Everyone said that it was the most incredible thing they had ever witnessed.

"Then let's summon the right person," said the princess. "The one who made the work of art, he shall be my husband and lord!"

And he stood in the church with all the people accompanying him. Everyone rejoiced, everyone blessed him. There was not one person who was jealous—yes, that was the most incredible thing of all!

Auntie Toothache

Where did we get this story?
Do you want to know?
We got it from the barrel, the one with the old paper in it.

Many a good and rare book has ended up at the grocer's or at the delicatessen, not as reading material but as a basic necessity. They need it to make paper twists to hold starch and coffee beans, and as wrapping paper for salt herring, butter, and cheese. Handwritten materials can also be used.

Things often end up in the bin that shouldn't be in the bin.

I know a grocery boy, the son of a delicatessen owner. He rose up from working in the cellar to the main shop; a boy who has read widely, paper-twist reading, both printed and handwritten. He has an interesting collection that includes many important documents from the wastepaper baskets of various busy and absentminded civil servants; several confidential letters from one girlfriend to another: scandalous reports that were not meant to go any further, were not to be discussed with anyone else. He's a regular rescue society for a not insignificant segment of literature that covers many topics. He has access to the shops of both his parents and employer, and there he has rescued many a book or pages of a book that would be worth reading twice.

He showed me his collection of printed and handwritten materials from the bin, the richest items coming from the delicatessen. There were several pages from a lengthy diary. The handwriting was particularly beautiful and clear; it attracted my attention at once.

"The student wrote that," he said. "The student who lived right across the street and died a month ago. He suffered from a terrible toothache, as you can see. It's quite amusing to read. There's only a small amount left of what he wrote; it used to be a whole book and even a little more than that. My parents gave the student's landlady half a pound of green soap for it. Here's what I've managed to salvage."

I borrowed it, I read it, and now I'm going to tell you what it said.

The title was: AUNTIE TOOTHACHE.

I.

Auntie gave me sweets when I was little. My teeth survived; they didn't get damaged. Now I've grown up and become a student. She still spoils me with sweets and tells me I'm a poet.

I have something of the poet in me, but not enough. Often when I walk along the city streets I feel as if I were walking through a great library. The buildings are bookshelves, each floor a shelf with books. Over there stands a book about everyday life, there a good old-fashioned comedy, and scholarly works in every field; over here risqué literature and entertaining stories. I can fantasize and philosophize about all those books.

There is something of the poet in me, but not enough. Many people have demonstrated that they possess just as much as I do, and yet they don't wear a sign or a collar that reads: POET.

Both they and I have been granted a gift from God, a blessing, large enough for ourselves but much too small to be handed out piecemeal to others. It appears like a ray of sunshine, filling soul and mind; it appears like the scent of a flower, like a melody that sounds familiar yet you can't remember where it's from.

On a recent evening I was sitting in my room, and I felt like reading but didn't have a book, not even a page. Suddenly a leaf, fresh and green, fell from the linden tree. The breeze brought it into my room.

I examined the branching veins; a little bug was moving over them, as if it wanted to make a thorough study of the leaf. That made me think about human wisdom. We too crawl around on the leaf, it's the only thing we know, and then we immediately start lecturing about the whole big tree, the roots, the trunk, and the crown. The big tree: God, the world, and immortality, yet of the whole we know only a little leaf!

As I sat there I had a visit from Auntie Millie.

I showed her the leaf with the bug, told her my thoughts, and her eyes lit up.

"You're a poet!" she said. "Perhaps the greatest we have! If it turns out to be true I will go to my grave contented. Ever since Brewer Rasmussen's funeral you've always astonished me with your tremendous imagination."

That's what Auntie Millie said, and then she kissed me.

Who was Auntie Millie and who was Brewer Rasmussen?

II.

My mother's aunt was known to us children as Auntie; we had no other name for her.

She gave us jam and sugar, even though they could cause great harm to our teeth, but she had a weakness for sweet children, she said. It was cruel to deny them the tiny amount of sweets that they loved so much.

And that's why we loved Auntie so dearly.

She had been an old maid for as long as I could remember, always old. Her age never changed.

For years she had suffered terribly from toothaches and was always talking about them, and that's why her friend, Brewer Rasmussen, used his wit and named her Auntie Toothache.

He hadn't done any brewing in the past few years, but lived on his interest payments. He often came to see Auntie, and he was older than she was. He had no teeth at all, just a few black stumps.

As a child he had eaten too much sugar, he told us children, and that's what happens.

Auntie had apparently never eaten sugar in her childhood; she had the loveliest white teeth.

She also used them sparingly, not even sleeping with them at night, Brewer Rasmussen said.

We children knew that was a wicked thing to say, but Auntie told us he didn't mean anything by it.

One day at lunch she told us about a horrid dream she had had in the night: that one of her teeth had fallen out.

"It means," she said, "that I'm going to lose a true friend."

"Was it a false tooth?" said the brewer with a chuckle. "If so, then it just means that you're going to lose a false friend."

"What an uncivil old man you are," said Auntie, more angry than I've ever seen her, either before or since.

Later she said that her old friend was just teasing her. He was the noblest person on earth, and one day when he died, he would become one of God's little angels in Heaven.

I gave a good deal of thought to this transformation and to whether I would be able to recognize him in his new form.

When Auntie was young and he was young too, he had proposed to her. She thought about it for too long and didn't make a move, made no move for too long a time, and remained an old maid but always his faithful friend.

And then Brewer Rasmussen died.

He was transported to his grave in the most expensive hearse and with a great procession, with people in uniform wearing medals.

Dressed in mourning Auntie stood at the window with all of us children, except for little brother; the stork had brought him only the week before.

Then the hearse and procession passed, the street was deserted, and Auntie prepared to leave, but I didn't want to leave. I was waiting for the angel, Brewer Rasmussen. He had now become a little winged child of God and would have to put in an appearance.

"Auntie," I said, "don't you think he'll come now? Or maybe when the stork brings us another little brother he'll bring us the angel Rasmussen?"

Auntie was quite overwhelmed by my imagination and said, "That child is going to be a great poet!" She repeated this during all my school years, yes, even after my confirmation and well into my university days.

She was and is the most devoted friend to me, when I have both poet-aches and toothaches. And I have attacks of both.

"Just write down all your thoughts," she said, "and put them away in your desk drawer. That's what Jean Paul did. He became a great poet, though I'm not especially fond of him; he doesn't excite me. You have to be exciting! And you *will* be exciting!"

The night following that speech I lay in bed, filled with longing and agony, with a craving and desire to become the great poet that Auntie saw and sensed in me. I lay there suffering from poet-ache. But there is a worse torment: a toothache. It mashed and gnashed me. I became a cringing worm, with an herb compress and a Spanish fly plaster.

"I know what that feels like," said Auntie.

There was a sorrowful smile on her lips, and her teeth gleamed so white.

But I have to start a new section in the story of my aunt and myself.

III.

I moved into new lodgings and had been living there for a month. I told my aunt all about it.

"I'm living with a quiet family. They don't give me a thought, even if I ring the bell three times. And by the way, it's a house full of tumult with the noise and din of wind and storms and people. I live right above the front gate. Every cart that drives in or out makes the pictures on my wall jump. The gate slams and shakes the whole house like an earthquake. If I'm lying in bed, the jolts shudder through all my limbs, but that's supposed to be fortifying to the nerves. If the wind is blowing, and it's always blowing in this country, then the long window latches outside swing back and forth, striking the wall. The bell on the neighbor's gate in the courtyard rings with every gust of wind.

"The lodgers come trickling home from late in the evening until well into the night. The lodger right above me, who gives trombone lessons during the day, is the last one home and never goes to bed until he has taken a little midnight stroll, with heavy footsteps and iron-shod boots.

"There are no double windows, but there is a broken pane over which the landlady has glued some paper. The wind still blows in through the crack, sounding like a buzzing botfly. That's my bedtime music. When I finally fall asleep, the crowing rooster soon wakes me up. The rooster and hens in the chicken coop kept by the cellar tenant announce that morning is about to arrive. The little ponies have no stable; they're tethered in the storeroom under the stairs, and they kick at the door and paneling as they try to move about.

"The day dawns. The porter, who sleeps in the garret with his family, thunders down the stairs. His wooden clogs clatter, the gate slams, the house shakes, and when that's over the lodger above me starts his exercises, lifting in each hand a heavy iron ball, which he can never hold on to. They drop over and over again, while at the same time the youths of the house, who are off to school, come rushing out, shrieking. I go over to the window and open it to get some fresh air. It's a relief when I can get it, provided the woman in the back building isn't washing gloves in stain remover, which is how she makes a living. And by the way, it's a nice place and I live with a quiet family."

That's the summary I gave Auntie about my lodgings. I told it in a much livelier fashion, since spoken words have a fresher sound to them than written words.

"You're a poet!" cried Auntie. "Just write down what you told me and you're as good as Dickens. Yes, now you're much more interesting to me. You paint when you speak. You describe your house so I can see it. It makes me shiver. Keep writing! Put something alive into it: people, charming people, preferably unhappy ones."

I actually did write down my description of the house, the way it stands there with all its din and defects, but I only put myself in it, without any plot. That came later.

IV.

One evening that winter, after the theaters had closed, a terrible storm blew in, a snowstorm, that made it almost impossible to move.

Auntie had gone to the theater and I was there to escort her home, but I was having trouble enough walking on my own, let alone accompanying anyone else. The hansom cabs had all been taken. Auntie lived a good distance away in the city, while my own lodgings were close to the theater; if that had not been the case, we would have had to seek shelter in the sentry box for the time being.

We staggered forward through the deep snow with whirling snowflakes rushing around us. I lifted her, I held her, I shoved her along. Only twice did we fall, but we fell softly.

We reached my gate, where we shook off the snow. On the stairs we shook ourselves again, yet still had enough snow to cover the floor in the entryway.

We took off our overcoats and undercoats and every garment that could be removed. The landlady loaned Auntie dry stockings and a dressing gown. She would need them, said the landlady, and added quite truthfully that it would be impossible for my aunt to return home that night. She invited Auntie to make herself comfortable in the parlor; there she would make up the sofa in front of the connecting door to my room that was always kept locked.

And that's what happened.

The fire burned in my stove, the tea urn was set on the table, the little room grew quite pleasant, although not as pleasant as Auntie's parlor in the wintertime, with its thick curtains over the doors, thick curtains at the windows, and double carpets with three layers of thick paper underneath. Sitting there is like being in a tightly corked bottle filled with warm air, although, as I said, it was also quite pleasant in my room. The wind was whistling outside.

Auntie talked and told stories; her youth reappeared, the Brewer reappeared, and old memories.

She could remember when I got my first tooth and how the family rejoiced.

My first tooth! The tooth of innocence, gleaming like a little white drop of milk, my baby tooth.

One appeared, more appeared, a whole row of them, side by side, top and bottom; the loveliest baby teeth, yet they were just the advance troops, not the real ones that would last my whole life.

They too appeared, along with my wisdom teeth, the flank guards in the row, born with pain and great trouble.

They'll leave again, every one of them. They'll leave before their time of service is over; even the very last tooth will leave, and that is not a day for celebrating, that is a day for grieving.

By then you're old, even though your spirits may be young.

Such thoughts and discussions are not enjoyable, yet we happened to talk about all these things. We returned to my childhood years, talking and talking. It was midnight before Auntie went to bed in the parlor next door.

"Good night, sweet child," she called. "I'm going to sleep as snugly as if I were in my own bed."

She settled in peacefully, but there was no peace either inside the house or outdoors. The storm rattled the windows, battered the long, dangling iron latches, and rang the neighbor's doorbell in the back courtyard. The lodger upstairs had come home. He was still taking a little nighttime stroll back and forth. Then he threw off his boots and got into bed to sleep, but he snores so loudly that anyone with good ears can hear it through the ceiling.

I couldn't sleep, couldn't find any peace. The weather couldn't find peace either; it was terribly lively. The wind whistled and sang in its own way. My teeth started to get lively too; they whistled and sang in their own way. They were getting ready for a bad toothache.

A draft came from the window. The moon was shining on the floor. The light came and went, the way clouds come and go in stormy weather. There was a restless shifting of shadow and light, but at last the shadow on the floor took shape. I looked at this moving form and felt an icy gust.

On the floor sat a figure, tall and thin, the kind a child draws with a pencil on a slate, something that is supposed to look like a person. A single thin line forms the body, one line and then another form the arms; the legs are each one line, the head a polygon.

Soon the figure grew more distinct. It was wearing a sort of gown, very thin, very fine, but this showed that the figure was female.

I heard a buzzing. Was it her or the wind that was droning like a botfly through the crack in the pane?

No, it was her, Madam Toothache! Her Horrible Highness, *Satania infernalis*. God save us from her visits!

"How nice it is here," she hummed. "Such nice quarters. Marshy ground, boggy ground. The mosquitoes have buzzed around here with poison in their stingers. Now I have the stinger, and it has to be sharpened on human teeth. They're shining so white in this fellow in the bed. They've braved sweet and sour, hot and cold, nutshells and plum pits. But I'll smack them and whack them, I'll mulch the roots with a drafty gust and give them cold feet."

What a horrible speech, what a horrible guest!

"Oh, so you're a poet," she said. "Well, I'm going to write you into all the verses of pain. I'm going to give you iron and steel in your body, put fiber into all the fibers of your nerves."

It felt as if a glowing awl were passing through my cheekbone. I twisted and writhed.

"What excellent teeth," she said. "An organ to play on. A mouth organ concert, how splendid! With kettledrums and trumpets, piccolos, and trombones in the wisdom tooth. Great poet, great music!"

Oh yes, she started playing, and how horrible she looked even though I could see no more of her than her hand, that shadowy gray, ice-cold hand with the long fingers as thin as awls. Each of them was a torture instrument: her thumb and index finger were the pincers and screw, her middle finger ended in a sharp awl, her ring finger was a gimlet, and her little finger a syringe full of mosquito poison.

"I'll teach you metered verse," she said. "A big poet will have a big toothache, a little poet a little toothache."

"Oh, let me be little," I begged. "Let me not be one at all. I'm not a poet, I just have attacks of poetry, attacks, like toothaches. Go away! Go away!"

"Then do you acknowledge that I'm mightier than poetry, philosophy, mathematics, and all music?" she said. "Mightier than all those painted and marble-carved sensations? I'm older than all of them. I was born close to the Garden of Eden, outside where the wind blew and the damp toadstools grew. I made Eve put on clothes in the cold wind, and Adam too. Believe me, the first toothache was a powerful one!"

"I believe everything," I said. "Go away! Go away!"

"Well, if you'll give up being a poet, never set verse to paper, slate, or any form of writing material again, then I'll let you go. But I'll be back if you ever start writing."

"I swear!" I said. "If only I never see or feel you again!"

"But you *will* see me, though in a more substantial form, one that is dearer to you than I am now. You will see me as Auntie Millie, and I'll say: 'Write, my sweet boy! You're a great poet, perhaps the greatest we have!' But believe me, if you start writing, then I'll set your verses to music and play them on your mouth organ. You sweet child. Think of me when you see Auntie Millie."

Then she vanished.

In farewell I got what felt like a glowing awl jabbed into my jaw, but it soon faded. I felt as if I were floating on gentle water. I saw the white water lilies with the broad green leaves droop, sink below me, wither, dissolve, and I sank with them, dissolving into peace and rest.

"Die, melt away like the snow!" is what I heard singing and ringing in the water. "Evaporate into the clouds, pass on like the clouds!"

Shining down through the water toward me were big, bright names, inscriptions on fluttering victory banners, the proclamation of immortality—written on the wings of a mayfly.

My slumber was deep, slumber without dreams. I didn't hear the whistling wind, the slamming gate, the neighbor's doorbell ringing, or the vigorous exercises of the lodger.

What bliss!

Then came a gust of wind so strong that the locked door to Auntie's room blew open. Auntie leaped to her feet, pulled on her shoes, put on her clothes, and came into my room.

I was sleeping like one of God's angels, she said, and she couldn't bear to wake me.

I awoke on my own, opened my eyes, and had completely forgotten that Auntie was in the house. But I quickly remembered, remembered my toothache vision. Dream and reality merged into one.

"You didn't happen to write anything last night, after we said good night, did you?" she asked. "How I wish that you had! You're my poet, and you always will be."

I thought she smiled so slyly. I couldn't tell if it was the real

Auntie Millie, who loved me, or the horrible one, to whom I had given my promise in the night.

"Have you written anything, sweet child?"

"No, no!" I cried. "But you're Auntie Millie."

"Who else?" she said. And she was Auntie Millie.

She kissed me, got into a hansom cab, and drove home.

I wrote all of this down. It's not in verse, and it will never be published . . .

And that's where the manuscript ended.

My young friend, the budding delicatessen owner, couldn't find the missing pages. They had gone out into the world as wrapping paper for salted herring, butter, and green soap. They had fulfilled their destiny.

The brewer is dead, Auntie is dead, and the student is dead, the one whose sparks of genius ended up in the bin.

Everything ends up in the bin.

And that's the end of the story, the story about Auntie Toothache.

Notes

A NOTE ON DANISH CURRENCY

In several stories, Andersen refers to *rigsdaler*. For most of his lifetime, Danish currency was denominated in *rigsdaler*, marks, and *skillings*. Multiplying one *rigsdaler* by about one hundred provides an equivalent in Danish kroner today. Multiplying one *rigsdaler* by about ten therefore provides an approximate equivalent in pounds sterling, multiplying by about fifteen provides an approximate equivalent in U.S. dollars.

THE TINDERBOX (1835)

"The Tinderbox" opened Andersen's first collection of stories, *Eventyr*. It is based on a Danish folktale called "The Spirit of the Candle," which has links with "Aladdin." Andersen also borrows from many other folktales—the princess in the tower from "Rapunzel," the cross on the soldier's door that the dog duplicates along the street from "Ali Baba and the Forty Thieves," the trail of grain from "Hansel and Gretel"—while adapting details of the Aladdin story such as the Arabian minarets, which become Copenhagen's Round Tower.

The Aladdin story had a special emotional significance for Andersen. While he was a poor schoolboy sponsored through grammar school, a turning point in his fortunes came when he was invited to stay with a leading Copenhagen family, that of Admiral Wulff, in his apartment in the royal Amalienborg Palace. He was given a copy of Shakespeare that Wulff had translated into Danish; ecstatic, he stood at the window of his room and in his diary (December 19, 1825) wrote out lines from Oehlenschläger's play *Aladdin*:

"It's going for me as it did for Aladdin, who says at the close of the work as he is looking out of a window of the palace:

Down there I walked when just a lad
Each Sunday, if I was but allowed,
And gazed with wonder at the sultan's palace.

Five or six years ago, I, too, was walking around on the streets down there, didn't know a soul here in town, and now I am gloating over my Shakespeare in the home of a kind and respected family. O Lord, I could kiss you!"

LITTLE CLAUS AND BIG CLAUS (1835)

The second story in Andersen's first collection is based on a Danish landlord-and-tenant folktale: the cunning little guy outwits the big stupid one. The farcical and grotesque devices such as the grandmother propped up in a cart as if alive are witness to the folk tradition. Andersen sanitizes the sexual innuendo of the traditional version by giving the farmer an irrational dislike of deacons, though the cuckold theme is clear to adult readers.

THE PRINCESS ON THE PEA (1835)

This is another adaptation of a Danish folktale that appeared in Andersen's first collection. Andersen's comic touch is to invent the conclusion about seeing the pea in a museum.

THUMBELINA (1835)

"Thumbelina" opened Andersen's second collection of *Eventyr*. Its inspiration was the folktale "Tom Thumb," and also the German writer E. T. A. Hoffmann's *Kunstmärchen* ("art fairy story") for adults, the hallucinatory, erotic *Meister Floh,* in which a tiny lady a span in length torments the hero. Andersen named Hoffmann as one of his three greatest influences.

THE TRAVELING COMPANION (1835)

In 1830, Andersen included an arch retelling of the Fyn folktale "The Dead Man's Help" as a story called "The Ghost: A Fairy Tale from Fyn" with a collection of his poems and an introduction reading, "As a child, it was my greatest pleasure to listen to fairy tales, and some of these are either very little or not at all known. I have retold one of these here, and if it wins approval, I mean to retell several, and one day to publish a cycle of 'Danish Folk Tales.'" The 1830 version fell on deaf ears, but the themes are so close to Andersen's heart—love, death, fate—that it is easy to see why he returned to it for his second volume of *Eventyr*, when he was a more confident teller of fairy tales.

The frigid princess recalls the cruel heroine in the ancient story of *Turandot*; her black- and white-winged transformations anticipate Odette and Odile in *Swan Lake*. This is the first of many Andersen tales that give symbolic significance to shoes or feet, in recognition of his father. The trio of shoe, glove, and head with which the hero answers the princess's riddles may also refer to Andersen's childhood home, which was a cottage divided into three occupied by his father the shoemaker, a glovemaker, and a hatter.

THE LITTLE MERMAID (1837)

"The latest tale, 'The Little Mermaid,' you *will* like; it is better than 'Thumbelina,'" Andersen wrote to his friend the poet B. S. Ingemann. "I don't know how other writers feel! *I* suffer with my characters, I share their moods, whether good or bad, and I can be nice or nasty according to the scene on which I happen to be working. This latest, third installment of tales for children is probably the best, and you're going to like it! . . . I have not, like de la Motte Fouque in *Undine,* allowed the mermaid's acquiring of an immortal soul to depend upon an alien creature, upon the love of a human being. I'm sure that's wrong! It would depend rather too much on chance, wouldn't it? I *won't* accept that sort of thing in this world. I have permitted my mermaid to follow a more natural, more divine path. No other writer, I believe, has indicated it yet, and that's why I am glad to have it in my tale."

The ancient myth of mermaids and sea-brides who marry mortals on certain conditions, silence often being part of the bargain, had an irresistible appeal in its pagan eroticism for the nineteenth-century Romantics.

Andersen was influenced by de la Motte Fouque's *Undine* (1811) and by the mermaid sagas of the German Romantic poet Ludwig Tieck and the Danish poets Ingemann and Oehlenschläger, as well as by Bournonville's ballet *La Sylphide*, about a woman in fairy form, which opened in Copenhagen in 1836. These in turn inspired the later romantic operas and ballets on the theme—Tchaikovsky's *Swan Lake,* Dvořák's *Rusalka,* Maeterlinck and Debussy's *Pelléas et Mélisande.*

Andersen, however, brought his own personal anguish to the tale; the Little Mermaid, as his letter suggested, was one of his characters with whom he particularly identified. In 1836, when he began the story initially called "The Daughters of the Sea," he was staying on the island of Fyn to avoid the wedding in Copenhagen of his friend Edvard Collin, with whom he was in love. He had spent years trying to express the feelings he was not allowed to speak out, and he empathized with his mermaid—in her sense of being a different species from humankind, as Andersen felt in his bisexual desires, and in her position with the prince: like Andersen with Edvard, she was held in affection but never considered an erotic possibility, and without a tongue was unable to declare her feelings. In a letter he never dared send, Andersen imagined himself and Edvard united "before God," and in the manuscript of "The Little Mermaid" there is an extended ending where the mermaid says "I myself shall strive to win an immortal soul . . . that in the world beyond I may be reunited with him to whom I gave my whole heart." Andersen deleted this; unique among versions of the mermaid myth, he separated the mermaid's double goal of love and an eternal soul and awarded her immortality as a consolation for sexual disappointment—much as he assumed his own immortality as a writer was a consolation for loneliness in life.

This disturbing tale has been interpreted in countless different ways. It is a tragic account of the permanency of female love versus male faithlessness. It is the drama of a social outsider—in 1907, Andersen's first biographer, Hans Brix, read the bottom of the sea as the lower class from which Andersen came and dry land as the Copenhagen bourgeoisie to which he aspired to belong. And it is a coming-of-age fairy tale in which a young girl—as in "Sleeping Beauty" and "Snow White"—is suddenly forced to cope with her own sexuality and the fears it arouses, symbolized by the blood and the knife that divides the mermaid's fish tail ("It will be painful. It will feel like a sharp sword is passing through you"). Feminist readers have seen it variously as a warning against men and a misogynistic vision in which self-sacrifice and silence are offered as ideal female patterns of behavior; others have seen the amphibian Little Mermaid as a homoerotic character. She has always been one of Andersen's most beloved characters; the story was one of the first to be translated into English (1846) and, transformed by a happy ending, is one of Disney's most popular adaptations of a fairy tale.

THE EMPEROR'S NEW CLOTHES (1837)

This was the companion piece to "The Little Mermaid" published in the third installment of *Eventyr*. Andersen took the outline from a medieval Spanish collection based on Arab and Jewish stories, *Libro de Patronio,* by Infante don Juan Manuel. This version tells the more risqué story of a Moorish king conned by weavers who claim to make clothes invisible to any man not the son of his presumed father.

Andersen's simple, classical tale only acquired its punch line at the last moment. The manuscript ends with everyone simply admiring the clothes; when it was already at the printer's Andersen hit on the now famous ending of the small child announcing "But he doesn't have anything on!" He sent a new last paragraph to the proofreader, asking for its insertion, "as it will give everything a more satirical appearance." Behind the comic masterstroke is Romanticism's ideal of the child as uniquely wise and pure, which inspired Andersen's entire oeuvre and his public persona, too. From an early age he had sold himself to the Danish bourgeoisie as the naive precocious child not usually admitted into the grown-up parlor; this was his exposé of the hypocrisy and snobbery he had found there.

THE STEADFAST TIN SOLDIER (1838)

"The Steadfast Tin Soldier" was a turning point for Andersen: It is the first tale he wrote that has neither a folktale source nor a literary model, but came straight out of his imagination, and it marks a new independence in his work. It is a high point of Andersen's perfectly chiseled evocation of the nineteenth-century nursery world, with its cast of toy swans and dancers. The soldier himself shares Andersen's fatalism, his faithfulness, and his one-legged sense of being different; sexual repression lies just beneath the nineteenth-century values of stoical endurance. Thomas Mann, like Andersen tormented by homoerotic desires, wrote at eighty that "I have always liked Andersen's fairy tale of the Steadfast Tin Soldier. Fundamentally, it is the symbol of my life."

THE WILD SWANS (1838)

Andersen adapted this folktale, popular across Europe, in direct compe-
tition to other retellings. He wrote to friends inviting them to compare
his version to one included in Matthias Winther's 1823 collection of
Danish folktales, and he would also have known "The Six Swans" and
"The Twelve Brothers," variations in the Grimm brothers' collections.
Andersen's particular contributions are his characteristic love of detail—
the princes "wrote on golden slates with diamond pencils"—and the
Christian motifs that debrutalize the essentially pagan story; in the
Grimms' version, by contrast, the wicked queen is burned at the stake.
Both this and "The Steadfast Tin Soldier" continue from "The Little
Mermaid" the theme of an upstanding central character, full of
integrity, who for a noble motive does not express his or her emotions
and therefore is misunderstood or sacrificed.

THE FLYING TRUNK (1839)

This was published as a Christmas story, and contains in-jokes intended
to amuse the Copenhagen intelligentsia. The matches are Johanne Luise
Heiberg, leading actress at Copenhagen's Royal Theater; according to
the choreographer Auguste Bournonville "on the Danish stage no star
. . . sparkled as strongly or as long . . . she outshone everyone." Dazzling
and proud, she was married to Andersen's enemy, the influential critic
Johan Ludwig Heiberg. Her kitchen companions are the chatterers of
Copenhagen literary society, while Andersen is the nightingale in a cage
outside the room, despised as an upstart: "she can sing. Of course, she
hasn't been trained, but tonight we won't even mention that!" The aging,
restless hero who "roams the world telling stories, though they're no
longer as merry as the one he told about the matches," is also a self-portrait.
Shortly after this story was written, Mrs. Heiberg played the lead in
Andersen's drama *The Mulatto* to critical acclaim, but then refused the
role in his next play *The Moorish Maid*, prompting a public row that made
Andersen a laughingstock and encouraged him to leave Denmark for a
year (1840–41).

THE NIGHTINGALE (1844)

"In Tivoli . . . began the Chinese tale," runs Andersen's almanac for October 11, 1843, and the next day "finished the Chinese tale." The story took its setting from the Chinese imagery—pagodas, peacocks, and colored lanterns—of Copenhagen's new pleasure garden, which opened in summer 1843. But although he wrote it in one frenzied day, it had been forming in Andersen's mind since September, when he had fallen in love with the singer Jenny Lind, the "Swedish Nightingale."

Like Andersen's, her artistry was rooted in folk culture—she sang Swedish folk songs in a way that made of them a high art form, to a rapturous international audience—and Andersen saw in her naturalness and simplicity the ideal of his own art, which also battled against artifice and reason. The story was a direct tribute to her—though Andersen liked the fact that he, too, had been called "the little nightingale of Fyn" as a child—and is his aesthetic manifesto, celebrating the transformative power of art.

THE SWEETHEARTS (1844)

Andersen wrote this bittersweet comedy in 1843 after he met by chance his first love, Riborg Voigt, on holiday thirteen years after she had turned down his marriage proposal. She was by then a middle-aged matron and he was a famous writer. The tale was published in a collection with "The Ugly Duckling" and "The Nightingale," both also strongly autobiographical works, and Andersen may have seen it as a complement to "The Nightingale"—a valediction to an old love affair and a celebration of a new one.

THE UGLY DUCKLING (1844)

"I was dejected, against my will, roamed around in the woods and fields, felt less than well. Had the idea of 'The Story of a Duck,' this helped my sunken spirits"—so Andersen wrote in his diary on July 5, 1842, while staying with aristocratic friends at Gisselfeldt Manor, noting three days later that "the swans have cygnets, and are very irritable." At another Danish estate, Bregentved, three weeks later, he wrote "Started on 'The Cygnet' yesterday," and over a year later, on October 7, 1843, in Copenhagen, "finished the tale of the young swan."

Into this much-worked masterpiece went the wish-fulfillment dreams of a lifetime, a rags-to-riches fantasy that is universally appealing. What child has not sometimes felt neglected, or believed that he is in fact the offspring of a much nicer family, and has ended up by mistake among those who undervalue and misunderstand him? Andersen's memories of his own humiliations—his mockers are even personalized here, with stay-at-home Ingeborg Drewsen, Edvard Collin's sister, as the clucking hen, for example—fused here with a Romantic view of genius over background and culture ("It doesn't matter if you're born in a duck yard when you've been lying inside a swan's egg"), and his ambition to triumph over the writers of the ancien regime: "They all said 'The new one is the most beautiful of all! So young and lovely!' And the old swans bowed to him."

"The Ugly Duckling" was published with "The Nightingale," "The Sweethearts," and another tale, "The Angel," as *Nye Eventyr (New Fairy Tales)* in December 1843, and sold out almost immediately. Andersen wrote on December 18, "The book has sold like hot cakes! All the papers praise it, everyone reads it! No books of mine seem to be appreciated as these fairy tales are!" To the poet Ingemann he said, "I think—and it would give me great pleasure if I were right—that I have now discovered how to write fairy tales. The first ones I wrote were, as you know, mostly old ones I had listened to as a child, and which I then usually retold and re-created in my own manner. Those that were my own creations . . . were the most popular, and that gave me inspiration. Now I tell stories out of my own breast, I seize an idea for the grown-ups—and then tell the story to the little ones while always remembering that Father and Mother often listen, and you must also give them something for their minds."

THE FIR TREE (1845)

"The Fir Tree," published in the second installment of *Nye Eventyr* in December 1844, is a tragic-comic self-portrait, harshly perceptive. Andersen like his tree was a fantasist, vain, restless, a trembling over-sensitive neurotic who swung madly from hope to despair.

THE SNOW QUEEN (1845)

"It has been sheer joy for me to put on paper my most recent fairy tale, 'The Snow Queen,'" Andersen told Ingemann on December 10, 1844. "It permeated my mind in such a way that it came out dancing over the paper." It took just five days to write—"the pace of inspiration rather than worked-out thought," according to the critic Naomi Lewis—and was published with "The Fir Tree" in *Nye Eventyr*.

The poetic construction is unrivaled in Andersen's oeuvre, the varied tones and picture paintings of its broad canvas almost symphonic in their richness, but the leitmotif is simple: that love conquers all, that a reliance on reason and learning is barren. Beyond it, "The Snow Queen" works on many different levels. It is a quest story, a tale of dangerous journeys through many seasons and strange landscapes; a battle between good and evil; and it is Andersen's variation on that classic nineteenth-century theme, woman's redemption of man, tempered by the Romantic myth of childhood—that Kai grows up, and Gerda doesn't, saving him by her innocence, is central to the plot. Much of the childhood idyll here is rooted in Andersen's by now rose-hued memories of his childhood: the roof garden where the children play, for example, recalls exactly a description of the one in Andersen's own home.

W. H. Auden used the scene in which Kai is found working on his ice puzzles to illustrate the difference between folktales and literature. It could never occur in a folktale, he wrote, "firstly because the human situation with which it is concerned is an historical one, created by Descartes, Newton and their successors, and secondly, because no folk tale would analyse its own symbol and explain that the game with the ice-splinters was the game of reason. Further, the promised reward, 'the whole world and a new pair of skates,' has not only a surprise and a subtlety of which the folk tale is incapable, but also a uniqueness by which one can identify its author."

THE RED SHOES (1845)

This gruesome story has innocuous origins in Andersen's memories of his own confirmation, when he could think only of his squeaky new boots. It associates feet and the human soul as in "The Little Mermaid," and it brings out in a particularly Andersenian class of masochism all the cruelty of the folktale tradition that he usually subliminates. The red shoes dancing off with Karen's feet may have been inspired by the Grimms' folktale "Snow White," where the queen dances herself to death in red-hot shoes.

THE SHEPHERDESS AND THE CHIMNEY SWEEP (1845)

This was published with "The Red Shoes" in the third installment of *Nye Eventyr* and is a gentle counterpoint to it, a classic story from the Biedermeier drawing room, delicate and whimsical as its porcelain heroine.

THE SHADOW (1847)

The germ of "The Shadow," written in a sweltering Naples in June 1846, appeared as far back as 1831, when Andersen met the German author von Chamisso in Berlin and read his *Peter Schlemihl's Strange Story* (1813), about a man who loses his shadow. That story, obliquely referred to at the beginning of this tale, was associated in Andersen's mind with an emotional trauma—on that visit to Berlin he received a letter from the love of his life, Edvard Collin, declining Andersen's suggestion that they use the intimate *du* form. This put-down, social as well as emotional/ sexual, rankled for the rest of Andersen's life, and the central scene in which the shadow refuses to let the learned man address him by the intimate form—rendered in English as being on first-name terms—uses the language of Edvard's letter fifteen years earlier: "How strange nature can be. Some people can't stand to touch gray paper without falling ill . . . I get the same feeling when I hear you using my first name."

"The Shadow" was written during a particular time of stress in Andersen's life, when he had been commissioned by a German publisher to write his autobiography and was busy constructing the fraudulent *The Fairy Tale of My Life*, which invents a ludicrously sunny life of high connections and public acclaim ("a star of good fortune shines upon me"). "The Shadow" was his release from this pretense. It was as if, having sent himself into the shadows in his factual account, his real creative self took revenge in the fairy tale and painted a demonic picture of self-annihilation, a true self-portrait of a man with no identity.

Symbolically, "The Shadow" is about how we accommodate, or don't accommodate, the darker side of our souls—the thwarted desires that get suppressed in the process of becoming civilized. Jung suggested that we all carry a shadow that becomes blacker and denser the less it is embodied in our conscious life. As Andersen was posturing, shadowless, to the world in his autobiography, the terrors he was suppressing came back in spades in "The Shadow."

THE OLD HOUSE (1848)

"I read that story over and over again, with the most unspeakable delight," Charles Dickens wrote of "The Old House." Written immediately after Andersen's first visit to London, it shows many Dickensian influences—the life breathed into inanimate objects, the mix of the grotesque and sentimental. The portrait of the laughing child was based on three-year-old Maria Hartmann, daughter of Andersen's friend the Danish composer J. P. E. Hartmann; three years later the child died.

THE LITTLE MATCH GIRL (1848)

Andersen wrote "The Little Match Girl" in a single day on November 18, 1845, when he was a dissatisfied guest staying with aristocratic Danish friends at Glorup Manor. Like "The Fir Tree" it is a bitter Christmas tale; its starting point was Andersen's poignant memories of his grandmother and the stories his own mother had told him of being sent to beg and staying out, cold and hungry, because she was too frightened to return home penniless. Its fierce social indignation and the surreal quality of its dying heroine's hallucinatory imaginings bring Andersen close to his contemporary Charles Dickens here.

THE STORY OF A MOTHER (1848)

Andersen's first published work, in 1827, was a poem called "The Dying Child," spoken in the voice of the child itself; it was a subject that obsessed him and to which he now returned with an adult perspective. The popularity of the subject in the nineteenth century must be seen in the context of mortality rates: one in five children did not reach their fifth birthday.

The manuscript reveals that originally Andersen gave the tale a happy ending. The mother bows her head and "As she did so, her lips touched the child's lips, as he lay in a sweet, sound sleep, and the sun shone on his cheeks, so they seemed red; and when the mother looked round she found herself sitting in her little room; the lark was sitting in its cage, as though it felt the coming of spring; and death was not in the room. Folding her hands, the mother thought of the house of the dead, and of the child's future, and said again 'God's will be done.'" At the last minute Andersen deleted this, replacing it with "And Death took her child into the unknown land." The alteration is a fine example of his ruthlessness as an artist—a ruthlessness carried over into life, for when, as was his custom, he read the tale aloud to friends to test it out, he chose as his victim Edvard Collin's wife, Henriette, who had lost two children in the past four years, and not till she broke down in tears was he persuaded to stop.

THE COLLAR (1848)

Another mocking self-portrait, "The Collar" was also inspired by Andersen's visit to England. Its ending answers the censorious Danish press, which criticized Andersen for boasting his way across England, and is also a joke on himself as a compulsive autobiographer.

THE BELL (1850)

The physicist Hans Christian Ørsted was the first to recognize the genius of the fairy tales, and "The Bell" is Andersen's tribute to him. The story is a parable about the search for wisdom, in which the prince represents science and Ørsted, the poor boy, poetry—and Andersen himself.

THE MARSH KING'S DAUGHTER (1858)

"The Marsh King's Daughter" was one of the long works with which Andersen in the 1850s experimented with a new style of tale. He rewrote the tale six times, and his sources included books about Africa and about the flights of birds as well as Viking legends, though the starting point is the animal fable of transformation, involving Andersen's favorite creatures, swans, and storks.

THE WIND TELLS OF VALDEMAR DAAE AND
HIS DAUGHTERS (1859)

This is another experimental work from the 1850s. The specifically Danish setting—the grand Borreby Manor was an estate in southern Sjælland, near two manor houses where Andersen was often a guest—is a feature of Andersen's tales in the 1850s (he also emphasizes the Danish element in "The Marsh King's Daughter"), and was the result of his increased patriotism after the Danish-Prussian war of 1848–51.

THE SNOWMAN (1861)

Andersen wrote "The Snowman" on New Year's Eve 1860 at a house party at the manor of Basnæs in southern Sjaelland, and its setting was inspired by the woods on the estate. It is another self-mocking auto-biography, lighthearted cousin of "The Fir Tree," and takes on a special pathos when one knows that Andersen was at the time contemplating the one homosexual love affair to bring him happiness, though social disapproval: thus the oddly paired couple of the Snowman and the Stove, as unlikely as the Owl and the Pussy Cat.

THE ICE MAIDEN (1862)

"His corpse lay on the bed . . . A cricket chirped the whole night through. 'He is dead,' said my mother, addressing it, 'you need not call him, the Ice Maiden has carried him off.' I understood what she meant. I recollected that in the winter before, when our windowpanes were frozen, my father pointed to them and showed us a figure like that of a maiden with outstretched arms. 'She is come to fetch me,' said he in jest, and now when he lay dead on his bed my mother remembered this."

The first germ of "The Ice Maiden" was this incident, fixed in Andersen's mind along with the trauma of his father's death when he was still a child. Nearly half a century later, in 1861, he wrote the story in Switzerland, which inspired its mountain setting—working titles were "The Mountain Hunter" and "The Eagle's Nest." It is a work in the high-Romantic tradition, the Ice Maiden a typical nineteenth-century femme fatale whose kiss is the kiss of death. In his ballet version of the tale, *Le Baiser de la Fée*, Stravinsky interpreted the kiss as the kiss of the muse, marking out the hero Tchaikovsky for tormented brilliance. Later commentators have seen the kiss as a symbol of the stigma of homosexuality; shortly after he finished the tale, Andersen began an affair with a male dancer from the Copenhagen ballet.

THE WOOD NYMPH (1868)

Andersen was spurred to write "The Wood Nymph" by a comment in a Danish newspaper that only Dickens could respond to the 1867 Paris World Exposition with the flair of an artist. Andersen took this as a challenge and visited Paris several times to write this story. His impression of Paris as the epitome of corrupt nineteenth-century urbanization, a modern "kingdom of Babel," set against the innocence of the countryside, is pronounced. His evocative portrayal of the city made "The Wood Nymph" extremely popular—an edition of three thousand sold out immediately when it appeared in December 1868, and a new edition was printed ten days later.

THE MOST INCREDIBLE THING (1872)

"The Most Incredible Thing" was inspired by the Franco-Prussian War and by earlier wars between Prussia and Denmark in the 1860s, which upset Andersen deeply because he loved the high culture and rapturous welcome he had found in Germany and was shocked by the country's descent into militarism. When Denmark admitted defeat in 1864 he wrote in his dairy, "Disaster, violation, oblivion and death are waiting for me . . . I've been tormented by the pressure of political events . . . I feel each kindness people in Germany have shown me, acknowledge friends there but feel that I, as a Dane, must make a complete break with them all, never will we meet again. My heart is breaking!"

This tale became especially important in Denmark during the Nazi occupation. It was the first Andersen story to appear in print during this time; an edition of July 1940 was introduced by Professor Paul Rubow, who suggested that Andersen had written the tale out of terror for the future. "But," the professor ended, "'The Most Incredible Thing' concludes with the certainty of victory. The demons of darkness must be vanquished! What we read here is the author's Holocaust Dream, a profound anxiety and doubt that is superseded by an even more profound faith."

In 1942, "The Most Incredible Thing" was published in a small volume of stories organized by scholars, including Elias Bredsdorff, who were to become leaders of the Danish Resistance Movement. Radical new illustrations were used to smuggle past the censors a message of hope and resistance to a wide readership. In the final picture, the night watchman who strikes down the destroyer is a Jewish rabbi with hat and beard, standing in condemnation of a brawny, seminaked Aryan pinned to the floor by the tablets of Moses inscribed in Hebrew letters, watched by a crowd of "ordinary" Danes in contemporary 1940s dress. "I think," Bredsdorff wrote just before his death in 2002, "Andersen would have been pleased to know that some of his work became a useful tool against the oppressors at a time when Denmark was not master in her own House."

AUNTIE TOOTHACHE (1872)

Andersen suffered from toothaches all his life, and the progress of his teeth had always been for him a tangible if comic indicator of the road to mortality. When he wrote this story, he was about to lose his last ones. Immediately after it was published, in November 1872, he suffered the first symptoms of the liver cancer that was to kill him, so "Auntie Toothache" became his last work.